Mikh

Born in a village of the Don region in 1905, Sholokhov was not himself a Cossack but knew and loved the Cossack tradition. Educated in Moscow, he returned to his home village as a school-teacher and there witnessed the savage civil warfare of the early 1920s. Sholokhov began writing when he was eighteen and published his first book – *Tales from the Don* – in 1925. He was awarded the State Prize for Literature in 1940, the Nobel Prize for Literature, in 1965, and the Order of Lenin on no less than three occasions. Sholokhov's great work is undoubtedly his epic of the Don and its people, published in two parts as *And Quiet Flows the Don* and *The Don Flows Home to the Sea*. *Virgin Soil Upturned* was planned as the first novel in a trilogy that never reached completion. Sholokhov's passionate realism, vivid lyricism, and genuine love for the Don Cossacks must weigh against those anti-intellectual denunciations that earned him the enmity of Solzhenitsyn and the new generation of dissident writers. After the Nobel accolade, Sholokhov published little, spending his time hunting and drinking on his large estate at Rostov-on-Don until his death in 1984.

PICADOR *Classics*

Photograph of Mikhail Sholokhov courtesy of Camera Press

MIKHAIL
SHOLOKHOV

Virgin Soil
Upturned

PICADOR *Classics*

published by Pan Books
in association with The Bodley Head

Podnyataya Tselina first published in the U.S.S.R.
1932
This translation published by Putnam 1935
This Picador Classics edition published 1988 by
Pan Books Ltd, Cavaye Place, London SW10 9PG
in association with The Bodley Head
9 8 7 6 5 4 3 2 1
ISBN 0 330 30329 5
Printed and bound in Great Britain by
Richard Clay Ltd, Bungay, Suffolk

Key to Principal Characters

Atamanchukov, Vasili. A cossack, member of the Gremyachy Collective Farm, but secretly hostile.

Bannik, Gregor Matveich. A cossack working his own land and antagonistic to the collective farm.

Batalshchikov, Ivan. A cossack member of the Collective Farm, but hostile.

Beskhlebnov, Akim. A cossack, member of the Collective Farm. Called 'the Older', to distinguish him from his son.

Beskhlebnov, Akim. Also member of the farm, called 'the Younger'.

Borodin, Titok. A rich cossack ('kulak'), formerly a Red army man.

Borshchev, Timofei. A poor cossack, supporter of the 'kulaks'.

Damaskov, Frol. A rich cossack ('kulak').

Damaskov, Timofei. Frol's son.

Davidov, Siemion. A metal worker, Communist, one of 25,000 workers mobilized by the Soviet Communist Party to organize collective farms, chairman of Gremyachy Collective Farm.

Diemid. A poor cossack, nicknamed 'the Silent'.

Dubtsiev, Agafon. A cossack, member of the Collective Farm, and in charge of the farm's third brigade of labourers.

Gayev. A 'kulak' with a large family.

Ignationok, Mikhail (Mishka). A cossack collective farmer.

Ignationok, Uliana. Mikhail's mother.

Kondratko, Osip. An Ukrainian worker, in charge of the column sent to the villages to make propaganda for the collective farms.

Korchinsky. Secretary of the Communist Party District Committee.

Lapshinov, Siemion. A rich old cossack ('kulak').

5

Liubishkin, Pavel. A cossack collective farmer, in charge of the collective farm first brigade.

Losiev, Arkady (Arkashka). A cossack collective farmer, notorious for his love of bargaining.

Lyatievsky, Vatslav Avgustovich. Formerly a lieutenant in the Imperial Army, now a member and organizer of an anti-Soviet conspiratorial organization.

Maidannikov, Kondrat. A middle-class cossack, member of the Collective Farm.

Nagulnov, Makar. Secretary of Gremyachy Communist Party group.

Nagulnova, Lukeria. Makar's wife.

Naidionnov, Ivan. A young Communist, member of Kondratko's Propaganda Column.

Ostrovnov, Yakov Lukich. A fairly rich, far-seeing cossack, who becomes manager of the Collective Farm in order to wreck it.

Polovtsiev, Alexander Anisimovich. Formerly a captain in the Imperial Army and regimental comrade of Ostrovnov's, now organizer of an anti-Soviet conspiratorial organization.

Poyarkova, Marina. Andrei Razmiotnov's mistress.

Razmiotnov, Andrei. A Communist, chairman of Gremyachy Village Soviet.

Shchukar. An old man, member of the Collective Farm, given to bragging.

Shaly, Ippolit. The village blacksmith.

Ushakov, Diemka. A cossack, collective farmer and in charge of the collective farm second brigade.

Contents

1. A Stranger Arrives in Gremyachy   9
2. The Mobilized Worker   12
3. The Conspiracy   24
4. A Village Meeting   31
5. Story of a Revolutionary   43
6. Evicted!   55
7. Taking Possession   62
8. Unexpected Resistance   67
9. An Important Decision   70
10. Parting of the Ways   82
11. Turned Out   86
12. Murder   94
13. A Name of Honour   111
14. Appointing the Manager   119
15. Wholesale Slaughter   127
16. Caught in the Act   139
17. A Painful Operation   144
18. Clothing Distribution   149
19. Troubles of the Farm   154
20. A District Bureaucrat   166
21. Plans for the Spring   171
22. Propaganda Column   180
23. A Wrecker at Work   185
24. Going too Far   199
25. Youth Shows the Way   210
26. A Well-Earned Reward   221
27. The Conspiracy Fails   229
28. The Party Line   240

29. Deserting the Farm   248
30. Two Lovers Part   252
31. A Misadventurous Life   261
32. Expelled from the Party   276
33. A Fight for Grain   292
34. The Ancient Mound   312
35. To the Rescue   317
36. Giving a Lead   326
37. A Fortnight of Changes   346
38. An Energetic Manager   356
39. Off with the Old Love ...   361
40. An Exile Returns   370

Chapter 1

A Stranger Arrives in Gremyachy

ENVELOPED in the scent of the first thaw at the end of January, the cherry orchards smell good. At noontide, when the sun is warm, here and there in the sheltered corners the mournful, hardly perceptible odour of cherry-bark is mingled with the vapid rawness of melting snow, with the mighty and ancient smell of the earth peering through the snow and the dead leaves. The delicate, mingled aroma hangs stubbornly above the orchards until the azure dusk is falling, until the green horn of the moon is thrust through the naked branches, until the fattening hares scatter the feathery speckles of their tracks over the snow.

But then from the steppe ridge the wind brings the bitter breath of the frost-burnt wormwood into the orchards, the scents and sounds of the day are engulfed, and over the mugwort, over the brushwood, over the dewgrass withered in the stubble, over the rolling fields of the ploughed land the night comes silently on from the east like a grey wolf, leaving the lengthening evening shadows behind her like tracks across the steppe.

One evening in January, 1930, a horseman rode along the path leading from the steppe into the village of Gremyachy Log. By the stream he halted his weary horse, shaggily coated with hoar-frost in the groin, and dismounted. The waning moon stood high above the black depths of the orchards stretching along both sides of the path, above the islands of poplar clumps. It was dark and quiet in the lane. Somewhere beyond the stream a dog howled noisily, a yellow point of light shone out. The horseman avidly inhaled the frosty air, unhurriedly drew off a glove, and lit a cigarette. Then he tightened the saddle-girth, thrust his fingers under the saddle-cloth, and after feeling the wet warmth of his sweating horse's back, easily hoisted his great body into the saddle. He began to ride through the shallow stream, which was not frozen over even in the deepest of winters. The horse's hoofs rang hollowly on the pebbles of the river-bed; it dropped its head to drink as it went, but its rider urged it on, and the horse, its belly rumbling, scrambled out on to the sloping bank.

Hearing the sound of talk and the scrape of sledge-runners coming towards him, the rider again halted his horse. At the sound the animal cautiously pricked up its ears, and turned. The silver-mounted breast straps, and the high, silvered pommel of the cossack saddle were caught by the moonlight, and suddenly broke into a white, dazzling gleam in the darkness of the lane. The horseman threw the reins over the pommel, hastily drew over his head the camel-hair cossack cowl which had been hanging around his shoulders, wrapped his face in it, and put his horse into a swinging trot. When he had passed the sledge he rode at a walking pace as before, but did not remove his cowl.

On reaching the village, he asked a passing woman:

'Tell me, auntie, where does Yakov Ostrovnov live?'

'Yakov Lukich, d'you mean?'

'M'yes.'

'That's his hut, the one with the tiled roof, beyond the poplar. D'you see it?'

'Yes, I see it. Thank you.'

Outside the spacious, tiled hut he dismounted, led the horse through the wicket gate, and, knocking gently with his whip-handle on the window, called out:

'Master! Yakov Lukich! Come out for a moment.'

Bareheaded, his coat flung across his shoulders, the master came out into the porch, closely examined the newcomer, and stepped across the threshold.

'Who the devil is it?' he asked, smiling into his grizzled whiskers.

'Can't you guess, Lukich? Put me up for the night. Where can I put the horse so that it's warm?'

'No, comrade, I don't recognize you. You're not from the District Committee, are you? Or the Land Department? I seem to know you ... Your voice sounds familiar.'

Wrinkling his shaven upper lip into a smile, the newcomer threw back his cowl.

'D'you remember Polovtsiev?' he asked.

And Yakov Lukich turned pale, suddenly glanced fearfully around, and whispered:

'Your Excellency! Where've you come from? Captain! We'll get the horse fixed up in a minute ... in the stable. How long it is since ...!'

'Now, now, quieter! It is a long time since ...! Have you got a horse-cloth? You haven't any strangers in the house, have you?'

The horseman gave Lukich the reins. Lazily submitting to the movement of the unfamiliar hand, raising its head on its outstretched neck and wearily dragging its hind legs, the horse went towards the stables. Its hooves clattered against the wooden flooring, it snorted as it caught the familiar scent of another horse. The stranger's hand lay on its nose, the fingers deftly and carefully freed the chafed gums from the damp iron of the bit, and the horse gratefully nuzzled into the hay.

'I've loosened the girths, but it can stand saddled until it's cooler, then I'll unsaddle it,' Yakov Lukich said, thoughtfully throwing a horse-cloth over the animal's back. While he was attending to the horse, from the tightness of the girths and the play of the strap joining the stirrup leathers he had easily reached the conclusion that his guest had come some distance, and had made no short journey that day.

'Got plenty of grain, Yakov Lukich?' the arrival asked.

'A little. We'll give him a drink, then we'll feed him. Come into the hut ... I don't know what to call you now. We've got out of the way of using the old titles, and they don't come easily ...' The master smiled awkwardly in the darkness, although he knew that his smile could not be seen.

'You can use my Christian name and patronymic. You haven't forgotten them, have you?' his guest replied, as he left the stable with Lukich behind him.

'How could I? We smashed up the whole German army together, and in the last war we had a ... I've often thought of you, Alexander Anisimovich. I've not heard a word of you since we got separated in Novorossiisk. I thought you had gone off with the cossacks to Turkey.'

They went into the well-heated kitchen. The newcomer removed his cowl and his white, lambswool cap, revealing a powerful, angular skull covered with scanty white hair. From under his steep, bald, wolfish brow he ran his eyes· around the room, and, smilingly screwing up his small, pale-blue eyes glittering seriously in their sockets, he bowed to the women – the mistress and her daughter-in-law – seated on the bench.

'I hope you're well, women !' he greeted them.

'Praise be !' the mistress cautiously replied, expectantly, interrogatively glancing at her husband as though asking: 'Who is this man you've brought in, and how are we to behave to him ?'

'Get supper ready,' the master curtly ordered, and invited his guest to the table in the best room.

As the visitor ate the cabbage and pork soup, in the women's presence he directed the conversation into talk of the weather and of former comrades in arms. His great, rock-hewn, lower jaw worked with difficulty; he chewed slowly, wearily, like an over-worked ox at rest. After supper he rose, said a prayer before the ikon in its dusty, paper flowers, and, brushing the breadcrumbs from his old, tight-fitting tunic-shirt, remarked :

'Thank you for your hospitality, Yakov Lukich. And now we'll talk.'

In response to the master's raised eye-brows the mistress and her daughter-in-law hurriedly cleared the table, then went into the kitchen.

Chapter 2

The Mobilized Worker

SHORTSIGHTED, and languid in his movements, the secretary of the Party District Committee sat down at the table, stared sidelong at Davidov, and, screwing up his eyes until the folds gathered in bags, began to read Davidov's documents.

Outside the window, the wind was whistling through the tele-phone wires; a magpie strutted lopsidedly and pecked at something on the back of the horse fastened by a bridle to the palisade. The wind ruffled the bird's tail and sent it flying off, but it settled again on the back of the ancient, emaciated, impassive nag and stared around victoriously with its rapacious eye. Ragged clumps of cloud were sailing low over the town. Occasionally slanting rays of sunlight fell through the openings in the clouds, a summery azure scrap of sky broke through, and then the bend of the Don visible from the window, the forest beyond it, and the distant ridge of hills with a tiny windmill on the horizon acquired an agitating softness of outline.

'So you were held up in Rostov owing to illness? Oh, well ... The other eight allotted to us out of the twenty-five thousand men mobilized for the work of collectivization arrived three days ago. We held a meeting, and the representatives of the collective farms met them.' The secretary thoughtfully chewed his lips. 'Things here are very complicated just now. The percentage of collectivization in the district is 14.8. And most of that is only associations for joint working the land. There are rich kulaks still behind with their grain collections. We badly need more men. Badly! The collective farms sent in demands for forty-three workers, and they have only allotted nine of you.' From under his puffy eyelids he took a new long and inquisitive stare at Davidov, as though estimating the man's capabilities.

'And so you're a locksmith, comrade? Very good! And have you been working long at the Putilov works? Have a smoke?' he continued.

'Ever since my demobilization. Nine years.' Davidov stretched out his hand for the cigarette, and the secretary, noticing the faded blue of tattoo marks on his hand, smiled at the corners of his pendulous lips.

'"The honour and pride of the country,"' he remarked. 'So you were in the fleet?'

'Yes.'

'I noticed the anchor on your hand ...'

'I was young, you know ... green and silly, so I let them poison me ...' Davidov angrily pulled down his sleeve as he thought: 'You see things that don't matter. But you couldn't see to your own grain collections!'

The secretary was silent, and the meaningless smile of welcome at once left his sickly, puffy face.

'You'll set out this very day as the district committee's delegate with full powers to carry through complete collectivization, comrade,' he announced. 'Have you read the Regional Committee's latest instruction? You have? All right, then you'll go to the Gremyachy Village Soviet. You can have a rest later, there's no time now. Your objective is 100 per cent collectivization. They've got a tiny agricultural association there, but we must set up giant collective farms. As soon as we've got a propaganda brigade organized we'll send it to you. But now, off with you, and set up a collective farm on the basis of a cautious squeezing of the kulaks. All the poorest and middling cossacks in the village must be brought into the farm. And then, set up a socialized grain fund for the entire area to be sown by the collective farm in 1930. But act with great care. Go easy with the middling cossacks ! There's a Party nucleus consisting of three communists in Gremyachy. The nucleus secretary and the chairman of the village Soviet are good lads, they were formerly members of Red Partisan bands.' He again chewed his lips, then added : 'With all the consequences that that implies. Understand? Politically they're not very literate, they can make blunders. If you meet with any difficulties, come to the district office. We haven't got telephonic communication with the village yet, that's the worst of it. And yes : the secretary of the nucleus holds the Order of the Red Banner; he's a bit crude, all angles and sharp ones at that.' The secretary drummed with his fingers on the lock of his document case, and, seeing Davidov stand up, added more animatedly :

'Wait a bit, one thing more : send us reports every day by horse messenger, and keep a tight hand on the lads there. Now go to the chief of the Organization Department, and then get off. I'll give orders for you to be supplied with District Executive Committee horses. And then you'll make a drive for 100 per cent collectivization. We shall judge your work by the percentage you achieve. We'll create a gigantic collective farm out of our eighteen village Soviets. An agricultural Red Putilov,' he smiled at his complacent comparison.

'You said something about my going cautiously with the kulaks. How am I to interpret that?' Davidov asked.

'Like this,' the secretary smiled patronizingly. 'There's the kulak who delivers the grain demanded of him, and there's the kulak who is obstinate. With the second the course is clear: apply article 107 of the grain collection law, and put the lid on them. But the position is more complicated with the first sort. How would you deal with them?'

Davidov reflected, then answered: 'I'd give them a further grain task to fulfil.'

'A fine method! No, comrade, that won't do! That way you may undermine all confidence in our activities. What would the middling peasant say then? He'd say: "That's what the Soviet government does! One way or another they put the lid on the peasant." Lenin taught us to take the peasant's attitude into serious account, and you suggest a second task! That's infantile, my boy!'

'Infantile, is it?' Davidov went livid. 'So according to you Stalin is wrong, is he?'

'What are you dragging Stalin into it for?'

'I've read his speech to the conference of the Marxist ... the what are they called ... when they were discussing the land question. Damn it, what do they call them ... land workers, isn't it?'

'Agrarians, d'you mean?'

'Yes, that's it!'

'Well, and what about it?'

'Get me the *Pravda* that printed his speech.'

The head of the department brought the *Pravda*. Davidov ran his eyes greedily over the pages.

Smiling expectantly, the secretary stared into his face.

'Here it is. Listen! "... so long as we stood for only a limited collectivization we could not allow the kulaks to be broken up ..." And further: here it is! "But now? Now the position is different. Now we are able to make a decisive attack on the kulaks, to smash their resistance, to liquidate them as a class ..." As a class, understand? Then why can't we make a second demand for grain? Why can't we put them completely between our thumb-nails?'

The smile vanished from the secretary's face, and he looked serious.

'And farther on he said that the middling and poor peasants who join the collective farms are to do the liquidating,' he retorted. 'Isn't that so? Read on!'

'Hm, you ...'

'None of your "hms",' the secretary angrily replied, his voice even trembling. 'And what is it you're suggesting? Administrative measures against every kulak without discrimination. And that in a district where there is only 14 per cent of collectivization, where the middling peasants are only just beginning to come into the collective farms. In this business we can trip up in a moment. People like you coming here and not knowing anything about local conditions ...' The secretary controlled himself, and went on more quietly:

'With those views you can chop up as much wood as you like ...'

'That's all very well ...'

'Oh, don't go on! If such measures were necessary and timely the Regional Committee would tell us straight: "destroy the kulak!" And then, by all means! In two twos! The militia and the whole of the government machinery are at our service. But for the present we only partially punish the kulak who conceals his grain, and that by economic measures, under article 107, before the People's Court.'

'And so in your opinion the labourers, the poor and the middling peasants are against liquidating the kulaks? They're on the kulaks' side? They've got to be led against the kulaks?'

The secretary noisily snapped the lock of his document case, and drily replied:

'It's up to you to interpret any speech of the leader how you like, but the District Committee Bureau, and I personally, are responsible for the district. You will see to it that you follow our line in the village we're sending you to, and not some line invented by yourself. And I've got other business to attend to besides you.' He rose to his feet.

The blood again flushed strongly into Davidov's cheeks, but he took himself in hand, and answered:

'I shall follow the line laid down by the Party, and I tell you straight out, in worker fashion; your line is wrong, it is politically incorrect. Fact!'

'I'll answer for my work . . . and that "worker fashion" business is out of date . . .'

The telephone bell rang. The secretary picked up the receiver. Others began to enter the room, and Davidov went off to see the head of the Organization Department.

'He's limping on the right leg . . . Fact!' he thought, as he left the office. 'I'll read that speech to the agrarians again . . . surely I'm not wrong? No, brother, excuse me! With your tolerance you've allowed the kulak to get out of hand. At the Regional Committee they said you're a "capable man", but your kulaks are behind with their grain. It's one thing to squeeze them, and another to root them out as a pest. Why aren't you leading the masses?' he mentally continued the discussion with the secretary. As always, his most convincing arguments occurred to him afterwards. In the office he had got excited and agitated, and had clutched at the first objection that came into his head. He ought to have kept calmer. He splashed in the frozen puddles as he walked, and stumbled over the icy clods of cow-dung in the market square.

'Pity we finished so quickly, or I'd have squeezed you!' he said aloud. Then he lapsed into a chagrined silence as he noticed a woman pass him with a smile on her face.

He hurried to the 'Cossack and Peasant House', and picked up his suitcase, smiling as he remembered that its chief contents, apart from two changes of linen, socks, and a suit, consisted of screwdrivers, pliers, a file, calipers, a bolt chisel, a spanner and other simple tools of his which he had hurriedly snatched up at Leningrad. 'Damn it, I'll have a lot of use for them!' he thought. 'I must have imagined I'd be digging myself into a collective farm and have to repair a tractor. And there aren't any tractors here. And it looks as though I shall be dashing all over the district as an organizer. I'll give them to a smith in some collective farm,' he decided as he threw the suitcase into the sleigh.

The oat-fed District Executive Committee horses easily drew along the sleigh, which had its back painted in bright colours. Davidov began to freeze almost before they had left the town. He vainly wrapped his face in the shabby sheepskin collar of his greatcoat, and pulled his cap down over his eyes. The wind and the damp sleet penetrated under the collar and up the sleeves, chilling him with the cold. In their light, well-worn town boots, his feet felt especially frozen.

From the district town to Gremyachy Log stretched twenty-eight kilometres of lonely upland ridges. The track, brown with melting dung, lay along the top of the ridges. All around, as far as eye could see, stretched snow-covered, virgin soil. At the sides of the road, the sparse tops of wormwood and thistles huddled miserably. Only from the slopes of the gullies did the earth peer out at the world with little clayey eyes. There, blown away by the wind, the snow had no hold. But the channels at the bottoms of the gullies and ravines were filled to their edges with solid drifts.

Davidov got out of the sleigh and ran for some time, holding on to the side, trying to get his feet warm. Then he jumped in again, and, huddling into the bottom, fell into a doze. The sleigh runners whistled, the calkers of the horse-shoes dug into the snow with a dry scrunch, the swing-tree of the right-hand shaft-horse rattled. Occasionally, from under his rimed eyelids Davidov saw the wings of rooks rising violently from the road and flickering like violet summer-lightning in the sun, then a pleasant drowsiness again closed his eyes.

He was awakened by the cold, which was gripping his heart like a vice. Opening his eyes, through the glittering rainbow-hues of his tears he saw the chilly sun, the majestic expanse of the silent steppe, the leaden-grey sky on the selvedge of the horizon. On the white cap of a mound close at hand was a ruddy tawny fox with a fiery tinge to its coat. It reared on to its hind legs, then, with a twist of its body, leaped up; dropping on its forepaws, it scooped away with them, enveloping itself in a glittering silver dust, while its tail lay softly and flexibly like a crimson tongue of flame on the snow.

They arrived at Gremyachy Log in the early evening. Several two-horsed sledges were standing empty in the spacious yard of

18

the village Soviet. Some seven or eight cossacks were crowded, smoking, around the porch. The horses, their coats covered with frozen sweat, came to a halt in front of them.

'Good evening, citizens. Where's the stable?' Davidov asked.

'Your good health!' an elderly cossack answered for them all, raising his hand to the edge of his hareskin cap. 'That's the stable over there, comrade, under that reed-thatched roof.'

'Stop over there,' Davidov ordered his driver, and he jumped, a stocky, thickset figure, out of the sleigh. Rubbing his cheeks with his glove, he followed the driver. The cossacks also went towards the stable, unable to understand why the new arrival, evidently an official, and speaking with the harder northern Russian accent, had followed the sleigh and not gone straight into the Soviet.

A dungy steam billowed out of the stable doors. The driver halted the horses. Davidov confidently set to work to free a swing-tree from its traces. The cossacks crowding around him exchanged glances. Scraping the icicles from his whiskers, an old fellow in a woman's white sheepskin slily winked and remarked:

'Look out or he'll kick, comrade!'

Davidov freed the strap from under the horse's tail, then, his bluish lips smiling and revealing the loss of a single tooth, he turned to the old man.

'I've been a machine-gunner, daddy, and I think I can manage these ponies!' he remarked.

'And the tooth you've lost, did a horse kick it out?' asked a cossack as black as a raven, with a curly beard growing right up to his nostrils. The others laughed good-naturedly, and as Davidov deftly removed the collar he also jested:

'No, I lost my tooth years ago in a drunken business. And I'm better off without it; the women won't be afraid of my biting them. Will they, daddy?'

They took the sally in good part, and with assumed regret the old man shook his head:

'I've done with biting too, my boy. My tooth fell out long ago!'

The black-bearded cossack roared like a stallion, opening wide his white-toothed jaws and seizing the crimson sash which tightly girdled his cossack coat, as though afraid of bursting with laughter.

Davidov handed his cigarettes around, lit one for himself, and went towards the village Soviet.

'You'll find the chairman in there. And the secretary of our party is there too,' the old man said, as he followed close on Davidov's heels. Smoking their cigarettes away in a couple of puffs, the other cossacks also followed. They had been delighted to find that the newcomer was not like those who usually came out from the district offices; he had not jumped out of his sledge and rushed past them into the Soviet, hugging his document case under his arm, but had lent a hand with unharnessing the horses, helping the driver and revealing long acquaintance and knack in handling horses. But at the same time they were surprised.

'How is it you don't mind seeing to the horses, comrade? That isn't an official's job, is it? What's the driver for?' The black-bearded cossack could not restrain his curiosity.

'It seems very strange to us,' the old man openly admitted.

But Davidov had no chance of answering. 'Why, he's a smith!' a young, yellow-whiskered little cossack exclaimed in a disillusioned tone, pointing to Davidov's hands, with their palms leaden-hued through contact with metal, and their nails marked with old scars.

'A locksmith!' Davidov corrected him. 'But what are you coming into the Soviet for?'

'We're interested,' the old man answered for them all, as he halted on the bottom step of the porch. 'We're curious to know what you've come for. If it's about the grain collections . . .'

'It's about the collective farm.'

The old man gave a long and bitter whistle, and was the first to turn away from the porch.

The low-ceilinged room smelt strongly of the sour warmth of thawing sheepskins and wood-ash. At the table, turning up the wick of a lamp, stood a tall, square-shouldered man with his face towards Davidov. The crimson ribbon of the 'Order of the Red Banner' was visible on his khaki shirt. Davidov guessed that he was the secretary of the Gremyachy Party nucleus.

'I'm the delegate from the District Committee,' he announced. 'Are you the secretary of the nucleus, comrade?'

'Yes, I'm the secretary. My name's Nagulnov. Sit down, comrade. The chairman of the Soviet will be here in a minute,' Nagulnov rapped with his fist on the wall, then came over to Davidov. He was broad in the chest, and had the bandy legs of a cavalryman. Above his yellow eyes with their extraordinarily large pupils, which looked as though filmed with oil, grew well-arched, black eyebrows. He would have been handsome in his negligent, but decidedly masculine features, but for the too rapacious slit of the nostrils of his small, abbreviated nose, and the muddy film over his eyes.

A stocky cossack wearing a grey, goatskin cap thrust to the back of his head, a short jacket of military material, and striped cossack trousers gathered into white woollen stockings, emerged from the other room.

'Here's the Soviet chairman, Andrei Razmiotnov,' said the secretary.

The chairman smilingly stroked his blond, curly whiskers with his palm, and dignifiedly stretched his hand out to Davidov.

'And who are you?' he asked. 'A delegate from the District Committee? Aha! Your documents ... Have you looked at them, Makar? You've come about the question of the collective farm, I suppose?' He scrutinized Davidov with a naïve lack of constraint, frequently winking his eyes, clear and blue as a summer sky. A look of impatient expectation passed frankly over his swarthy, long unshaven face. Across his forehead ran a livid, crooked scar.

Davidov sat down at the table, told them of the tasks which the party had set in connection with the two months' advance towards complete collectivization, and proposed that a meeting of the poor cossacks and active workers be called for the very next day.

Nagulnov explained the local situation to him, particularly telling him about the Gremyachy Association for joint working the land. While he talked, Razmiotnov listened attentively, occasionally interpolating a remark, without removing his hand from his darkly flushed face.

'We've got an Association for joint working the land here,' Nagulnov began, speaking with obvious agitation. 'And I tell you, comrade worker, it's nothing but a mockery of collectivization and a dead loss to the government. There are eighteen farms in it, all of them the poorest of the poor. And what's the result of it all? It's inevitably a laughing-stock. When it was started the eighteen farms had only four horses and a yoke of oxen between them, and 107 mouths to fill. And how are they going to justify their existence? Of course, they get long-term credits for purchasing machinery and draught animals. They take the credits, but they'll not be able to pay them back even though they are long-term. And I'll tell you why: if they had a tractor it'd be another matter, but they weren't given a tractor, and you don't get rich quickly with oxen. And I tell you, too, they've gone wrong in their policy, and I'd have sent them all packing long ago for lying down to the government like an ailing calf: it can suck all right, but it doesn't grow at all. And they think among themselves: "They'll help us in any case! But they can't take anything from us in payment of the debts." And so their discipline's gone all to pieces, and the Association will be a corpse before long. It's a sound idea to get everybody into a collective farm. That would be heaven, and not earthly life! But the cossacks are a wooden-headed lot, I tell you, and they'll have to be broken...'

'Is there any party member in the Association?' Davidov asked, looking from one to the other.

'No,' Nagulnov replied. 'I joined a commune in 1920, but after a time it broke up owing to some of its members ratting. I gave up what belonged to me. I was filled with anger against all property, so I gave my oxen and stock to a neighbouring commune, which still exists, and I and my wife have got nothing. Razmiotnov couldn't set any example: he's a widower, and he's only got his old mother. If he'd joined, the reproaches would have stuck to him like burrs. They'd have said: "He's shoved his old mother on to us, and he doesn't do any work on the land himself." We've got to be careful here. And the third member of the nucleus – he's away just now – he's one-handed. A thresher tore off the other.

And he doesn't like to join the Association; he thinks they've got enough mouths to feed without his.'

'Yes, our Association is in a bad way,' Razmiotnov confirmed. 'It's chairman, Arkashka Losiev, is a bad manager. They chose the best man all right! We must admit we were at fault in the matter. We ought not to have let him take the job.'

'Why not?' Davidov asked as he ran his eyes over a list of kulak farm property.

'Because he's a sick man,' Razmiotnov said with a smile. 'He was just made to be a merchant. That's what he suffers from: he'd exchange and resell everything. He's ruined the Association completely. They bought a blood bull for breeding, and he decided to change it for a motor-cycle. He got round the members, didn't consult us at all, and the next thing they sent out this motor-cycle from the district town. We groaned and clutched our heads! Well, it was brought out, and nobody knew how to drive it. And what did they want it for, anyhow? It would have been funny if it hadn't been tragic. Back to the district it went. There the experts looked at it and said: "It would be cheaper to scrap it." It had certain parts missing which could only be made at a factory. They ought to have had Yakov Ostrovnov for chairman. He's got a good head! He had some wheat of a new, finer sort sent him from Krasnodar, which lives through the worst of drought; he always keeps the snow on his autumn ploughed land, and his harvest is always among the best in the village. He's raised first-class cattle, too. He groans a bit when we press him for his taxes, but he's a good farmer, and has a letter of praise from the Agricultural Department.'

'He's like a wild goose among his gander; he's always on his own, and keeps himself at a distance,' Nagulnov dubiously shook his head.

'No, he doesn't. He's all right,' Razmiotnov confidently declared.

Chapter 3

The Conspiracy

THE night Yakov Lukich Ostrovnov was visited by his former company commander, captain Polovtsiev, the two men had a long talk. In Gremyachy village, Yakov was regarded as a man of great intelligence, and as crafty as a fox in his caution and behaviour, yet even he could not avoid the raging struggle which had broken out in the villages, for like a whirlpool it drew him into its events. From that night his life began to descend a dangerous slope.

After supper Lukich took out his pouch, sat down on the chest, crossing his legs clad in their thick, woollen stockings, and began to talk, pouring out all that the years had piled up bitterly in his heart.

'What is there to talk about, Alexander Anisimovich?' he said. 'There's no joy or pleasure in life, these days. The cossacks had begun to build up their farms again, and to get rich. In 1926, and even in 1927, the taxes were, well, comparatively bearable. But now they've turned the clock back again. How are things in your district; is there any talk of collectivization there?'

'There's talk,' his guest briefly replied, licking a cigarette paper and staring attentively from under his brows at Lukich.

'So everywhere tears are falling because of that cheerful song, are they?' Lukich said. 'I'll tell you my story. I returned from the retreat in 1920. I left a pair of horses and all my goods down by the Black Sea. I came back to a bare hut. Ever since then I've worked day and night. The first time the comrades troubled me with their grain requisitions, they raked up every bit of my grain. I've lost count of the wrongs I've suffered since then. I could reckon them up, though: they do you a wrong and then write you out a receipt so that you won't forget.' He rose, slipped his hand behind the mirror, and, smiling into his clipped moustache, drew out a sheaf of papers. 'Here they are; here are the receipts for what they took in 1921, and I gave up grain, and meat, and butter, and skins, and wool, and fowls, and I took whole oxen into the collections office. And here are the receipts for the single agricultural tax, for self-taxation, and these are for insurance. I've even paid for the smoke that came out of the chimney and for the cattle standing alive in the yard. I'll have a sackful of such papers soon. In a word, Alexander Anisimovich, I've lived, and fed myself from the earth, and fed others around me too. They've skinned me again and again, but I've grown a new skin every time. I got a yoke of young oxen to begin with, and they grew up. I sold one at a smart price for meat, but I bought another with my wife's sewing-machine. After a time, in 1925, I got another yoke of oxen from my own cows. So I had two yoke of oxen and two cows. They didn't take my vote from me, but for the future they wrote me down among the middling to rich peasants.'

'And have you got any horses?' his guest asked.

'Wait a bit, and I'll tell you about the horses. From a neighbour, I bought a yearling filly born of a thoroughbred Don mare (the only one left in the whole village). The filly grew up a beauty. Not many hands high, no good for the army, an inch short, but spirited beyond belief! At a district exhibition of agricultural life I won a prize for her, and a certificate that she was a blood-mare. I began to listen to the agricultural inspectors, started a proper rotation of crops, and looked after my land as though it was a sick wife. My maize is the finest in the village, and I get the best harvest of all. I chemically treated my grain, and took steps to keep the snow on my fields. I sowed the spring seed grain immediately after ploughing, without any spring tilling, and my sown fallow was always the first. In a word, I became a scientific farmer, and I've had a letter of praise from the District Agricultural Department. Have a look at it.'

The guest glanced fleetingly in the direction indicated by Yakov's finger, and saw a letter with a wax seal, in a wooden frame, hanging at the side of the ikons and a portrait of Voroshilov.

'Yes, they sent me that letter, and the inspector even took

away a handful of my fine wheat to show the authorities at Rostov,' Yakov Lukich proudly continued. 'During the first years after my return I sowed five hectares, then, as I got on, I bent my back to it even more. I sowed twelve, then twenty, and even thirty hectares, think of that! I worked, and my son and his wife. I only hired a labourer a couple of times at the busiest season. What was the Soviet government's order in those years? Sow as much as you can! And I sowed until my back well-nigh broke, by the true Christ! And now, Alexander Anisimovich, my friend, believe me I'm afraid. I'm afraid that because of my thirty hectares they'll drag me through the needle's eye, and call me a kulak. The chairman of our Soviet, the Red Partisan comrade, Razmiotnov, it was he who led me into this sin, damn him! "Sow," he used to say, "sow the maximum you can, Yakov Lukich; help the Soviet government, it badly needs grain now." I was doubtful about it at the time, but now I'm beginning to think that his maximum will get my legs tied up to my neck, God defend me!'

'Is anybody putting his name down for the collective farm in your village?' the guest inquired. He stood by the bed, his hands behind his back, broad-shouldered, big-headed, and solid like a sack of grain.

'The collective farm? They haven't troubled us much about it so far, but there's to be a meeting of the poor cossacks tomorrow. They went round telling everybody just before sunset. They've been talking about it ever since Christmas. Nothing but "Join!" and "Join!" But everybody flatly refused, nobody put his name down. Who's going to hit himself in the eye? I expect they'll try to bring off the match again tomorrow! They say some worker has arrived from the District this evening, and he will drive us all into the collective farm. The end of our life is coming. I've built up my farm, and got a hump on my back and calluses on my hands into the bargain, and now have I got to give everything into the common stock: my cattle, and grain, and fowls, and my home too? That way it works out that you give your wife up to others, and you go yourself to the whores, that's all. Judge for yourself, Alexander Anisimovich. I'll be giving the collective farm a yoke of oxen (I've managed to get rid of one yoke to the Meat Co-operative), a mare with foal, all my implements and grain. And another will be giving only his lousy pants. We each give what we've got, and we shall share the profits equally. And isn't that unjust to me? Maybe another man's lain on the stove all his life dreaming of owning a farm, while I ... But why talk about it? Look!' And he drew the edge of his hairy hand across his throat. 'Well, enough of that. How are you getting on? Are you working in an office, or are you an artisan?'

The guest drew closer to Yakov Lukich, sat down on a stool, and began to roll another cigarette. He stared fixedly into his tobacco-pouch, and Yakov stared at the tight collar of his guest's old tunic shirt which cut into his swarthy, swollen neck, causing the veins to stand out on both sides of the Adam's apple.

'You served in my company, Lukich ... D'you remember how, in Yekaterinodar, I think it was, when we were retreating, I had a talk with the cossacks about the Soviet government? Even then I warned them, you remember? "You're bitterly mistaken, my boys!" I said. "The communists will squeeze you, will twist you into a ram's horn. You must wake up or it'll be too late!"' He was silent, the tiny, pinhead pupils contracted in his blue eyes, and he smiled a thin smile. 'Wasn't I right? I didn't leave Novorossiisk with the others. I couldn't manage it; the volunteers and allies betrayed us, abandoned us. I joined the Red Army, and was put in command of a squadron, but on the road to the Polish front they had a commission for weeding out and testing former officers. The commission removed me from my position, arrested me, and sent me to the Revolutionary Tribunal. The comrades would have shot me without a doubt, or else put me in a concentration camp. And can you guess what for? Some son of a bitch from my home village informed them that I had taken part in the execution of Podtielkov. On the way to the Tribunal I escaped ... I hid for a long time, living under a different name, but in 1923 I returned to my village. I had managed to preserve the document showing I had been a Red Commander, and I found some good lads. In a word, I was left to live. To begin with I was dragged to the Regional Political Bureau of the Don Cheka, but I wriggled my way out of it, and became a teacher. I was teaching until quite recently. But now ... Now I'm on a different business. I'm riding to Ust-Khopersk district on various matters, and dropped in to see you as an old comrade in arms.'

'So you've been a teacher? So ... You're a well-read man, you've studied books, tell me what's going to happen now? Where shall we get to with these collective farms?'

'To communism, brother! To the true and genuine! I've read Karl Marx and the famous Communist Manifesto. D'you know what the end of the collective farm business will be? It will start with the collective farm, but it will go on to the commune, to the complete abolition of property. Not only your oxen, but your children will be taken away from you to be brought up by the state. Everything will be in common: children, wives, cups and spoons. You'd like to eat vermicelli and goose giblets, but they'll feed you on sour beer. You'll be a serf tied to the land.'

'But supposing I don't want to be?'

'They won't even ask you.'

'What d'you mean?'

'I mean what I say.'

'Fine!'

'So you say! Now I ask you: can you go on living like that?'

'No, I can't.'

'Then if you can't, you've got to act; you've got to fight!'

'What are you saying, Alexander Anisimovich? We've tried that, we did fight ... It's not possible, anyhow. I can't even imagine it.'

'But you try!' Polovtsiev moved right up to his companion, glanced at the fast-closed door, and, suddenly turning pale, went on in an undertone: 'I tell you straight I'm counting on you: in our district the cossacks are getting ready to revolt. And don't you think that's all there is to it! We've got connections with Moscow, with generals who're now serving in the Red Army, with engineers who're working in factories and works, and even further, with abroad. Yes, yes! If we organize solidly and act at once, with the help of foreign powers the Don will be cleared by the spring. You'll sow your land with your own grain and for yourself. Wait; speak when I'm finished. There are many

28

sympathetic to us in your district. They must be united and collected. That's what I'm going to Ust-Khopersk for. Will you join us? We've already got over three hundred front-line cossacks in our organization. We've got militant groups in Dubrovsky, and Voiskovoi, Tubyanskoe and other villages. A similar group must be organized in Gremyachy. Well, now you speak.'

'The people are grumbling against the collective farms and against giving up their grain . . .'

'Wait a bit! We're not talking about the "people", but about yourself. I ask you, well?'

'Can I settle such a question in a moment? You're asking me to put my head under the axe.'

'Think! On the order, we shall attack simultaneously in all the villages. We'll seize your district town, deal with the militia and the communists one at a time in their quarters, and after that we'll be sailing along without any need for wind.'

'But where are the weapons coming from?'

'They'll be found. You've got something left, I expect.'

'Who knows? . . . I think there's a souvenir lying around somewhere. An Austrian pattern . . .'

'We've only got to begin, and within a week foreign ships will bring guns and rifles. And aeroplanes, too. Well?'

'Let me think it over, captain! Don't force me at once to . . .'

His face still pale, the captain bent towards the bed and said thickly:

'We're not calling on you to join a collective farm, and we aren't forcing anybody. It's as you will, but keep a watch on your tongue, Lukich! There's six for you, and the seventh . . .' With his finger he spun the barrels of the revolver rattling in his pocket.

'You needn't fear for my tongue. But yours is a risky business. And I don't sweat about it: it's terrible to have to take such a road, but my life is finished, anyhow.' He was silent. After a minute or two he went on: 'If they didn't hunt the rich cossacks I might now, with my efforts, be the first man in the village. In a free life I might be driving my own car. But to take that road alone . . .'

'But why alone?' the captain disagreeably interrupted him.

'Well, I keep my word; but how about others? What is the world like? Will the people take it up?'

'The people are like a flock of sheep. They must be led. Have you decided?'

'I said, Alexander Anisimovich . . .'

'I want to know definitely, yes or no.'

'I can't get out of it, so I must decide. All the same, give me time to think it over. I'll say my final word tomorrow morning.'

'In addition you must talk over reliable cossacks. Seek out those who are baring their teeth against the Soviet government.' Polovtsiev was already issuing orders.

'With things as they are everybody is doing that.'

'And how about your son?'

'What can the finger do without the hand? Where I go, he goes.'

'Is he a good lad, and dependable?'

'He's a good cossack,' Yakov Lukich replied with quiet pride.

A grey sledge rug and sheepskin were spread by the stove in the best room for the guest. He removed his boots, but did not undress, and he fell asleep as soon as his cheek touched the cold, smelly feather pillow.

Before dawn next morning Yakov Lukich awoke his eighty-year-old mother, who was sleeping in the little side room. He briefly told her what his former company commander had come to see him about. The old woman listened, letting her black-veined legs, the joints distorted with cold, hang from the stove, and thrusting her yellow ear forward with her palm.

'Have I your blessing, mother?' Yakov Lukich went down on his knees.

'Rise, rise against them, the enemies, my child! God bless you! They're shutting up the churches ... They won't let the priests live ... Attack them!'

In the morning, Yakov awoke his guest and told him:

'I've decided. What are your orders?'

'Read this and sign it.' Polovtsiev pulled a paper out of his breast pocket. Yakov Lukich read:

'God with us. I, a cossack of the Almighty Don Army, hereby

join the Alliance for the Emancipation of the Native Don, and pledge myself to the last drop of my blood to fight with all my strength and means on the order of my superior officers against the communist bolsheviks, the accursed enemies of the Christian faith and the oppressors of the Russian people. I pledge myself unreservedly to obey my superior officers and commanders. I pledge myself to place all my possessions on the altar of the Russian orthodox fatherland. To which I set my hand.'

Chapter 4

A Village Meeting

THIRTY-TWO people, active workers and poor cossacks of Gremyachy, breathed with a single breath. Davidov was no great speaker, but from the beginning they listened to him more attentively than if he had been the most artistic of story-tellers.

'I am a worker from the Red Putilov works, comrades,' he opened his speech. 'I have been sent to you by our Communist Party and the working class, in order to help you organize a collective farm and to destroy the kulaks, our common bloodsuckers. I shall not say much. You must all join together in a collective farm, socialize the land, and all your implements and cattle. Why must you join a collective farm? Because it is impossible to go on living as we are! The difficulties we're having with the grain have arisen because the kulak lets it rot in the ground. We have got to get the grain from him by force! But you would be glad to give your grain, only you haven't got much. You can't feed the Soviet Union on the grain of the poor middling peasants. We've got to sow more. But how are you going to sow more with only a wooden or a single-share plough? Only the tractor can get us out of that difficulty. Fact! I don't know how much you can plough here in the Don with one plough during the autumn . . .'

'With your hands glued to the plough-handle from daybreak

31

to sunset you'll turn over some twelve hectares during the aut
umn,' someone answered.

'Ho! Twelve! And supposing the earth is hard?' another cossack objected.

'What are you talking about?' came a shrill female voice. 'You
want three or even four yoke of good oxen to the plough to do
that, and where have we got them? Some of us, and not every
one of us, have got a yoke of bullocks, but most of us have got
the sort of oxen that have udders. The rich now, they have the
wind at their backs.'

'That's not the point! You'd better shove your apron end
into your mouth and shut up!' came a hoarse bass voice.

'You talk sense! Go and teach your wife, and not me!' the
woman replied.

'And how much could you plough with a tractor?' someone
asked.

Davidov waited until there was silence, then he answered:

'With a tractor, with one of our Putilov manufacture say,
and good, expert drivers we could plough up those twelve hectares in a day of two shifts.'

The meeting gasped. Someone remarked in a tone of stupe-
faction: 'Well, I'm damned!'

'Now that's fine! That's the horse to plough with,' came an
envious whistle.

Davidov wiped his hand over his lips, which were dry with
his agitation, and went on:

'Supposing we build a tractor for you at our works. It's not
easy for a poor or middling peasant to buy a tractor by himself.
He couldn't digest it! So, in order to buy it the labourers and
the poor and middling cossacks must unite collectively. You
know that a tractor's a machine which if you use it on a small
bit of ground it's only a loss. It needs a large area. And even
with your small land-working associations you get about as
much service from it as milk from a goat.'

'Even less,' a bass voice barked from the back rows.

'So what's to be done?' Davidov went on, ignoring the reply.

'The Party proposes complete collectivization, so as to hitch you
on to the tractor and lift you out of your want. What did com-

rade Lenin say just before his death? "Only in the collective farm can the peasant find salvation from his poverty. Otherwise he is doomed. The vampire kulak will suck him as flat as a board." And you must walk quite firmly along the road he pointed out. In alliance with the workers the collective farmers will sweep away all the kulaks and enemies. I'm speaking the truth. And now I must talk about your Association. It's too small and weak, and so it's in a very miserable state. And that means you're pouring water down a drain. It's nothing but a loss. But we must include the Association in the collective farm and make it the backbone, and around that backbone the middling peasants will grow . . .'

'Wait a bit! Let me chip in!' shock-headed and squinting Diemka Ushakov, who had once been a member of the Association, rose to his feet.

'Ask to speak, and then speak,' Nagulnov, who was sitting with Davidov and Razmiotnov, sternly instructed him.

'I'll tell you without asking,' Diemka waved him down, squinting so terribly that it appeared as though he were looking simultaneously at the table and at the meeting. 'Whose fault is it, if you'll excuse me, that the Association has been a loss and the Soviet government's had the burden of it? Whose fault was it that we lived like beggars on credit? It was through your dear chairman of the Association, through Arkashka and his bargaining.'

'You're lying like a counter-revolutionary element!' came a tenor cock-crow from the back of the room. And Arkashka elbowed his way to the table.

'I'll prove it!' Diemka went pale, and his eyes turned in towards the bridge of his nose. Taking no heed of Razmiotnov knocking with his fist, he turned to Arkashka. 'You can't get out of it! We and our collective farm didn't fall on evil times because there were so few of us, but because of your bargains. And I'll give it to you all the more for your "counter-revolutionary element". Did you change the bull for a motor-cycle without asking permission? You did! And who thought of exchanging our laying-hens for . . .'

'You're lying again!' Arkashka defended himself on the run.

'Wasn't it you who got us to exchange three sheep and a young cow for a light cart? A snotty-nosed trader, that's what you are!' Diemka triumphantly shouted.

'Steady now! Are you a couple of cocks?' Nagulnov urged, his cheek muscles working under his flushed skin.

'Let me have my turn to speak,' Arkashka asked, as he stood at the table. He had gathered his ruddy beard into his fist in readiness to speak when Davidov interrupted him with:

'Let me finish, and don't butt in, please! Well, as I was saying, comrades, only through a collective farm can you ...'

'You needn't try to work us up with your propaganda! We'll join the collective farm down to our giblets,' the Red Partisan Pavel Liubishkin, who was sitting nearest to the door, broke in.

'We agree with the collective farm!' another shouted.

'With an Association we can beat the devil himself!'

'Only we must run it properly!'

The same Liubishkin outshouted all the rest. He rose from his chair, took off his black, forbidding fur cap and, tall and broad-shouldered, leaned against the door.

'You're queer, aren't you, agitating among us on behalf of the Soviet government? It was us who set it on its feet during the war, it was us who supported it with our shoulders, so that it didn't break down. We know what a collective farm is, and we're all for it. Give us machines!' He stretched out a fist the size of a turnip. 'A tractor's fine, we know, but you workers have only made a few of them, and that's what we swear at you for. We haven't got anything to lay hold of, that's the trouble. And we can plough with oxen, one hand driving, the other wiping away our tears, without joining a collective farm. I myself was thinking of sending Kalinin a letter before the collective farm movement began, to ask them to help the grain-growers to begin a new life. For the first few years were just like the old regime – pay your taxes, live as best you can, and what was the Russian Communist Party for? Well, we won the civil war, and then what? Again the old style: follow the plough, those who had anything to harness to a plough. And those who hadn't ... Were they to stretch out their hands and beg at the church door? Or to wait with a wooden club under a bridge and frighten

Soviet merchants and co-operative managers? They allowed the rich to rent land, they allowed them to hire labourers. Was that what the revolution dictated in 1918? You've closed the eyes of the revolution! And when we say: "What did we fight for?" the officials, who never smelt powder, sneer at us, and behind their backs all the white swine burst out laughing! No, you needn't try to teach us! We've heard many fine speeches in our time. You give us a machine on credit or for grain, and not a ploughshare or a horse-plough, but a good machine! Give us the tractor you talked about. What did I get these for?' Right across the knees of those sitting on the front benches he strode up to the table, unbuttoning his loose, ragged trousers as he went. At the table he pulled up the edge of his shirt, and held it against his breast with his chin. Terrible scars which puckered the skin were revealed on his belly and thigh.

'What did I get these souvenirs of Cadet hospitality for?' he demanded.

'You shameless devil! Why don't you let your trousers drop altogether?' widow Anisya, who was sitting next to Diemka Ushakov, exclaimed in a shrill, indignant voice.

'And you'd like him to, wouldn't you?' Diemka squinted contemptuously at her.

'You shut up, auntie Anisya! I'm not ashamed of showing my wounds to a working man. Let him look! And if we have to go on living as we are, there'll be nothing for this poor devil to cover all these scars up with! Even now they're only trousers in name. I can't go past any girls during the daytime, I'd frighten them to death.'

Those at the back began to laugh, and a hubbub arose; but Liubishkin swept them with his harsh eyes, and again it was quiet enough for the faint spluttering of the burning lamp-wick to be heard.

'It seems I fought the Cadets for the rich to live better than me. For them to have the sweets, and I get bread and onion. Is that so, comrade worker? Don't you wink at me, Makar! I only speak once a year, so I can speak now.'

'Go on!' Davidov nodded his head.

'I'm going on! This year I sowed three hectares of wheat.

I've got three little children, a lame sister and a sick wife. Did I hand over my grain according to the plan, Razmiotnov?'

'You did, but don't make a song about it!'

'Yes, I shall! And how about the kulak Frol, the devil take him?'

'Now, now!' Nagulnov knocked with his fist.

'Did Frol hand over his grain according to plan? He didn't.'

'And the court fined him and took the grain,' Razmiotnov intervened, his filmy eyes glittering as he listened with obvious enjoyment.

'You ought to be here, my easy-going friend,' Davidov thought, as he remembered the District Committtee secretary.

'But this year he'll be "Frol Ignatich" again! And in the spring he'll come and hire me again!' Liubishkin threw his black fur cap at Davidov's feet. 'What are you talking to me about the collective farm for? Cut the veins of the kulaks, and then we'll join! Give us their machines, their oxen, give us their strength, then we shall have our equality! But now it's all talk and talk about "destroy the kulak", while he grows from year to year like a burdock, and keeps the sun off us.'

'Give us Frol's property and Arkashka will exchange it for an aeroplane!' Diemka interrupted.

'Ha – ha – ha – ha!'

'That's just what he would do!'

'You're witnesses of their insults,' Arkashka shouted.

'Quiet, we can't hear!'

'Can't you speak in turns, you devils?'

With considerable effort Davidov at last succeeded in restoring order.

'That is the policy of our party,' he declared. 'What are you knocking at an open door for? Destroy the kulak as a class, hand over his property to the collective farms! Fact! And you, comrade Partisan, you threw your cap under the table for nothing, you'll still need it for your head. The renting of land and hiring of labourers can't go on any longer! We put up with the kulaks because of our need, they supplied more bread than the collective farms did. But now it's the other way round. Comrade Stalin has reckoned it all up to the last figure and said:

"Free the kulak of his life! Hand his property to the collective farms." You've all been crying out for machines. Five hundred million whole roubles are going to be given to the collective farms to get them on to their feet. What d'you think of that? Have you heard about that? Then what are you shouting about? First you've got to start your collective farm, and then worry about machinery. But you want to buy the collar first, and when you've got it you'll buy a horse! What are you laughing at? That's true!'

'Liubishkin wants to go arse forward!'

'We're heart and soul for the collective farm.'

'He hit the mark with his collar!'

'We'll join tonight. Write our names down at once.'

'Lead us to smash up the kulaks!'

'All who want to join the collective farm, put up your hands,' Nagulnov proposed. Thirty-three hands were counted. Someone had absent-mindedly put up two.

The stifling heat had peeled Davidov out of his greatcoat and jacket. He unbuttoned the collar of his shirt, and smiled as he waited for silence.

'You're class conscious all right. Fact! But do you think you've only got to join the collective farm, and that's all? Well, it isn't! You poor peasants are the basis of the Soviet government. You're the green kernel, and you've got to join the collective farm yourselves, and bring in the hesitating middling peasant after you.'

'And how are you going to get him in if he doesn't want to come? Is he an ox, that you can tie the reins to his horns and lead him?' Arkashka asked.

'Persuade him! You're a fine fighter for our truth if you can't convert another. There'll be a meeting tomorrow. You vote in favour yourself, and persuade your middling peasant neighbour to do the same. Now we'll turn to consideration of the kulak. Shall we pass a resolution to expel them all from the boundaries of the North Caucasian area, or what?'

'Agreed!'

'Dig under their roots!'

'No, better dig up their roots, and not under them,' Davidov corrected the remark. He turned to Razmiotnov and asked: 'Read out the list of kulaks. Then we'll confirm that they're to be destroyed as kulaks.'

Andrei Razmiotnov drew a sheet of paper out of his document case and handed it to Davidov.

'Frol Damaskov. Is he worthy of this proletarian punishment?' Davidov asked.

Hands were raised at once. But when they were counted Davidov discovered that someone had refrained from voting.

'Aren't you in favour?' he demanded, raising his sweating eyebrows.

'I'm not voting,' the cossack who had abstained, a quiet-looking and undistinguished man, curtly replied.

'Why aren't you?' Davidov questioned him.

'Because he's my neighbour, and he's been very kind to me. So I can't put up my hand against him.'

'Leave the meeting at once!' Nagulnov ordered in a quivering voice, rising as though in stirrups.

'No! that won't do, comrade Nagulnov!' Davidov sternly intervened. 'Don't go, citizen! Explain your position. In your view is Damaskov a kulak or not?'

'I don't understand what you mean. I'm not an educated man, and I must ask you to let me leave the meeting.'

'No! You tell us how he's been kind to you.'

'He's always helped me, let me have his oxen, lent me seed ... Isn't that something? But I'm not a traitor ... I'm in favour of the Soviets ...'

'Did he ask you to stand up for him? Has he given you money, or grain? Speak up now, don't be afraid!' Razmiotnov joined in. 'Now, tell us what he's offered you,' and he smiled awkwardly, out of shame for the man and for his own blunt question.

'Maybe he hasn't promised me anything, for all you know.'

'You're lying, Timofei! You're a bought man, and so you're a supporter of the kulaks,' someone shouted from the benches.

'Call me what you like, as you will ...'

As though he were setting a knife against the man's throat, Davidov asked him:

'Are you for the Soviet government or for the kulaks? Don't

bring shame on the poorer class, citizen, but say straight out on whose side you are.'

'Why waste time on him?' Liubishkin indignantly interrupted. 'You can buy him, old clothes and all, for a bottle of vodka. You make my eyes ache to look at you, Timofei!'

At last, with assumed submissiveness, the non-voter, Timofei Borshchev, replied:

'I'm for the government; what are you attacking me for? My ignorance made me go wrong.' But when the vote was taken a second time he raised his hand with obvious reluctance.

Davidov briefly made the note in his notebook: 'Timofei Borshchev is a muddled class enemy. Must work on him.'

The meeting unanimously confirmed the names of four more kulaks. But then Davidov read out:

'Tit Borodin.'

'Who's in favour?' he asked.

The meeting was oppressively silent. Nagulnov exchanged an embarrassed glance with Razmiotnov. Liubishkin took to mopping his wet brow with his cap.

'What's the silence about? What's the matter?' Davidov looked with astonishment over the rows of seated men and women, and, unable to catch anybody else's eye, turned his gaze on Nagulnov.

'You see,' Nagulnov began irresolutely. 'This Borodin – we call him Titok – voluntarily joined the Red Guards together with us in 1918. He was the son of a poor cossack, and fought bravely. He was wounded and was given a distinction, a silver watch, for his revolutionary conduct. So you see, comrade worker, how he has touched our hearts. When he came home he got his teeth into his farm like a hound into carrion. And he began to get rich, although we warned him again and again. He worked day and night, grew a shaggy beard all over him, went about in a single pair of canvas trousers winter and summer. He got himself three yoke of oxen and ruptured himself through lifting heavy weights, and still it wasn't enough for him! He began to hire workers, two or three at a time. He got a windmill, and then he bought a five-horse-power steam motor, set up an oil-mill and began to trade in cattle. He doesn't eat much himself, and he starves his labourers, although they work twenty hours a day, and have to get up five

39

times a night to see to the horses and cattle. We've had him before the nucleus and at the Soviet more than once, we've tried to make him feel ashamed of himself, we've told him: "Stop it, Tit, don't stand in the way of our own Soviet government. You've suffered for it yourself fighting the Whites at the fronts ..."' Nagulnov sighed and spread out his hands. 'What can you do when the devil gets hold of a man? We could see he would be eaten up with his property. We called him before us again, reminded him of the civil war and our common sufferings, argued with him, threatened we would trample him into the earth if he stood in our way, became a bourgeois and didn't want to wait for the world revolution ...'

'Don't be so long-winded !' Davidov impatiently demanded.

Nagulnov's voice trembled as he went on more quietly:

'I can't cut it any shorter. It ... hurts till the blood comes. But he always replies: "I'm carrying out the orders of the Soviet government. I am increasing my sowings. And I'm allowed by law to have labourers, my wife is ill with women's sickness. I was nothing and I've become all; I have got everything, and that's what I fought for. And it isn't the likes of you who keep the Soviet government going. With my hands I give it something to chew, and you're only paper spoilers. I see you for what you are." When we speak about the war and the difficulties we suffered together, sometimes a tear comes to his eyes. But he won't let it come out, he turns away, hardens his heart and says: "The past has overgrown the past." And we took away his vote. He tried to ride the high horse, wrote letters to the District and to Moscow. But as I understand it there are old revolutionaries sitting in the chief positions in the central institutions, and they realize that once a man's become a traitor he's an enemy, and there's no mercy for him.'

'But do cut it shorter !'

'I'll be finished in a minute. And they didn't give him back his vote, but he's gone on just the same, only he's got rid of his labourers ...'

'Well, but what's all this leading up to?' Davidov stared fixedly at Nagulnov's face. But he hid his eyes behind their short, sun-scorched lashes, and replied:

'That's why everybody was silent. I was only explaining what the kulak Tit Borodin was like in the past days.'

Davidov pressed his lips together, and his face darkened.

'You know how we dealt with Trotsky, don't you?' he demanded. 'What are you telling us these pitiful stories for? He was a Partisan, and all honour to him for that. But now he's become a kulak, become an enemy, crush him! What is there to talk about?'

'It wasn't out of pity for him. That's a silly charge to make, comrade.'

'Who's in favour of destroying Borodin as a kulak?' Davidov swept the rows with his eyes. Hands were raised: not all at once, not unitedly, but they were raised.

After the meeting Nagulnov invited Davidov to spend the night with him. 'And we'll find quarters for you tomorrow,' he said, as they groped their way out of the dark porch of the Soviet house. They walked side by side over the scrunching snow. Nagulnov talked in low tones:

'I can breathe more easily, comrade worker, since I've heard that all the grain-producing property is to be drawn solidly into the collective farm. I've hated property ever since I was a child. All the evil is because of it, the educated comrades Marx and Engels were right there. And even under the Soviet regime there are people who're like swine at a trough: they tug and shove and squeal, and all because of that accursed disease! And yet, what was it like in the former days, under the old regime? Terrible to think of! My father was a cossack fairly well off, he had four yoke of oxen and five horses. We had an enormous area under cultivation, sixty, seventy, and even a hundred hectares. Our family was large and hard working. We did everything ourselves. But then, to begin with I had three married brothers. And what made me turn against private property still sticks in my memory. Some neighbour's swine had got into our orchard and had dug up several roots of potatoes. My mother saw it, poured some boiling tar from a pot into a mug, and told me: "Chase it off, Makar, and I'll stand behind the gate." Well, of course I chased the unfortunate swine. And my mother splashed the tar over it. How its bristles began to smoke! It was summer–time, the worms got into the sores, and it got worse and worse till it died. Our neighbour showed no sign of his anger. But within a week twenty-three stooks of wheat of ours were burnt down in the steppe. My father knew who had done it, and wouldn't sit down under it, but went to court. And they came to hate each other so much that they couldn't stand the sight of each other. They'd only got to get a little drunk, and at once there'd be a fight. Five years this dragged on, until at last it ended with a death. Our neighbour's son was found dead on their threshing floor at Shrovetide. Some-one had jabbed a pitchfork through his breast in several places. And from various things I guessed it was my brothers who had done it. There was an investigation, but they didn't find out the murderers. So it was officially reported that he had been killed in a drunken brawl. But from that time I left my father and became a labourer. I was taken for the war. And there I'd lie, while the Germans fired their heavy shells at us, and the black smoke would fly up to heaven from the earth. I'd lie and think: "Who am I suffering this fear and death for, whose property am I saving?" And because of the firing I wished I could turn into a nail, and drive myself right up to my head into the earth. My beloved mother! I had a whiff of their gases, and was poisoned. And now if I have to go up the smallest hill I get palpitations, the blood rushes to my head, and I can't manage it. Even at the front there were intelligent men explaining what it was all about, and I came back a Bolshevik. And in the civil war I cut the rep-tiles down without mercy. In one battle I got a contusion, and then I began to have fits. But look at this sign.' He laid his enormous palm over his decoration, and a new tone of terrible warmth entered into his voice. 'It makes me feel warmer at once. At once I'm back in the days of the civil war, back in the positions, comrade. We must dig ourselves into the ground, but we must draw everybody into the collective farm. Always a step nearer to the world revolution.'

'Do you know Tit Borodin well?' Davidov thoughtfully asked, as they strode along.

'Of course I do; we used to be friends, but he's so fond of property that we quarrelled. In 1920 he and I were in the same squadron putting down a rising in one of the districts of the Donietz area. There were lots of Ukrainians killed outside the village. One night Tit turned up in his hut carrying sacks. He shook them and turned eight frozen dismembered legs on to the floor. "Have you gone mad, you accursed devil?" a comrade asked him. "Clear out with them at once!" And Tit said: "The bastards won't rise again! And their four pairs of boots will be useful to me. I'll shoe all my family." He thawed out the legs on the stove and began to pull off the boots, ripping up the seams of the boot-tops with his sword. Then he carried the bare legs outside and pushed them under a pile of straw. " I've buried them," he said. If we'd known at the time we'd have shot him like a dog. But his comrades didn't give him away then. Afterwards I asked him if it was true. "It was true," he said. "I couldn't get the boots off any other way, the legs had gone hard with the frost, so I hacked them off with my sword. As a cobbler I couldn't bear to think of good boots rotting in the ground. But now's the worst of it," he went on. "Sometimes I wake up at night, and ask my wife to let me sleep by the wall because I'm afraid lying on the edge..." Well, here are my quarters.' Nagulnov strode into a yard and fumbled at the door latch.

Chapter 5

Story of a Revolutionary

ANDREI Razmiotnov was seen off to his military service in 1913. According to the conditions of cossack service at that time, he should have taken his own horse with him. But he had nothing to buy a horse with, nor even the equipment required of a cossack. From his dead father he had inherited only his grandfather's sword in its broken, rusty scabbard. Never would Andrei forget his bitter humiliation. At the district assembly the elders decided to send him off to his service at the cost of the Cossack Council;

they bought him a cheap russet nag, a saddle, two greatcoats, two pairs of trousers, and boots. 'We're sending you at the cost of the community, Andrei,' the elders told him. 'Don't forget our kindness, don't dishonour the district, serve the Tsar in faith and truth.'

But at the regimental races the sons of wealthy cossacks would lord it on blood horses from the Korolkovsky stud farm, or on thoroughbred stallions from the Provalsky stables, with expensive saddles, silver-mounted bridles and the newest of uniforms. The district administration took over Andrei's land, and during the years he was being flung from front to front in defence of others' riches and comfortable lives, it was rented out. Andrei won three Crosses of St George in the war, and sent the extra pay home to his wife and mother. On this the old woman and her daughter-in-law lived, and Andrei was able to give his mother belated comfort in her tearful old age.

Towards the end of the war Andrei's wife, who had hired herself out for threshing in the autumn, saved up sufficient money to travel to the front to see her husband. She stayed there several precious days (the 11th Don Cossack Regiment, in which Andrei was serving, was resting behind the lines) and lay on her husband's arm. The nights flashed by like summer lightning. But is much time required for a transient sin, for the satisfaction of woman's hungry happiness? She went back home with shining eyes, and at the appointed time, without cries or tears, almost incidentally, in the middle of the ploughing season, she bore a little son cast in the mould of Andrei.

In 1918 Razmiotnov returned to Gremyachy Log for a short period. He did not stay long in the village; he mended the rotting wooden plough, put new rafters in the sheds, and ploughed two hectares of land, then spent a whole day dandling his little son, seating him on his bull-neck, which smelt of army life, and ran laughing about the kitchen. But his wife noticed tears standing in the corners of his light, usually rather angry-looking eyes, and turned pale. 'Are you going off again, Andrei?' she asked. 'Yes, tomorrow; get some victuals ready,' he replied.

And the next day he, and Makar Nagulnov, Liubishkin of the Ataman's regiment, Tit Borodin and eight other front-line cossacks of the village assembled outside his hut. Their saddled, vari-coloured horses carried them away beyond the windmill, and the light spring dust driven up by the horses' lightly-shod hoofs was left a long time dancing on the track.

That same day, over Gremyachy Log, over the flooded fields, over the steppe, over all the azure earth from the south to the north, high in the heavens flocks of black-winged barnacle geese and wild geese went hurrying, flying without cry or voice.

At Kamenska Andrei was separated from his comrades. With one of the Voroshilov divisions he marched on Morozovsky and Tsaritsin, while Makar Nagulnov, Liubishkin and the others found themselves in Voroniozh. Some three months later Andrei was slightly wounded by a fragment of shell, fell in with a fellow villager at the dressing station, and learnt that after the destruction of the Podtielkov detachment the White cossacks, Andrei's neighbours in Gremyachy Log, had taken vengeance for his joining the Reds, by making a ferocious sport of his wife. All the village had come to know of it, and Yevdokia had been unable to bear the terrible shame and had laid hands on herself.

... It was a frosty day in December. In Gremyachy Log the huts, the sheds, wattle-fences, and trees were covered with a white blush of rime. Fighting was going on beyond the distant hills, and there was a muffled thunder of guns. Towards evening Andrei galloped on a foaming horse into the village. And to this day he remembers, he has only to close his eyes and the passionate flight of memory carries him into the past ... The wicket-gate scraped. Panting, he pulled on the reins and led his weary, stumbling horse into the yard. His mother ran bareheaded out of the porch.

And oh, how the mournful tears in her voice pierced Andrei's ears!

'Oh, my son, my darling! Her dear bright eyes are closed...!'

Razmiotnov rode in as though into a stranger's yard. He wound the reins over the balustrade of the steps, and went into the hut. With sunken, deathly eyes he stared around the empty kitchen, at the empty cradle.

'Where's the child?' he asked.

Wrapping her face in her apron, his mother shook her scanty-haired, grey head. He forced a reply out of her.

'I couldn't save the little one!' she told him. 'He died a week after Dunia ... of a convulsion!'

'Don't shout ... that's for me to do! If I could find the tears! Who was it raped Yevdokia?'

'Anikei Dievyatkin dragged her into the threshing-floor ... he whipped me off ... called the others to him. All over her white little arms they beat with their scabbards, she came in all black ... only eyes ...'

'Is he at home now?'

'He's retreated with the Whites.'

'Is there anybody of his at home?'

'His wife and father. Andrei! Don't kill them! They can't answer for the sins of others ...'

'Are you telling me?' Andrei scowled, and he choked with his anger. He tore open the fastenings of his greatcoat and the collar of his tunic and shirt. With his bare, bony chest firmly pressed against the iron water pot, he drank, biting the rim with his teeth. Then he stood up, and asked without raising his eyes:

'Mother! What message did she leave for me before she died?'

His mother went to the corner and drew a fading scrap of paper from behind the ikons. And his wife's death-bed words seemed to him to sound in her own voice:

'My darling Andrei! They've defiled me, curse them! They have made a mock of me and of my love for you. I cannot look you in the face, and will not see another day. My conscience will not let me live and suffer the filthy disease. My Andrei, my darling flower! These many nights I have not slept, and have wetted my pillow with my tears. I remember our love, and shall remember it in the next world. And I have only one regret: for the child and you, and because our life and love together were so short. If you bring another home, for the love of God let her have pity on our little lad. And, you, too, have pity on him, my orphan child. Tell mother to give my skirts and shawls, and my jacket to my sister. She is to be a bride, she will need them ...'

Andrei galloped furiously to the Dievyatkin farm, dismounted drew his sabre from its scabbard, and rushed into the porch. When Anikei Dievyatkin's father, a tall, greyheaded old man, saw him, he crossed himself and dropped to his knees beneath the ikons.

'Andrei Stepanich!' was all he said as he bowed himself at Andrei's feet. And he uttered not another word, nor did he raise his rosy, bald head from the floor.

'You will answer to me for your son! Pray to your Gods, to your Cross!' Andrei shouted. With his left hand he seized the old man's grey beard, then he kicked open the door and noisily dragged him into the porch. The old wife had fallen down in a swoon by the stove, but their daughter-in-law, Anikei's wife, gathered the children into a heap (she had six altogether) and ran weeping out into the porch. Andrei. as white as dead, wind-weathered bone, had swung his body sideways, and already had his sabre raised above the old man's neck. But at that moment the snotty, bellowing and howling children flung themselves at his feet.

'Cut them all down! They're all Anikei's whelps! Cut me down!' their mother shrieked. She went right up to Andrei, un-buttoning her rose-coloured shirt, her dry, withered breasts tossing like those of a bitch with a numerous litter. And the children large and small crawled around his feet. Staring wildly around, he stepped back, thrust his sabre into the scabbard, and, stumbling even on the level ground, went towards his horse. As far as the wicket-gate the old man followed him, weeping with joy and his past terror, trying continually to fall on him and kiss his stirrup. But, frowning contemptuously, Andrei pulled away his foot and hoarsely said:

'Lucky for you . . . and the children . . .'

For three days he remained at home in a stupor, weeping and drinking. The second night he set fire to the shed in which Yevdokia had hanged herself, and on the fourth day, his face swollen and ghastly, he took a quiet farewell of his mother. As she pressed his head against her breast she noticed the first feathery threads of grey in her son's shock of flaxen hair.

Two years later Andrei returned home from the Polish front. For another year he wandered over the upper Don area with a grain-requisitioning detachment, then he took up farming again.

He silently ignored his mother's advice to take another wife. But one day she insistently demanded an answer.

'Get married, Andrei!' she said. 'I haven't got the strength to lift the pots any longer. Any girl would have you. Who shall we call on with a proposal?'

'I'm not going to, mother; don't keep on about it!'

'The same old story! Look at you, the frost is already showing in your hair. When will you think about it? When you're gone quite white? You don't care much for your mother! But I did think I should nurse my grandchildren. I've gathered the down from two goats to knit stockings for the children. Washing and bathing them's my job; I find it difficult to milk the cow now, my fingers don't answer properly.' Her voice acquired a tearful note: 'And what wicked child have I given birth to? Sulking and sniffing! Can't you speak? You devil!'

Andrei picked up his cap and silently went out of the hut. But the old woman would not be appeased; she had talks with her neighbours, whisperings, councils . . .

'I won't bring anybody else home after Yevdokia,' Andrei obstinately stuck to his guns. And his mother's anger was transferred to her dead daughter-in-law.

'That snake has bewitched him,' she told the old women as they met on the road to the pasturage, or sat of an evening outside the yard. 'She hanged herself, and now she's sucking the life out of him. He doesn't want to take another. And is that easy for me? Ah, my dears! When I look at other women's grandchildren the tears come to my eyes, and I am ashamed. Other old women have joy and comfort, but I am alone like a marmot in its hole.'

That same year Andrei took up with Marina, the widow of sergeant Mikhail Poyarkov, who had been killed near Novocherkass. She had passed her fortieth year that autumn, but she still retained a vague steppe beauty in her full, strong body and her swarthy features.

Andrei spent one day in October thatching the roof of her hut with rushes. As dusk was falling she called him into the hut, swiftly laid the table, set a bowl of soup before him, threw a clean, embroidered towel across his knee, and sat down opposite him, supporting her cheek with its angular cheekbone on her palm. Andrei silently glanced sidelong at her proud head with its burden of glossy black hair. It was thick, and looked as coarse as a horse's mane, but it curled with a childlike turbulence and softness around her little ears. She screwed up one long, rather slanting black eye at Andrei.

'Will you have some more?' she asked him.

'Don't mind if I do,' he assented, wiping his fair whiskers with his palm. He was about to renew his attack on the soup, and Marina sat down opposite him and watched with a bestially cautious and expectant gaze. But he happened to notice a little blue vein pulsing strongly in her full neck, and for some reason he was embarrassed and put down his spoon.

'What's the matter?' she swept up the black wings of her eyebrows in astonishment.

'I've had enough. Thank you. I'll be along early tomorrow morning to finish the roof.'

Marina passed round the table. Slowly baring her close-set teeth in a smile, pressing her large, soft breast against him, she asked him in a whisper:

'But maybe you'll stop the night with me?'

'I could do,' the flabbergasted Andrei could find nothing else to say. And in revenge for his foolish reply Marina bent her waist in a bow:

'For that I thank you, benefactor! You have shown regard for a poor widow ... And I, sinful that I am, was afraid you would refuse.'

She deftly blew out the guttering wick, made the bed in the darkness, bolted the outer door, and, with contempt and hardly perceptible chagrin in her voice, declared:

'You've not got a drop of cossack blood in you. A Tambov tinker made you.'

'What makes you say that?' Andrei took offence, and even stopped pulling off his boots.

'It's true; you're like all the rest. Judging by your eyes you're spirited enough, but you're too timid to ask a woman for anything. And you won crosses at the war!' She spoke less distinctly as she unbraided her hair and held the hairpins between her teeth. 'D'you remember my Mishka? He was shorter than me.

You're just my height, but he was a little shorter. Well, I loved him just for his pluck. He wouldn't give in to the strongest in the tavern, though his nose might be all blood; he wouldn't ever admit he was beaten. Maybe that's why he died. And he knew why I loved him,' she ended with pride in her voice.

Andrei recalled the stories of the village cossacks who had been regimental comrades of Marina's husband, and witnesses of his death. He had been out on a reconnaissance expedition, and had led his troop into an attack on a Red Army patrol twice as numerous. The patrol had put them to flight with a Lewis gun, had sent four cossacks flying out of their saddles in the pursuit, and had cut Mikhail Poyarkov off from the others and attempted to overtake him. He shot point-blank three of the Red Army men pursuing him, and curvetted his horse (he had been the finest trickrider in his regiment) in order to avoid the bullets. He would have escaped, but the horse put its hoof into a hole and broke its master's leg as it fell. And that was the end of the plucky sergeant.

Andrei smiled as he remembered the story.

Marina lay breathing hard, pressing her body against Andrei. Some half-hour later she took up the thread of their talk, and whispered:

'I loved Mishka for his pluck ... but you I love ... for no reason at all,' and she pressed her little, burning ear against Andrei's chest. In the dusk it seemed to him that her eye shone as fierily and unsubmissively as that of a restive, unbroken horse. Just before dawn she asked:

'Will you be coming tomorrow to finish the roof?'

'Why, of course!' Andrei replied in surprise.

'Don't bother.'

'Why not?'

'You're a fine thatcher, you are! Old daddy Shchukar thatches better than you,' and she laughed aloud. 'I asked you to do it for a good reason! How else could I have got you here? As it is you've been an expense. The hut will have to be thatched all over again.'

Two days later old Shchukar rethatched the hut, grumbling continually at Andrei's bad work as he did so.

But after that Andrei visited Marina every night. And sweet

seemed to him the love of this woman ten years older than himself: as sweet as a forest winter apple touched with the first frost.

Their association was quickly discovered by the village, and was received in various ways. Andrei's mother wept and complained to her neighbours: 'It's a disgrace; he's taken up with an old woman.' But after a time she grew reconciled to the situation, and held her peace. For a long time Niura, a neighbour's single daughter with whom Andrei had occasionally joked and flirted, avoided meeting him. But one day she ran into him on a field path when cutting down brushwood, and turned pale.

'So an old woman has saddled you?' she asked, smiling with quivering lips, and not attempting to hide the tears glistening under her eyelashes.

'I've got no time to breathe now!' he tried to jest.

'Couldn't you have found anyone younger?' she asked as she passed on.

'But look what I'm like, myself.' He removed his cap, and pointed with his gloved hand to his hair streaked with grey.

'Yet I, fool that I am, fell in love with you, you old hound! Well, it's good-bye then.' And she walked off, carrying her head offendedly high.

Makar Nagulnov curtly told him:

'I don't approve of it, Andrei. She'll make a sergeant of you and a small property owner. Now, don't get upset; you know I was joking; you can see that, can't you?'

'Marry her properly,' his mother once said in a burst of generosity. 'Let her become my daughter-in-law.'

'It wouldn't do,' Andrei evasively answered.

Marina seemed to have thrown twenty years off her shoulders. Her slanting eyes restrainedly glittering, she met Andrei at night, embracing him with masculine strength; and until the coming of daylight the bright, cherry flush did not leave her angular, swarthy cheeks. It was as though the days of her girlhood had returned. She embroidered tobacco-pouches made of colourful pieces of silk for him, devotedly watched his every movement, ingratiated herself with him. Then jealousy and the fear of losing him awoke with terrible force in her. She began to attend meetings only in order to watch him there, to see whether he was playing about with the young wives, or was casting glances at any woman. At first he was oppressed by this unexpected tutelage, cursed her, and even beat her several times; but then he got used to it, and the circumstance flattered his self-esteem. To please him she gave him all her dead husband's clothes. And Andrei, who previously had been a ragamuffin, was not ashamed to have the rights of succession, and swaggered about the village in the sergeant's cloth trousers, and in shirts with sleeves and collars obviously too short and tight for him.

He helped Marina with her farm, and after a day's hunting always brought back a hare or a brace of partridges for her. But Marina never abused her power over him, and did not deprive his mother of her share, although secretly she felt hostility for her.

For that matter, she was quite capable of managing her farm by herself, and could easily have dispensed with male assistance. With secret satisfaction Andrei would sometimes watch her raising a pitchfork a hundredweight stook of wheat entangled with rosy convolvulus, or, seated on a reaper, tossing the swathes of full-grained barley from under the rattling wings. She had a good deal of masculine grip and strength. She even harnessed a horse masculine fashion, putting her foot against the rim of the collar and drawing the thong tight with a single pull.

As the years passed, Andrei's feeling for Marina became firmly deep-rooted and constant. Occasionally he remembered his first wife, but the memory no longer brought the former stabbing pain. Once, when he happened to meet the eldest son of Anikei Dievyatkin, who had emigrated to France, Andrei turned pale, so striking was the son's resemblance to his father. But afterwards his anger was dissipated in work, in the struggle for bread, in his daily anxieties; and the dull, nagging pain, resembling the pain he sometimes felt in the scar on his forehead (a souvenir of a Hungarian officer's sword) left him altogether.

After the meeting of the poor peasants Andrei went straight to Marina. While waiting for him she was spinning wool. The spinning wheel hummed drowsily in the little, low and well-heated room. As Razmiotnov entered a mischievous, curly-haired kid clattered its tiny hoofs over the earthen floor with the intention of jumping on to the bed.

Andrei frowned irritably and said:

'Stop spinning that wheel!'

Marina removed the pointed toe of her high-heeled shoe from the treadle, and stretched herself luxuriously, arching her back, like a horse's crupper in its breadth.

'What happened at the meeting?' she asked.

'We're going to start pulling the kulaks' giblets tomorrow.'

'Really?'

'All the poor peasants at the meeting have joined the collective farm.'

Without removing his jacket Andrei lay down on the bed, and caught the kid, a warm little bundle of wool, in his hands.

'You take your application along tomorrow,' he added.

'What application?' Marina asked in surprise.

'To be taken into the collective farm.'

She pushed the spinning-wheel vigorously away from her towards the stove, and burst out:

'Have you gone barmy? What should I get out of that?'

'Don't let's argue about it, Marina. You've got to join the farm. Otherwise they'll be saying of me that I get others to join, but I keep my Marina out. My conscience will prick me.'

'I'm not going to join. Say what you like, I'm not going to.' She walked past the bed, enveloping him in the smell of her hot sweaty body.

'Well, we'll have to part in that case.'

'Threats!'

'I'm not threatening you, but I can't do anything else.'

'Well, clear out, then! I take them my one cow, and what shall I get? And afterwards you'll come and ask me to feed you.'

'The milk will be communal.'

'And perhaps the women will be communal, too? Is that why you're trying to frighten me?'

'I could give you a good hiding, but I don't feel like it,' Andrei said. He threw the kid to the floor, reached for his cap, and whipped his woollen scarf around his neck as though it were a hangman's noose.

'Every blessed devil has got to be persuaded and pleaded with! And even Marina is getting up on her hind legs! What's going to happen at the general meeting tomorrow? They'll beat us if we squeeze them too hard,' he angrily thought, as he strode through the orchards to his own hut.

For a long time he was unable to sleep, but tossed and listened as his mother twice got up to look at the dough. A devilishly noisy cock crowed in the shed. Andrei thought anxiously of the coming day, of all the village agriculture now on the eve of complete reconstruction. He was troubled by the fear that Davidov, a dry, hard chap as he thought, would frighten the middling peasants away from the collective farm by some incautious step. But then he recalled his thickset, solidly built figure, his face, tense and gathered into a knot and with harsh folds down the sides of his cheeks, the humorously intelligent eyes; he recalled how Davidov had leant across behind Nagulov's back while Liubishkin was speaking at the meeting, and, breathing the clean, bitter-wine scent of his gap-toothed mouth into his face, had remarked: 'That Partisan's a tough fellow, but you've neglected him. You haven't taken him in hand. Fact! We've got to work at him!' Remembering this, he decided more cheerfully: 'No, he won't get us into difficulties. Makar's the one who's got to be bridled. In the heat of the moment he could easily give someone a crack. Let him get the rein under his tail, and there'll be no holding back the cart. No holding back what? The cart ... What cart? Makar ... Titok ... tomorrow ...' Sleep stole upon him and robbed him of consciousness. He dozed off, and the smile slowly slipped from his face like a dewdrop from the rib of a leaf.

Chapter 6

Evicted!

WHEN Davidov arrived at the village Soviet about eight o'clock the next morning, he found fourteen of the Gremyachy poor cossacks already assembled.

'We've been expecting you a long time, ever since sunrise,' Liubishkin smiled, as he collected Davidov's hand in his own healthy palm.

'We couldn't wait,' old Shchukar explained.

Shchukar was the man dressed in a woman's white sheepskin, who had bandied jokes with Davidov in the Soviet yard on the evening of his arrival. From that moment he had regarded himself as an old acquaintance of Davidov, and, unlike the others, had spoken to him in a tone of friendly familiarity. Just before Davidov came into the Soviet he had been saying: 'As I and Davidov decide, so it will be. He had a long chat with me a couple of days ago. Of course we were joking at times, but we had a serious talk, and chiefly discussed how we were to organize the collective farm. He's a bit of a joker, like myself.'

Davidov recognized Shchukar by his white sheepskin, and, without knowing it, seriously offended him by remarking:

'And so it's you, grand-dad! Now you see! Two days ago you got annoyed when you heard what I'd come for, and now you're a collective farmer already! Brave lad!'

'I hadn't time to stop then, that's why I went off,' Shchukar mumbled as he edged away from Davidov.

It was decided to divide into two groups to eject the kulaks from their farms. The first group was to go to the upper part of the village, the second to the lower part. But when Davidov proposed Nagulnov as leader of the first group Makar categorically refused. He was greatly embarrassed by the exchange of glances which followed, and called Davidov aside.

55

'What are you abandoning your post for?' Davidov coldly asked him.

'I'd rather go with the second group to the lower part of the village,' Makar replied.

'What's the difference?'

Makar bit his lips, and said as he turned away:

'I'd rather not say ... But you'll find out all the same! My wife has relations with Timofei, the son of Frol Damaskov the kulak. I don't want to go there, there's sure to be talk about it if I do. I'll go with the second group, and let Razmiotnov go with the first.'

'Ah, brother, afraid of talk! But I shan't insist. Come with me in the second group,' Davidov replied.

Suddenly he remembered that when Nagulnov's wife had given him his breakfast that morning, he had noticed that she had an old green and yellow bruise over her eyebrow. Frowning, and wriggling his neck as though a wisp of hay had got down behind his collar, he asked:

'Was it you who gave her that bruise? Do you beat her?'

'No, I didn't.'

'Then who did?'

'He did.'

'Yes, but who's "he"?'

'Why, Timofei, Frol's son.'

In his perplexity Davidov was silent for some moments, then he wrathfully answered:

'Oh, well, the devil take it! I don't understand. Come on. We'll talk about that later.'

Nagulnov, Davidov, Liubishkin, daddy Shchukar and three other cossacks left the village Soviet together.

'Where shall we start?' Davidov asked Nagulnov without looking at him. Each felt awkward after their talk.

'With Titok,' Makar answered.

They went silently along the street. Women stared inquisitively out of the windows after them. Some lads began to fall in behind them, but Liubishkin pulled a switch out of a wattle fence, and the quickwitted youngsters dropped behind. As they were approaching Titok's house Nagulnov remarked to nobody in particular:

'This house will make a good centre for the collective farm administration. It's large. And the sheds will do for farm stables.'

The house certainly was large. Titok had bought it in the neighbouring village of Tubyanskoe in the famine year of 1922, in exchange for a dry cow and a hundredweight of flour. All the family of the former owners died, so nobody was left to sue Titok afterwards for his shady deal. He had the house carried to Gremyachy, gave it a new roof, added timbered sheds and a stable, and built himself a home for ever. From the ochre-painted cornice an inscription of ingenious design in old Slavonic stared down at the street:

'T. K. Borodin. A.D. 1923.'

Davidov ran his eyes inquisitively over the house. Nagulnov was the first to pass through the wicket gate. At the sound of the latch an enormous chained dog the colour of a wolf rushed out from under a barn. Without a sound it tore towards them and reared on to its hind legs, revealing its fluffy white belly, then, choking with the pressure of its collar, began to growl. It threw itself forward and fell over on to its back several times in attempts to snap its chain. But the iron was too strong, so it dashed towards the stable, sending the chain clattering against a wire stretching to the stable door.

'Let that devil seize you and you won't get away,' old Shchukar muttered, nervously watching the animal out of the corner of his eye, and keeping close to the fence in case of accidents.

They entered the kitchen in a bunch. Titok's wife, a tall, thin woman, was giving a calf drink from a tub. She scrutinized the unexpected guests with a look of angry suspicion. In reply to their greeting she snorted something which sounded like: 'What the devil's brought you here?'

'Titok at home?' Nagulnov asked.

'No.'

'Where is he, then?'

'I don't know,' she snapped.

'You know what we've come for! We ...' old Shchukar was

beginning enigmatically, but Nagulnov rolled his eyes so violently at him that the old man convulsively swallowed down his spittle, gave vent to a croak and sat down on the bench, throwing open his white, untanned sheepskin with a gesture of importance.

'Are the horses in the stables?' Nagulnov queried, as though he had not noticed the ungracious reception.

'Yes.'

'And the oxen?'

'No. What do you want?'

'With you we can't . . .' Shchukar was beginning again. But this time Liubishkin strode towards the door, seized him by the edge of his sheepskin, and hauled him violently into the porch, so that the old man was unable to finish the sentence.

'Then where are the oxen?' Nagulnov continued.

'Titok has driven somewhere with them.'

'Where to?'

'I just told you I didn't know.'

Nagulnov winked to Davidov and went out. As he passed Shchukar he raised his fist to the level of the old man's beard, and advised him:

'You keep your mouth shut until you're asked to speak!' Turning to Davidov, he said: 'It looks bad! We must find out where he's taken the oxen. I'm afraid he'll get rid of them.'

'Then we must leave the oxen . . .'

'What?' Nagulnov exclaimed in alarm. 'His oxen are the finest in the village. You can't reach to the tips of their horns, they're so big. We can't let them go! We must search for Titok and the oxen.'

He and Liubishkin held a whispered consultation, then they went to the cattle yard, passing under the shed and on to the threshing floor. Some five minutes later Liubishkin, armed with a wooden post, forced the dog to retreat and drove it under the barn. Then Nagulnov led a high-standing horse out of the stable, bridled it, and, seizing it by the mane, vaulted on to its bare back.

'What are you doing, Makar, using other people's property without asking their permission?' the mistress shouted, running with arms akimbo out on to the porch. 'When my husband returns I'll tell him! He'll settle accounts with you!'

'Don't bawl! I'd settle accounts with him if he was here. Comrade Davidov, come here, will you?'

Completely nonplussed by Nagulnov's conduct, Davidov went across to him.

'There are fresh oxen tracks running from the threshing floor on to the road,' Nagulnov pointed out. 'It's clear Titok got wind of our coming, and he's driven off the oxen to sell them. And all the sledges are under the shed. The woman's lying! Go and deal with the Kochetovs, and I'll ride to Tubyanskoe. There's nowhere else he could have driven them to. Break me off a switch to tickle up the horse with.'

Straight across the threshing floor Nagulnov made for the track. A white dust arose behind him, then slowly settled on the fences and the scrub in dazzlingly brilliant, crystalline silver. The traces of oxen and the hoofmarks of a horse at their side stretched as far as the track, then disappeared. Nagulnov galloped some two hundred yards in the direction of Tubyanskoe. As he went he noticed the same traces and a slight sprinkling of dung on the shallow snow-drifts, and rode on, reassured that he was taking the right direction. He had covered just over a mile in this way when the traces suddenly ceased at a gulley. He turned the horse sharply round, jumped off, and attentively examined whether the hoofmarks had been obliterated by snow. But the gulley was untouched and virginally white. At the very bottom he could see the criss-crosses of magpies' feet. Cursing, he rode back at a walking pace, looking all around him. He quickly came across the tracks again, and found that the oxen had turned off the road just by a stretch of pasturage land. He had over-run the turn through riding at a swift trot. At once he realized that Titok had struck straight across the hills in the direction of Voiskovoi village. 'Going to a friend, it looks like,' he thought as he followed the tracks, holding in the horse. On the farther side of the hill, close to a ravine he noticed ox dung on the snow, and halted. The dung was fresh, and only a fine flake of ice from the frost lay on it. Nagulnov felt for the cold stock of his revolver in the pocket of his sheepskin jacket. He dropped down into the ravine at a walking pace. He rode another half-mile, and only then saw a horseman and a couple of oxen beyond a clump of bare oaks quite close at hand. The horseman waved the oxen reins at the animals, and bent low in the saddle. Blue tobacco smoke floated across his shoulder and melted away towards Nagulnov.

'Turn back!' the pursuer shouted.

Titok halted his whinnying mare, looked round, spat out his cigarette, and slowly rode to the front of the oxen, quietly saying:

'What's the matter? Hey, stop!'

Nagulnov rode up. Titok greeted him with a long stare.

'Where are you going?' Makar demanded.

'I was going to sell the oxen, Makar. I won't hide the fact.' Titok blew his nose on his hand and carefully wiped his ruddy, drooping walrus whiskers with his glove. The two men sat without dismounting, face to face. Their horses sniffed snortingly at each other. Nagulnov's wind-burnt face was flushed and angry. Outwardly Titok was calm and quiet.

'Turn the oxen round and drive them back home!' Nagulnov ordered, riding to one side.

For one moment Titok hesitated. He sat fingering the reins, his head sunken drowsily, his eyes half-closed, and in his grey, homespun coat with the hood pulled over his ragged earflapped cap he was like a dozing hawk. 'If he's got anything under his coat, he'll be slipping back the safety catch in a moment,' Nagulnov thought, not removing his eyes from the motionless Titok. But as though he had woken up, Titok waved the oxen reins. The oxen returned in their tracks.

'Are you taking everything? Are you going to treat me as a kulak and smash me?' Titok asked after a long silence, flashing the bluish whites of his eyes at Nagulnov from under the hood drawn down over his forehead.

'You've had your day! I'm driving you back like a captured snake!' Nagulnov shouted, unable to restrain himself any longer.

Titok bristled up. He was silent until they reached the hill. Then he asked:

'What do you intend to do with me?'

'We shall send you out of the district. What's that sticking up under your coat?'

'A gun.' Titok glanced sidelong at Nagulnov, and threw his

coat open. The roughly-planed stock of a rifle with the barrel sawn off short looked like a white thighbone.

'Give it here!' Makar stretched out his hand. But Titok calmly pushed it away.

'Not me!' he said, and smiled, laying bare his black, tobacco-stained teeth beneath his drooping whiskers. He stared at Nagulnov with sharp, ferrety, yet merry eyes. 'Not me! You'll take my property, and even my last rifle? A kulak's always got a gun, so they say in the newspapers. Without exception he has a gun. Maybe I shall get my daily bread with it, don't you think? The village correspondents may find me ...' He laughed and shook his head, not removing his hands from the pommel, and Nagulnov did not insist on his handing over the gun. 'I'll break you when we get to the village!' he mentally decided.

'I expect you're asking yourself what he took a gun with him for?' Titok went on. 'Damn it! I've had it ever since I brought it back from the Ukrainian revolt, d'you remember? Well, it lay about and got rusty. I cleaned it up and oiled it, thinking it might come in useful against an animal or a wicked man. Then yesterday I learnt that you were intending to shake up the kulaks. Only I didn't hear you were to begin today, or I'd have gone off with the oxen last night ...'

'Who told you?'

'Now you're asking! The earth is full of rumours. Yes, and I talked it over with my wife during the night and decided to put the oxen into safe hands. I took the gun with me, thinking to bury it in the steppe so that it shouldn't be found in the yard; then I thought that was a pity, and then you turned up! And how my finger itched!' He talked animatedly, his eyes twinkling humorously, as he rode his mare's breast hard against Nagulnov's horse.

'You'll be joking later, Titok! But now you'd better keep a straight face.'

'Ha! Now's the time for me to make jokes. I won myself a comfortable life, I defended the just government, and now it's taking me by the throat!' Titok's voice suddenly broke off. From that moment he said no more, but deliberately reined in his horse, trying to let Makar ride at least half a length in front. But Makar also hung back in his fear. The oxen plodded on far ahead of them.

'Step it out, step it out!' Nagulnov said, tensely staring at Titok and clutching the revolver in his pocket. He knew Titok only too well! He knew him better than anyone else. 'No dropping behind! If you're thinking of shooting, you'll not get a chance.'

'You have grown nervous,' Titok smiled, and, whipping up his horse with the oxen reins, he galloped ahead.

Chapter 7

Taking Possession

ANDREI Razmiotnov and his group arrived at Frol Damaskov's hut just as the family were having their midday meal. At the table sat Frol himself, a little, ailing old man with a small, wedge-shaped beard and a torn left nostril (he had disfigured his face by falling from an apple tree when a child), his wife, a corpulent and stately old woman, his son Timofei, a lad about twenty-two, and his daughter, a marriageable maiden.

Timofei, dignified and handsome like his mother, rose from the table. Wiping the bright crimson lips under his youthful, fluffy moustache with a rag, he screwed up his insolent, protruding eyes, and, with the jauntiness of the village's finest accordion player and the girls' favourite, beckoned with his hand.

'Come in and sit down, my dear government officials!' he invited them.

'We haven't got time to sit down!' Andrei Razmiotnov replied, pulling a paper out of his document case. 'The meeting of the poor peasants has decided to evict you from your house, Frol Damaskov, and to confiscate all your property and your stock. So finish your meal, and then get yourselves out of the hut. We shall make an inventory of the property at once.'

'What's all this for?' Throwing down his spoon, Frol rose to his feet.

'We intend to destroy you as a kulak class,' Diemka Ushakov enlightened him.

His solid, leather-soled felt boots creaking, Frol went into the sitting-room and brought back a document.

'Here's the statement; you signed it yourself, Razmiotnov.'

'What statement?'

'The statement that I handed over my grain tax.'

'The grain tax has got nothing to do with this.'

'Then what am I being driven out of my home and my property confiscated for?'

'That's what the poor peasants have decided, as I've already told you.'

'There's no law which allows it!' Timofei sharply exclaimed. 'You're organizing robbery. Father, I'll ride to the District Executive Committee at once. Where's a saddle?'

'You'll go to the Committee on foot, if you want to. I shan't let you have a horse.' Andrei sat down at the edge of the table, and took out a pencil and paper. Frol's torn nose was flooded with blue, and his head began to shake. He suddenly crumpled to the floor where he stood, and muttered, with difficulty moving his swollen, blackened tongue :

'Sons of bitches ! Sons of bitches ! Rob on ! Cut us down !'

'Father, get up for the love of Christ !' the girl burst into tears and tried to lift her father with her hands under his armpits.

Frol recovered, got up, and lay down on the bench, listening impassively as Diemka Ushakov and the tall, sheepish Mikhail Ignationok dictated to Razmiotnov :

'An iron bedstead with white balls, a feather bed, three pillows, and two wooden bedsteads . . .'

'A cupboard full of crockery. Am I to go all through the crockery? Damn the whole lot !'

'Twelve chairs, one long armchair with a back. A three-tiered accordion.'

'I'm not going to let you have my accordion,' Timofei shouted, snatching it out of Diemka's hands. 'Hands off, boss-eye, or I'll smash your nose in !'

'I'll smash you so that your mother won't be able to wash you clean,' Diemka retorted: 'Hand over the keys to the chests, old woman!'

'Don't give them to them, mother. Let them break the chests open, if they've got the right.'

'Have we got the right to break them open?' Diemid the Silent suddenly bestirred himself. He was known to speak only when it was absolutely necessary; the rest of the time he worked silently, smoked silently with the other cossacks gathered for a walk on holidays, sat silent at meetings, and was in the habit of only rarely answering questions, wearing a guilty and mournful smile. For Diemid the whole wide world was full of unnecessary noises. They flooded life to the brim, not even dying away at night, and prevented his listening to the silence, disturbed the sage silence with which the steppe and forest overflow in autumn. Diemid did not like the hubbub of humanity. He lived apart at the end of the village, was hard working, and the strongest man in the whole district. But somehow fate had scarred his life with wrongs, had cheated him as though he were a stepchild. For five years he had lived as a labourer with Frol Damaskov, then he married and turned to farming for himself. He had not finished building his farm when it was all burnt down. Within a year a second fire left him with only a plough reeking with smoke in the yard. And soon after that his wife left him, declaring: 'I've lived with you two years and I haven't heard you say two words. Live by yourself in future! I'd find it more cheerful living in a forest with a wolf. Living with you is enough to drive a woman mad. I've already begun to talk to myself . . .'

Yet the woman had grown accustomed to Diemid. It is true that during the first few months she had wept and nagged at him with: 'Diemid, my dearest! Do talk to me at least! Say one little word!' Diemid had only smiled his quiet, childlike smile, and scratched his hairy chest. But when he could no longer bear his wife's nagging, in his chesty voice he had said: 'You're just a magpie!' and had gone off. For some reason Diemid was reputed to be a proud and cunning man, one of those who 'had their own thoughts'. Maybe that was because all his life he had shunned clamorous folk.

So Andrei threw up his head when he heard the dull thunder of Diemid's voice above him.

'Got the right?' he cross-questioned, staring at Diemid as though he were seeing him for the first time. 'Of course we've got the right!'

Moving with a straddling gait, marking the floor with his wet, badly worn boots, Diemid went into the best room. He smilingly pushed Timofei aside from the doorway as easily as though he had been a twig, and passing the cupboard, making its crockery rattle beneath his heavy tread, he went to the chests. Squatting down, he turned the heavy padlock over in his hand. The next moment it was lying with a broken hasp on top of the chest, and Arkashka stared at Diemid with unconcealed astonishment, exclaiming in admiration:

'I'd like to change my strength for yours!'

Andrei could not get all the items written down. From the best room and from the hall Diemka Ushakov, Arkashka and auntie Vasilisa, the only woman in Andrei's party, outvied one another with their shouts:

'A woman's fur coat.'

'A sheepskin.'

'Three pairs of new boots and goloshes.'

'Four lengths of cloth.'

'Andrei! Razmiotnov! You'll never get all these goods on to one sledge, old man. There's calico, and black satin, and all sorts of other stuff ...'

As he went towards the best room Andrei heard a girl's lamentations, the housewife's voice, and Ignationok's persuasive tones coming from the porch. He threw open the door.

'What's up here?' he demanded.

Her face swollen with tears, the snub-nosed daughter was leaning against the front door, bellowing like a calf. Her mother was bustling and cackling around her, while Ignationok, his face crimson and wearing an embarrassed smile, was pulling at the girl by the edge of her skirt.

'What the ...? Damn you!' Not realizing what was the trouble, Andrei began to choke with rage, and gave Ignationok a violent push. His long legs engulfed in his ragged felt boots,

Ignationok fell on his back. 'Fine politics that!' roared Andrei. 'We're attacking the enemy, and you're pawing girls in corners? But you'll answer to a court for your ...'

'Here, hold on, wait a bit!' Ignationok jumped up from the floor in alarm. 'As if she could turn my head! Pawing her! Look at her: she was just drawing on the ninth skirt around her. I was trying to stop her, and you flare up like that!'

Only then did Andrei notice that the girl, who, under cover of the general confusion, had dragged a bundle of clothes out of the best room, had already managed to wrap a heap of woollen dresses around her. Hampered in her movements by the abundance of her clothes, looking strangely awkward and dock-tailed as she huddled in the corner, she was adjusting the hem of the top skirt. Andrei felt pity and aversion for her with her wet eyes, which were pink like a rabbit's. He slammed the door and said to Ignationok:

'You can't undress her. What she's managed to put on she can keep, but take the bundle away from her.'

The inventory of the goods in the house was finished at last. 'The keys of the granary,' Andrei demanded.

Frol, as black as charred wood, waved his hand. 'We haven't got them,' he declared.

'Go and break the door open,' Andrei ordered Diemid, who went to the barn, pulling a swivel-bolt out of a cart as he went. The fivepound-weight padlock was broken off with difficulty by resort to an axe.

'Don't smash the doorpost! It's our barn now, so take care with it. Gently, gently!' Diemka counselled the sweating Diemid.

They began to measure out the grain. 'Perhaps we'd better sift it at once? There's a sieve lying in the bin,' Ignationok, drunk with joy, proposed. The others laughed at him, and the jokes continued as they poured the heavy wheat into the measure.

'We can give another two hundred poods out of this for the grain collection,' Diemka Ushakov remarked as he waded up to his knees in the grain. With a spade he threw the wheat towards the mouth of the cornbin, caught some up in his hand, and let it trickle through his fingers.

'It ought to weigh heavy on the scales,' he added.

'It's wheat of pure gold, only it's gone a bit fusty through lying. See there?'

Arkashka and a youngster were lording it in the yard. Stroking his little ruddy beard, Arkashka pointed to some ox dung in which undigested grains of millet were showing.

'No wonder they worked well!' he commented. 'They ate pure grain, and in our Association even the hay was given out in driblets.'

From the granary came the sound of animated voices, laughter, the scent of the strong-smelling corn dust, sometimes a juicy oath. Andrei returned to the house. The mistress and her daughter were collecting pots and utensils into a sack. Frol was lying on the bench with only his stockings on his feet, his fingers crossed over his chest as though he were dead. Timofei, rather more composed, gave him a hateful glance and turned to the window.

In the best room Andrei found Diemid squatting on his heels. On his feet were Frol's new, leather-soled felt boots. As Andrei entered unnoticed, Diemid scooped up a tablespoon of honey from a large iron bucket and ate it, screwing up his eyes with delight, smacking his lips, and letting the sticky yellow drops run down his beard.

Chapter 8

Unexpected Resistance

IT was mid-day when Nagulnov and Titok returned to the village. During their absence Davidov had made inventories of the property in two kulak farms, and had expelled the owners. Then he had returned to Titok's yard, and, with Liubishkin's help, had measured and weighed the grain found in a fuel shed. Old Shchukar put the remains in a manger for the sheep, and promptly hurried out of the sheep-pen when he saw Titok coming.

Borodin strode across the yard with his coat thrown open and his head bare. He was making his way to the threshing floor, when Nagulnov shouted after him:

'Come back at once, or I'll lock you in the barn.'

Makar was angry and agitated, his cheek was twitching more violently than usual. He had failed to notice how and where Titok had managed to get rid of his gun. As they were drawing near to the house he had demanded:

'Will you give up that gun? We'll take it from you in any case.'

'Enough of that joke!' Titok smiled. 'You must have dreamt you saw a gun.'

And Nagulnov could not find any weapon under his coat. It was useless riding back to look for it: he would never find it in the deep snow or among the scrub. Angry with himself, he reported the incident to Davidov, who had been staring at Titok inquisitively ever since his arrival.

Davidov at once went across to Titok. 'Give up your gun, citizen!' he said. 'You'll have more peace without it.'

'I never had a gun. Nagulnov made up that story to spite me.' Titok smiled, and his ferrety eyes twinkled.

'Well, we shall have to arrest you and send you to the District.'

'Arrest me?'

'Yes, you. What did you think we should do? Take your past into account? You hide grain, you prepare . . .'

'Me?' Titok repeated in a hissing voice, crouching as though in readiness to spring.

At that moment all his forced gaiety, his self-possession and restraint left him. Davidov's words supplied the impulse needed to unloose the savage anger which had accumulated and hitherto had been held in check. He strode towards Davidov, who fell back before him. As he advanced, his foot stumbled over a yoke lying in the middle of the yard, and, stooping, he suddenly tugged the iron bolt out of the yoke. Nagulnov and Liubishkin flung themselves towards Davidov, while old Shchukar turned and ran out of the yard. But, as though of malice, the old man's feet were entangled in the overlong edge of his sheepskin, and he fell, wildly crying:

'Help, help, good people! There's murder being done!'

Davidov seized Titok by the wrist of his left arm, but Titok managed to strike him a blow on the head with his right. Davidov staggered, but kept his feet. The blood from the wound poured into his eyes and blinded him. He dropped Titok's arm, stumbled, and covered his eyes with the palm of his hand. A second blow sent him headlong into the snow. At the same moment Liubishkin seized Titok around his waist. Tearing himself away, Titok ran with great bounds towards the threshing floor. At the gate Nagulnov overtook him, and with the butt of his revolver struck him on the flat, hairy back of his head.

Titok's wife added to the turmoil. Seeing Liubishkin and Nagulnov running after her husband, she fled to the granary and unchained the dog. Rattling its iron collar, the animal rushed around the yard, and, attracted by Shchukar's terrified shouts and the sight of his sheepskin spread over the snow, it fastened upon it. With a rending sound fragments of skin, clumps of wool and clouds of dust flew out of the white sheepskin. Shchukar jumped to his feet, lunged furiously at the dog with his foot, and tried to break a stake out of the fence. Staggering under the animal's powerful tugs, he dragged it hanging on to his collar for some four or five yards, then with a desperate effort he managed to pull out a stake. The dog fled off howling, but with its last tug it succeeded in tearing the old man's sheepskin into two.

The old man's eyes stared out of his head; but as his courage returned he roared in a throaty voice: 'Give me a revolver, Makar! Give it me while my blood's hot! I'll kill him and his mistress too.'

Meantime Davidov had been assisted into the kitchen, and the hair had been cut away from the wound, from which the dark blood was still streaming and bubbling. In the yard Liubishkin harnessed Titok's horses into the two-horsed sledge. Nagulnov sat down at the table and hurriedly wrote:

To the District Officer of the State Political Police: I hand Titok Konstantinovich Borodin into your disposition as a counter-revolutionary and poisonous element. While we were making an inventory of this kulak's property he formally made an attack on comrade Davidov, one of the twenty-five thousand sent into the country, and managed to hit him twice on the head with an iron bolt.

In addition, I must inform you that I saw him in possession of a rifle of Russian pattern, with a sawn-off barrel, which I was unable to take from him owing to conditions in which I was out on the steppe and afraid of bloodshed. He threw the gun into the snow without my noticing. When found we shall send it to you as material evidence.

Secretary of the Gremyachy Nucleus of the All-Union Communist Party, and member of the Order of the Red Banner,

M. Nagulnov

They put Titok into the sledge. He asked for a drink, and also for Nagulnov to come to him. From the porch Makar shouted:

'What d'you want?'

'Makar! Remember!' Titok cried, shaking his bound hands as though drunk. 'Remember! Our roads will cross! You've trampled on me, but then I shall trample on you. Whatever happens I shall kill you. Our friendship is buried!'

'Off with you, counter-revolutionary!' Nagulnov waved his hand.

The horses dashed impetuously out of the yard.

Chapter 9

An Important Decision

EVENING was coming on when Razmiotnov dismissed the group of poor peasants who had been working with him, and dispatched the last sledge of confiscated goods from the kulak Gayev's yard to Titok's hut, where all the kulaks' property was being collected. Then he went to the village Soviet, where in the morning he had agreed to meet Davidov about an hour before the general meeting, which was to begin at nightfall.

As he went up the steps he saw a light in the corner room of the Soviet, and he went in, flinging the door wide open. At the sound Davidov raised his white, bandaged head from his notebook, and smiled.

'And here's Razmiotnov,' he remarked. 'Sit down. We're reckoning up how much grain we've found in the kulaks' possession. Well, and how did things go with you?'

'All very well. But what's your head bound up for?'

Nagulnov, who was fashioning a lampshade from a sheet of newspaper, reluctantly said:

'Titok gave him that. With a yoke bolt. I've sent Titok to the district Political Police Office.'

'Wait a little, and we'll tell you all about it in a minute,' said Davidov, pushing an abacus across the table. 'Add a hundred and fifteen. Got it? A hundred and eight . . .'

'Steady, steady!' Nagulnov anxiously muttered, very carefully pushing the beads across the abacus with one finger.

His lips trembling, Andrei stared at them and thickly declared:

'I'm not going on.'

'What d'you mean, "not going on"?' Nagulnov pushed the abacus to one side.

'I'm not going to do any more of this breaking up the kulaks. Well, what are you staring at? Do you want to send yourself into a fit?'

'Are you drunk?' Davidov asked, looking anxiously and attentively at Andrei's face, which was expressive of angry determination. 'What's the matter with you? What d'you mean by "you're not going on"?'

His calm tenor voice infuriated Andrei, and, stuttering with his agitation, he shouted:

'I've not been trained! I've not been trained to fight against children! At the front it was another matter. There you could cut down who you liked with your sword or what you liked . . . And you can all go to the devil! I'm not going on!' His voice rose higher and higher like the note of a tautened violin string, and seemed about to snap. But, taking a hoarse breath, he unexpectedly lowered his tone to a whisper:

'Do you call it right? What am I? An executioner? Or is my heart made of stone? I had enough at the war . . .' And he again began to shout. 'Gayev's got eleven children. How they howled when we arrived! You'd have clutched your head. It made my hair stand on end. We began to drive them out of the kitchen . . . I

71

screwed up my eyes, stopped my ears and ran into the yard. The women were all in a dead fright, and pouring water over the daughter-in-law ... The children ... Oh, by God, you ...'

'Cry! It'll ease you!' Nagulnov counselled him, pressing the twitching muscle in his cheek until it swelled, his inflamed eyes staring fixedly at Andrei.

'And I shall cry! My own little lad maybe ...' Andrei broke off, bared his teeth, and abruptly turned his back on the table.

There was a silence.

Davidov slowly rose from the table. And just as slowly was his unbound cheek flooded with a deathly blue, and his ear went white. He went up to Andrei, took him by the shoulder, and gently turned him round. Breathing heavily, not removing his eyes from Andrei's face, he began to speak:

'You're sorry for them ... You feel pity for them. And have they had pity on us? Have our enemies ever wept over the tears of our children? Did they ever weep over the orphans of those they killed? Well? After a strike at his factory my father was sacked and sent to Siberia. My mother was left with four children. I was the oldest, and I was nine. We had nothing to eat, and so my mother went ... You look at me! ... She went on the streets so as we shouldn't die of starvation. She brought her guests into our little room – we were living in a cellar. We had only one bed left. And we children slept on the floor behind the curtain ... And I was nine years old ... Drunken men came home with her. And I had to put my hands over my little sisters' mouths to prevent them from crying ... Who wiped away our tears? Do you hear? In the morning I would take the accursed rouble ...' Davidov raised his leathery palm to the level of Andrei's face, and tormentedly ground his teeth. '... the rouble my mother had earned and would go to get bread ...' Suddenly he swept his leaden-hued fist down on the table and shouted: 'How can you pity them?'

And again there was a silence. Nagulnov dug his nails into the table-top and clung to it like a kite to its prey. Andrei said nothing. Panting violently, Davidov paced up and down the room for a minute, then embraced Andrei around the shoulders and sat down with him on a bench. In a breaking voice he said:

'You've lost your senses! You come and start bellowing "I won't work ... children ... pity ..." Well, that slanderous attack of yours just now, do you take it back? Let's talk it over. You think it's a pity we're clearing out the kulak families? Think again! We're clearing them out so as they shan't prevent our organizing a life without any of those ... so as it shan't happen again in the future. You're the Soviet government in Gremyachy, and yet I've got to make propaganda on you!' He smiled forcedly. 'We'll send the kulaks to the devil, we'll send them to Solovky in the White Sea. They won't die, will they? If they work we'll feed them. And when we've built the new life their children will no longer be kulak children. The working class will re-educate them.' He pulled a packet of cigarettes out of his pocket, but for a long time his trembling fingers could not grip one.

While Davidov was speaking Nagulnov's face had broken into a deathly sweat. Andrei sat watching him, not taking his eyes off him for a moment. Now, to Davidov's surprise he swiftly rose to his feet, and at the same moment Nagulnov jumped up as though tossed into the air by a springboard.

'Snake!' he gasped out in a penetrating whisper, clenching his fists. 'How are you serving the revolution? Having pity on them? Yes ... You could line up thousands of old men, women and children, and tell me they'd got to be crushed into the dust for the sake of the revolution, and I'd shoot them all down with a machine-gun.' Suddenly he screamed savagely, a frenzy glittered in his great, dilated pupils, and the foam seethed at the corners of his lips.

'Here, stop shouting! Sit down!' Davidov took alarm.

Sending the chair flying as he went, Andrei hurriedly strode towards Nagulnov. But Makar huddled against the wall, threw back his head, rolled his eyes and shouted piercingly, protractedly:

'I'll cut you down!'

But he himself crumpled up sideways, his left hand clutching the air by his hip in search of a scabbard, his right convulsively groping for an invisible sword-hilt.

As Andrei caught him in his arms he felt the terrible tension

73

of all the muscles in Makar's heavy body, and the steely rigidity of his legs.

'He's in a fit! You hold his legs!' he cried to Davidov.

When the three of them arrived at the school they found it packed to overflowing with people come to the meeting. The building could not hold all who wanted to be present. Men, women and girls were standing pressed tightly together in the passage and on the porch. Steam mingled with tobacco smoke was billowing out of the cavern of the wide open door.

Pale, with blood caked on his broken lips, Nagulnov was the first to pass along the passage. The sunflower-seed husks scrunched beneath his measured footsteps. The cossacks stared discreetly as they made way for him. When they saw Davidov they began to whisper among themselves.

'Is that Davidov?' a girl in a colourful shawl asked in a loud voice, pointing at him with her handkerchief full of sunflower seeds.

'The one in the overcoat . . . He's not so big to look at . . .'

'No, but he's strongly built. Look, he's got a neck like a prize bull! They've sent him to us for breeding purposes,' one girl laughed, screwing up her round grey eyes at him.

'And he's broad in the shoulders, isn't he? He can squeeze the waists a bit, I expect, girls!' Natalia the grass-widow said shamelessly, working her painted eyebrows.

A youngster's rough, smoke-rasped voice remarked caustically:

'Our Natalia free-of-her-body would take anything in trousers.'

'So someone's pecked at his head already. He's got it bound up . . .'

'Perhaps he's got toothache.'

'No, Titok . . .'

'Girls! Sweets! What are you staring your little eyes out of your heads at a stranger for? Am I any worse than him?' an elderly, close-shaven cossack roared with laughter as he caught a whole drove of girls in his long arms, and pressed them against the wall. There was a chorus of shrieks. Girls' fists drummed hollowly on the cossack's back.

By the time Davidov reached the classroom door he was sweating. The crowd breathed out a reeking odour of sunflower-seed oil, onions, home-cured tobacco, and vodka fumes. From the girls and young women came the spicy smell of pomade and of clothes long stored in chests. A dull hum as of a myriad bees filled the school. And indeed the people seethed in a black, solid mass just like a swarm of bees.

'Your girls are cheeky,' Davidov said disconcertedly, when he clambered on to the platform. On the boards of the platform stood a couple of school desks. Davidov and Nagulnov sat down, and Razmiotnov opened the meeting. After a few preliminaries he announced:

'The representative of the Party District Committee, comrade Davidov, will speak first on the subject of the collective farm.'

His voice died away, and the roaring waves of conversation sharply subsided and ebbed into silence. Adjusting the bandage on his head, Davidov rose. He spoke for half an hour, and towards the end his voice grew hoarse. The meeting listened quietly. The stuffiness of the room grew more and more palpable. By the meagre light of the two lamps he could see the faces shining with sweat in the front rows, but beyond them everything was hidden in a murky twilight. Not once was he interrupted; but when he ended and stretched out his hand for the glass of water the questions came thick and fast like a downpour:

'Has everything got to be socialized?'

'How about the houses?'

'Is the collective farm only for a time, or for ever?'

'What will happen to those who go on their own? Their land won't be taken from them, will it?'

'And shall we eat together?'

Davidov answered them fully and to the point. When difficult problems of agriculture were involved Nagulnov and Andrei came to his aid. The draft collective farm constitution was read out, but still the questions did not cease. At last a cossack in a three-cornered fox-skin cap and a black sheepskin flung wide open rose from the middle rows and asked permission to speak. The hanging lamp threw a slanting light over his cap, and the ruddy fur seemed to flame and smoke.

'My farm's a middling one,' he declared, 'and what I say is, citizens, that the collective farm is a good idea, there's no other word for it, but we've got to think it over a lot! We can't go into it as though we'd only got to open our mouths and eat the fruit as it falls into them. The comrade from the party says all we've got to do is put our forces together, and we shall get the benefit. That's what comrade Lenin said too, he declares. But the comrade delegate doesn't know much about agriculture, I don't suppose he ever followed a plough in all his factory life, and I expect he wouldn't know which side to approach a bullock from. And because of that he's missed the mark a little. In my view we've got to get the people into the collective farms like this: those who're hard working and have got animals go into one farm, and the poor into another, and those who're well off into another, and the idlers must be sent off for the State Police to teach them how to work. It's no good lumping everybody together, no sense will ever come of that. It'll be like in the fairy-tale: the swan flapping its wings and trying to fly, the crayfish seizing it by its parson's nose and pulling it back, while the pike tries to crawl into the water.'

The meeting responded with a restrained laugh. A girl at the back gave a sudden squeal, and at once someone's indignant voice roared:

'Hi, you there who can't behave yourselves! You can squeeze one another in the yard. Clear out of here!'

The owner of the fox-skin cap wiped his brow and lips with his handkerchief, and continued:

'People have got to be sorted out like a good master sorts his oxen. He yokes together oxen equal in strength and size. But harness up unequal oxen, and what's the result? The stronger will pull his guts out while the weaker stands still, and through him the stronger one will have to stop too! What work will you get out of them? The comrade said all the village except the kulaks must go into one collective farm. And what's the result? The strong and the weak are yoked together!'

Liubishkin rose, angrily stroked his spreading black whiskers, and turned to the speaker:

'You can talk the hind leg off a donkey, Kuzma ... If I was a woman I could sit and listen to you for ever!' There was a ripple of laughter. 'You're talking over the meeting as if it was Pelagea Kuzmichova.' The laughter burst in a salvo. A sharp sting of flame flickered snake-like from the lamp. All the meeting understood the allusion, which was probably indecently amusing. Even Nagulnov smiled with his eyes. Davidov was about to ask him the reason for the laughter, but Liubishkin outshouted the roar of voices:

'The voice is yours, but the song's another's! It's all right for you to sort out the people like that! You learned how to do it when you belonged to Frol's machinery Association, didn't you? They took your motor from you last year. But now we've disembowelled your Frol with fire and smoke! You gathered a sort of collective farm around Frol's motor too, only it was a kulak one. I suppose you haven't forgotten how much you fleeced the peasants of for threshing? Not one quarter in every eight, was it? Maybe you would like to do the same again: to lean up against the rich . . .'

Such a hubbub arose that Razmiotnov had difficulty in restoring order. And for a long time the furious shouts came like a spring hail:

'They did well out of their association!'

'You can't crush lice with a tractor!'

'The kulaks have got hold of him!'

'Give him a lick!'

'You could husk sunflower seed with his head.'

Nikolai Lushnia, a cossack just above the poverty level, asked to be allowed to speak.

'But no arguments! The question's quite clear!' Nagulnov warned him.

'How d'you make that out? Maybe I do want to object! Or aren't I allowed to speak against your opinion? I say this: the collective farm's a voluntary matter. If you want to, you join, and if you want to, you watch it from outside. And we want to look on from outside.'

'Who are "we"?' Davidov asked.

'Those who grow the grain, I mean.'

'You speak for yourself, daddy. Each has got a free tongue and will speak for himself.'

'And I can for myself. It's for myself I'm speaking. I want to see what sort of life there'll be in the collective farm. If it's good, I'll sign on; and if not, why should I join it? It's a stupid fish that swims into the net...'

'That's true!'

'We'll wait before we join.'

'Let others try the new life first!'

'Come in for the love of it! What is there to try? It isn't a girl, is it?'

'Akhvatkin's to speak next. Go ahead, Akhvatkin,' Razmiotnov announced.

'I'll tell you about myself, fellow-citizens. Me and my brother Piotr, we lived together. But we couldn't agree. First the women quarrelled among themselves, you couldn't part them with water. They tore one another's eyes out. Then me and Piotr, we couldn't get on together. And here they want to throw the whole village into one little heap! You'll get such a muddle as we won't ever be able to get out of. There'll be fights every time we go out to plough in the steppe. It'll be, "Ivan's overdriven my oxen, I haven't looked after his horses". The militia will have to live here all the time. One will work more, another less. Our work isn't like standing at a bench in a factory; it's different. In a factory you do your eight hours and then off you go, pipe between your teeth...'

'Have you ever been in a factory?'

'No, I haven't, comrade Davidov, but I know.'

'You know nothing whatever about the workers. And if you've never been in a factory and never seen one, why are you wagging your tongue? Kulak talk about the worker with his pipe!'

'Well, let it be without a pipe; he's done his work, and off he goes. But with us you get up and plough while it's still dark. And by the time night comes you've sweated all the sweat out of you, you've got blood-blisters the size of a hen's egg on your feet, but you've got to pasture the oxen during the night, and there's no sleep for you; if the ox doesn't get its fill, it won't pull the plough. In the collective farm I shall work hard, but someone else, our Koliba for instance, will sleep in a furrow. The Soviet government says there are no idlers among the poor, that it's the kulaks have made that story up, but it isn't true.

Koliba's spent all his life lying on the stove. All the village knows that one winter he was lying on the stove with his feet stretched towards the door, and by the morning his legs were covered with hoarfrost, but his side was burnt as red as a brick. It showed he had grown so lazy he couldn't get off the stove and go outside even to relieve himself. How am I to work with a man like him? I'm not putting my name down for the collective farm.'

'Kondrat Maidannikov speaks next. Out with it, Maidannikov.'

A medium-sized cossack in a grey coat slowly made his way from the back rows on to the platform. The faded cloth helmet of a Budionny cavalry man swayed above the fur and the three-cornered caps, above the women's vari-coloured shawls and kerchiefs. He went on to the platform, turned his back to the table, and unhurriedly groped in his trouser pocket.

'Going to read your speech?' Diemka Ushakov asked with a smile.

'Take your hat off!'

'Spout it by heart!'

'He writes all his life down on paper.'

'Ha, ha! He's educated!'

Maidannikov found his greasy little notebook, and hastily turned over the scribbled leaves.

'You wait with your laughing, you may have to cry before you're finished,' he said angrily. 'Yes, I write down what I feed on. And I'll read it out to you in a moment. We've had several speeches, but not one to the point. You think little about your life...'

Davidov pricked up his ears. Smiles were visible on the faces in the front rows. Voices rippled through the school.

'My farm's a middling sized one,' Maidannikov began confidently, without any embarrassment. 'Last year I sowed five hectares. As you all know, I own a yoke of oxen, a horse, a cow, a wife and three children. Our working hands – there they are, all of them! From my five hectares I harvested ninety poods of wheat, eighteen of barley and twenty-three of oats. I need sixty poods to feed my family, ten poods for the fowls, and the oats go to feed the horse. What is left for me to sell to the State?

Thirty-eight poods. Reckon one rouble ten kopeks a pood all round, and you get forty-one roubles net profit. Well, I sell some fowls, take the ducks to market and get another fifteen roubles.' And, with a mournful look in his eyes, he raised his voice: 'With that amount can I get boots and clothes, buy paraffin, matches and soap? And doesn't it cost money to have the horse shoed? What are you silent for? Can I go on living like that? And that's all right if the harvest is poor or good. But supposing we get a failure of crops? Then who am I? An old man! What right have you, damn you, to try to argue me and push me away from the collective farm? Will my life be any worse then than what it is now? You lie! And all the middling peasants will tell you the same. And I'll tell you in a minute why you're against it yourselves, and are trying to befog others.'

'Give it to the sons of bitches, Kondrat!' Liubishkin roared in delight.

'And I will give it to them! Let them listen! You're against the collective farm because you can't see anything beyond your own cow and your chicken-coop of a hut. It's snotty, but it's my own! The Communist Party is pushing you into a new life, and you're like a blind calf: lead it to the cow's udder, and it kicks and shakes its head. But if the calf doesn't suck at the teat it'll never live to see the light of day. And that's all. I shall sit down this very day to write that I want to join the collective farm, and I call on others to do the same. But those who don't want to shouldn't interfere with those who do.'

Razmiotnov rose to his feet.

'The matter is quite clear, citizens,' he said. 'The lamps are going out and it's getting late. Those who're in favour of the collective farm, raise their hands. Only heads of households can vote.'

Out of the two hundred and seventeen heads of households present only sixty-seven raised their hands.

'Who's against?'

Not one hand was raised.

'So you don't want to put your names down for the collective farm?' Davidov asked. 'So it's true what comrade Maidannikov said?'

'We don't want it,' came a woman's snuffling voice.

'Don't hold your Maidannikov up to us.'

'Our fathers and grandfathers lived ...'

'You'd better not try to force us in!'

When the cries had died away, from the back rows, from the darkness lit only by the gleam of cigarette ends, came someone's belated, rancorous voice:

'You can't drive us like sheep. Titok's let your blood once, and it can happen again ...'

Davidov started up as though he had been lashed by a whip. In the terrible silence he stood for a minute speechless, paling, his gap-toothed mouth half-open. Then he hoarsely shouted:

'You! The enemy who spoke then! Titok hasn't let enough of my blood! I shall still live to see all such as you buried. But if it is necessary, for the party, for my party and the cause of the workers I'll give every drop of my blood. Do you hear, you kulak reptile? All, to the very last drop.'

'Who shouted that out?' Nagulnov straightened up in his seat.

Razmiotnov jumped down from the platform. A bench creaked in the back rows, a crowd of some twenty men went noisily out into the passage. Some in the middle rows also began to get up. There was a jangling and crashing of glass: someone had broken out a window pane. The fresh wind blew in through the opening, and the white steam whirled like a waterspout.

'That wasn't Timofei, Frol's son, who shouted out, was it?'

'Turn them out of the village!'

'No, it was Akimka. There are cossacks here from Tubyan-skoe."

'The brawlers! Let their blood! Turn them out!'

The meeting came to an end long after midnight. For and against the collective farm speeches were made, until throats were hoarse and eyes were dimmed. Here and there, even right under the platform, the opponents came together and seized one another by the breast of their shirts as they argued their views. A neighbour and relation of Kondrat Maidannikov's tore his shirt down to the navel. The affair came almost to blows; Diemka Ushakov rushed to Kondrat's help, jumping across benches, over the heads of those still sitting. But Davidov separated the combatants. And Diemka himself at once remarked venomously to Maidannikov:

'Well, Kondrat, reckon up with your brains how many hours you'll have to plough to pay for your torn shirt.'

'You reckon up how many your wife's got . . .'

'Now, now! Start making jokes of that sort and I'll turn you out of the meeting.'

Diemid the Silent slept peacefully under a bench in the back rows, lying like an animal with his head towards the draught coming under the door, his head wrapped in his coat to keep out the unnecessary noise. Elderly women who had come to the meeting with unfinished knitted stockings dozed like hens on a perch, letting their needles and balls of wool drop to the floor. Many had left long before. And when Arkady, who had already spoken more than once, wanted to make yet another speech in defence of the collective farm, a sound like the vicious hissing of geese burst from his throat. He clutched at his Adam's apple and bitterly waved his hand. But he could not control his feelings, and, sitting down where he had been standing, he mutely showed the raging opponent of the collective farm, Nikolai Akhvatkin, what would happen to him after wholesale collectivization. He laid one tobacco-stained thumbnail on the other, and – crack! Nikolai merely spat, and swore under his breath.

Chapter 10

Parting of the Ways

AS Kondrat Maidannikov strode away from the meeting, right above him the stars of the Great Bear smouldered their unextinguished fires. The night was so still that the cracking of the earth splitting with the frost, and the rustle of freezing twigs could be heard for some distance. When he reached his hut Kondrat went across the yard to the oxen, and put a meagre armful of hay in their manger. But, remembering that tomorrow he would be driving them to the communal yard, he gathered an enormous load of hay, and said aloud:

'Well, so we're going to part ... Move over, baldhead! Four years we've worked, the cossack for the ox, and the ox for the cossack. And nothing has come of it. Half-starved you've been, and I've not been much better. That's why I'm changing you for the communal life. Here, what are you yawning for, as though you really understood what I was saying?' He pushed the brindled ox with his foot, and turned its chewing, dribbling jaws with his hand. As his eyes met the animal's lilac eye, he suddenly remembered how he had waited for this ox to come some five years before. The old cow had taken the bull so secretly that neither Kondrat nor the herdsman had seen them together. And for a long time that autumn she showed no sign of having been up to any tricks. 'She's gone dry, curse her!' Kondrat thought, turning cold as he looked at her. But, like all old cows, she began to show signs a month before calving, at the end of November. How often during the cold nights towards the end of Advent Kondrat had woken up as though someone had nudged him, had thrust his feet into his felt boots, and, wearing only his drawers, had run to the warm stable to see whether she had calved yet. The frosts were heavy that year, and the calf might freeze before its mother had time to lick it clean. Towards the end of the fast Kondrat had hardly any sleep. Then, one morning his wife Anna came in gaily, all but triumphantly, and said:

'The old girl's emptied her veins. It ought to come tonight.'

That evening Kondrat lay down without undressing, and did not put out the light in the lantern. Seven times he went out to the cow! And only at the eighth time, just before dawn, as he was opening the little door into the cattle-shed he heard a deep and painful groan. He went in, and found the cow evacuating the after-birth, while a tiny, shaggy, white-nostrilled calf, already cleaned, and trembling miserably, was seeking the mother's teat with its clammy lips. Kondrat snatched up the after-birth to prevent the cow eating it, for he shared the general belief that if she did her milk could not be used for twelve days. Then he lifted the calf in his arms, warming it with the warmth of his breath, wrapping it in the edge of his coat, and rushed with it into the hut.

'It's a bull!' he shouted joyfully.

Anna crossed herself. 'Glory to God!' she said. 'The Merciful One has seen our need.'

And certainly, possessing only one sorry nag, Kondrat was up to his eyes in need. And the bull had grown and worked well for Kondrat, in summer and in the winter cold, setting down its cloven hoofs innumerable times on the roads and the tillage, dragging the cart or the plough.

As he looked at the bull Kondrat suddenly felt a painful lump in his throat, and a smarting in the eyes. He burst into tears and left the yard, as though they had given him relief. He did not sleep all that night, but lay smoking.

'How will things go in the collective farm? Do they all feel and see as I see that this is the only way, that there can be no turning back? That no matter how painful it is to hand over to strangers the lean animal which has grown up together with the family on the earthen floor of the hut, yet it has got to be done? And this shameful regret for my own goods must be crushed, must not be allowed to get hold of my heart!' So Kondrat thought as he lay beside his snoring wife, and stared with unseeing eyes into the blackness of the night. And then he thought: 'But where shall we put the lambs and goats? They need a warm hut, and a good deal of looking after. How are they to be picked out from the others when they're almost all alike? Their mothers will mix them up, and so will the people. And the cows? How is their food to be carried? How many shall we lose? And supposing everybody clears out again after a week, in fear of the difficulties? Then it's the mines for me, and good-bye to Gremyachy for ever. I shall have nothing left to live on.'

Just before dawn he dozed off. But even in his dreams he found things difficult and heavy. The principle of the collective farm did not come easily to Kondrat. With tears and blood he tore away the umbilical cord connecting him with ownership of property, with his oxen, with his own stretch of land.

After breakfast next morning he sat a long time with his sunburnt brow knitted, writing his application. The result read:

To comrade Makar Nagulnov in the Communist Gremyachy Party
   Nucleus:

Application.

I, Kondrat Maidannikov, a middling cossack, ask to be accepted
in the collective farm, with my wife and children, and my property, and with all our livestock. I ask you to let me come into the
new life, as I entirely agree with it.

K. Maidannikov

'Are you joining?' his wife asked.

'Yes.'

'Are you taking the cattle along?'

'I'm taking them at once. Well, what are you raising your
voice for, you dolt? I've talked to you and wasted a lot of time
on you, and yet you still cling to the old life, don't you? And
you agreed yourself.'

'I'm only sorry about the cow, Kondrat. I do agree. Only it
gives me a heart-ache,' she said, smiling and wiping away the
tears with her apron. And Khristishka, their four-year-old
daughter, began to cry like her mother.

Kondrat bridled the horse, let the cow and the oxen out of the
yard, and drove them down to the river to drink. The oxen
turned to go back home, but with wrath boiling in his heart
Kondrat rode the horse at them, barred their road, and drove
them in the direction of the village Soviet.

The women stared openly out of their windows after him, and
the cossacks watched across the fences, without coming into the
street. Kondrat felt more and more beside himself. But as he
turned the corner he saw a great crowd of oxen, horses and
sheep outside the Soviet. It was like a market day. Liubishkin
came out of a side alley dragging a cow by a rope tied to its
horns. And behind them hurried a calf with a rope dangling
around its neck.

'Let's tie their tails together and drive them side by side,' Liubishkin tried to jest, but he was himself obviously stern and pre-
occupied. He had had no small difficulty in getting the cow along,
as the fresh scratch on his cheek witnessed.

'Who's been scratching you?' Kondrat asked him.

'I won't hide my sin! It was my wife. The devil of a woman

85

flung herself after the cow.' Liubishkin thrust the end of his whisker into his mouth and added discontentedly through set teeth: 'She advanced to the attack like a tank. There was such a shedding of blood all over the yard that all our neighbours will know of it. You'd hardly believe it, but she came at me with a frying pan. "Ah," I said, "you'd strike a Red Partisan, would you? We gave it hot to generals," I said. And I hit her one on the temple. Someone was watching us outside. I expect he enjoyed the show . . .'

From the village Soviet they set out for Titok's farm. During the morning twelve middling cossacks who had spent the night thinking it over brought applications for membership and drove in their cattle.

With the aid of two carpenters Nagulnov cut down alders in order to make mangers, the first communal mangers in Grem-yachy Log.

Chapter 11

Turned Out

IT took Kondrat a long time to break through the frozen earth with a pickaxe, and to dig holes for the manger uprights. Liubishkin worked at his side. His face burned, and from under his black fur cap, which hung over his forehead like a menacing cloud, the sweat poured down. His mouth gaping, he swung the pick furiously, and the clumps and clods of frozen earth flew upward and sideways, rattling like shot against the wall. The mangers were hastily knocked together, and after being valued by a commission the twenty-eight yoke of oxen were driven into the shed. His khaki shirt clinging to his wet shoulders, Nagulnov followed them into the shed.

'You've only swung an axe a little, and you can squeeze the water out of your shirt! You'd make a poor workman, Makar,' Liubishkin remarked with a shake of his head. 'Look how I work! Smash, crash! This is a good pick of Titok's! Come and put your fur coat on quickly, or you'll catch cold, and the next thing you'll be laid out.'

Nagulnov flung on his coat. The blood-red flushes in his cheeks slowly ebbed away.

'It's because of the poison gas,' he replied. 'As soon as I do a bit of work or start going uphill I begin to pant, and my heart thumps away. Is that the last tether-post? That's fine! Look what a stock we've got!' With burning, glittering eyes he swept the long row of oxen ranged in front of the new, fresh-smelling mangers.

While the cows were being distributed around the open cattle-yard Razmiotnov and Diemka Ushakov arrived. Andrei called Nagulnov aside and took his arm.

'Makar, old friend,' he said, 'don't be angry about what happened yesterday. As I listened to the children's crying I remembered my own little lad, and it pinched me a bit.'

'You devil! You ought to be pinched, you saint!'

'Well, it's all over. I see from your eyes that you don't feel the same to me as before.'

'Oh, drop that, jaw-me-dead! Where are you going? We must get in some hay. Where's Davidov?'

'He's at the Soviet looking through the applications with Arkashka. And I'm going . . . I've still got one kulak farm left untouched. Siemion Lapshinov's . . .'

'And when you come back will you carry on like you did yesterday?' Nagulnov smiled.

'Drop it! Who can I take with me? There's so much going on that everything's upside down, like in a battle. Dragging cattle, bringing hay! Some of them have already brought in seed-corn. I sent them back with it. We'll deal with the seed afterwards. Who could I take to help me?'

'There's Kondrat Maidannikov. Kondrat, come over here! Go with the chairman to take over Lapshinov's farm. You're not afraid, are you? There are others who don't want to, they're all conscience, like Timofei Borshchev! He's got no scruples about crawling to the kulaks, but when it's a question of taking back what they've stolen he finds he's got a conscience.'

'No, why shouldn't I go?' Kondrat replied. 'I'll go willingly.'

Diemka Ushakov joined Kondrat and Andrei, and all three went into the street. Glancing at Kondrat, Razmiotnov asked:

'What are you scowling for? You ought to be glad; see how the village has come to life, just as though someone had upset an anthill.'

'There's nothing to be pleased about yet. It's going to be difficult,' Kondrat drily answered.

'How?'

'With the sowing, and with watching the cattle. Just now I saw three men working and a dozen sitting on their heels under the fence and smoking . . .'

'They'll all work sure enough! This is only the start. When there's nothing for them to eat they'll smoke less.'

At a bend in the road they came upon a sledge turned over on its side. A heap of scattered hay lay beside it, and the uprights used to retain loads on the sledge were broken. The yoke of oxen had been unharnessed, and were chewing the brilliant green couch-grass showing through the snow. The young son of Siemion Kruzhenkov, a cossack who had joined the collective farm, was languidly scraping up the hay with a three-pronged fork.

'Hi, what are you working like a corpse for? I was all on the go when I was your age. Is that the way to work? Here, give me that fork!' Diemka Ushakov tore the pitchfork out of the smiling youngster's hands, and, with one gasp, balanced a whole stook of hay on the prongs.

'How did you manage to turn the sledge over?' Kondrat asked.

'It struck against something coming down the hill. Don't you know how it's done?'

'Well, run and fetch an axe. Get one from the Donietskovs.'

The three men lifted the sledge on to its runners, refashioned and replaced the uprights in their sockets, then Diemka neatly piled the load of hay on the sledge and tidied it with a rake.

'Kruzhenkov, ah, Kruzhenkov!' he chided the lad. 'You ought to have your greasy hide tanned without your being allowed to cry out. Look how much hay the oxen have trodden! You should have taken up an armful, driven them over to the fence and let them eat. Whoever lets them wander about like that?'

The youngster laughed and drove on the oxen, remarking as he went: 'The hay isn't ours any longer, it's the collective farm's.'

'Did you ever see such a swine?' Diemka looked at Kondrat with eyes squinting both ways, then swore unpleasantly.

Some thirty people gathered in Lapshinov's yard while they were making the inventory. The majority were women neighbours, and there was only a sprinkling of cossacks among them. When Lapshinov, a tall, grey-haired man with pointed beard, was invited to leave the hut, a murmur arose from the crowd which had thronged into the room, and someone muttered:

'Yes, but why should he? He's saved and saved, and now it's out into the steppe for him!'

'It's a sad business...'

'Do you feel sorry for him?'

'A pain's a pain, whoever feels it.'

'He doesn't seem to like it, but under the old system he took all Trifonov had in payment of a debt, and he didn't think of whether Trifonov liked it then.'

'How he's bawling...!'

'And so he ought, the bearded old goat! They've tied a fire under his tail!'

'It's a sin to rejoice in others' misfortunes. You may have some yourself some day.'

'How the devil can we? All we own is a heap of stones. You don't get rich on them!'

'Last summer he stung me for ten roubles for two days' use of his mowing machine. Where's the conscience in that?'

Lapshinov had long been regarded in the village as a man of substance. It was known that even before the war he had had no little property, for the old man had never scorned to lend money at usurious interest and quietly to buy up stolen property. At one time there had been obstinate rumours that stolen horses were to be found in his stables. Occasionally, usually at night, gipsy horse-dealers visited him. It was said that through Lapshinov's hands the horses passed along the broad road to Tsaritsin, Taganrog and Uriupinsk. The village knew beyond doubt that in the old days he had driven two or three times a year to the district town to change paper roubles for gold imperials. In 1912 there had been an attempt to hold him up on the road, but Lapshinov, who was a strong and desperate old man, had beaten off the robbers with only a cudgel and had galloped away. He was too clever to be caught: he had been caught once in the steppe with some-one else's stooks, but that was in his youth. As he grew old he adopted a simple attitude to other men's property: he picked up anything left lying about. He was so grasping that he would set a farthing candle before the picture of Nikolai Mirlikisky in the church, and hardly had it been lit when he would go and put it out, cross himself, and thrust it into his pocket. Thus one little candle would last him a whole year, and if anyone reproached him for such niggardliness and negligence in regard to God he replied: 'God's wiser than you, you fool! It isn't candles he needs, but respect. There's no point in God letting me in for expense. He even beat the traders in the temple with a whip.'

Lapshinov received the news of his dispossession quite calmly. He had nothing to be afraid of. Everything of value had been previously hidden or delivered into trusty hands. He helped to draw up the inventory of his property, stamped his foot men-acingly at his lamenting old wife, and in the next breath sub-missively said:

'Don't cry, mother! The Lord will take notice of our sufferings. The All-merciful sees everything . . .'

'But he doesn't see where you've hidden your new sheepskin coat, does he?' Diemka asked in a serious tone, imitating Lap-shinov's voice.

'What sheepskin?'

'The one you went to church in last Sunday.'

'I wasn't wearing a new sheepskin.'

'You were, but now you've put it away somewhere.'

'Before God I tell you I never had one, Dementii.'

'God will punish you, old man! He'll teach you!'

'And in the name of Christ I tell you you're wrong,' Lapshinov crossed himself.

'You're taking a sin on your soul,' Diemka winked at the crowd, forcing smiles from the women and cossacks.

'I am not guilty in God's sight, I swear it.'

'You've hidden the coat! You'll answer for it on Judgement Day!'

'What, for my own sheepskin?' Lapshinov burst out.

'You'll answer for hiding it.'

'Do you think God's got a mind like yours, you twaddler? He won't even interfere in such matters. I haven't got a sheepskin. You ought to be ashamed of mocking at an old man. Ashamed before God and man.'

'But you weren't ashamed to take three measures of millet in return for the two measures I borrowed for sowing, were you?' Kondrat asked. His voice was quiet and a little hoarse, almost inaudible in the general hubbub, but Lapshinov turned to him with youthful agility:

'Kondrat! Your father was a worthy man, but you ... If only out of respect for his memory you oughtn't to sin! In the sacred book it is written: "Hit not a man when he is down," but how do you behave? Whenever did I take three measures for two from you? And what of God? He sees all.'

'He'd like us to give him the millet for nothing, the ragged-arsed idol!' Lapshinov's wife shouted in a heartrending voice.

'Don't cry, mother! The Lord suffered, and he commanded us to suffer. He put on a crown of thorns, and wept bloody tears.' Lapshinov wiped away his own muddy little tears with his sleeve. The women ceased their hubbub, and sighed. Razmiotnov finished his writing, then said harshly:

'Well, daddy Lapshinov, clear out of here. Your tears aren't so pitiable as all that. You've done wrong to many in your time, and now we're going to settle with you ourselves, without God's help. Out with you!'

Lapshinov put his three-cornered cap on his head, took his stuttering, half-witted son by the hand, and left the hut. The crowd rushed after him. In the yard the old man spread the edge of his fur-skin jacket out over the snow, and fell to his knees. He signed the cross before his furrowed forehead, and bowed down to the ground in all four directions.

'Get on! Get on!' Razmiotnov ordered. But the crowd began quietly to boo, and shouts were heard:

'Let him say good-bye to his own farm at any rate!'

'Don't be a fool, Andrei! A man with one foot in the grave, and you...'

'After the life he's lived he ought to crawl in with both feet,' Kondrat shouted. He was answered by old Gladilin, the churchwarden:

'Currying favour with the government? Men like you ought to be whipped.'

'You old fox, I'll give you such a blow that you'll forget your way home,' Kondrat replied.

Lapshinov bowed, crossed himself, and, appealing to the easily affected women's hearts, said stentoriously, so that all could hear:

'Good-bye, true believers! Good-bye, dear kindred! May God give you health ... to enjoy my property. I lived, I worked honestly, I...'

'Bought stolen goods,' Diemka prompted him from the porch.

'In the sweat of my brow I earned my bread...'

'Ruined other men, took interest, and even stole! Go on, confess! You old lecher, you ought to be taken by the throat and your head knocked against the ground.'

'My daily bread, I say, and now in my old age...'

The women began to snivel, and drew the ends of their kerchiefs up to their eyes. Razmiotnov was about to raise Lapshinov and push him out of the yard, and had got as far as: 'Don't you try to work up an agitation here, you...' when there was a sudden tumult on the porch, where Diemka had been leaning against the balustrade. Lapshinov's wife came running out of the kitchen; in one hand she had a basket containing a clutch of goose eggs, in the other was a goose lying quiet and blinded by the snow and sun. Diemka had no difficulty in taking the basket from her, but the old woman clung on to the goose with both hands.

'Let go, you wretch! Let go!' she shouted.

'The goose belongs to the collective farm now,' Diemka roared, seizing the bird by its outstretched neck.

The woman hung on to its legs. They each pulled in the opposite direction, and furiously dragged each other about the porch.

'Give it back, boss-eye!' she screamed.

'I won't.'

'Let go, I say!'

'It's a collective farm goose,' Diemka pantingly shouted. 'It'll give us goslings in the spring. Get away, old woman, or I'll kick you in the ribs. You've eaten your fill of goose . . .'

Dribbling with spittle, her feet firmly planted against the step, the dishevelled woman pulled the bird towards her. The goose had at first given voice to a stupid cry, but now it was silent, and evidently Diemka was choking it. But it flapped its wings madly, and white down and feathers whirled like snowflakes about the porch. It seemed that in another minute Diemka must be victorious, and tear the half-dead goose out of the woman's knotted hands. But at that moment the bird's feeble neck quietly cracked at the joints and came apart from the body. The woman's skirt flew over her head, and she tumbled thunderously down from the porch, her body bumping heavily on each step. Groaning with surprise, Diemka, holding only the goose's head in his hands, fell into the basket on the floor just behind him, and crushed the half-hatched eggs. A tremendous outburst of laughter shook the icicles from the roof. Lapshinov rose from his knees, pulled on his cap, furiously tugged his dribbling, impassive idiot son by the arm, and dragged him out of the yard almost at a gallop. Black with anger and pain, his wife scrambled to her feet. After dusting her skirt, she stretched out her hand to pick up the beheaded goose, which was still writhing by the steps. But a tawny Borzoi hound hanging around the porch steps saw the blood spurting out of the goose's neck, and, its hair on end, made one sudden spring, seized the bird from under the woman's nose, and dragged it around the yard to the whistling and hallooing of the lads.

Throwing the goose's head with its eternally astonished orange eyes still staring out on the world, after the woman, Diemka went into the hut. And for a long time the sound of voices, of laughter, and excitement hung about the yard and the street corner, frightening the sparrows out of the dry brushwood.

Chapter 12

Murder

LIFE in Gremyachy Log was turned upside down; it reared on end like a restive horse before an obstacle. During the day the cossacks gathered in the sidelanes and in the huts, arguing, discussing the collective farm, expressing their opinions. For four days in succession meetings were held every evening, and continued until cock-crow.

During those days Nagulnov grew so thin that he looked as though he had had a long and dangerous illness. But Davidov retained his previous outward calm, only the deep, obstinate folds at the sides of his cheeks above his lips grew sharper. Somehow he had managed to instil confidence into Razmiotnov, who normally was quick to take fire and as easily prone to unjustified panic. With a confident smile playing in his ill-natured eyes, Andrei walked around the village inspecting the communal cattle-yards. To Arkady, who was placed in charge of the collective farm until the election of the management committee, he frequently remarked:

'We'll show them ! They'll all come into the farm !'

Davidov dispatched a mounted courier to the District Committee, to inform them that at the moment only 32 per cent of those eligible had been brought into the collective farm, but that the work of bringing in the others was continuing at high pressure.

The kulaks expelled from their own huts went to live with their relations and friends. After sending his son Timofei direct to the Regional Public Prosecutor, Frol went to live with his friend Borshchev, the man who had not wanted to vote at the meeting of the poor cossacks. And in Borshchev's small, two-roomed hut the more active of the kulaks began to gather. In the daytime they usually made their way to the hut in ones and twos, going by the backways and through the threshing floors, in order to avoid being overheard or seen or attracting the attention of the Soviet authorities. David Gayev came, and the hardened old fraud Lapshinov, who, after his dispossession, had become a 'beggar in the name of Christ'. Occasionally Yakov Lukich Ostrovnov came to see the lie of the land. Some of the middling peasants who were resolutely opposed to the collective farm, such as Nikolai Lushnia, also frequently dropped in at the kulak 'staff headquarters'. Besides Borshchev there were even a couple of poor cossacks: tall, eyebrowless Vasili Atamanchukov, always taciturn, as bareheaded as an egg and completely clean-shaven, and Nikita Khoprov, an artilleryman of the former Guards' battery, who had served in the army with Podtielkov, had always evaded military service during the civil war, but none the less in 1919 had found himself in the punitive detachment of the Kalmik White colonel Ashtimov. And this had determined all Khoprov's future life under the Soviet regime. Three men from Gremyachy: Yakov Lukich Ostrovnov and his son, and old Lapshinov, had seen Khoprov in the Ashtimov detachment during the 1920 retreat, wearing the white band of an ensign on his shoulder-straps. And they had seen him in charge of three Kalmik cossacks driving arrested workers from the railway depot at Kushevka to Ashtimov for examination. They had seen him ... And how much it cost Khoprov, when he returned from Novorossiisk to Gremyachy and learnt that Ostrovnov and Lapshinov had seen him! What terrors the broad-chested artilleryman endured during the years of ferocious settlement with the counter-revolution! And he who could hold still any horse while it was being shoed, seizing it by the hoof of one hind leg, trembled like a late oak-leaf caught by the frost whenever he met the craftily smiling Lapshinov. He was more afraid of him than of anyone else. Whenever he met him he said hoarsely through numbed lips:

'Daddy, don't let a cossack soul perish, don't give me away!'

And with studied indignation Lapshinov would reassure him:

'Why, Nikita! God be with you! Why, don't I wear a cross at my breast? And what did the Saviour teach: "Have pity on your neighbour as yourself." You mustn't even think I should tell! Cut my throat if I tell a lie. I'm not that sort. Only, you support me if ever ... At a meeting, maybe, someone will be against me, or the government may attack me ... You defend me if necessary ... "One good turn," you know ... And those who take the sword shall perish by the sword. Isn't that so? And another thing: I wanted to ask you to give me a hand with the ploughing. God's given me a son who's a little touched, he's no help. And hiring a man's expensive.'

Year after year Nikita Khoprov 'helped' Lapshinov, ploughing for him, fetching and carrying, serving Lapshinov's wheat into Lapshinov's thresher. Afterwards he would go home, sit down at the table, bury his broad, ginger-whiskered face in his iron palms, and think: 'How long is this to go on? I'll kill him!'

Yakov Lukich did not oppress him with demands, nor did he ever threaten him, for he knew that if he should have to ask Khoprov even for something on a big scale, and not merely for a bottle of vodka, Khoprov would not dare to refuse. But Yakov Lukich frequently drank a bottle of vodka with him, and invariably said: 'Thank you for treating me.'

'I hope it chokes you!' Khoprov would think, clenching his weighty fists under the table in his hatred.

Polovtsiev was still living with Yakov Lukich in the little room where Yakov's old mother had previously slept. She transferred herself to the top of the kitchen stove, while in her room Polovtsiev smoked almost incessantly, lying on the short couch, with his bare feet thrust against the hot back of the stove. At night he often walked about the sleeping house, and not a door creaked, for the hinges had all been carefully greased with goose-fat. Sometimes he would throw his fur jacket across his shoulders, put out his cigarette, and go to see his horse, which was concealed in the chaff-shed. The long-standing horse would welcome him with a quivering, stifled whinny, as though it knew that now was not the time to express its feelings too loud. Its master would run his hands over it, feeling the joints of its legs with his inflexible, steely fingers. On one occasion, on a particularly dark night, he led the horse out of the shed and galloped off into the steppe. He returned just before dawn. The horse was wet as though it had been washed with sweat, its flanks were heaving, and it was shaken with a heavy, infrequent trembling. In the morning Polovtsiev said to Yakov Lukich:

'I've been in my home town. They're searching for me there. The cossacks are ready to rise and are only waiting for the order.'

It was at his instigation that, when a second general meeting of the Gremyachy inhabitants was summoned to discuss the collective farm, Yakov Lukich made an appeal for everybody to join, and delighted Davidov inexpressibly with his intelligent, practical speech, and by the fact that after Lukich, who carried much weight in the village, had announced his intention to join, thirty-one further applications were at once handed in.

At the meeting Lukich spoke fine words about the farm, but he talked very differently the next day, when he went around the huts, using Polovtsiev's money to treat reliable middling cossacks who were hostile to the collective farm, though he drank but little himself.

'You're a mug, my boy,' he said. 'It's much more necessary for me to join than for you, and I daren't speak against it. I've done pretty well, and I might easily be turned out of my farm as a kulak. But what do you need to join for? Don't you see the yoke? In the collective farm they'll tie your head down so that you'll never see the sun.' And he quietly began to repeat the lesson he had learnt by heart: that a rising was imminent, that the women would be socialized in the farm. And if his audience proved to be pliable, angrily ready for anything, he cajoled, implored, threatened with reprisals when 'our people' returned from abroad, and at last gained his end: he left assured of one more member for the 'Alliance'.

Everything went well and easily. Yakov Lukich recruited some thirty cossacks, strictly enjoining them not to talk to anyone about their having become members of the 'Alliance', or about their talk with him. But one evening he happened to go along to the kulak 'staff' to complete the enrolment. He and Polovtsiev had an unshakable hope of the dispossessed kulaks and those who had gathered around them, and they had left them till the last, thinking it would be easy enough to enlist their support. But there he had his first setback. Muffling himself in his greatcoat, he went to Borshchev's hut in the early evening. A stove had been lit in the unused best room. He found all the kulak group already gathered. The master of the house, Timofei Borshchev, was on his knees, thrusting some chopped brushwood into the stove. On the benches, and on a heap of pumpkins piled in one corner, which, with their black and orange stripes, looked like Cross of St George ribbons, sat Frol, Lapshinov, Gayev, Nikolai Lushnia, Vasili Atamanchukov and the artilleryman Khoprov. Timofei, Frol's son, was standing with his back to the window. He had returned only that day from the regional town, and was telling of his harsh reception by the Public Prosecutor, who, instead of considering his complaint, had wanted to arrest him and send him back to the District. As Lukich entered Timofei lapsed into silence, but his father said encouragingly:

'He's one of us, Timofei. You needn't be afraid of him.'

Timofei ended his story, and said, his eyes glittering:

'Things are so bad that if there was any organization to join I'd get on my horse and begin to let the Communists' blood flow.'

'These are hard times, hard times,' Yakov Lukich assented. 'But if that was all we'd still have to thank God ...'

'But is there any worse to come?' Frol grumbled. 'They haven't touched you, you're comfortable enough; but they're already eating my bread. You and I lived almost the same under the Tsar, but now you're all blown up, while they've taken my last pair of felt boots from me.'

'I wasn't thinking of that. I'm afraid of something else happening.'

'What else can happen?'

'War, perhaps.'

'God grant it! Smile on it, St George the victorious! This very moment if you like! As it is said in the writings of the apostle ...'

'We'd go out with staves, as the Vioshenska men did in 1919.'

'I'd disembowel them alive ...'

Atamanchukov, who had been wounded in the throat during the civil war, and whose voice in consequence was inarticulate and thin, like the sound of a shepherd's pipe, remarked:

'The people are become very devils. They'd bite with their teeth.'

Yakov Lukich cautiously hinted that there appeared to be unrest in the neighbouring districts, that in some places the people were already teaching the Communists sense in the cossack fashion, as in the old days the unwanted atamans who had associated with the Muscovites were taught – and they were taught simply enough, by the people thrusting their heads into sacks and throwing them into the water. He spoke quietly, measuredly, weighing each word. He mentioned in passing that there was unrest everywhere in the North Caucasus area, that in the districts of the lower Don the women had been socialized, that the Communists were the first to sleep openly with other men's wives, and that an invasion was expected by the spring. He had been told so by an officer acquaintance, a regimental comrade who had passed through Gremyachy the previous week. Only one thing did Yakov Lukich conceal: that this officer was still hidden in his hut.

Nikita Khoprov, who had not spoken before, asked him:

'Yakov Lukich, tell us this: supposing we do rise and kill off our own Communists, what then? We can deal with the militia, but what if troops are sent out from the railway? Who is going to lead us against them? We haven't got any officers, we're ignorant folk, we know our road by the stars. But soldiers don't move at random in war-time, they look up their roads and maps, and plans are drawn up by the staff. We'll have plenty of hands, but no head.'

'There'll be a head, too,' Yakov Lukich fierily assured him. 'The officers will turn up. They're better trained than the Red commanders. They passed into the command out of the old Junkers' corps, and they learned the noble sciences. And what commanders have the Reds got? Take our Makar Nagulnov. He can cut off a head, but is he any good at leading a regiment? Not on your life. Is he any good at reading maps?'

'But where will the officers turn up from?'

'Women will give birth to them!' Yakov Lukich grew annoyed. 'Why, Nikita, you've fastened on me like a burr on a sheeps fleece. "Where from?" and "where from?" How do I know where they'll come from?'

'They'll come from abroad; of course they'll come.' Frol plucked up hope, and, foretasting the revolt and the bloody sweetness of revenge, he satisfiedly dilated his one sound nostril, and noisily inhaled the smoke-laden air.

Khoprov rose, pushed away a pumpkin with his foot, and smoothing his broad, ginger whiskers, said impressively :

'That's as may be ... But the cossacks have grown educated now. They were punished unmercifully for the last rising. They won't revolt. The Kuban won't support it ...'

Yakov Lukich laughed into his grizzled whiskers, and declared:

'They'll rise like one man! And all the Kuban will be set ablaze. And in a fight, one moment you're underneath with your shoulder-blades pressed to the ground, and the next you're lying on top of the enemy, crushing him down.'

'No, brothers; say what you like, I don't agree to that.' Khoprov spoke, turning cold with his access of resolution. 'I'm not going to rise against the government myself, and I'm not advising others to. And it's no use your urging the people on to such games, Yakov Lukich. The officer who spent the night with you was a stranger, and not to be trusted. He stirs up the muddy water and then clears off. But we've got to drink it again. In the last war they drove us on against the Soviet government, they sewed epaulettes on to the cossacks' shoulder-straps, and turned them into half-baked officers. But they themselves kept in the rear, in the staffs, giving themselves over to playing about with spindle-shanked young ladies. You remember who paid for the general sins, when it came to a settlement? In Novorossiisk the Reds cut off the Kalmiks' heads on the quays, but meantime the officers and the other gentry were already on the steamers sailing to warm, foreign countries. All the Don army was herded in Novorossiisk like a flock of sheep, but the generals? Ah! And yes, there's one point I wanted to ask you about. The "excellency" who spent the night with you – isn't he still hiding with you? More than once I've noticed you carrying a bucket of water into the chaff-shed. "What is Lukich carrying water in there for?"

I thought. "What the devil can drink it in there?" And then as I listened I heard a horse whinnying.' With inward satisfaction Khoprov noticed that Ostrovnov's face was turning the colour of his grizzled whiskers. There was a general feeling of embarrassment and anxiety in the room. A furious joy swelled Khoprov's breast; as he spoke he heard his voice as though it were someone else speaking.

'I haven't got any officer staying with me,' Lukich said thickly. 'And it was my mare that whinnied, and I've never carried any water into the chaff-shed, only swills sometimes. We've got a hog in there.'

'I know the voice of your little mare, you can't take me in like that. But what does it matter to me? Only I'm not taking any part in your game.' Khoprov put on his fur cap, and, looking around him, made towards the door. Lapshinov barred his way. The old man's grey beard was shaking, and he stood in a queer, crouching position, stretching out his arms, as he asked:

'Going to inform on us, Judas? Sold yourself, have you? But supposing someone tells them you were in a punitive detachment with the Kalmiks . . .'

'Don't you mumble, old man!' Khoprov said in a cold fury, raising his cast-iron fist to the level of Lapshinov's beard. 'I'll start by informing against myself; I'll say "I was in a punitive band. I was an ensign, judge me". But,' he said the word with a drawl, 'you look out for yourselves, too! And you, you old hound! And you . . .' Khoprov panted, and the breath wheezed hoarsely from his chest like the air from a smithy's bellows. 'You've sucked the blood out of me! Now I'll have my own back on you for once!'

He struck Lapshinov in the face with a short-arm jab, and went out, slamming the door, without a glance at the old man crumpled on the floor by the doorpost. Timofei Borshchev brought an empty bucket, and Lapshinov knelt down with his head hanging over it. The dark blood poured out of his nostrils as though from an open vein. In the disconcerted silence only Lapshinov sobbing and grinding his teeth, and the drip, drip of the blood falling from his beard against the side of the pail, were to be heard.

'Now we are done for, and no mistake!' Gayev, the kulak

with the large family, remarked. Nikolai Lushnia immediately jumped to his feet, and, without a word of farewell, not even stopping to put on his fur cap, he rushed out of the hut. Atamanchukov strode more sedately after him, saying in his thin, hoarse voice as he went :

'We must break up, or we'll be caught here.'

Yakov Lukich sat on for several minutes without speaking. He felt as though his heart had swollen and risen into his throat. He found it difficult to breathe. The blood beat violently in his head, and a cold sweat stood out on his brow. He rose to his feet only when many had already left, and, passing squeamishly around Lapshinov hung over the pail, quietly said to Timofei :

'Come along with me.'

Timofei silently put on his jacket and cap. They went out. In the village the last lights were being extinguished.

'Where are we going?' Timofei asked.

'To my hut.'

'What for?'

'You'll see. Let's step it out.'

Yakov Lukich deliberately took the way past the village Soviet. It was in darkness, and the windows yawned blackly. They went on into Yakov's yard. Close to the porch he halted, and touched the sleeve of Timofei's jacket.

'Wait here a bit,' he said. 'Then I'll call you.'

'All right.'

Yakov knocked, and his daughter-in-law drew the bolt back from its socket.

'Is that you, father?' she asked.

'Yes.' He shut the door fast behind him and, not going into the kitchen, knocked at the door of Polovtsiev's room. A hoarse bass voice asked :

'Who's there?'

'It's me, Alexander Anisimovich. May I come in?'

'Yes, come in.'

Polovtsiev was sitting writing at the table opposite the window, which was curtained with a black shawl. He covered the writing with his large, veiny hand, and turned his head.

'Well, what's the matter?' he asked. 'How are things going?'

'Bad! Something's happened . . .'

What? Out with it quickly!' Polovtsiev jumped to his feet, thrust the written sheet of paper into his pocket, hurriedly buttoned up the collar of his tunic, and, his face flooding with blood and turning livid, he tensely bent forward, like a great rapacious beast ready to spring.

Yakov Lukich confusedly told him what had occurred at Borshchev's. Polovtsiev listened without uttering a word. His little blue eyes stared fixedly at Lukich from their deep sockets. Clenching and unclenching his fists, he slowly straightened up, and at the end writhed his shaven lips terribly and strode towards Lukich.

'You scoundrel! You grey-headed monster, do you want to destroy me, damn you? Do you want to ruin the cause? You've already half-ruined it with you idiotic imprudence. What did I order you? What did I order you?' he repeated, emphasizing every word. 'You should have tested them all out one by one to see beforehand what they thought. But you go at it like a bull down a bank!' His stifled, gurgling, deep-toned whisper made Lukich turn pale, and still further increased his terror and dismay. 'What are we to do now? Has he informed them yet, this Khoprov? Yes? Or no? Oh, speak up, you Gremyachy blockhead! He hasn't? Where did he go? Did you follow him?'

'No . . . Alexander Anisimovich, your Excellency, we're done for now!' Yakov clutched his head. A little tear tickled his brown cheek and ran over his grey whiskers. But Polovtsiev only ground his teeth.

'You woman! We must do something. We must act, and not . . . Is your son at home?'

'I don't know . . . I brought someone along with me.'

'Who?'

'Frol's son.'

'Aha! Why did you bring him?'

Their eyes met, and they understood each other without need for words. Yakov Lukich was the first to turn away his eyes, and, at Polovtsiev's question, 'Can the lad be trusted?' he only silently nodded his head. Polovtsiev furiously snatched his sheepskin jacket from the nail, pulled his freshly-cleaned pistol out from under the pillow, and spun the barrel round. The nickel of bullet-heads glittered in the openings of the chambers.

As he buttoned up his jacket Polovtsiev sharply ordered, as though on a battle-field:

'Get your axe. Take us by the very shortest way. How many minutes will it take?'

'It's not far off, some eight huts along.'

'Has he got a family?'

'Only a wife.'

'Are the neighbouring huts close to his?'

'There's a threshing floor on one side, and a garden on the other.'

'And the village Soviet?'

'It's a long way off...'

'Come on!'

While Lukich went to the wood-shed to fetch his axe, Polovtsiev squeezed Timofei's elbow with his left hand, and quietly said:

'Do what I tell you implicitly! When we get there, you, my lad, alter your voice and say you're the watchman from the village Soviet, and that you've got a document for him. We must get him to open the door himself.'

'You look out, comrade ... I don't know what to call you ... This Khoprov's as strong as a bullock. If you aren't careful he can make the blood flow with his bare fist so that ...' Timofei began to say disconnectedly.

'Hold your tongue!' Polovtsiev interrupted him, and stretched out his hand to Lukich. 'Give it here! Lead on!'

He thrust the ash handle of the axe, warm and wet from Yakov's hand, through his trouser belt under his sheepskin, and turned up his collar.

They went along the by-lane in silence. Compared with Polovtsiev's great, well-built figure Timofei looked a stripling. As he walked along beside the uncertainly striding officer, he importunately stared into his face. But the darkness and the raised collar prevented his getting a good view.

They crawled through a wattle fence into a threshing floor.

'Keep in one another's tracks, so that we leave only one footprint,' Polovtsiev ordered in a whisper.

Like a trail of wolves, step after step, they went across the virgin snow. By the wicket gate leading to Khoprov's yard Lukich pressed his hand against his left side, and whispered miserably:

'Oh, my God!'

Polovtsiev pointed to the door.

'Knock!' Timofei not so much heard as guessed the order by the movement of Polovtsiev's lips. He quietly rattled the latch, and immediately heard the fingers of the stranger in the white fur cap at his side furiously groping and tearing at the fastenings of his sheepskin. Timofei knocked again. Yakov Lukich stared, terror-stricken, at a small dog which crawled from under a plough standing in the open yard. But frozen with the cold, the puppy quietly yelped, began to whimper, then went off towards the reed-thatched cellar.

Khoprov returned home burdened with irresolution, but somewhat tranquillized as the result of his walk. His wife got his supper ready for him. He ate without appetite, and sadly remarked:

'I could eat a salted water-melon this minute, Maria.'

'Got a headache through drinking?' she smiled.

'No; I haven't had a drink all day. Tomorrow, I'm going to tell the government I was in a punitive detachment. I can't stand this any longer.'

'That's a fine idea! What are you all sort of dreamy about today? I don't understand.'

Nikita smiled, tugged at his broad ginger whiskers, and said in a serious tone as he was lying down to sleep:

'You'd better get some dry toast ready for me or bake some fresh victuals. I'm going to do time.'

And then, ignoring his wife's expostulations, he lay with open eyes, thinking: 'I'll tell about myself and about Ostrovnov. Let them sit in prison, too, the devils! But what will they do to me? I don't suppose they'll shoot me. I'll do three years or so, chop down trees in the Urals, and come out clean. And then no one will fling my past up at me. I shan't have to work any more for others because of my sin. I shall tell them straight out how I found myself in Ashtimov's band. I'll tell them: "You see, I was saving myself from the front; who wants to put his head up against a bullet?" Let them judge, it's so long ago that they'll let me off lightly. I'll tell them everything. I didn't shoot anyone myself, that's true, but as for flogging ... Well, I laid the whip on cossack deserters and on some for being bolsheviks. At that time I was darker than night, I didn't know what was what or which way to go.'

He dozed off. He was soon awakened out of his first sleep by a knock. He lay and listened, wondering who had taken it into his head to call at that time of night. The knock was repeated. Groaning with annoyance, he began to get up and was about to light the lamp, but he disturbed his wife, and she whispered:

'Is it for another meeting? Don't light the lamp. No peace day or night ... They've gone stark raving mad, damn them!'

Nikita went barefoot into the porch.

'Who's there?' he asked.

'It's me, daddy Nikita, from the Soviet.'

Nikita felt a feeling of anxiety, a hint of alarm, and he asked:

'Yes, but who is it? What d'you want?'

'It's me, Nikolai Kuzhenkov. I've got a note for you from the chairman; he said you were to go to the Soviet at once.'

'Push it under the door.'

There was a second of silence on the outside of the door. A threatening, inciting glance from beneath the white, lambswool cap, and Timofei, who momentarily had been at a loss, found a way out. 'You've got to sign for it; open the door,' he said.

He heard Khoprov impatiently step back, heard the bare soles of his feet shuffling over the earthen floor of the porch. There was a clatter as the bolt was shot free of its socket. Against the black background, framed in the doorway, Khoprov appeared. At the same moment Polovtsiev put his left foot over the threshold, and, swinging the axe, struck Khoprov with the blunt end just above the bridge of the nose.

Like a bullock stunned by a blow from the poleaxe in the slaughter-house, Nikita crumpled to his knees and gently toppled over on to his back.

'In with you! Bolt the door!' Polovtsiev ordered almost inaudibly. He groped at the handle, and, with the axe still gripped in his hand, threw open the inner door of the porch. From the bed corner came the rustle of sacking, and a woman's anxious voice:

'Have you knocked something over? Who is it, Nikita?'

Polovtsiev dropped the axe, and rushed with outstretched arms towards the bed.

'Oh, good people . . . ! Who's that? Help!'

Timofei painfully stumbled over the doorstep, and ran into the hut. He heard the sound of choking and struggling in the corner. Polovtsiev had fallen on the woman, had smothered her face with a pillow, and was twisting and tying her hands together with a towel. His elbows slipped over the woman's shifting, flabbily soft breasts, beneath him her chest bent springily inward. He felt the warmth of her strong body as she struggled to free herself, her heart beating violently like that of a captured bird. Suddenly and only momentarily a sharp desire flamed up within him, but he snarled, and furiously thrust his hand under the pillow, forcing the woman's mouth open as though she were a horse. Beneath his crooked fingers her torn lip yielded like rubber, then slowly slipped away; his fingers felt the warm blood. But the woman no longer emitted long, muffled screams, for he gathered her skirt into a ball and stuffed it into her mouth as far as her throat.

He left Timofei by the bound woman, and went into the porch, breathing stertorously, like a horse with glanders.

'A match!' he demanded.

Yakov Lukich struck a match. By the feeble light Polovtsiev bent down over Khoprov, who was lying on his back, his legs tucked up awkwardly, his cheek pressed against the earthen floor. He was breathing, and his broad chest rose and fell irregularly. With each breath his ginger whiskers dropped into a pool of crimson. The match went out. Polovtsiev groped to feel the place where the axe had struck Khoprov. The splintered bone grated beneath his fingers. A swelling covered the lid of the left eye.

'Let me go . . . I can't stomach blood,' Yakov Lukich whispered. He was shivering as with ague, his legs were on the point of giving way beneath him. But, without answering his request, Polovtsiev ordered:

'Fetch the axe. It's in there by the bed. And water.'

The water revived Khoprov. Polovtsiev set his knee on the cossack's chest, and demanded in a whistling whisper:

'Have you told, traitor? Speak!' He turned to Yakov. 'Hey, you, a match!'

The match again lit up Khoprov's face and his half-open eyes for a couple of seconds. Yakov's hands trembled, and the tiny flame trembled also. Yellow points of light danced on the wisps of reeds hanging down from the roof of the porch. The match burnt to its end and scorched Yakov's fingernail; but he felt no pain. Twice Polovtsiev repeated his question, then he began to bend Khoprov's fingers back. The injured man groaned and suddenly turned over on to his belly, then, slowly and painfully, he struggled on to his hands and knees. Grunting with the strain, Polovtsiev endeavoured to throw him on to his back again, but the artilleryman's bear-like strength helped him to his feet. With his left hand he seized Lukich by the belt, with his right he clutched Polovtsiev around the neck. Polovtsiev jammed his chin down on to his breast to save his throat from Khoprov's cold fingers, and shouted:

'A light! Curse you! A light, I say!' In the darkness he was unable to feel the axe with his hands.

Poking his head through the kitchen door, Timofei said in a loud whisper:

'Hey, you! Under his ribs, under his ribs with the axe, the sharp edge. Then he'll speak.'

Polovtsiev now had the axe in his hand; with a tremendous effort he tore himself out of Khoprov's clutch and struck him with the sharp edge: once, twice. The cossack fell, and in falling knocked his head against the porch seat. A pail was sent flying off the seat, the sound of its fall was like a shot. Grating his teeth, Polovtsiev finished off Khoprov as he lay, groping for the man's head with his foot and smashing away with the axe. He heard the blood gurgling and bubbling as though liberated. Then he forcibly thrust Lukich into the hut, closed the door behind himself, and said in an undertone:

'You're a dribbling coward! Hold the woman by her head;

we've got to find out whether he had time to inform or not. And you hold her legs down, my lad.'

Polovtsiev threw himself chest downwards on the bound woman. The acrid, musky smell of sweat came from him. Carefully enunciating every word, he demanded:

'After your husband came home this evening, did he go to the Soviet or anywhere else?'

In the dusk of the hut he saw eyes crazy with fear, swollen with unwept tears, and a face black with suffocation. He began to feel uncomfortable, wanted to get out into the air. Mastering his anger and revulsion, he pressed his fingers behind her ears. She struggled against the sickening pain, and lost consciousness for a few moments. Then, coming round, she suddenly thrust the spittle-sodden gag out with her tongue. But she did not cry out, only asked in a thin, sobbing whisper:

'Friends, friends! Spare me! I'll tell all!'

She recognized Yakov Lukich, and he had been joint godparent with her; seven years previously she and he had acted as godparents at the christening of her sister's son, and with difficulty, as though she had an impediment in her speech, she moved her hideously lacerated lips:

'Kinsman! My dear! What's this for?'

Aghast, Polovtsiev covered her mouth with his broad palm. In sudden hope of mercy she tried to kiss his palm with her bloody lips. How she wanted to live! She was mortally afraid.

'Did your husband go anywhere or not?' he asked.

She shook her head negatively. Yakov Lukich caught Polovtsiev's arm.

'You ... your ... Alexander Anisimovich!' he stuttered. 'Don't touch her! We'll threaten her, and she won't tell! She'll never tell!'

Polovtsiev pushed him away. For the first time during all these minutes he wiped his face, using the back of his hand, as he thought: 'She'd tell tomorrow! But she's a woman, a cossack woman, and it would be shameful for me, an officer ... Damn her! I'll cover her eyes so that she doesn't see the end ...'

As he wrapped her sack-cloth shirt around her head, his glance momentarily rested on the well-proportioned body of this thirty-year-old woman who had never borne a child. Like a great white, shot bird she lay on her side, one leg drawn up. In the dusk Polovtsiev suddenly noticed that the hollow between her breasts and her swarthy belly was beginning to shine, and as he looked it was swiftly covered with sweat. 'She's guessed why I've wrapped up her head. Damn her!' With a snort Polovtsiev brought the axe-blade down on the shirt enveloping her face.

Yakov Lukich suddenly felt a protracted shudder rack her body. The nauseating scent of fresh blood filled his nostrils. He stumbled across to the stove, and, shaken by a terrible attack of vomiting, painfully brought up his inside.

Out in the porch Polovtsiev swayed as though drunk; he pressed his lips against and licked up the fresh, feathery snow lying on the balustrade. They went to the wicket gate. Timofei fell behind, and, passing round the hut, made towards the sound of an accordion coming from the direction of the school. A group of villagers was gathered for a sing-song and dance close to the school. Pinching the girls as he went, Timofei made his way into the circle, and asked the accordion player for his instrument.

'Timofei, play us the gipsy chain-dance,' one of the girls requested.

He attempted to take the accordion from its owner's hand, but dropped it. He quietly laughed, again reached out his hand, and again let it drop before he could get the strap over his left shoulder. His fingers would not obey him. He tried to run them over the keys, laughed, and handed back the accordion.

'He's filled himself up somewhere!' one of the girls remarked.

'Look, surely he's not drunk?'

'And he's been sick all over his jacket. A fine sight.'

The girls drew away from him. Dissatisfiedly blowing the snow from the leather folds of the bellows, the owner of the accordion uncertainly began to play the 'gipsy' dance. The tallest of all the girls, Uliana Akhvatina, 'just made for a lifeguard', as they said of her, went into the ring, the low heels of her shoes scrunching and squeaking in the snow, her arms held out sideways and bent like a yoke. 'I must sit until sunrise,' Timofei thought as though of someone else, 'then if there's an investigation nobody will think of me.' He rose, and, now deliberately pretending to be drunk, lurched across to a girl sitting on the school steps, and laid his head on her warm knees.

'Catch my lice, my darling,' he said.

But Yakov Lukich vomited to his heart's content, and then, as green as a cabbage leaf, fell on to the bed as soon as he reached his hut and did not lift his head from the pillow. He heard Polovtsiev wash his hands in a basin, splashing the water and snorting, then go into his own room. It was midnight when the captain came out, awoke the housewife, and asked:

'Have you got any fruit juice? Get me some to drink.'

He drank. (From the pillow Yakov Lukich watched him with one eye.) He picked out a stewed pear, munched it, then went out, smoking a cigarette and stroking his womanishly smooth, fluffy chest. Going to his room, he stretched his bare feet out to the still warm back of the stove. He enjoyed warming his rheumatically aching legs at night. He had got them frozen swimming across the river Boog in the winter of 1916, when serving his Imperial Majesty in faith and truth, and defending the fatherland. Since then captain Polovtsiev had always been attracted to warmth, to the warmth of felt boots...

Chapter 13

A Name of Honour

DURING Davidov's week in Gremyachy many problems had arisen like a wall before him. On returning at night from the village Soviet or the collective farm office, which was housed in Titok's spacious hut, he walked up and down his room smoking for hours, read *Pravda* and *Molot*, then turned again in thought to the people of Gremyachy, to the collective farm, to the events of the past day. Like a hunted wolf, he sought to escape from the circle of thought connected with the collective farm, recalling his shop at the Putilov works, his friends, his work. He felt the least tinge of sadness as he thought that many changes must have been made there, and all in his absence, that he could no longer sit all night over the plans for a caterpillar tractor, trying to find a new method of reconstructing a gear-box, that another, probably the self-confident Goldschmidt, was standing at his capricious and exacting bench, that evidently they had already forgotten him, despite the fervent speeches they had made when seeing off the twenty-five thousand mobilized workers. And abruptly his thoughts turned once more to Gremyachy, as though someone had boldly pushed over a switch in his brain, and redirected the current of his meditations. He had been by no means a naive town dweller before he went to work in the country, but he had not realized all the complexities of the class struggle, its tangled knots and frequently secret courses, until he arrived in Gremyachy. He could not understand the stubborn reluctance of the majority of the middling peasants to join the collective farm despite the tremendous advantages of collective agriculture. He could not find the right key to an understanding of many of the people and their inter-relationships. There was Titok, formerly a Partisan and now a kulak and enemy. There was Timofei Borshchev, a poor cossack, who had openly defended the kulaks. A highly intelligent farmer like Ostrovnov had deliberately joined the collective farm, yet Nagulnov adopted a cautiously antagonistic attitude towards him. All the inhabitants of Gremyachy passed before Davidov's mental vision. And there was much in them that was incomprehensible to him, that was hidden behind a kind of impalpable curtain. The village was like a new type of complicated motor, and Davidov studied it intently and tensely, trying to understand its mechanism, to see clearly every detail, to note every interruption in the daily, incessant throbbing of this involved machine.

The mysterious murder of the poor cossack Khoprov and his wife prompted him to deduce that some secret mechanism was at work within the machine. Sadly he realized that Khoprov's death was causally connected with collectivization, with this new element which had smashed through the crumbling walls of small individual farming. The morning the two bodies were discovered he had a long talk with Razmiotnov and Nagulnov, but they were just as much at the mercy of guesses and surmises as himself. Khoprov was a poor peasant, formerly a White, who had played no active part in the life of the village community, but in some queer fashion was a hanger-on of the kulak Lapshinov. The suggestion that robbery was the motive for the murder was absurd on the face of it, for none of his goods had been touched, nor indeed was there anything to take. Razmiotnov dismissed the problem with :

'He must have got across somebody over a woman. He must have had someone else's wife in his arms, and they've had his life for it.'

Nagulnov was silent; he was not fond of saying the first thing that came into his head. But when Davidov surmised that some of the kulaks had had a hand in it, and proposed that they all be immediately expelled from the village, Nagulnov resolutely supported him.

'It was one of their brood that killed off Khoprov, no doubt of that,' he declared. 'Send the reptiles to the Arctic regions !'

Razmiotnov laughed and shrugged his shoulders.

'Of course they must be sent out of the village,' he replied. 'They're stopping the people from joining the collective farm. But Khoprov didn't suffer through them. He wasn't mixed up with them. It's true he hung on to Lapshinov, and worked for him regularly, but wasn't that so that he could get his belly full? He was forced by his need, and that's why he went to Lapshinov. We can't lay everything to the door of the kulaks; don't try to be original, brothers ! No, a woman was mixed up in it, whatever you care to say.'

An investigating officer and a doctor arrived from the district town. A post-mortem was held on the two bodies, and Khoprov's and Lapshinov's neighbours were examined. But the investigating official was unable to get hold of a single thread that might have led to the discovery of the murderers and their motives. The next day, 4 February, a general meeting of the collective farm members unanimously passed a resolution to expel all the kulak families from the territory of the Northern Caucasus. The same meeting confirmed the collective farm management committee elected by the temporary delegates. Yakov Lukich was also elected on to the committee, his candidature being vigorously supported by Davidov and Razmiotnov, despite Nagulnov's objections. The other members were Pavel Liubishkin, Diemka Ushakov, and Arkady, who just scraped through, while Davidov made the fifth, being elected by a unanimous and undiscussed vote. His election was greatly facilitated by a letter received from the district office of the agricultural co-operative, which stated that the District Party Committee, in agreement with the District Co-operative, proposed the committee's representative, comrade Davidov, as chairman of the collective farm management committee.

The meeting spent some time discussing a name for the farm. Razmiotnov was the last to speak.

'I object to the name "Red Cossack",' he declared, 'because it is a dead and defiled name. In the old days the workers used to frighten their children with the word "cossack". I propose, comrades and fellow collective farmers, to give our road to socialism, our collective farm, the name of comrade Stalin. We all know about him, we know that from the very beginning he has taken a straight road, turning aside neither to the right nor the left. And we shall follow him in a broad stream towards that same dear socialism for which we fought and left our wives and children, careless of our young lives, and mercilessly wetting our hands in our own blood and others'.'

Andrei was visibly agitated, the scar on his forehead was livid. For a brief moment his ill-natured eyes were misted with tears, but he recovered his control and firmly declared:

'Brothers, long live our comrade Yusef Vissarionovich Stalin to lead us! I propose we rise and take off our caps in his honour.'

The meeting stood up; bared bald heads gleamed, matted heads of hair in all hues were revealed. Razmiotnov went on:

'And let us agree to call ourselves by his name. And besides, comrades, I can report on facts. When we were defending Tsaritsin, I personally saw and heard comrade Stalin in the front line of fire. At that time he was the Revolutionary Military Council with Voroshilov; he wore civilian clothes, but I must say he was an expert! Both at reviews and in the firing line he would talk to us fighters about standing firm . . .'

'You're not sticking to the point, Razmiotnov,' Davidov interrupted him.

'Not to the point? Then I'm sorry, of course. But I am firmly in favour of our taking his name.'

'We all know that, and I'm in favour of calling the collective farm after Stalin also,' Davidov said. 'But it's a responsible name to take. There must be no bringing shame on it. If we do take it we shall have to work so as to do better than any other farm in the district.'

'We're quite agreed on that,' old Shchukar declared.

'Of course!' Razmiotnov smiled. 'Comrades, I declare authoritatively, as chairman of the Soviet, that there could be no better name than that of comrade Stalin. I'd call all the collective farms after him. Our Communist Party stands so closely and so firmly solid around comrade Stalin, and is so proud of him, that it would be impossible to find a better name. For instance, in 1919 I happened to see our Red infantry capture the dam across the river Tsulin by the village of Topolka, close to a water mill ...'

'There you go again with your memories,' Davidov said in a vexed tone.

'I'm sorry. We'll take the vote, citizens. But when you recall those days of war your heart begins to itch and you long to talk about them,' Razmiotnov smiled guiltily and sat down.

The meeting unanimously adopted the name of 'Stalin' for the collective farm.

Davidov was still living with the Nagulnovs. He slept on a chest, which was screened from the married couple's bed by a low cotton curtain. The front room was occupied by the owner of the hut, a childless widow. Davidov realized that he was inconveniencing Makar, but the bustle and anxieties of his first few days in Gremyachy left him no time to look for other quarters. Nagulnov's wife Lukeria was invariably friendly to Davidov, but after the talk with Makar in which he had learnt that she associated with Timofei he could hardly conceal his hostility, and found his temporary stay with them irksome. Although he would not enter into conversation with her, he would often take a sidelong glance at Lukeria of a morning. She appeared to be no more than twenty-five years old. Her rather long cheeks were thickly spotted with fine freckles, and her speckled face reminded him of a magpie's egg. But there was an alluring and unclean beauty in her coal-black eyes, in her somewhat lank but shapely figure. Her arched, delicate brows were always the very least bit raised; she seemed always to be awaiting some joyous event; her bright lips held a smile ready in their corners, and did not completely hide the firm horseshoes of her prominent teeth. And she walked, swinging her sloping shoulders, just as though every moment she was expecting someone to squeeze her from behind, to embrace her girlishly slender back. She dressed like all the other cossack women of the village, though she may have been a little neater and cleaner.

Early one morning Davidov heard Makar's voice behind the curtain. 'I've got something in my jacket pocket for you,' he said. 'You must have given Siemion an order for it. When he came back from the town yesterday he asked me to hand it to you.'

'Makar dear, are you telling the truth?' Lukeria's warmly drowsy voice quivered with joy. Wearing only her shirt, she jumped out of the bed, and reached for her husband's fur jacket hanging on the nail. Out of the pocket she drew, not the elastic garters which constrict the legs, but proper suspenders such as city women wear, with a belt hemmed in blue. Davidov saw her reflection in a mirror. Craning her boyishly lean neck, she stood measuring the suspenders against her slender leg. In the mirror he noticed the line of a smile above her shining eyes, a faint flush on her freckled cheeks. As she was admiring the black stocking drawn tightly up over her leg she turned towards Davidov, and he saw her firm, swarthy breasts, protruding downward and away like a goat's udders, trembling in the opening of her shirt. At the same moment she noticed Davidov across the curtain; she drew the points of her shirt collar together with her left hand, and, without turning away, screwed up her eyes and smiled a long, slow smile. 'See how beautiful I am !' her unembarrassed eyes invited.

Blushing vividly, Davidov fell back on to the creaking chest. He threw the glossy black hair back from his forehead with his

116

fingers, and thought: 'Damn it! Now she'll think I was spying on her. She'll get it into her head that I'm interested in her!'

'You needn't run about in your skin in front of a stranger,' Makar discontentedly muttered, as he heard Davidov give a disconcerted cough.

'He can't see,' she replied.

'Yes, I can.' Davidov again coughed behind the curtain.

'If you can, then look and do your eyes good,' she said unconcernedly, as she drew her skirt on over her head. 'There aren't any strangers now, Makar. He's a stranger today, but if I feel like it he'll be mine tomorrow.' She laughed, and ran and flung herself on to the bed. 'You're my quiet little one, Makar!' she added. 'My little calf, my dear, sweet little calf!'

Hardly had the two men left the yard after breakfast when Davidov hit out hard.

'Your woman's a good-for-nothing hussy,' he declared.

'That's nothing to do with you,' Nagulnov quietly answered, not looking at Davidov.

'But it is something to do with you! I'm shifting my quarters this very day. It makes me feel sick to see it. A fine chap like you, and you're letting her make a fool of you! You told me yourself that she plays about with Timofei.'

'Am I to beat her, then?'

'No, but you can influence her! I tell you straight, I'm a Communist, I know, but I easily get worked up. And I'd beat her and send her to the devil! She's discrediting you in the eyes of the masses; and you say nothing. Where does she get to all night? She's still out when we come back from a meeting. I'm not going to interfere in your private affairs ...'

'Are you married?'

'No. And after seeing your family life I never shall be married to my dying day!'

'You regard a woman as your own property ...'

'Oh, damn you! You lopsided anarchist! Property, property! It still exists, doesn't it? And how are you going to abolish it? The family still exists, doesn't it? But you ... they crawl after your woman ... You're spreading immorality in the name of toleration. I'll raise the matter at the nucleus meeting. An example to the peasants like you ought to be put an end to. You'd make a fine example!'

'Well, then, I'll kill her!'

'Congratulations!'

'Well, you listen ... Don't interfere for the present,' Makar pleaded, halting in the middle of the street. 'I'll tackle the matter myself, but now's not the time. If it had only started yesterday it would be different, but I've got used to it now ... Wait a little, and then we'll see. I've got very fond of her, or I'd have stopped it long ago. Where are you going, to the Soviet?' he changed the subject.

'No. I want to go and see Ostrovnov. I'd like to have a talk with him in his own home. He's an intelligent peasant. I want to make him the farm manager. What do you think about it? We need a manager who can make our collective farm kopek ring like a rouble. Ostrovnov's clearly that sort.'

Nagulnov waved his hand and angrily replied:

'Again throwing good money after bad! You and Andrei are completely taken in by Ostrovnov. The collective farm needs him about as much as a bishop needs his ... I'm against the proposal. I'll get him expelled from the collective farm! For two years he's paid the agricultural tax with the extra percentage, the prosperous reptile. He lived like a kulak even before the war, and are we to shove him forward?'

'He's a scientific farmer. D'you think I want to defend a kulak?'

'If his wings hadn't been clipped he'd have been a kulak long ago.'

They parted without reaching agreement, profoundly dissatisfied with each other.

Chapter 14

Appointing the Manager

THE earth was crushed, contracted with the cold. The sun rose each morning in a white, frosty incandescence. Where the wind had swept the snow away, the bare earth cracked hollowly at night. Like over-ripe water-melons the mounds in the steppe were scarred with serpentine cracks. Beyond the village, along the frozen furrows the snowdrifts dazzled blindingly, unbearably. The poplars by the banks of the stream were chased with silver. Of a morning the straight, orange columns of smoke arose like timber from the chimneys. But because of the frost the wheat straw in the threshing floors was even more scented with azure August, with the burning breath of the midsummer wind and the summer sky.

The bullocks and cows roved around the cold yards all the night. By sunrise not a single stalk of scrub was left in the mangers. The lambs and kids of the winter litters were no longer left out in the yards. At night the sleepy women would carry them out to their mothers, then carry them back in their aprons into the steaming warmth of the huts, and the kids' shaggy fur would smell tenderly, primitively of the frosty air, the mingled hay grasses, and sweet goats' milk. Under its crust the snow was a granular, sparkling, brittle salt. Midnight was so still, so empty was the frigid sky with its fine sprinkling of innumerable stars, that it seemed as though life were abandoning the world. A wolf roamed over the snowy virginity of the azure steppe. No imprint of its cushioned paws was made on the snow, but where its claws had torn away an icy piece of the crust a sparkling scar, a pearly trace was left.

Let a mare in foal neigh as she felt the milk flowing into her satiny black udder, and if the night were still her neigh could be heard for many miles around.

February...

The azure stillness before the dawn.

The wilderness of the Milky Way was fading.

The flickering crimson glow of fires, the reflection of lighted stoves, began to appear in the dark windows of the huts.

The ice of the stream rang hollowly under the blows of a pick-axe.

February . . .

Dawn had not yet come when Yakov Lukich aroused his son and the women. They lit the stove. Yakov's son Siemion sharpened knives on the whetstone. Captain Polovtsiev carefully wrapped strips of rag around the woollen stockings on his legs, and drew on his felt boots. Then he went with Siemion to the sheep-yard. Yakov Lukich possessed seventeen sheep and two goats. Siemion knew which of the sheep were in lamb, and which had already borne. He caught and by the feel sorted out the rams, sheep and lambs, pushing them one by one into the warm shed. Drawing his white fur cap down over his eyes, Polovtsiev caught a gelded ram by its cold twisted horn, and threw it to the ground. Then, lying with his breast against the outstretched animal, he pulled back its head and cut its throat with a knife, setting free the dark, streaming blood.

Yakov Lukich had a good eye to business. He did not want the meat from his sheep to feed Red Army soldiers, or workers in some factory dining-room. They were Soviet, and for the past ten years the Soviet government had burdened him with taxes and exactions, and had not allowed him to develop his farming on a large scale, to grow rich and fatter than the fat. The Soviet government and Yakov Lukich were mutual enemies, at daggers drawn. All his life Yakov Lukich had been attracted to riches like a child to fire. Before the revolution came he had begun to build up his position. He had thought of having his son educated in the Novocherkass Junkers' school, he had dreamt of buying an oilseed mill and had already begun to save his money for that purpose, he had dreamt of having three workers to feed on his farm, and in those days his heart had sometimes stopped beating out of joy at the fabulous things life had in store for him. He had planned to open a little shop, and then to buy a half-derelict mill from an unsuccessful local cossack landowner. In his thoughts

Yakov Lukich used to picture himself attired not in the cossack trousers of cheap leather, but in a pair made of silk, with a gold chain across his belly, and not with calloused, but with soft white hands from which the dirty black nails would be shed like a sloughed reptile skin. His son would become a colonel and wed an educated young lady, and Yakov Lukich would go to fetch them from the station not in a britzka, but in his own motor-car, like the one the landowner Novopavlov had ... Not few were the daydreams Yakov had indulged in during those unforgettable years when life had sparkled and crackled in his hands like a rainbow-hued rouble-note. The revolution had breathed the chill breath of unseen shocks upon him, the ground had rocked beneath his feet, but he had never been at a loss. With all his characteristic sobriety and cunning he had succeeded in discerning the approaching anarchy from afar, and, unnoticed by his neighbours and fellow-villagers, had swiftly disposed of his accumulated property. He had sold the steam engine bought in 1916, had buried thirty gold ten-rouble pieces and a leather bag of silver in a jug, had sold his surplus livestock, had reduced the area of his sowings. He had made his preparations. And the revolution, the war and the fronts passed over him like a black steppe whirlwind over the grass; if they could bend him he bent, but they could not break or cripple him. In a storm only poplars or oaks are broken and torn up by the roots, but the iron bush only bows to the ground, and afterwards stands upright again. But it so happened that Yakov Lukich was given no chance of standing upright again! And that was why he was against the Soviet government: because his life was as dreary as a castrated bull's. No building up for him, nor the drunken joy of such building. And so at the moment Polovtsiev was closer to him than was his own wife, closer than his own son. He must either take sides with Polovtsiev, in order to bring back the life which formerly had glittered and crackled like a hundred-rouble note, or he must throw up his present life!

And that was why Yakov Lukich, a member of the management committee of the Gremyachy Collective Farm 'Stalin', was slaughtering fourteen of his sheep. 'Better to throw the carcasses to that black hound which is greedily licking the steaming sheep's blood at Polovtsiev's feet, than allow a single sheep to pass into the collective farm pen, for it to grow fat and multiply to feed the enemy government,' thought Lukich. And the educated captain Polovtsiev was right when he said: 'You must slaughter your cattle! The ground must be cut from under the Bolsheviks' feet. Let the oxen die from lack of attention, we'll get more oxen when we seize the power! They'll send us oxen from America and Sweden. We'll strangle the Communists with famine, ruin, insurrection! And don't be sorry about your mare, Yakov Lukich! It's a good thing that the horses have been socialized. It's convenient and advantageous to us. When we rise and capture the village it will be easier to lead the horses out of the communal stables and saddle them, than to have to run from hut to hut in search of them.' Golden words! Captain Polovtsiev's head served him as trustily as his arms!

Yakov Lukich stood by the shed and watched Polovtsiev and Siemion getting on with the job, flaying a carcass hung to the crossbeam. The lantern clearly lit up the white sheepskin. The carcasses were easily flayed. Yakov Lukich looked at one carcass hanging neck downward, with the sheepskin turned back and freed down to the blue belly; then he glanced at the black head rolling close to the trough, and turned pale, tottering as though struck behind the knees. The sheep's yellow eye with its enormous, still unglazed pupil was frozen into a mortal terror. Lukich suddenly remembered Khoprov's wife, her stuttering, terrible whisper: 'Kinsman! Old friend! What's this for?' With loathing he looked at the violet and rose-hued carcass, at its lower tendons and bunches of muscles. The acrid stench of blood evoked an attack of vomiting, just as it had on that previous occasion, and he began to heave. He turned to hurry out of the shed.

'I can't stand dead meat ... Lord! I can't even bear the smell,' he muttered.

'What the devil did you come and look for? We can manage without you, thin-skin!' Polovtsiev smiled, and began to roll a cigarette in his blood-stained, smelly hands.

By dint of hard work they finished the slaughtering by breakfast time. The flayed carcasses were hung in the granary. The women put the fat sheeps' tails on to boil. Polovtsiev locked himself into his room, from which in the daytime he never emerged. They took him some fresh cabbage soup made with broth from the boiled sheeps' tails. Yakov's daughter-in-law had hardly removed his empty plate when the wicket gate creaked.

'Father! It's Davidov coming in!' shouted Siemion, who was the first to see who was coming into the yard. Yakov Lukich went whiter than the finest of white flour. Davidov was already wiping the snow off his boots with the besom in the porch. He gave a hollow cough, and entered with a confident stride.

'I'm done for!' thought Yakov Lukich. 'The way he walks in, the son of a bitch! Just as though he owned the whole world! As though he was in his own hut! Oh, I'm done for! I expect he's come to arrest me for the murder of Nikita Khoprov. He's found out, the swine!'

There was a knock on the door, and a hoarse tenor voice asked:

'May I come in?'

'Come in!' Yakov Lukich meant to call out, but his voice trailed off into a whisper.

Davidov waited a moment, then opened the door. Lukich did not rise from the table, for he could not. And he even had to lift his trembling, helpless legs from the floor so that the heels of his boots should not be heard knocking on the boards.

'Your health, master!' Davidov spoke first.

'Your health, comrade!' Lukich and his wife replied in one voice.

'There's a heavy frost today . . .'

'Yes, it's a heavy frost.'

'The rye won't be killed by the frost, will it? What do you think?' Davidov asked. He slipped his hand into his pocket, and, pulling out a handkerchief as black as soot and burying it in his hand, he blew his nose.

'Come right in, comrade!' Yakov invited him.

'What's he got the wind up about, the dolt?' Davidov wondered, as he noticed Ostrovnov's pale face and quivering lips.

'So what d'you think about the rye?' he asked.

'No, it oughtn't to be . . . it's well covered by the snow. It may get nipped a bit where the wind's blown the snow off . . .'

'He's going to begin with the corn, and then suddenly he'll say: "Well, get ready!" Perhaps someone's informed him about Polovtsiev. There'll be a search!' Yakov Lukich thought. He recovered a little from his fright and the blood abruptly flowed back into his face; the sweat started from the pores of his skin, and rolled down over his forehead on to his grizzled whiskers and his prickly chin.

'You'll have something to eat with us, won't you? Come into the front room,' he invited.

'I want to have a talk with you, Yakov Lukich. You spoke very well and to the point about the collective farm at the meeting. Of course you were right in saying that the farm needs complicated machinery. But you were wrong in regard to the organization of labour. Fact! We're thinking of putting you forward as manager of the farm. I've heard that you're a first-class scientific farmer ...'

'Come in, come right in, comrade! Gasha, get the samovar going. Or would you like to have a drop of cabbage soup? Or some salted water-melon, perhaps? Come in, dear guest. Our leader towards the new life ...' Yakov began to choke with joy; he felt as though a mountain had been removed from his shoulders. 'Yes, I've worked my farm scientifically, you were right there. I wanted to get our ignorant cossacks out of their grandfathers' ways. Look how they plough! They merely rake the earth! I received a letter of praise from the Regional Land Department. Siemion! Bring the letter I framed. No, don't bother, we'll be going into the room ourselves.'

Giving Siemion a hardly perceptible wink, Yakov Lukich led his guest into the best room. His son understood, and went out into the corridor to lock the door of Polovtsiev's room. He glanced inside, and was startled to find the room was empty. He went into the hall. With only his woollen stockings on his feet, Polovtsiev was standing by the door leading to the best room. He beckoned to Siemion to go out, and set his gristly ear, erect like that of a preying animal, against the door. 'Fearless devil!' Siemion thought as he left the hall.

The large, cold hall of Ostrovnov's hut was not used in winter. In one of the corners of the painted floor hempseed was piled up from one year to another. At the side of the door stood a barrel of pickled apples. Polovtsiev sat down on the rim of the barrel. Here he could catch every word of the conversation between Davidov and Lukich. A rosy, dusky light peered through the frosted window-panes. Polovtsiev's legs were frozen, but he sat on without stirring, listening with corrosive hatred to the hoarse tenor voice of the enemy who was separated from him by only a door. 'He's got husky at his meetings, the hound! I'd give him ... If only I could, this minute ...' Polovtsiev pressed his fists, swollen with blood, to his chest, and the nails cut into his palm.

From the other side of the door came:

'This is what I say, my dear collective farm chairman. It's no use our farming in the old ways. Take only the corn! Why is it killed off by the frost, and if we get twenty poods to the hectare we call it a good crop, while many don't even get enough back for seed? But you can never make your way through the corn on my fields. I've known times when I've saddled my mare, and the ears have come above the saddlebow. And you couldn't lay the spikes of the ears on your palm. And it's all because I've kept the snow on my fields, and watered the earth. Another citizen cuts down his sunflowers right to the roots: he's greedy, and argues that it will be good for burning in the stove. The swine hasn't got time in the summer to cut dung from his yard for fuel! He was born lazy, and the habit clings to him. And he doesn't understand that if he cuts off only the flowerheads the stalks will hold the snow on the fields; the wind won't go driving through them and sweep the snow into the hollows. In springtime such earth is better than the finest autumn ploughing left to lie fallow for the winter. And if you don't keep the snow on the fields it runs off to waste, the rich flood water is lost, and neither man nor land gets the benefit of it.'

'That's perfectly true.'

'Our nursing mother, the Soviet government, didn't give me a letter of praise for nothing, comrade Davidov. I know what's what! Some of its agricultural specialists get a little off the mark sometimes, but there's a good deal of truth in their learning. For instance, I subscribed to an agricultural journal, and in it one highly educated man who teaches students wrote that the corn doesn't even die from the frost, but is lost because when the bare earth hasn't got any snow to cover it up it cracks and tears up the roots with it.'

'That's very interesting. I've never heard that!'

'And he wrote the truth. I agree with him. I've even tested the theory out myself. I dug some corn up, and saw that the fine and tiny roots that feed the main root, the ones with which the germinating seed sucks in the black blood and gets its food, were all broken and split. The seed had nothing to feed with, and so it died. Cut a man's veins and he won't go on living, will he? And so it is with the grain.'

'Yes, Yakov Lukich, you're telling me facts. The snow must be kept on the fields. Let me have those agricultural journals of yours to read, will you?'

'They'll be no good to you,' Polovtsiev thought. 'You won't have time to read them. Your days on this earth are numbered.' And he smiled to himself.

'And again, how is the snow to be kept on the fallow during the winter?' Lukich continued. 'You need screens for that. I've already thought of making screens of brushwood. We've got to fight the drifts in the ravines; every year they rob us of more than a thousand hectares.'

'That's all true. Tell me now, what's the best way of keeping the cattle-pens warm? A way that's both cheap and good, you understand?'

'The yards, you mean? We can do that all right! We must put the women on to plastering up the fences with mud, to begin with. Or if not, we must heap up dry dung between two rows of fences.'

'Yes. And what about chemically treating the seed corn?'

Polovtsiev wanted to seat himself more comfortably on the barrel. But the lid slipped from under him and fell with a clatter. He grated his teeth as he heard Davidov ask:

'What's that fallen in there?'

'I expect the cat's knocked something over. We don't use the hall during the winter. And by the way, I'd like to show you my selected hempseed. I had it sent specially. It's in that hall for the winter. Come in and look at it.'

Polovtsiev sprang towards the door leading into the passage, and the well-oiled hinges gave no sound as he opened it, but let him pass out noiselessly.

Davidov left Ostrovnov's hut with a packet of journals under his arm, satisfied with the results of his visit and still more convinced of Ostrovnov's value. 'With a man like that, in a year we could transform the village. A clever peasant, the devil, and well read. And how he knows farming and the land! That's a real qualification! I don't understand why Makar's so suspicious of him. He'll be of great value to the collective farm. Fact!' So Davidov thought as he made his way to the village Soviet.

Chapter 15

Wholesale Slaughter

THROUGH the influence of Yakov Lukich livestock began to be slaughtered every night in Gremyachy. Hardly had darkness fallen when the brief and stifled bleating of a sheep, the mortal scream of a pig or the bellowing of a calf would be heard piercing the silence. Not only those who had joined the collective farm, but individual farmers also slaughtered. They killed oxen, sheep, pigs, even cows; they slaughtered animals kept for breeding. In two nights the horned cattle of Gremyachy were reduced to half their number. The dogs began to drag entrails and guts about the village, the cellars and granaries were filled with meat. In two days the co-operative shop sold some two hundred poods of salt which had been lying in the warehouse for eighteen months. 'Kill, it's not ours now!' 'Kill, they'll take it for the meat collection tax if you don't.' 'Kill, for you won't taste meat in the collective farm.' The insidious rumours crept around. And they killed. They ate until they were unable to move. Everybody, from the youngest to the oldest, suffered with stomach-ache. At dinner-time the tables groaned under the weight of boiled and roasted meat. At dinner-time everybody had a greasy mouth, everybody belched as though they had been at a funeral repast in memory of the dead. And all were owlish with their intoxication of eating.

Old Shchukar was one of the first to slaughter a calf born the previous summer. With his wife's help he tried to hang the carcass from a crossbeam in order to flay it the more easily. They struggled long and vainly, for the fattened calf was heavy; the old woman even sprained her back as she tried to lift the hind-quarters, and for a week afterwards Mamichikha, the old simples woman, kept an iron pot on her back. But old Shchukar himself did the cooking next day, and, whether annoyed because his old wife had hurt herself, or from extreme greediness, he ate so much of the stewed breast that for some days he did not go farther than the yard, did not fasten up his sack-cloth trousers, and suffered for twenty-four hours on end in the terrible cold among the sunflower stalks behind the shed. Everyone who passed by Shchukar's tumbledown hut during those days saw the old man's fur cap sticking up motionless among the sunflower stalks in the garden. Then Shchukar himself would abruptly emerge from the sunflowers, and would crawl painfully towards the hut without giving a glance into the lane, holding up his unfastened trousers with his hands as he walked. Plodding wearily, hardly dragging his feet along, he would get as far as the gate, then suddenly, as though he had remembered something urgent, he would turn and run with little steps back to the sunflowers. Once more the old man's fur cap would stick up immovably and importantly among the sunflower stalks. And how the frost nipped! And the ground wind swept up sharp-pointed drifts all around him.

Towards evening of the second day, as soon as Razmiotnov heard that the slaughter of cattle was occurring on a wholesale scale, he ran to Davidov.

'Not doing anything?' he asked.

'I'm reading.' Davidov turned the page of a small, yellowish book, and smiled meditatively. 'There's a book for you, my boy! It takes your breath away!' He laughed, baring his gap-toothed jaws and throwing out his short, sturdy arms.

'Reading novels! Or some song book! While in the village ...'

'You fool! Fool! Novels! Where's the song book?' Davidov

burst into a roar of laughter, sat Andrei down on a stool opposite him, and thrust the book into his hand. 'That's Andreev's report to the Rostov Party active members. That book's worth a dozen novels, my boy! Fact! I started to read and then forgot my grub. I read on and on. Oh, damn it, I'm fed up. I expect it's all cold now.' His swarthy face was tinged with vexation and annoyance. He rose, thrust his hands into his pockets, gloomily hitched up his short trousers, and went into the kitchen.

'Will you listen to me or won't you?' Razmiotnov demanded, growing indignant.

'Why, of course, of course I will. One minute.'

He brought an earthenware bowl of cold cabbage soup back from the kitchen, and sat down. Fixing his wearily screwed-up grey eyes on Razmiotnov, with one bite he disposed of an enormous hunk of bread, and chewed away, working the muscles above his cheekbones. Gleaming yellow spots of mutton fat floated on top of the cold soup, and a streak of meat showed like a crimson flame.

'Meat in the soup?' Andrei spitefully asked, pointing his tobacco-stained finger at the bowl.

Choking, and smiling with difficulty, Davidov contentedly nodded.

'But where's the meat come from?'

'I don't know, but what does it matter?'

'This, that they've slaughtered half the cattle in the village.'

'Who have?' Davidov screwed up a lump of bread and pushed it away.

'The devils!' The scar on Razmiotnov's forehead went crimson. 'Chairman of the collective farm!' he sneered. 'You'll organize a giant, all right! It's your collective farmers who're doing it, that's who! And individual farmers, too. They've gone crazy, the bloody swines! They've slaughtered everything outright, and I hear they're even killing off the bulls.'

'You've got a bad habit of shouting as if you were at a meeting,' Davidov said with annoyance, betaking himself to his soup. 'Tell me quietly and to the point, who's doing it, and why they're doing it.'

'How do I know why?'

'You always roar and shout. I could shut my eyes and think it was dear old 1917 all over again.'

'You'll be roaring in a minute, I expect!'

Razmiotnov told all he knew concerning the slaughter of the livestock. Towards the end Davidov ate almost without chewing. His facetious mood left him, a radiation of furrows gathered around his eyes, and his face seemed to age.

'Go at once and call a general meeting,' he ordered. 'Get Nagulnov ... but don't bother, I'll go along to him myself.'

'What's the meeting for?'

'What's it for? We'll forbid them to slaughter the stock! We'll turn them out of the collective farm and bring them to trial. This is a terribly serious matter. Fact! It's the kulaks have shoved their spoke into our wheel again. Here, take a cigarette and get on with it! Ah, yes, I've forgotten to sing my own praises!' A happy smile slipped across Davidov's face and warmed his eyes; no matter how much he pursed up his lips he could not conceal his joy.

'I received a parcel from Leningrad today. Yes, a little parcel from the boys ...' Crimson with pleasure, he bent down, dragged a small box out from under his bed, and raised the lid. In the box lay packets of cigarettes, biscuits, books, a carved wooden cigarette case, and other things in packets and bundles heaped in disorderly confusion.

'The comrades remembered me, and look what they've sent ... These are our Leningrad cigarettes, my boy. And they've even sent chocolate, d'you see it? What's the good of it to me? I'll have to give it away to somebody's children ... But that's not the point, it's the fact that they've sent it that's important. Isn't that so? The main thing is that they've remembered me and sent me the box, and a letter with it ...'

Davidov's voice was unusually gentle. Such an embarrassedly happy comrade Davidov Andrei had never seen before. In some strange way his agitation was communicated to Razmiotnov, and in the desire to say something pleasant Andrei barked:

'Well, that's fine! You're a great lad, and that's why they've sent you the box. Look at it, that lot wasn't bought for one rouble.'

'That's not the point. It's like this: I, poor devil, am a kind of orphan, with no wife or anybody. Fact! And then this parcel suddenly arrives! A touching fact! Look how many have signed the letter.' With one hand Davidov held out a box of cigarettes, in the other he held a letter decorated with innumerable signatures. His hands trembled.

Razmiotnov lit the Leningrad cigarette, and asked:

'Well, and how do you like your new quarters? The mistress is all right, isn't she? What have you done about your washing? You could bring it along for mother to do, if you like. Or you could arrange with the woman here. You couldn't cut through that shirt you're wearing with a sword, and it stinks with sweat like a worn-out nag.'

Davidov flushed and burst out with:

'Yes, I must do something about it. It wasn't very easy for me to do anything while I was living with Nagulnov. I did any sewing I needed myself, and I did my own washing, too, somehow. I haven't had a good wash since I arrived, that's a fact. And my sweater, too . ... The village shop hasn't got any soap. I've already asked the woman here to wash for me, and she said: "Give me the soap and I will." I'll write to the boys to send me some household soap. But the quarters aren't bad, there aren't any children. I can read without being disturbed, and altogether ...'

'You bring your washing along to mother, and she'll do it. Don't feel shy about it. Mother's a good sort.'

'Don't worry, I'll manage somehow. Thank you all the same. We must get a bath-house built for the collective farm, that's the idea! We'll do it! Fact! Well, off with you and organize that meeting.'

Razmiotnov finished his cigarette and went out. Davidov aimlessly rearranged the packets in the box, sighed, adjusted the well-stretched collar of his dirty, yellowish-brown sweater, and, smoothing his black, upstanding hair, began to dress to go out.

On the way he called to see Nagulnov, who greeted him with knitted brows and averted eyes.

'They're slaughtering the cattle,' he muttered, after they had exchanged greetings. 'They're sorry about their property. There's such dismay among the petty bourgeoisie that words can't describe it.' He turned sternly to his wife and told her: 'You clear out of here at once, Lukeria. Go and sit with the mistress for a while, I don't feel up to talking with you around.'

Sorrowfully Lukeria went into the kitchen. Ever since the day Timofei had ridden away with the kulak families she had gone about looking sadly crestfallen. Mournful pools of blue lay under her eyes, even her nose had peaked like a corpse's. It was clear that her heart was heavy at the separation from her dear one. The day the kulaks were sent off to the icy Polar region she had openly and unashamedly hung about the Borshchevs' yard from early morning, waiting to see Timofei. And when towards evening the sledges carrying the kulak families and their goods had set out from Gremyachy, she had given an ill-boding, hysterical scream and flung herself down in the snow. Timofei had been about to jump off the sledge and run towards her, but his father had called to him with a threatening shout. Timofei had strode off behind the sledge, biting his lips, white with his burning hatred, and looking back at Gremyachy again and again.

Like the leaves on the poplars Timofei's caressing words murmured repiningly in Lukeria's mind: it was clear she would never hear them again. How could the woman help withering with impotent yearning, how could she avoid feeling crushed? Who would say to her now, gazing lovingly into her eyes: 'That green skirt suits you perfectly, Lukeria! You look finer in it than any officer's wife of the old days'? Or, in the words of the women's song: 'Forgive me and farewell, my beautiful. Thy beauty is unending joy to me.' Only Timofei could stir Lukeria to the depths of her soul with flattery and heart-felt effrontery.

From that day she had been completely alienated from her husband. And calmly and weightily, with unusual eloquence, Makar had said to her:

'Live a few last days with me, live them out! And then gather together your bits and pieces, your garters and pots of pomade, and go where you like. I have suffered much shame through my love for you, but now my patience is broken. You played about with a kulak's son, and I held my tongue. But now that you've wept after him in front of all the class-conscious people of the collective farm, I've no more patience with you. It isn't that I'll never reach the world revolution while I'm tied to you, but I may go downhill altogether. You're an unnecessary load on my back. And I'm throwing off that load. You understand?'

'I understand,' Lukeria had replied, and said no more.

The same evening Davidov and Makar had had a secret talk together.

'That woman's brought you into the mud! How are you going to face the collective farm people now?' Davidov had demanded.

'That old trouble again...'

'You're a blockhead! You ox-stomach!' Davidov crimsoned down to his neck, and the veins stood out on his forehead.

'How is a man to talk to you?' Nagulnov paced up and down the room, cracking his fingers, and quietly, craftily smiling. 'You've hardly said a word when you try to pin me down with: "Anarchist! Deviator! Trotskyist!" You know what I think about my wife, and why I've stood all this. I've already told you I've no thought for her. Have you ever stopped to wonder about a sheep's tail?'

'No!' Davidov slowly replied, taken aback by the sudden turn of Nagulnov's remarks.

'Well, I have. I've often wondered what use a sheep's tail is to it. It's extra heavy by nature. But it seems to be of no use whatever. A bullock or a horse, or a dog can drive the flies off with their tails. But the sheep is burdened with eight pounds of fat, it can shake it, but it can't drive off the flies. It's hot to carry around in the summer, and the burrs stick in it.'

'What are you driving at with all this talk about sheep's tails and other tails?' Davidov again began to grow quietly angry.

But Nagulnov imperturbably continued:

'I think it's been stuck on it to hide its shame. It's inconvenient, but what could you put in its place? And my woman, my wife I mean, is as necessary to me as a tail is to a sheep. I'm all whetted for the world revolution. I'm waiting for it, for the beloved. But my woman's only a gob, and no more. She's just by the way. Yet you can't get on without her, you've got to cover your shame.

I'm a man down to my roots, even if I am sick, and in between whiles I can answer my purpose. If she can't get satisfaction out of me, well, peace be with her! I once told her: "If you must play about with other men, do as you like; but don't bring home the stains on your skirt, and don't show the signs of where you've been lying on your clothes, or I'll knock your head lopsided." But you now, comrade Davidov, you don't understand anything of this. You're like a folding footrule. And you don't listen for the coming of the revolution in the same way as I do. But what do you rail at me for because of my wife's sins? She's got enough for both of us. But as for her hanging on to a kulak and crying after him, after a class enemy, because of that she's a reptile and whatever happens I'll drive her out of my yard. But I've got no strength to beat her. I'm going on to the new life, and I don't want to dirty my hands. You'd beat her, wouldn't you? But, then, what difference is there between you, a Communist, and some man of the old days, some official, say? They always used to beat their wives! And that's the whole point. No, brother, you stop talking to me about Lukeria. I'll settle scores with her myself, your help isn't wanted in this business. A wife's a pretty serious matter. A good deal depends on her.' Nagulnov smiled dreamily, then heatedly went on: 'Wait till we break down all the frontiers, and I shall be the first to shout: "Lay on with you, marry yourselves off to the women of foreign blood!" Everybody will get mixed up, and there won't be the scandal of one man having a white body, another having a yellow, and a third having a black, and the whites reproaching the others with the colour of their skin and regarding them as lower than themselves. Everybody will have pleasantly swarthy faces, and all alike. I've often thought about it at night . . .'

'You live in a kind of dream, Makar!' Davidov said dissatisfiedly. 'There's a lot I can't understand about you. The racial differences . . . that's true enough, but as to the rest . . . I can't agree with you on the problems of existence. Well, damn you! Only I'm not going on living with you any more. Fact!'

Davidov had dragged his suitcase out from under the bed, making the tools lying inside it rattle hollowly, and had gone out. Nagulnov had accompanied him to his new quarters, to the childless collective farmer Filimonov and his wife. All the way to the Filimonovs' yard they had talked about the spring sowing, and they had not returned to the problems of family and life. From that time there had been an even more perceptible coolness in their relationships.

And so, on the occasion of the slaughtering of the stock Nagulnov welcomed Davidov with a sidelong, downcast look. But after Lukeria had gone out he talked more animatedly.

'They're slaughtering the stock, the reptiles!' he declared. 'They're ready to choke themselves with meat rather than hand the animals over to the collective farm. What I propose is that we hold a meeting and pass a resolution asking permission to shoot those found deliberately slaughtering.'

'What?' Davidov drawled.

'Shoot them, I say. Whose permission do we have to ask to shoot them? The People's Court can't do it, can it? Kill off a couple of those who've slaughtered cows in calf and I reckon the rest'll come to their senses. We must act with the utmost severity now.'

Davidov threw his cap down on the chest, and strode up and down the room. A tone of discontent and irresolution sounded in his voice.

'There you go deviating again! You're in a bad way, Makar! Think it over: can you really shoot people for slaughtering their own cows? There aren't any laws to cover that. Fact! There was a resolution of the Central Executive Committee, and it said in so many words: "imprisonment for two years, deprivation of land, the ill-intentioned exiled from the district". And you suggest asking permission to shoot them! Really you're ...'

'Well, what am I? I'm not anything of the sort. You're always scheming and planning. But what are we going to do the sowing with? What with, if they kill off their bullocks before they join the collective farm?' Makar strode right up to Davidov, and put his hand on the latter's broad shoulder. He was almost a head taller than Davidov, and as he stared down at him he added:

'Siemion! I'm sorry for you. What have you got such a lazy brain for?' Then he almost shouted: 'Can't you see we're done for if we can't manage the sowing? Don't you realize that? We simply must shoot two or three of the reptiles for this business!

We must shoot the kulaks! It's their work! We must ask the higher authorities for permission.'

'You fool!'

'There you are again with your "fool"!' Nagulnov gloomily drooped his head. But he threw it up again at once, like a horse feeling the rider's knees, and shouted: 'They're all slaughtering! We've come to a time of position warfare, like it was in the civil war. The enemy's rising all around us, and you? It's such as you who'll ruin the chances of the world revolution. It'll never come through you, you slow-wits! All around us the bourgeoisie are torturing the working people, are blowing up the Red Chinese in smoke, are beating up the blacks, and here you are being tender to the enemies! Shame on you! It's a terrible disgrace! My blood runs cold as I think of our own blood brothers that the bourgeoisie abroad are torturing! I can't read the papers because of it. All my inside turns over when I look at them. And you ... what do you care about our blood brothers that our enemies are leaving to rot in prisons? You've got no pity for them!'

Tousling his gleaming black hair with his fingers, Davidov hoarsely snorted:

'To hell with you! How haven't I pity for them? Don't bawl like that, please! You're a little touched in the head yourself, and you want to make others like you. Was it because of Lukeria's eyes that I settled accounts with the counter-revolutionaries in the war? What is it you're proposing? Come to your senses! There can be no talk of shooting! You'd be better occupied in mass work, explaining our policy. But shooting – anybody can do that! And you're always like that! The least upset and you at once run to extremes. Fact! But where were you before this started?'

'Where you've been!'

'And that's the very point! We've had our eyes shut during this campaign, but now we must put things right, and not talk about shootings! You've done enough hysterics. Get yourself to work. You're a girl, damn you! You're worse than a girl who stains her nails!'

'Mine are stained with blood!'

'Like all who fought with the gloves off. Fact!'

'Siemion, how could you call me a girl?'

'It wasn't serious!'

'Take that word back!' Nagulnov quietly asked.

Davidov stared silently at him for a moment, then laughed.

'All right. You calm down, and let's get off to the meeting. We must put in some hard propaganda about this slaughtering business.'

'I spent all day yesterday going from hut to hut, arguing with them about it.'

'Now that's a good method. We must go round again, and all of us.'

'There you go again! As I was leaving one yard yesterday I thought: "Well, it seems I've talked them over." But as soon as I got outside I heard a pig squealing under the knife. And I'd spent a whole hour talking to the reptile of an owner about the world revolution and Communism! And how I talked! Until I was so moved I brought the tears to my own eyes. No, it's no good arguing with them, they've got to be clouted on the head, clouted and told: "Don't listen to the kulak, you dangerous reptile! Don't learn from him to be fond of property. Don't kill off your animals, you scum!" He thinks he's killing a bullock, but in reality he's stabbing the world revolution in the back.'

'Some must be clouted, and others taught,' Davidov insisted.

They left the yard. A fine, damp snow was powdering the ground. The sticky flakes were covering the old snow, and melting on the roofs. Through the slaty darkness they made their way to the school. Only half the villagers had turned up to the meeting. Razmiotnov read out the decision of the Council of People's Commissars concerning 'Measures for fighting the wilful slaughtering of stock'. Then Davidov spoke. At the end of his speech he told the meeting in so many words:

'Citizens, we have received twenty-six more applications to join the collective farm. At tomorrow's meeting we shall sort them out, and those who've allowed themselves to be caught on the kulaks' hook and have killed their cattle before joining will not be accepted. Fact!'

'But supposing someone who's already joined kills a young animal, what then?' Liubishkin asked.

'We'll kick him out!'

The meeting groaned, and a hollow murmur arose.

'Then you can break up the collective farm! There isn't a hut in the village where an animal hasn't been killed,' Borshchev shouted.

Shaking his fists, Nagulnov fell on him.

'You hold your tongue, you little kulak! Don't stick your spoke into the collective farm's affairs. We can manage without you. Of course you haven't killed your young bullock, have you?'

'I can do what I like with my own cattle.'

'Fine! I'll send you off to prison tomorrow where you can do what you like all right!'

'You're too harsh! Too harsh in your decisions!' someone roared in a hoarse voice.

Although the meeting was small, it was stormy. As they broke up the villagers went off in silence, and only when they had left the school and scattered into groups did they begin to exchange views as they went.

'The devil got me to kill two sheep!' the collective farmer Siemion Kuzhenkov complained to Liubishkin. 'You pull that meat out of my throat now...'

'I've made a mess of things myself, my boy. I killed a goat,' Liubishkin sighed heavily. 'Now how can I stand up in front of the meeting? It's all that wife of mine, damn her! She argued me into sin, curse the devil! Nothing but "Kill!" and "Kill!" She wanted to eat meat! Oh, the petticoated devil! When I get home I'll knock her teeth out!'

'She ought to be taught better, she ought!' Liubishkin's father-in-law, the ancient Akim Beskhlebnov, advised him. 'It's very awkward for you, my son, for you're a member of the collective farm.'

'That's just it,' Liubishkin sighed, wiping the snow from his whiskers in the darkness, and stumbling over a rut.

'And you killed your piebald bull, didn't you, old Akim?' Diemka Ushakov, who lived next door to Beskhlebnov, coughed and asked.

'I did, my boy. But what else was I to do? The bull broke its leg, the damned devil! The unclean powers led it to the cellar, and it fell in and broke its leg.'

'I thought I saw you at dawn with your daughter-in-law driving the bullock towards the cellar with sticks . . .'

'What are you saying? What are you saying, Diemka? Take that back!' Old Akim got alarmed and halted in the middle of the street, blinking again and again in the impenetrable nocturnal darkness.

'Come on, come on, old man!' Diemka said soothingly. 'What are you standing there like a half-buried plough share for? You drove the bullock into the cellar . . .'

'It went of its own accord, Diemka! Don't sin like that! It's a mortal sin!'

'You're cunning, but no more cunning than a bullock. A bullock can reach under its own tail with its tongue, but I don't suppose you can, can you? You thought you'd lame the bullock and get away with it, didn't you?'

A humid wind raged over the village. The poplars and willows howled noisily in the meadows along the stream. A darkness so black that it made the eyes smart enveloped everything. Muffled by the dampness, voices were to be heard a long time in the by-lanes. The snow fell and fell. Winter was shaking out her last, belated gifts.

Chapter 16

Caught in the Act

DAVIDOV and Razmiotnov left the meeting together. The falling snow was thick and damp. Here and there tiny points of light glittered through the darkness. Broken by gusts of wind, a dog's bark sounded mournfully and incessantly across the village. Davidov recalled what Yakov Lukich had said about keeping the snow

139

on the fields, and sighed: 'No, this year we can't manage that. And in such a storm what a lot of snow would lie on the fallow land. It's a shame! Fact!'

'Let's go along to the stables and have a look at the collective farm horses,' Razmiotnov proposed.

'All right!' Davidov agreed.

They turned into a by-lane. Soon a point of light appeared: outside Lapshinov's hay barn, which had been converted into a stable, a lantern was hanging. They went into the yard. Under the eaves by the stable door some seven or eight cossacks were standing.

'Who's on duty today?' Razmiotnov asked. One of the men put his cigarette out with his boot, and answered:

'Kondrat Maidannikov.'

'But why is all this crowd hanging around? What are you all doing here?' Davidov asked.

'Well, comrade Davidov ... We're just standing and having a general smoke.'

'We brought the hay across from the threshing floor this evening.'

'We stood here to have a smoke and talk. We thought we'd wait for the snow to stop.'

The horses were munching regularly in their stalls. A smell of sweat, horse-dung and urine was mingled with the light, steaming scent of wormwooded steppe hay. On wooden racks opposite the stalls hung horse collars, reins, or traces. The passage along the stalls was swept clean, and lightly sprinkled with yellow sand.

'Maidannikov!' Andrei called.

'Hullo!' a voice replied from one end of the stable.

Maidannikov was carrying a load of corn straw on a pitchfork. He went into the stall fourth from the door, brought a black horse to its feet with his boot, and scattered the straw.

'Turn round, you devil!' he angrily shouted, and swung the pitchfork handle at the dozing horse. In alarm the animal clattered and slipped with its hoofs on the wooden floor, then snorted and stretched its head towards the manger, evidently thinking better of lying down again. Saturated with the smell of the stable and straw, Kondrat came up to Davidov and held out his hard, rough hand.

'Well, how are things going, comrade Maidannikov?'

'All right, comrade Collective Farm Chairman.'

'You've got very official with your "comrade Collective Farm Chairman,' Davidov smiled.

'I'm on duty now, you see.'

'Why is that crowd hanging around the stable?'

'Ask them yourselves!' A note of bitter vexation sounded in Kondrat's reply. 'No sooner do I start feeding the horses at night than the devil brings them all around here. The people can't get rid of their feeling of ownership no-how. They're all owners out there! They come and ask: "Have you given my bay horse some hay?" "Have you put down straw for my dun?" "Is my little mare in the stall all right?" But where else could his little mare have gone to, anyway? I can't shove it down my throat, can I? They all come and ask: "Let me help to feed the horses." And each tries to give his own horse more hay. It's bad! We must pass a resolution to prevent people hanging around who're not wanted.'

'D'you hear that?' Andrei winked to Davidov and shook his head regretfully.

'Clear them all off!' Davidov harshly ordered. 'No one is allowed here except the man on duty and his assistants. How much hay do you give the horses? Do you weigh the feed each time?'

'No, I don't. Each animal gets about half a pood, by guess.'

'Do you put down straw for all of them?'

'Why, of course, by God!' Kondrat furiously nodded his head with its cloth army helmet, and the fine hairs sprinkled over the swarthy pillar of his neck and on to the collar of his well-worn padded coat. 'Our manager Ostrovnov, Yakov Lukich I mean, came along and said: "The hay the horses leave after eating is to be put down for bedding in the stalls." And is that a good order to give? He's regarded as a scientific farmer, the devil, and he gives me a silly order like that!'

'Why, what's wrong with it?'

'Of course it's wrong, comrade Davidov! The hay the horses leave is all good food. Any wormwood in it is soft and eatable, and the scrub, too. The sheep and goats would eat every bit of it down

141

to the last stalk, they'd pick it all over. And he told me to put it down for the horses to lie on! I began to argue with him about it, and he said it wasn't my business to teach him.'

'Don't put it down for bedding, you're quite right there! We'll twist his tail for him tomorrow,' Davidov promised.

'And there's another thing. They've started on the hay that was stacked down by the well. What for, I want to know.'

'Yakov Lukich told me it was poor hay. He wants to feed the animals with the poor stuff during the winter, and to leave the good until the spring ploughing.'

'Well, if that's so, he's right,' Kondrat agreed. 'But you tell him about putting down good hay for bedding.'

'I shall. Well, now here's a Leningrad cigarette to smoke.' Davidov coughed. 'My comrades at the works sent them to me ... Are all the horses in good condition?'

'Thank you. Give me a light. Yes, all the horses are pretty fit. Our saddle-horse, the one that was formerly Lapshinov's, dropped down last night, but they noticed it. Otherwise they're all in order. There's one little devil won't lie down at all. He remains standing all night, they tell me. We shall have them all re-shoed on their forefeet tomorrow. It's been slippery, and the ice has worn all the calks smooth. Well, so long! I haven't bedded down all the horses yet.'

Razmiotnov went along with Davidov to his hut. But at the turning leading to the hut, outside the yard of the individual farmer Luka Chebakov, Razmiotnov stopped Davidov, touched his shoulder, and whispered:

'Look!'

A man's figure was silhouetted by the wicket gate some three paces away from them. Suddenly Razmiotnov ran swiftly up to him. Gripping the butt of his revolver with his right hand, with his left he seized the man standing on the inside of the gate.

'Is that you, Luka?' he demanded.

'It isn't you, is it, Andrei Stepanich?'

'What have you got in your right hand? Now then, hand it over. Quickly!'

'Why, what's the game, comrade Razmiotnov?'

'Hand it over, I say, or I'll shoot!'

At the sound of the raised voices Davidov came up, blinking shortsightedly. 'What are you taking from him?' he asked.

'Hand it over, Luka! I'll shoot if you don't!' Razmiotnov insisted.

'Here, take it! What have you gone barmy about?'

'Look what he was standing holding at the gate! Oh, you devil! What were you doing, standing in the night with a knife in your hand? Who were you waiting for? Not Davidov, were you? I ask you, what were you doing standing here with a knife? Are you a counter-revolutionary? Planning to become a murderer?'

Only Andrei's keen hunter's eyes could have discerned the white blade of a knife in the hand of the man at the wicket gate. He had rushed to disarm him. But when, panting, he began to question the dumbfounded Lukasha, the man opened the gate and said in a changed voice:

'If that's the twist you're giving to it, I can't keep it quiet. You may suspect me of worse than it is, and that God forbid! Come in with me, Andrei Stepanich.'

'Where to?'

'Into the sheep shed.'

'What for?'

'You come, and you'll see then why I was looking down the road with a knife in my hand.'

'Let's go and see,' Davidov proposed, leading the way into Luka's yard. 'Where are we to go?'

'You follow me.'

In the sheep shed, which was littered with a crumbling pile of dung-fuel, was a stool with a lantern on it. By it was squatting Lukasha's wife, a handsome, full-faced woman with fine eyebrows. She rose in alarm when she saw the strangers, and placed herself in front of two pails of water and a basin standing by the wall. Beyond her, right in the corner, a fat hog was trampling on clean straw evidently only just put down. Its head thrust into a huge trough, it was chewing and guzzling swills.

'You see what's the trouble,' Luka said confusedly and disconnectedly, pointing to the hog. 'We thought we'd quietly kill the old hog. The wife was feeding it, and I was just about to throw it and cut its throat when I heard a noise out in the street. So I thought I'd go out for a moment to see if anyone was listening. I went to the gate just as I was, with my sleeves rolled up, an apron on and the knife in my hand. And there you were! What did you think I was doing? Do you go out to knife a man in an apron and with your sleeves rolled up?' Taking off his apron, Luka smiled sheepishly, and shouted at his wife with suppressed anger: 'Well, what are you standing there for, little fool? Drive the hog out!'

'Don't kill it,' Razmiotnov said, feeling somewhat embarrassed. 'We've just had a meeting, and you aren't allowed to slaughter your livestock.'

'Well, I shan't now. You've killed all my desire . . .'

All the rest of the way to his hut Davidov was quizzing Andrei.

'Stopped an attempt on the life of the collective farm chairman! Disarmed a counter-revolutionary! Seven at a stroke! Fact! Ho-ho-ho!'

'But I saved the hog's life!' Razmiotnov jested back.

Chapter 17

A Painful Operation

NEXT day, at a private meeting of the Gremyachy Party nucleus it was unanimously decided to socialize all the animals, whether large or small, belonging to the members of the Gremyachy 'Stalin' collective farm. It was also decided to socialize the fowls, in addition to the livestock.

At first Davidov stood out stubbornly against socializing the smaller animals and the fowls, but Nagulnov resolutely declared that if such a decision were not passed at the next collective farm meeting the spring sowing campaign would be wrecked, for all the animals would be slaughtered and the fowls into the bargain. Razmiotnov supported him, and after some vacillation Davidov agreed.

In addition it was decided and recorded in the minutes that an extensive propaganda campaign must be put in hand to bring to an end all wilful slaughtering, for which purpose each member of the party voluntarily undertook to visit every hut that same day. As for legal measures against those caught slaughtering livestock, it was decided not to proceed against anyone for the time being, but to await the results of the propaganda campaign.

'The cattle and fowls will be safer this way. Otherwise there won't be a cow's low or a cock's crow to be heard in the village by the spring,' Nagulnov said in delight, as he slipped the minutes of the meeting into a folder.

The collective farm general meeting willingly passed the resolution socializing all the animals, for the draught animals and dairy cows had already been so treated, and the decision affected only the young cattle, sheep and pigs. But long and heated discussions arose over the proposal to include the fowls. The women particularly objected. But at last their obstinacy was overcome. Nagulnov was largely responsible for this. He it was who, pressing his long palms against the medal on his breast, said feelingly:

'Women, my dear women! Don't hanker after your chickens and geese. You didn't hold us back before, and you mustn't hold us back now. Let the fowls live in the collective farm. By the spring we'll have subscribed for an incubator, and instead of handfuls it'll turn out chicks for us by the hundred. An incubator's a machine which hatches chicks marvellously. Please don't stick to your point. They'll still be your chickens, only they'll be in the communal yard. There ought not to be any private ownership in hens, my dears. And besides, what use are the chickens to you? They won't lay eggs at present in any case. And look at all the bother you'll have with them before spring comes. They'll be jumping into the garden and pecking up the seedlings, and the next moment you'll find the devils have hidden their eggs away somewhere under the granary, or a pole-cat is twisting the neck of one of them. There's no end to the accidents that happen to them, and you've got to be always crawling into the chicken-house, to feel which has got an egg and which is barren. You crawl in and you pick up the chickens' lice, or some disease. They're nothing but a worry and misery to you. But how will they live when they're in the collective farm? It'll be splendid! They'll be properly looked after; we'll put some old widower, like Akim Beskhlebnov for instance, in charge of them, and let him feel them the whole long day, and crawl on to the perches. He'll find it a pleasant and easy job, just suited to an old man. He'll never rupture himself doing that in all his born days! Let's come to agreement, my dears!'

The women laughed, sighed a little, talked it over among themselves, and came to agreement.

Immediately the meeting was over Nagulnov and Davidov set off to visit the huts. From the results of their inquiries in the first few huts it became evident that there was meat in every one. Just before dinner-time they looked in on old Shchukar.

'He's an active supporter of the farm, and he said himself that the young cattle ought to be spared. He won't have slaughtered any of his stock,' Nagulnov assured Davidov as they went into Shchukar's yard.

They found the 'active supporter' lying on the bed with his legs drawn up. His shirt was rolled back as far as his tangled little beard, and the sharp rim of an earthenware pot of some six litres capacity was pressing into his pale, emaciated belly overgrown with shaggy grey hair. Two cupping glasses were sticking like leeches to his sides. He did not look up as the newcomers entered. His hands were trembling, and were crossed on his chest as though he were dead; his eyes were staring out of their sockets, and, delirious with pain, were slowly rolling in their orbits. Nagulnov thought he noticed a cadaverous smell in the hut. Shchukar's corpulent wife was standing by the stove, and Mamichikha the simples woman, an agile and mousey-grey old hag, was bustling around the bed. Mamichikha was well known throughout the district for her skill in applying cupping glasses, piling on iron pots, bonesetting, letting and stanching blood, and performing abortions with a knitting-needle. And she it was who at this moment was 'doctoring' the thrice unhappy Shchukar.

Davidov's eyes almost started out of his head as he entered. 'Good morning, old man!' he said. 'What's that you've got on your belly?'

'I'm in terrible pain! With my stomach!' the old man said with difficulty, making two bites of the sentence. And at once in a thin voice, he squealed like a puppy and screamed: 'Take the pot off! Take it off, you old witch! Oh, my stomach's bursting!'

'Hold on, hold on! It'll be easier in a minute,' the old woman argued with him in a whisper, vainly trying to pull away the rim of the pot, which with the suction had sunk deeply into the skin.

But old Shchukar suddenly roared like a wild beast, lunged out at the woman with his foot, and seized the pot with both hands. Davidov hastened to his help; snatching up the wooden rolling pin from the top of the stove, he pushed the old woman away, and struck with the rolling pin at the bottom of the pot. The vessel smashed to pieces, and the air rushed from the shards with a whistle. Old Shchukar gave one hiccough from the very depths of his body, and, panting heavily, heaving a sigh of relief, easily tore away the cupping glasses. Davidov glanced at the old man's belly with its enormous blue-black navel sticking up among the fragments of the earthenware, and fell back on to the bench, choking with a furious spasm of laughter. The tears rolled down his cheeks, his cap fell off, and the strands of black hair hung into his eyes.

A tenacious hold on life had old Shchukar! Hardly had Mamichikha begun to lament over the broken pot when he dropped his shirt over his bare body and got up.

'Oh, you old ruffian!' the woman screamed between her sobs. 'The devil's broken my vessel! I heal men like you, and you're never grateful!'

'Get outside, woman! Get outside at once!' Shchukar pointed to the door. 'You all but killed me that time. You ought to have had your pot broken over your head. Clear out, or it may come to murder. I'm a desperate man when I'm roused.'

'What was all this about?' Nagulnov asked almost before Mamichikha had closed the door behind her.

'Oh, my sons, kind friends, believe me! I was all but gone that time. For two whole days I didn't set foot outside my yard, and I went about keeping my trousers up with my hands. My bowels were so loose I couldn't hold myself! I'm afraid I've gone thin, it came away as if I'd been a mangy gosling?'

'Have you been cramming yourself with meat?'

'Meat ...'

'Have you killed your calf?'

'The calf's gone ... It didn't do me any good ...'

Makar coughed, hatefully looked the old man up and down, and hissed:

'You old devil, what you ought to have had was not an earthenware pot but a six-gallon drum on your belly. So that it would have sucked you all in right down to your intestines! Wait till we kick you out of the collective farm, then you won't be able to hold yourself even so much! What did you kill your calf for?'

'I was drawn into sin, Makar dear! The old woman talked me into it, and you know the cuckoo that calls at night always calls the loudest. Have pity ... Comrade Davidov! You and I have been good friends, you won't turn me out of the collective farm, will you? I've already suffered enough for my sins ...'

'Well, what are you to do with him?' Nagulnov waved his hand. 'Come on, Davidov! You old bag of sickness, you mix some gun grease with salt and drink that up, it'll do you good.'

Shchukar's lips quivered with umbrage. 'Are you poking fun at me?' he asked.

'It's the truth I'm telling you. In the old army we used to get rid of the belly-ache that way.'

'What, do you think I'm made of iron? Am I to use what they clean a lifeless gun with? I won't! I'd rather die among the sunflowers, but I won't take grease!'

The very next day, having failed to die, Shchukar was hobbling around the village, telling everyone he met how Davidov and Nagulnov had visited him, and had asked his advice concerning the repair of implements for the spring sowing, and other collective farm matters. At the end of his story the old man made a long pause, then, removing his cigarette, he sighed:

'I wasn't well, and so they came to see me. They can't get things to go right without me. They suggested some medicine for me to take. "Get well, old man," they said, "or, God forbid, you'll die, and we shall be lost without you." And they would

148

be, true Christ ! The least thing they call me to the nucleus to take a look at something, and to give them advice. I'm not a big talker, but I speak to the point. My words won't be lost on them, I hope !' And he raised his faded, exulting eyes to his hearer, trying to discover what impression he had made.

Chapter 18

Clothing Distribution

GREMYACHY Log, which had begun to quieten down after the first days of collectivization, again began to seethe with excitement. The slaughtering of livestock ceased. During two whole days sheep and goats of all kinds were dragged and driven to the communal yards, and chickens were carried there in sacks. The village groaned with the bellowing of cattle and the clucking and crowing of fowls.

Already one hundred and sixty farms had been brought into the collective farm. Three brigades were established. The farm management committee empowered Yakov Lukich to distribute the kulaks' sheepskins, boots and other wearing apparel to the poor cossacks who had need of them. A preliminary list of necessitous persons was drawn up, from which it appeared that the committee was not in a position to satisfy everybody.

In Titok's yard, where Yakov Lukich distributed the confiscated kulak clothing, an incessant roar of voices was heard all day until nightfall. The cossacks undressed on the spot, by the granary entrance, and tried on the well-made kulak boots, pulled on coats, jackets, women's jackets and sheepskins. The fortunate ones whom the commission had granted clothes or boots on account of future work laid themselves bare right outside the granary, and, grunting contentedly, their eyes glittering, their swarthy faces shining with chary, trembling smiles, hurriedly bundled up their old patched and repatched rags and invested themselves in the new garments through which their bodies were no longer visible. And even before anything was chosen what talks there were, what advice given, what expressed doubts, what curses! Davidov gave orders for Liubishkin to be supplied with a jacket, trousers and boots. The scowling Yakov Lukich pulled a heap of clothing out of a chest and threw them at Liubishkin's feet with the remark:

'Take what you feel you can!'

Liubishkin's whiskers quivered, his hands trembled. He began to turn the clothes over, and selected a jacket. By that time he was sweating terribly. He tried the cloth in his teeth, held it up to the light to see whether the moths had got into it. And all around him the crowd breathed hotly, and a hubbub arose:

'Hurry up, or your children will have to wear it out!'

'Why, where are your eyes? Can't you see that's been turned?'

'You're lying!'

'Look for yourself.'

'Take that one, Pavel.'

'I shouldn't; you try another one on!'

Liubishkin's face was as red as a well-burnt brick. He chewed his black whiskers, stared around him with a hunted look, and stretched out his hand for another jacket. He selected one. A good jacket on all counts. He thrust his rather long arms into the sleeves and they only reached to his elbows, while the seams began to split at the shoulders. And again, with a confused and agitated smile, he rummaged among the heap of clothing. His eyes started out of his head like those of a little child before an abundance of toys at a fair, and there was such a clear, childlike smile on his lips that anyone would have felt inclined to give the six-foot Liubishkin a fatherly pat on the head. Noon passed, and he was still undecided. He put on the trousers and boots he had chosen and, swallowing a sigh, told the scowling Yakov Lukich:

'I'll come again tomorrow to try on a coat.'

Wearing his creaking boots and new trousers with stripes down the legs, he left the yard, at once looking ten years younger. Although it was not his quickest way home, he deliberately went into the main street, and stopped again and again at the corners to smoke, or to talk with passers-by. It took him three hours to get home, boasting all the way, and by the evening the rumour was circulating all through Gremyachy that 'Liubishkin's got fitted out as though for his army service. He spent all day today choosing his clothes. He went home all dressed up in new clothes, and wearing Sunday trousers. He minced along like a crane, I don't suppose he felt his legs under him.'

Diemka Ushakov's little wife was frozen motionless over one chest, and had to be removed by force. She put on a flounced woollen skirt which formerly had belonged to Titok's wife, thrust her feet into new shoes, and enveloped herself in a brilliantly coloured shawl. Only then was everybody struck by the fact that Diemka's wife was not at all ugly of feature, and had a shapely figure. And what else could she do but swoon over the collective farm property, poor wretch, when all her bitter life she had never had a good meal, and had never worn a new jacket over her shoulders? How could the blood remain in her lips which were faded with continual need and insufficient food, when Yakov Lukich turned a pile of women's finery out of the chest? From year to year she had borne children, wrapping her sucklings in rotting rags and a worn-out scrap of sheepskin. And, her former beauty, health and freshness faded with sorrows and everlasting want, she herself went all summer in one short skirt as thin as a sieve, and in wintertime, while her one louse-infested shirt was in the wash, she would sit naked on the stove with the children, because she had nothing else to put on.

'My dears ... my dearest ... Wait a bit, perhaps I won't take this skirt after all ... I'll change it ... Something for the children perhaps ... for Misha ... Dunia ...' she whispered ecstatically, clinging to the lid of the chest, not removing her flaming eyes from the variegated heap of clothes.

As Davidov, who happened to be present, watched her, he felt his heart quiver. He went across to her and asked:

'How many children have you got, citizeness?'

'Seven,' Diemka's wife answered in a whisper, afraid to raise her eyes in the sweetness of her expectation.

'Have you got any children's clothes?' Davidov quietly asked Yakov Lukich.

'Yes.'

'Give this woman all she asks for for her children.'

151

'She'll be rich then!'

'What's that you said? Well?' Davidov angrily bared his teeth, and Yakov Lukich hurriedly bent over the chest.

Behind his wife stood the usually garrulous and sharp-tongued Diemka Ushakov, now silently licking his dry lips and holding his breath. But at Davidov's last remark he glanced up at him. From his slanting eyes the tears suddenly spurted like juice from ripe fruit. He started from where he was standing and ran to the granary entrance, pushing the people away with his left hand and covering his eyes with his right. Jumping down the granary steps, Diemka strode out of the yard, shamefacedly trying to hide his tears. But over his cheeks they rolled down from the black screen of his hand, chasing one another, sparkling and glittering like dewdrops.

Late in the afternoon old Shchukar managed to get along to the distribution. He burst into the collective farm office, and, hardly taking breath, cried to Davidov:

'Your very good health, comrade Davidov! I see you're alive.'

'Good afternoon.'

'Write an order for me.'

'What sort of order?'

'An order for me to receive clothing.'

'And what are you to have clothing for?' Nagulnov, who was sitting beside Davidov, raised his brows. 'For slaughtering your calf?'

'What's past ought to be forgotten, Makar; don't you know that? What d'you mean, "what for?"? Who suffered when we turned Titok the kulak out? Me and comrade Davidov! He got his head broken, but that was nothing. What did that hound do to my sheepskin? There was nothing left of it but rags to wipe your feet on. Here I am a martyr for the Soviet government, and you say I don't need anything? I'd rather Titok had smashed my head to bits than have touched my sheepskin. The sheepskin was my old woman's, wasn't it? She might put me out of this world because of it, and then what would happen? Aha, that's just it!'

'If you hadn't run your sheepskin would have been whole to this day.'

'But why wasn't I to run? Didn't you see what Titok's old witch of a wife did? She set the dog on me, and shouted: "Seize him, bite him! He's the worst of the lot!" Comrade Davidov could tell you that that's true.'

'You're an old man, but you lie like a trooper,' Makar declared.

'Comrade Davidov, I appeal to you.'

'I don't remember that happening . . .'

'That's what she shouted, true Christ! Well, the terror was coming at me, and, of course, I turned and left the yard. If the dog had only been like any other dog – but it was more terrible than a tiger.'

'Nobody set the dog on you; you're making the whole story up.'

'Makar, you just don't remember, my boy! You were so frightened yourself that you were beside yourself, so how are you to remember? Sinful that I am, I thought even at the time: "In a moment Makar will be turning and running." And how the dog dragged me around the yard! I remember it all down to the last details. If it hadn't been for that dog Titok wouldn't have escaped my hands alive, I swear it! I'm a desperate man, I am!'

Nagulnov screwed up his face as though he had got toothache, and said to Davidov:

'Give him an order quickly, and let him run off.'

But on this occasion old Shchukar was more than ever inclined to indulge in conversation.

'When I was a youngster, Makar, in a fight I could give anyone . . .'

'Oh, don't go on chattering, we've heard you before! We'll write you out an order for an iron pot, shall we? What will you cure your belly-ache with?'

Bitterly offended, Shchukar silently took the order, and went out without a word of parting. But after he had received an ample tanned sheepskin from Yakov Lukich he recovered his good-humour. His little eyes contentedly narrowed and lit up exultingly. As though taking a pinch of salt he took the edge of the sheepskin in his finger and thumb, raising it on one side as though it were the skirt of a woman about to cross a puddle, clicked his tongue, and boasted before all the cossacks:

'There's a fine sheepskin for you! With my own back I earned it. Everybody knows that when we turned Titok out he attacked comrade Davidov with a bolt. "My friend's done for," I thought. And in a moment I flung myself like a hero to save him, and beat Titok off. If it hadn't been for me Davidov would have been in his coffin.'

'But they say you ran away from a dog and fell over, and it began to tear at your ears as if you were a swine!' one of his audience insisted.

'That's all lies. What the people have come to; they'd twist anything. What's a dog? A dog's a stupid and filthy animal. It doesn't understand a syllable.' And old Shchukar cleverly turned the conversation into other channels.

Chapter 19

Troubles of the Farm

NIGHT...

Northward from Gremyachy Log, far, far beyond the rolling, shadowy steppe uplands, beyond the ravines and valleys, beyond the solid masses of forest, stands the capital of the Soviet Union. Above it lies a flood of electric lights. Like the reflection of a noiseless fire, their flickering azure gleam rises above the many-storied houses, eclipsing the unneeded light of the midnight moon and stars.

Fifteen hundred kilometres distant from Gremyachy Log, stone-bound Moscow also has its night life. The locomotive sirens shriek challengingly, the car horns sound like the notes of an enormous accordion, the trams clank, squeak and grind. But behind the Lenin Mausoleum, behind the wall of the Kremlin, in the icy, whirling wind, the red flag flutters in the irradiated sky. Lit up from below by the white incandescence of electric light, it burns and streams like spurting crimson blood. The wind eddies like a whirlpool and momentarily winds up the heavily hanging flag, then it is unwound again, its end streaming now to the west, now to the east, flaming with the lurid fire of insurrection, calling to the struggle.

One night two years before, Kondrat Maidannikov, who was in Moscow attending the All-Russian Congress of Soviets, walked into the Red Square. He looked at the mausoleum, at the red flag triumphantly gleaming in the sky, and hurriedly removed his cap from his head. A long time he stood motionless thus, with bare head, in his open, homespun jacket.

But in Gremyachy Log the night was cold with a profound silence. Sprinkled with the swansdown of young snow, the bare surrounding uplands sparkled. Deep blue shadows flooded all the valleys, the hillsides, the bushes. The shaft of Charles' Wain almost touched the horizon. Like a candle the poplar growing near the village Soviet stretched up to the oppressively lofty, sombre sky. The spring-fed stream flowing into the river tinkled and murmured magically. In the flowing river water you could see the falling stars that no longer illumine the earth. Listen to the apparent stillness of the night, and you will suddenly hear the hare feeding, gnawing and scraping at a twig with his sap-stained teeth. Under the moon the amber beads of frozen gum glisten dully on the trunk of the cherry. Tear one off and look: like a ripe, untouched plum, the little clot of gum is covered with a tender, smoky bloom. Occasionally an icy crust falls from the branch; and the night wraps the crystal tinkle in silence. Deathly immobile are the sprouts of the cherry twigs with the seamy grey tassels which the children call 'cuckoo's tears'.

Silence . . .

And only at dawn, when under the clouds the Moscow wind comes flying from the north, fanning the snow with its chilly wings, do the morning voices of life begin to sound in Gremyachy Log; the bare branches of the poplars rustle in the riverside groves, the partridges wintering around the village, which have fed in the threshing floors during the night, begin to twitter and call to one another. They fly off to spend the day in the scrub of the wormwood on the sandy slopes of ravines, leaving behind them heaps of straw and an embroidered crisscross of footprints on the snow by the chaff-sheds. The calves begin to low, demanding to be allowed to go to their mothers, the socialized fowls crow more furiously, and the pungently bitter smoke of burning dung-fuel hangs over the village.

But while night had lain over the village, certainly Kondrat Maidannikov was the only one in all Gremyachy who had not slept. In his mouth he had the bitter taste of home-grown tobacco, his head felt like a ton weight, he was nauseated with smoking.

Midnight. Kondrat thought he could see the exultant reflection of fires above Moscow, the menacing and angry scroll of the crimson linen stretched over the Kremlin, over the boundless world, where tears flow so copiously from the eyes of workers like Kondrat himself, who are living beyond the frontiers of the Soviet Union. He recalled the words his dead mother had once spoken in order to dry his childish tears:

'Don't cry, dear little Kondrat, don't make God angry. All over the world poor people cry like that every day, they complain to God of their need, and against the rich who have taken all the good things for themselves. But God ordered the poor to be patient. And so now he gets angry when the poor and hungry cry and cry, and he takes and gathers their tears and makes a mist of them and throws it over the blue sea, hiding the sky in it. And then the ships begin to wander over the sea, and lose their watery road. And a ship strikes against a burning rock in the sea and is drowned. Or sometimes the Lord makes dew out of the tears. In a single night all over the earth the salty dew falls on the grain, both ours and others', and the grain is burnt up by the bitter tears, and a great famine and plague goes over the world. So the poor mustn't cry out at all now, for they only hurt themselves ... Do you understand, little one?' And she ended sternly: 'Pray to God, Kondrat! Your prayers will reach Him quicker.'

'But are we poor, mummy? Is daddy poor?' little Kondrat had asked his pious mother.

'Yes, we're poor,' she had answered.

Falling on his knees before the dark ikon of the Old Believers, Kondrat had prayed and wiped his tears dry, in order that an angry God should not see them.

Kondrat lay untangling the past as though it were a fishing net. He was the son of a Don cossack, and now he was a collective farmer. He thought a great deal during those first nights of the collective farm existence, which were as many and long as the steppe tracks. When his father had been serving as a conscript, his company had knouted and sabred the striking weavers of Ivanovo-Voznesensk, and had defended the millowners' interests. His father died, Kondrat grew up, and in 1920 he had cut down the Polish Whites and Wrangel's soldiers, defending his Soviet government, the government of those same Voznesensk workers, from the attacks of the millowners and their hirelings.

Kondrat had long since ceased to believe in God, and now he believed in the Communist Party which was leading the toilers of all the world towards freedom, towards the sunlit future. He took all his cattle to the collective farmyard, carried along all his fowls down to the last feather. He was in favour of only those who worked being allowed to eat and walk the earth. He was firmly and inseparably grafted into the Soviet regime. Yet he could not sleep at night. And he could not sleep because he still felt a cankerous yearning for his property, for the goods which he had himself voluntarily renounced. The cankerous regret grew in his heart, chilling it with yearning and boredom.

Formerly he had been occupied from dawn to dusk; in the morning he would feed the bullocks, cows, sheep and horses, and take them down to drink; at noontide he would once more scrape up hay and straw out of the threshing floor, afraid of losing a single stalk. And later he had to tidy up again for the night. Even during the night he would go out several times into the cattle yard to see that all was well, and to gather back into the mangers the hay trodden underfoot. His heart rejoiced in his farmer's anxieties. But now his yard was empty and dead. There was nothing to go out to attend to. The mangers stood empty, the wattle-gates stood wide open, and not even a cock-crow was to be heard all through the long night. There was nothing by which to tell the time and the passing of the hours of darkness.

He got rid of his boredom only when his turn came to look after the collective farm stables. In the daytime he would get away from his hut at the first opportunity, in order to avoid the sight of the terribly deserted yard, to avoid his wife's afflicted, reproachful eyes.

Now she was sleeping at his side, breathing regularly. On the stove their little daughter Khristishka was tossing, sweetly smacking her lips, and muttering in her sleep: 'Daddy, gently ... gently ...' In her sleep she was seeing her own bright, childish dreams; she lived easily, breathed easily. She could be delighted with an empty matchbox, and turn it into a sledge for her rag doll. She could play with the sledge all day, and the following day would bring her the smile of a new amusement.

But Kondrat had his own thoughts. He struggled in them like a fish in a net. 'When will you leave me, accursed yearning? When will you dry up, you dangerous devil? But what's it all for? I pass by the stalls, and other men's horses are standing there and they mean nothing to me. But when I reach my own horse, and glance at its clipped left ear, and its back with the black strap running right to its tail, I begin to choke, and then he seems dearer than my own wife. And I still try to give him sweeter, finer grass. And others are just the same: each pines after his own horse, and doesn't care a fig for the others. Yet there aren't any "others" now, they're all ours. But there it is ... They don't want to look after the property, many of them aren't used to it. Kuzhenkov was on duty yesterday; he didn't take the horses out to drink, but sent a lad with them. The boy mounted one horse bareback, and drove the whole lot down to the river at a gallop. Whether they'd all drunk or not, he rounded them up and galloped them back to the stables. And you can't speak to anybody about it, for they simply bare their teeth and say: "Ha, you want more than all the rest of us." And it's all come of the struggle we've had to get property. I expect those who've always had their fill don't mind so much. I mustn't forget to tell Davidov tomorrow how Kuzhenkov watered the horses. If they're looked after like that they won't be able to shift a harrow when the spring comes. And tomorrow I must go and see how they're caring for the fowls; the women say that seven have died already through being overcrowded. Oh, it's difficult! And why did they have to collect all the fowls at once? They might have left a cock in each yard to serve instead of a clock. There's nothing in the co-operative shop, and Khristishka's going about barefoot. You can do what you like, but she must have a pair of shoes at least. My conscience won't let me ask Davidov for a pair. Oh, well, let her spend this winter on the stove, and by the summer she won't need them.'

Kondrat thought of the want which the country was suffering in carrying through the Five Year Plan, and he clenched his fists under the sacking, hatefully waging a mental argument with the workers in the west who were not Communists. 'You've sold us for good wages from your masters! You've betrayed us, brothers, to have your bellies well filled. Why haven't you got a Soviet government? Why are you so late? If you'd had a rotten life of it you'd have made your revolution by now; but it's clear the fiery cock hasn't pecked at your arses yet. You've got no guts, you can't get a move on no-how, and you're slow, you're all wobbly and uncertain. But it will peck at you! It'll peck you into sores! Can't you see across the frontiers how hard it is for us to build up our economic life? What want we're suffering, how we go half-naked and half-barefoot, but how we grit our teeth and work? You'll be ashamed to come in when everything's done, brothers! I'd like to have a great post made so as you could all see it; I'd climb to the top of it, and then I'd lay my tongue about you!'

He dropped off to sleep. The cigarette slipped out of his mouth and burnt a great black hole in his only shirt. The smart of the burn awoke him, and he got up, cursing under his breath, and fumbled in the dark for a needle in order to sew up the hole. Otherwise Anna would see it in the morning and would nag away at him for a couple of hours. But he could not find a needle.

He fell asleep again.

He awoke at dawn, and went into the yard to relieve himself. As he went he suddenly heard an extraordinary din. Shut in one shed for the night, the socialized cocks were all bawling at once in a myriad-voiced and mighty choir. Opening wide his swollen eyelids in his astonishment, Kondrat listened for a couple of minutes to the massed, incessant crowing, and when the last belated 'cuck-curroo' had died away he sleepily smiled. 'How they're bawling, the devils!' he thought. 'Just like a brass band. Anyone living near them will have no sleep or quietness. And in the old days one would start at one end of the village, and another at the other, without order or harmony. Ah, life!' and he went to do his duties.

After breakfast he went along to the fowl-yard. Old Akim Beskhlebnov greeted him with an angry shout:

'Well, what are you wandering around so early in the morning for?'

'I've come to visit you and the fowls. How are you getting on, daddy?'

'I used to live, but now . . . God preserve me!'

'Why, what's the matter?'

'Looking after the fowls is slowly killing me.'

'How?'

'You come and spend a day here, and you'll soon find out! The devilish cocks fight the whole long day, I've got tired out through running after them. You'd say hens were of the female sex, but these seize one another by the crest and they're all over the yard. This sort of service can go to hell for all I care. I'm going this very day to Davidov to ask him to let me mind the bees.'

'They'll get used to it, daddy.'

'While they're getting used to it daddy will be turning up his toes! And anyway, is it a man's job? Whatever I may look like, I'm a cossack, I took part in the Turkish campaign. But here I'll have you know that I've been made commander-in-chief of the chickens! It's two days since I took up my duties, but there's no getting away from the brats. As I go home they shout after me: "Daddy hen-feeler," "Daddy Akim hen-feeler." Have I had everybody's respect only to die in my old age with the nickname of "Hen-feeler"? That's not what I want.'

'Drop it, daddy Akim. Why worry about the brats?'

'If it was only the kids who make game of me! But some of the women join in with them. As I was going home to dinner yesterday Nastia Donietskova was standing drawing water from the well. "Are you managing the chickens all right, daddy?" she asked. "Yes, I'm managing," I said. "And are any of the hens laying, daddy?" "Some are laying," I said, "but not too well."

160

And how she snorted, the Kalmik mare! "See that there's a basket of eggs laid by ploughing time," she said, "or we'll make you ride the hens yourself." I'm too old to listen to such jokes. And the job's too unpleasant.'

The old man was going to say something more, but two cocks began to fight breast to breast by the fence, the blood started to stream from the comb of one of them, a handful of feathers flew from the other's crop. Old Akim rushed towards them at a run, arming himself with a switch as he went.

Despite the early hour, the collective farm office was crowded with people. By the porch a pair of horses harnessed to a sledge stood waiting for Davidov, who was getting ready to drive to the district town. Lapshinov's saddled trotting-horse was pawing the snow, while Liubishkin busily tightened the girths. He was getting ready to ride to Tubyanskoe, where he was to have a talk with the local collective farm manager concerning a grain-sorter.

Kondrat went into the first room. A book-keeper recently arrived from the town was rummaging through his books. Yakov Lukich, grown hollow-cheeked and gloomy during the past few days, was sitting writing opposite him. In the same room were crowded the collective farm workers whom the foreman had assigned to cart hay. In one corner Arkady and pockmarked Agafon Dubtsiev, the leader of the third brigade, were arguing with Ippolit Shaly, the only smith in the village. Razmiotnov's sharp and jovial voice came from the farther room. He had only just arrived, all bustle and laughter, and was telling Davidov:

'Four old women came to see me very early this morning. Old Uliana, Mishka Ignationok's mother, was their ringleader. Do you know her? No? She's getting on in years, weighs a good seven poods, and has a wart on her nose. Well, they came along, and mother Uliana stormed and stormed. I couldn't understand what she was saying, she was so angry and the wart on her nose began to go purple. And she attacked me like a fury: "Ah, you ..." and all the rest of it. I had a crowd of people with me in the Soviet, and there she was cursing and swearing. Of course I sternly told her: "Shut your mouth and stop using such expressions, or I'll send you to the district for insulting the government." Then I asked her: "What are you in such a rage about?"

And she answered: "What are you trying to take a rise out of old women for? How can you poke fun at our old age?" It took me all my time to find out what was the matter. At last it appeared that they'd heard that in the spring the collective farm management committee was to set apart all the old women who couldn't work, those who were gone sixty, to . . .' Andrei almost choked in the attempt to control his laughter. '. . . it appeared that owing to the shortage of steam machinery for hatching eggs the old women were to be given that little job! They were raving mad about it. Old mother Uliana bawled as though she was being killed: "You son of a bitch! Sit me on eggs, would you? There isn't an egg I'd sit on! I'll give you all a good hiding with my frying pan, and then I'll drown myself." I out-shouted the lot of them: "Don't drown yourself, mother Uliana; in any case our river hasn't got enough water in it to drown you. It's all lies, all kulak yarns." But what a trick, comrade Davidov! Our enemies are spreading lies like that in order to stop our work. I began to question them to find out where the story had come from, and learned that a nun had come from Voiskovoi the day before yesterday, had spent the night at Timofei Borshchev's hut, and told them the chickens were being collectivized in order to be sent into the towns to make soup. And she said that little chairs of a special sort, with straw in the bottoms, were to be made for the old women, and they would be forced to hatch out the eggs, and those who refused would be tied on to the chairs!'

'Where is this nun?' Nagulnov, who had been listening vigorously, asked.

'She's hopped it. She's no fool! Told her lies and then cleared off.'

'Black-tailed magpies like her ought to be arrested and sent where they belong to. Good job I didn't get hold of her. I'd have tied her skirt above her head and laid on the knout. But you're chairman of the Soviet, and anybody who likes can spend the night in your village. That's a fine state of things!'

'Damn it, I can't keep a watch on everybody!'

Wearing a huge sheepskin over his greatcoat, Davidov sat at the table taking a last glance at the plan for spring field work confirmed by the collective farm meeting. Without raising his eyes, he said:

'Slandering us is an old trick of the enemy. He's a parasite, and he wants to mess up all our constructive work. And sometimes we play right into his hands, as we have over the fowls ...'

'What about the fowls?' Nagulnov dilated his nostrils.

'By standing out for socializing the fowls.'

'That's not true.'

'It is true! It's a fact. We oughtn't to have worried about the small change. Here we haven't got our sowing materials ready yet, and we took on the fowls! Sheer idiocy! I could kick myself now. And the District Committee will lay it on about the seed grain fund when I get there. Fact! But a very unpleasant fact ...'

'Tell me why the fowls oughtn't to have been socialized. The meeting agreed, didn't it?'

'It isn't a question of the meeting,' Davidov frowned. 'Why can't you understand that the fowls are a detail, and we ought to decide the main point: to strengthen the collective farm, raise the membership percentage to a hundred, and finally sow the corn. And I seriously suggest that we've gone politically wrong in regard to the damned fowls. Fact, we've gone wrong! Last night I was reading something dealing with the organization of collective farms, and I realized where we'd gone wrong. You see, we've got a collective farm, and that's a co-operative association. But we've been trying to turn it into a commune. Isn't that right? And that's a left-wing deviation. Fact! You think it over. If I were in your place (you proposed it and got round us to accept it) I'd admit the mistake with Bolshevik courage, and would give the order for the chickens and other fowls to be redistributed to their farms. And if you won't do it, I'll do it off my own bat as soon as I get back. Well, I'm off. Good-bye.'

He clapped on his cap, turned up the high collar of his kulak sheepskin, which stank of naphthalene, and said as he fastened his document case:

'There are plenty of nuns still walking about alive and telling yarns about us, trying to get the women and the old men against us. But the collective farm job is so young and so terribly necessary. Everybody ought to be on our side. The old women, and the other women, too. The women also have their part to play in the collective farm. Fact!' He went out with long and heavy strides.

'Come on, Makar, send the chickens back to their homes. Davidov's said the truth.' As he waited, expecting an answer, Razmiotnov gave Nagulnov a long stare. Makar sat on the window-ledge, unbuttoning his sheepskin, turning his cap round in his hands, his lips moving soundlessly. Thus three minutes passed. Then Makar swiftly raised his head, and Razmiotnov met his open gaze.

'Come on, then,' he said. 'We've gone wrong. That's true enough. Davidov hit the nail on the head, the gap-toothed devil!' He smiled a little sheepishly.

As Davidov got into the sledge Kondrat Maidannikov stood talking to him, waving his arms as he fiercely told his story. The driver impatiently gathered up the reins and adjusted the knout thrust under his seat. Davidov listened, biting his lips. As Razmiotnov went down the steps he heard him say:

'Don't get agitated! Don't take things so much to heart. Everything's in our hands, and we'll get it all straight. Fact! We'll introduce a system of punishments, and we'll make the brigade leaders personally responsible. Well, so long.'

The knout spiralled and whistled over the horses' backs. The sledge marked the round, blue tracks of its runners across the snow, and disappeared through the gate.

Hundreds of hens were scattered like pebbles of a myriad hues in the fowl-yard. Old Akim, carrying a switch, was on duty in the yard. The breeze played with his grey beard, and dried the beads of sweat on his forehead. The 'hen-feeler' walked about the yard, thrusting the hens out of his way with his felt boots. Over his shoulder hung a sack half-full of coarse grain, which he poured out in a narrow trail from the granary to the shed. Under his feet the chickens seethed like boiling soup, incessantly uttering their hurriedly anxious cries.

In the threshing floor, railed off by a palisade from the rest of the yard, the flock of geese showed white like solid heaps of chalk. From them came a full-throated, sonorous cackle, the flapping of wings, and hissing as though the threshing floor were the flooded fields during the spring migration.

A large crowd of men was gathered by the shed. From outside, there showed only a ring of backs and bottoms. All their heads were bent downward, their eyes were fixed on something at their feet in the centre of the ring.

Razmiotnov approached them and glanced across their backs, attempting to discover what was happening in the ring. The men breathed heavily, and talked to one another in undertones.

'The red will win.'

'The hell it won't! Look, its comb is already hanging crooked.'

'Did you see that whack it gave the other?'

'It's mouth's wide open, it's tired out.'

Then old Shchukar's voice sounded above the others:

'Don't keep poking him. He'll begin of his own accord. Don't poke him, you idiot. I'll give you a poke under the windpipe.'

In the ring two cocks were strutting with outspread wings; one was a bright red, the other was feathered, with bluish-black, raven plumage. Their combs were torn with pecks and black with clotted blood, their feet trod over black and red feathers. The two fighters were tired. They separated and made a pretence of pecking at something, scratched at the half-melted snow with their claws, eyeing each other with cautious glances. Their feigned indifference did not last long. The black cock suddenly sprang off the ground, flying up like a spark from a flame; the red cock also sprang up. Again and again they clashed in mid-air.

Completely oblivious of the world, old Shchukar watched them. A bead of chilly water trembled on the tip of his nose, but he did not notice it. All his attention was concentrated on the red cock. The red simply must win, for Shchukar had taken on a bet with Diemid the Silent. His tense concentration was abruptly disturbed by someone's hand: it dragged the old man roughly by the collar of his sheepskin jacket, and hauled him out of the circle. His face distorted with anger, Shchukar turned round, and with all a cock's determination he threw himself on the offender. But his expression suddenly changed and became affable and welcoming: the hand was Nagulnov's. With a frown on his face, Makar dispersed the audience, separated the cocks, and morosely said:

'Setting cocks at each other, are you? Get off to your work, you drones. Go and carry hay to the stables if you haven't anything else to do. Or carry dung out to the gardens. Two of you go round the huts and tell the women to come and collect their chickens.'

'So you're breaking up the collective fowl farm?' asked one of the watchers of the cock-fight, a man who had decided to remain an individual farmer. 'It's clear their class-consciousness isn't strong enough for a collective farm. But tell me, will the cocks go on fighting under socialism or won't they?'

His face paling, Nagulnov measured the questioner with a heavy stare.

'You're being funny, but do you know what you're joking about?' he asked. 'The finest flowers of the human race have perished for socialism, and who are you to joke about it, you dog's muck? Clear out, counter-revolutionary, or I'll give you one that'll send you flying out of this world. Clear off, reptile, before I turn you into a corpse. You see, I can be funny, too!'

He walked away from the abashed cossacks, took a last look at the yard and its swarming fowls, and slowly, with bowed shoulders, suppressing a deep sigh, went towards the gate.

Chapter 20

A District Bureaucrat

THE District Committee room was blue with tobacco smoke, a typewriter clattered, the Dutch stove breathed out its warmth. The committee was due to meet at two o'clock. The secretary of the District Committee, clean-shaven, sweating, with the collar of his cloth shirt unbuttoned owing to the heat of the room, was in a hurry. Pointing Davidov into a chair he scratched his bare, puffy white neck, and said:

'I haven't got much time, get that clear. Well, how are things going? What is the percentage of collectivization? Will you soon reach the hundred? Speak briefly.'

'We shall soon,' Davidov replied. 'But it's not a question of percentages, but of what's going to happen inside the farm. I've brought the plan for the spring field work; would you like to see it?'

'No, no!' The secretary took alarm, and, painfully screwing up his baggy eyes, he wiped the sweat from his forehead with his handkerchief. 'Take it to Lupetov in the District Agricultural Union. He'll look at it and confirm it; I haven't got time. A comrade has arrived from the Regional Committee and there's to be a meeting of the Bureau in a few minutes. But we've got to ask what the devil you sent the kulaks to us for? You're in for it now! Didn't I tell you in good Russian and warn you: "Don't hurry with that business so long as we haven't got clear instructions." And instead of chasing after the kulaks and beginning to dispossess them before you'd set up your collective farm, you'd have done better to have got on with complete collectivization. Yes, and what about your seed grain fund? Did you receive the District Committee's instruction to set up a fund immediately? Then why haven't you done anything so far to carry out that instruction? I shall have to raise the question of you and Nagulnov in the Bureau this very day. I shall have to insist that this matter is set down against you in black and white. It's a positive disgrace! You look out, Davidov! Nonfulfilment of the District Committee's most important instruction will lead to very unpleasant organizational results for you. How much seed grain have you collected down to your last report? I'll look it up at once!' He picked up a ruled sheet of paper lying on the table, ran his narrowed eyes over it, and immediately went a vivid red. 'Well, of course! Not a single pood more. What are you silent for?'

'Why, you won't let me get a word in edgeways. It's true we haven't taken up the question of the grain fund yet. I'm returning today, and we'll begin then. All this time we've been spending every day holding meetings, organizing the collective farm, the administration, and brigades. Fact! We've had an awful lot to do, we can't do it just as you want, by orders: one, two and the farm's organized, and the kulaks turned out, and the grain fund collected. We'll get it all done; and don't be in too much of a hurry to have it put down against me, you'll have plenty of time.'

'What d'you mean, "don't be in a hurry"? When the Regional and Provincial Committees are pressing all the time, and not giving us a moment to breathe! The grain fund should have been established by the first of February, and you ...'

'And I'll have it done by the fifteenth! Fact! We aren't going to sow in February, are we? I sent a member of the management committee to Tubyanskoe for a sorter today. The chairman of the collective farm there is drunk; when we wrote and asked him when they'd be finished with the sorter he wrote back: "In the future." Another self-educated wit for you! Fact!'

'You needn't tell me tales about others. Talk about your own collective farm.'

'We've carried on a campaign against the slaughter of animals, and it's stopped now. A day or two ago we passed a resolution to socialize the fowls and smaller animals, because we were afraid they'd be slaughtered, too, and because in general ... But I told Nagulnov today to hand the fowls back again.'

'What for?'

'I consider the socialization of the smaller animals and fowls a mistake; they're not needed in the collective farm just yet.'

'Did the collective farm meeting pass the resolution to socialize them?'

'It did.'

'Well then, what's wrong?'

'We haven't got any chicken-houses, and the collective farmers got down in the mouth about it. Fact! There's no point in getting them worked up over petty details. It isn't compulsory to socialize the fowls; it's not a commune we're organizing, but a collective farm.'

'A very fine theory! But what's the point of giving the fowls back? Of course you shouldn't have laid your hands on them, but once it's done there's no point in going back on it. There's some sort of marking time and double-dealing going on among you. You must definitely pull yourselves together! You haven't established a grain fund, you haven't got a hundred per cent collectivization, you haven't got your implements repaired ...'

'I made arrangements with the smith about that today.'

'There you are; that's just what I'm saying. You're not getting any pace on. Unquestionably we must send you a propaganda column, they'll teach you how to work.'

'By all means ! That will be very good. Fact !'

'But where it wasn't necessary to hurry you trod hard on the pedal right away. Have a cigarette.' The secretary stretched his case out to Davidov. 'Your sledges with the kulaks arrived here like a bolt from the blue. Zakharchenko rings me up from the G.P.U., asking: "What am I to do with them? I've had no word from the Region. We need trucks for them. Where am I to send them to, how am I to send them?" You see what you've done? There was no agreement, no instruction for you to do that ...'

'Well, what ought I to have done with them?' Davidov grew angry. And when in his anger he began to talk faster, he lisped a little, because his tongue slipped into the gap between his teeth and made his speech indistinct. And now he began to lisp slightly and make peculiar sucking noises as he passionately raised his rough tenor voice: 'Had I got to hang them round my neck? They killed the poor peasant Khoprov and his wife ...'

'The investigation didn't prove that,' the secretary interrupted him. 'There might have been other causes for that.'

'He was a poor sort of investigator, and that's why it wasn't proved. And your "other causes" is just nonsense ! It was the kulaks' work. Fact ! They were continually interfering with our organization of the collective farm, and carried on an agitation against it. So I exiled them to the devil ! I don't understand why you're raking all this up. Just as though you weren't satisfied ...'

'That's a silly remark. Choose your words more carefully. I'm against independent action when the plan and the planned work are replaced by guerilla activities. First you were clever enough to throw the kulaks out of your village, so putting us in a terribly difficult position in regard to their exile. And then, all you think of is your own local interest, so you sent them on your sledges only as far as the District centre. Why not straight to the station, to the Regional town?'

'We needed the sledges.'

'That's just what I was saying – local interest! Oh, that's enough. Here are your tasks for the immediate future: collect the grain fund in its entirety, get the implements repaired by sowing time, and obtain a hundred per cent collectivization. Your collective farm will be quite independent. It's a long way from the other centres of population in your district, and, unfortunately, it won't come into the area of the "Giant" farm. And they're all mixed up in the Regional Office, now, damn them! First they ask for "Giants", then they say: "make them smaller." It's enough to drive you mad!' He clutched his head and sat silent for a moment, then said in an altered tone:

'Go and get your plan confirmed in the District Agricultural Union, then have dinner in the dining-room. Or if you're too late for dinner there, go along to my rooms and my wife will give you some food. Wait a second. I'll write a note for you.'

He swiftly scribbled something on a sheet of paper, thrust it at Davidov, and, burying his nose in his documents, stretched out a cold, clammy hand.

'And then get back to Gremyachy at once,' he added. 'Goodbye. I shall bring your case up at the Bureau. But perhaps I shan't. Only, pull yourself up. Otherwise, it'll be organizational results for you!'

Davidov went out, and opened the note. With blue pencil in a flowing hand was written:

'Liza! I categorically instruct that you immediately and unconditionally supply the bearer of this note with dinner. Korchinsky.'

'No! I'd rather go without dinner than get it with such an order,' hungry Davidov miserably decided, as he turned to go to the District Agricultural Union.

Chapter 21

Plans for the Spring

ACCORDING to the plan laid down, 472 hectares of land were to be ploughed in Gremyachy that spring, and 110 of these were to be virgin soil. In the autumn 643 hectares had been ploughed by individual farmers, and 210 hectares of winter rye had been sown. Of the total area to be sown in the spring, 667 hectares were allotted to wheat, 210 hectares to rye, 108 to barley, 50 to oats, 65 to millet, 167 to maize 45 to sunflowers and 13 to hemp. This made a total of 1,325 hectares, exclusive of 91 hectares of sandy soil allotted to melons.

At a production conference held on 12 February, at which over forty active members of the collective farm were present, the formation of a seed grain fund, the rates of output for field workers, the repair of implements in time for the sowing period, and allocation of fodder for the spring field labour were all discussed. On Ostrovnov's advice Davidov proposed that a round figure of seven poods to a hectare should be set aside for the grain fund, making an aggregate of 4,669 poods. At once a deafening outcry arose. Everybody roared away on his own account, heedless of anyone else, and the glass of the windows in Titok's hut quivered and rang with the hubbub.

'It's too much.'

'Mind you don't overdo it !'

'We've never sown so much to a hectare before, not even in sandy soil.'

'It's enough to make a hen laugh !'

'Five poods to a hectare at the most.'

'Or say five and a half.'

'We've got as much good earth needing seven poods to a hectare as would cover a sparrow's beak ! We ought to plough the land the animals have been dunging; what's the government going to do with that?'

'Or the fields by Paniushkin's hut.'

'Ho! You want to plough up the most grassy spots. That's asking for trouble.'

'Tell us how many kilos of grain are needed to your hectare.'

'Don't get us muddled up with your kilos. Tell us in poods.'

'Citizens! Citizens! Not so much noise!' Liubishkin, the leader of the second brigade, shouted at the top of his voice. 'Citizens, damn the lot of you! You've gone barmy, you darned fools. Let me say one word!'

'Say as many as you like. We'll let you!'

'What a lot, blast their kidneys! A lot of cattle! Ignat, what are you bellowing like a bull for? You've gone blue with shouting . . .'

'Well, and you're foaming at the mouth like a mad dog.'

'Let Liubishkin speak.'

'I can't stand this, it's deafening.'

The conference was ferocious in its tumult. And finally, when the noisiest had grown a little quieter, Davidov roared in unwonted frenzy:

'Whoever heard of a conference like this? What are you all bawling for? Let each speak in turn, and the rest shut up. Fact! There's no point in behaving like a lot of bandits. You want to use your intelligence.' A little more calmly he continued: 'You ought to learn from the working class how to hold a meeting in an organized fashion. We hold meetings in our shop, for instance, or at the club, and they're quite orderly. Fact! One man speaks and the others listen. But you all shout at once, and no one can understand a word.'

'If anyone starts quacking when someone else is speaking I'll give him a crack on the head with this stick, by God I will! So that he turns his toes up!' Liubishkin stood up and brandished a stout oaken stick.

'Then you'll put us all out by the end of the meeting!' Diemka Ushakov expressed his opinion.

The conference laughed, lit cigarettes, and turned to serious consideration of the amount of seed to be sown to a hectare. And, as it transpired, there proved to be no justification for so much shouting and arguing. Yakov Lukich spoke first, and he at once disposed of all the contradictory opinions.

'You've shouted yourselves hoarse, and all for nothing,' he began. 'Why did comrade Davidov propose seven poods? That's very simply answered: it was our general advice. Are we going to clean the grain and treat it chemically? We are. Will there be any waste? There will. And there may be a lot of waste, for you'll get seed grain that you can't distinguish from chicken food being brought in by some farmers who don't trouble. It's all mixed up with food grain, and that's how they sow it. Well, and if there is any over after sowing will it be wasted? No; we'll feed the fowls and cattle with it.'

The conference agreed to allow seven poods to the hectare. But matters did not go so easily when the question of the amount of land to be turned over by each plough was discussed. Such a conflict of opinion arose that Davidov was flabbergasted.

'How can you decide in advance how much land I'm to turn over with each plough, if you don't know what the spring's going to be like?' the leader of the third brigade, the pockmarked and stalwart Agafon Dubtsiev, shouted at Davidov. 'Do you know how the snow will melt, and what sort of soil will come from under it, damp or dry? Can you see through the earth?'

'Then what do you propose, Dubtsiev?' Davidov asked.

'I propose we don't waste paper and don't write anything down now. We'll soon find out when the sowing begins.'

'Call yourself a brigade leader, and you talk such nonsense against having a plan? Do you think a plan unnecessary?'

'You can't say how much and what beforehand,' Yakov Lukich unexpectedly came to Dubtsiev's support. 'You may have three yoke of good, old bullocks, and mine may be three-year-olds, not fully developed. Can I keep up with you? Not on your life.'

But Kondrat Maidannikov put in his spoke:

'It's very strange we should hear such words from Ostrovnov, the manager. How are you going to work without a task to work to? Just as God tells each one of us? I shan't take my hand off the plough handle all day, but you'll warm your back in the sun. And are we both to receive the same payment? You'll do well, Yakov Lukich!'

'Glory be, Kondrat Kristoforich! But how are you going to compare a bullock's strength with land? Supposing you've got soft earth and I've got hard, your field lies in a hollow, and mine's on the hillside. Tell me, what then, since you're so clever?'

'One task for the hard and another for the soft. The bullocks can be compared in harness. Everything can be allowed for, don't try to teach me!'

'Ushakov wants to speak,' someone announced.

'All right.'

'What I'd suggest, brothers, is that we must do as we've always done. A month before sowing time we must begin to feed up the animals with good fodder: good hay, maize and barley. That's a little problem for you, how we are going to manage about feeding the animals. The grain collection has eaten up too much grain...'

'We'll talk about the cattle later,' Davidov interposed. 'That's not the main question at the moment. Fact! We must settle the question of the amount of land to be ploughed each day. How many hectares of hard earth, how many for a plough, how many for a sower, and so on.'

'There are differences in sowers, too. I can't do as much with an eleven-row as with a seventeen-row sower.'

'Fact! Then what do you suggest? And you, citizen, why are you silent all the time? You're one of the active members, but I haven't heard your voice once yet.'

Diemid the Silent stared at Davidov in amazement, and replied in his rumbling bass voice:

'I agree.'

'What with?'

'That we've got to do the ploughing... and the sowing.'

'Well?'

'That's all I have to say.'

'All?'

'Hm!'

'You've said it!' Davidov smiled, and the rest of his words

were inaudible in the general roar of laughter. Then old Shchukar explained on Diemid's behalf:

'He's known as Diemid the "Silent" in the village, comrade Davidov. All his life he's been silent; he only speaks very rarely, and his wife left him because of it. He's not a stupid cossack, but he's a bit of a fool, or, to put it better, he's a little touched, or it's like as if he'd been dropped on his head when he was a baby. I remember when he was a kid he was snotty-nosed and good-for-nothing, he ran about without any trousers, and nobody noticed that he was at all clever. But now he's grown up and holds his tongue. Under the old regime the Tubyanskoe priest even refused him the sacrament because of that. At confession he covered him with a black kerchief – it was in Lent, in the seventh week of the fast, I think – and he asked: "Do you steal, child?" Diemid was silent. "Do you fornicate?" He was still silent. "Do you smoke?" "Do you commit adultery with women?" He was still silent. The fool had only to say, "I'm a sinful man, father," and from that moment his sins would have been forgiven him . . .'

'Oh, shut up!' came a voice and laughter from the back of the room.

'I'll be finished in one second! Well, and he only snivels through his nose and stares like a sheep at a new gate. The priest was desperate; he got frightened and began to tremble, but he went on asking: "Perhaps you've coveted another man's wife, or your neighbour's ass, or his other cattle?" And all sorts of other questions according to the gospels. Diemid still kept silent. And what could he say? No matter whose wife he might have coveted, nothing would have come of it. No woman, not even the lowest in the village . . .'

'Cut it short, daddy! Your story's got nothing to do with the business,' Davidov sternly ordered.

'It will have in a minute, I'm coming to the business now. This is only leading up to it. One more second! You interrupted me . . . Ah, you've got a heart as firm as a cabbage's. I've forgotten what I was saying. God help me to remember! Curse my bad memory! I've got it!' Shchukar smacked his hand against the bald spot on his head and poured out the sentences staccato like a machine-gun. 'So that in regard to another man's wife Diemid's case was hopeless, and what would he want an ass for, or any other sacred animal? He might have coveted it, for he hadn't got a horse for his farm, but we haven't got an ass in the village, and he'd never seen one all his life. And I ask you, citizens, where have we got any asses? From the beginning of the ages we've never had any. A tiger or an ass, or even a camel ...'

'Will you shut up now?' Nagulnov asked, 'or shall I put you outside?'

'On May day you talked about the world revolution from noon to sunset in the school, Makar. And you bored us, there's no other word for it; you kept on saying the same thing over and over again. I quietly rolled myself up on the bench and went to sleep, but I couldn't bring myself to interrupt you. Yet you're interrupting ...'

'Let the old daddy finish. Time will wait for us,' remarked Razmiotnov, who was fond of a joke and a funny story. The old man's time was extended by two minutes, and, swallowing his words, he finished up:

'Perhaps that was why he was silent. Nobody knows. The priest was lost in surprise. He put his head under the kerchief and asked Diemid: "You're not dumb, are you?" At that Diemid told him: "No, I'm not, I've had enough of you." The priest got mad, there's no other word for it, and his face went green, and he quietly whispered so that the old women near by shouldn't hear: "Then why are you as silent as a post, damn you?" And he gave Diemid one between the eyes with a candlestick.'

Above the roar of laughter rose Diemid's rumbling bass:

'You're lying! He didn't strike me.'

'Surely he did?' Old Shchukar was terribly surprised. 'Well, all the same he wanted to, I expect. And so he refused him the sacrament. Well, citizens, Diemid is silent, but we'll talk, that's nothing to do with us. Although a good word, like mine, is silver, silence is gold.'

'You ought to change all your silver into gold. It would be more peaceful for others then,' Nagulnov counselled him.

Like dead wood bursting into flame the laughter arose, then died away. Shchukar's story seemed likely to destroy the business-like mood of the meeting. But Davidov swept the smile from his face and asked:

'What did you want to say about the work rates? Come to the point.'

'Me, d'you mean?' Shchukar wiped his sweating brow with his sleeve, and blinked. 'I didn't want to say anything about them. I was clearing up the point about Diemid. But the rates had nothing to do with it.'

'I forbid you to say any more at this conference. You must talk to the point, you can do your gossiping afterwards. Fact!'

'A hectare a day for each plough,' one of the collective farmers, Ivan Batalshchikov, proposed.

But Dubtsiev indignantly shouted:

'You're barmy! Tell your fairy stories to your old woman! You can sweat all over, but you'll never do a hectare in a day.'

'I've done it before. A little bit less, perhaps . . .'

'Yes, a little less!'

'Half a hectare of hard ground to each plough.'

After long argument the daily ploughing rates were fixed at three-fifths of a hectare on hard ground, and three-quarters of a hectare on soft ground. The rates for sowing were fixed at $3\frac{1}{4}$ hectares with an eleven-row sower, 4 hectares with a thirteen-row, and $4\frac{3}{4}$ with a seventeen-row sower.

As there were 184 yoke of bullocks and 73 horses in Gremyachy, the plan for spring sowing was not excessive. And so Yakov Lukich pointed out:

'We'll get all the sowing done early, if we put our backs into it. It works out that each team has to do $4\frac{1}{2}$ hectares during the whole of the spring. That's nothing to speak of.'

'And in Tubyanskoe it worked out at eight for each team,' Liubishkin stated.

'Let them sweat till they're wet between the legs if they want to! Last autumn we were ploughing until the first frosts in November, and by the beginning of October they were starting to share out the brushwood for firing.'

It was next decided that the seed grain fund must be collected within three days. Then they listened to a joyless statement made by the smith, Ippolit Shaly. Being a little deaf, he spoke in a loud voice, and stood turning his sootily greasy, three-cornered cap round and round in his black, work-worn fingers, for he was shy of speaking in front of such a large audience.

'We can get everything repaired,' he said. 'The work won't halt through me. But so far as iron's concerned, everything must be done to get some at once. We've got no iron for the shares and the coulters. There's nothing we can work with. I'll start on the sowers tomorrow. I need an assistant, and coal. And what payment shall I get from the collective farm?'

Davidov reassured him in regard to payment, and proposed that Yakov Lukich should go the next day to the district town to get coal and iron. The question of establishing fodder reserves for the spring sowing was quickly settled. Then Yakov Lukich made a speech:

'We've got to consider carefully, brothers, where to sow and what to sow, and we must choose a good agriculturist, one who's educated and knows his job. You know that before the collective farm we had five agrarian officials, but there's nothing to show that they ever did anything. We must choose an agriculturist from the older cossacks, one who knows all our land, both near and far. Until our new method of working the land is well organized he'll be of great use to us. This is what I say: we've got almost the whole village in the collective farm now. They're all coming in, little by little. Only some fifty farms are left to be worked by individual peasants, and they'll wake up and find themselves collective farmers tomorrow. And so we must sow scientifically, as science teaches us. I'm in favour of using half the two hundred hectares which have been set apart for thorough ploughing to try the "Kherson" fallow on. We're going to turn over 110 hectares of virgin soil this spring, we shan't get a good harvest from it this year in any case, so I suggest we try out the "Kherson" fallow on it.'

'What is this Kherson fallow you're talking about?'

'We've never heard of it.'

'Explain how it works in practice,' Davidov asked, proud of the knowledge displayed by his highly-experienced manager.

'Why, it's a kind of fallow; sometimes it's called the "corridor" or the "American" fallow. It's very interesting and well thought out. For example, this year you sow your land with maize or sunflowers, and you sow them in rows much farther apart, twice as wide as usual, so that instead of getting the normal harvest you get only fifty per cent. Then you take off the heads of the maize, or you break off the sunflower caps, and you leave the stalks standing. And the same autumn you sow winter wheat in between the stalks along the corridors.'

'But how do you sow it? Surely the sower will break the stalks?' Kondrat Maidannikov, who was listening open-mouthed, eagerly asked.

'Why should it break them? The rows are far apart, and so it doesn't touch the stalks, but passes between them. And then the snow falls and lies among the stalks. It'll thaw slowly and give more moisture. Then in the spring, when the wheat begins to grow, these stalks die and wither off. It's very attractively thought out. I hadn't tried it myself, but I was intending to this year. It's sound reckoning, and can't go wrong.'

'I say yes to that proposal. I support it!' Davidov nudged Nagulnov's leg under the table, and whispered: 'You see? And you were against him...'

'And I'm still against him.'

'That's only your obstinacy. Fact! You're as stubborn as an ox.'

The conference adopted their manager's proposal. After discussing and deciding a number of minor matters, they began to disperse. Davidov and Nagulnov had not quite reached the village Soviet when a stocky youngster in an open leather jerkin strode towards them from the Soviet yard. Holding on his checkered town cap with one hand, and struggling against the gusty wind, he swiftly drew nearer.

'Someone from the district, it looks like,' Nagulnov screwed up his eyes.

The youngster walked right up to them, and put his hand to the peak of his cap in a military salute as he asked:

'You're not from the village Soviet, are you?'

'And who do you want?'

'The secretary of the local nucleus, or the chairman of the Soviet.'

'I'm the nucleus secretary, and this is the chairman of the collective farm.'

'Ah, that's fine ! I'm a member of the propaganda column, comrades. We've just arrived, and we're waiting for you at the Soviet.'

The snub-nosed and swarthy-featured youngster ran his eyes over Davidov's face, and smiled interrogatively. 'You're not Davidov, are you, comrade?' he asked.

'Yes, my name's Davidov.'

'I thought I recognized you. We met at the Regional Committee office a couple of weeks ago. I work in the town as a presser at an oil works.'

Only then did Davidov realize why he had caught the sweetish scent of sunflower seed oil as the lad approached them. The youngster's greasy leather jerkin was saturated with the ineradicable, flavourous smell.

Chapter 22

Propaganda Column

A THICKSET man was standing on the porch of the Soviet, with his back to the yard. He was wearing a pleated black leather, fur-lined jacket, and a black cap with ear-flaps making a white cross on the top. His shoulders were remarkably broad, and his ample back filled all the doorway between the posts. He stood straddling his short, sturdy legs, and looked as stocky and powerful as a steppe elm. His high boots with their creased legs and heels worn one-sidedly seemed to be growing into the floor of the porch, and crushing it under the weight of his bearish body.

'That's comrade Kondratko, the commander of our propaganda column,' the youngster remarked as he strode alongside Davidov. And noticing Davidov's smile, he added in an undertone:

'We jokingly call him "daddy Quadratko". He's a turner from the Lugansk locomotive works. He's old enough to be my father, but he's a great lad.'

At that moment Kondratko, hearing voices, turned his crimson face in their direction, and the white teeth gleamed in a smile beneath his hanging brown whiskers.

'Aha, I expect you're the local authorities,' he exclaimed. 'How are you, brothers?'

'Good day, comrade,' Davidov replied. 'I'm the chairman of the collective farm, and this is the secretary of the party nucleus.'

'Good! Come into the hut, where all my boys are waiting for you. I'm in charge of this propaganda column, so I can talk with you at once. My name's Kondratko. And if any of my lads tell you I'm called Quadratko, don't believe them, for they're such a lot of idiots as you wouldn't believe,' he said in a thunderous bass voice, as he squeezed sideways through the door.

Osip Kondratko had worked for more than twenty years in Southern Russia. He had been employed at Taganrog, at Rostov-on-Don, and finally at Lugansk, where he had joined the Red Guard in order to support the youthful Soviet government on his shoulders. During the years he had lived among Russians he had lost the purity of his native Ukrainian tongue, but his features and his drooping Shevchenko whiskers still betrayed his origin. In 1918, together with the Donietz miners he had marched under the leadership of Voroshilov through the blazing counter-revoluntionary and insurrectionary cossack villages to Tsaritsin. And ever afterwards, whenever the conversation happened to turn to talk of the years of civil war, whose echoes live undying in the hearts and memories of its participants, Kondratko would say with quiet pride: 'Our Klementy's from Lugansk. We used to know each other quite well, and maybe we shall meet again sooner or later. With me it's a case of "once seen, never forgotten". When we were fighting the Whites outside Tsaritsin time and again he joked with me. "Well, Kondratko, how's things?" he'd ask. "So you're still alive, you old wolf?" "Still alive," I'd say, "Klementy Voroshilov. I can't stop to die just yet, while we've got the mad counter-revolutionaries to fight." If we were to meet again he'd give me a hug at once,' Kondratko confidently ended.

After the war he found himself back in Lugansk, and worked in the transport department of the Cheka. Then he was transferred to party work, and finally sent back to the locomotive works. Then he was mobilized by the party and sent to assist in the work of collectivizing the villages. Of recent years he had grown stout, and even broader in the shoulders. None of his old comrades would have recognized him as the same Osip Kondratko who, during the attack on Tsaritsin in 1918, had cut down four cossacks, and a captain whom Wrangel himself had given a gold-chased sabre for bravery'. Osip had developed 'middle-age spread', and was beginning to look old; little blue and violet veins were showing in his face. As a horse is covered with grey foam after a swift and wearying gallop, so time had touched Osip with grey; even among his drooping whiskers the treacherous colour was settling. But his will and strength still served him, and as for his immeasurably increasing corpulence, that was nothing. 'Taras Bulba was fatter than me, and yet look how he cut down the Poles! That's the point. If I have to fight again, I'll still be able to turn one officer into two! And what are my half a hundred years? My father lived to be a hundred under the Tsarist regime, and under our own government I'll see a hundred and fifty!' So he declared, when anyone remarked on his age and growing fatness.

Kondratko led the way into the village Soviet. 'Quiet, boys!' he roared, 'here's the chairman of the collective farm and the nucleus secretary. They must tell us at once how things are going here, and then we'll know what we've got to do. Sit down, all of you.'

Some fifteen of the propaganda column members seated themselves around the room, while two more went out into the yard to attend to the horses. As he scanned the newcomers' faces, Davidov recognized three workers from the district: an agricultural specialist, a teacher from the secondary school, and a doctor. The others had been sent from the regional centre, and, judging by their appearance, some of them were industrial workers. While they were sitting down to the accompaniment of shifting chairs and coughing, Kondratko whispered to Davidov:

'Give orders for hay to be put down for our horses, and for the drivers to stay by them.' Winking cunningly, he added: 'Or maybe you've got some oats you can spare?'

'We haven't any oats left, except for sowing,' Davidov replied. The next moment he turned cold and had an acute feeling of embarrassment and dislike for himself. There were still over a hundred poods of fodder oats left, but he had refused Kondratko's request because he was keeping the oats for the beginning of the spring sowing campaign, and was watching over them as the apple of his eye. Yakov Lukich doled out this precious grain only to the farm administration horses, and to them only after long and difficult journeys, all but weeping even then.

'There's the petty property instinct coming out! It's beginning to affect even me!' Davidov thought. 'I never felt anything like that before. Fact! Perhaps I could let them have some oats after all? No, it would be awkward now.'

'Then maybe you've got some barley,' Kondratko asked.

'We haven't any barley either.'

That was certainly true, but before Kondratko's smiling, knowing gaze he burst out:

'I mean it seriously. We haven't got any barley.'

'You'd make a fine farmer. And even a kulak ...' Kondratko said, smiling into his whiskers. But seeing that Davidov was frowning, he embraced him, slightly raising him off the floor. 'Now, now, I'm only joking. If you haven't got any, well, you haven't. Save all you can so that you've got something for your own stock. Now then, brothers, to business. And dead silence, please.' Turning to Davidov and Nagulnov, he said: 'We've come in order to give you a hand; you know that, I expect. So tell us how things stand with you.'

After Davidov had made a circumstantial report on the course of collectivization and the establishment of a seed grain fund, Kondratko decided:

'There's nothing we can do here.'

Clearing his throat, he pulled a notebook and a map out of his pocket, and ran his fat finger over the map. 'We'll go on to Tubyanskoe,' he remarked. 'It's quite a short distance to that village, I see, and we'll leave three men here to give you a hand with the work. As for collecting the grain fund quickly, I'd advise you to hold a meeting first and tell the workers what it's all about, and then develop your mass work,' he unhurriedly continued.

Davidov listened with satisfaction to his speech, and although at times he could not understand some of Kondratko's Ukrainian phrases, he strongly felt that in general the man was laying down a sound plan of campaign for the collection of the seed grain. And Kondratko as unhurriedly indicated the course it was necessary to take in regard to the individual peasants and the richer sections of the village, if, contrary to expectations, they continued to be obstinate and resisted the collection of the grain. He mentioned the methods which had been found most effective in the propaganda column's experience of other villages. And throughout his remarks he spoke gently, without the least suggestion that he desired to direct and teach. In the course of his talk he turned to consult Davidov, or Nagulnov, or Razmiotnov, who had also arrived. 'This matter's got to be developed like this. What do you people of Gremyachy think?' 'And that's just what I was thinking,' were phrases frequently on his lips.

As Davidov smilingly watched the turner Kondratko's crimson, heavily-veined face, and the crafty twinkle in his deep-set eyes, he thought: 'He's a clever devil! He doesn't want to cramp our initiative, so he seems to be giving us advice. But make any objection to his sound attitude and he'll turn you into his way of thinking just as easily. Fact! I've met men like him before!'

One further little incident strengthened his warm feeling for Kondratko. Before the Ukrainian drove off with his column he called aside one of the three men he was leaving behind in Gremyachy, and had a brief talk to him.

'What are you wearing your pistol outside your jacket for?' he asked. 'Take it off at once!'

'But, comrade Kondratko, the kulaks . . . the class struggle . . .'

'What are you trying to tell me? The kulaks! Well, what about the kulaks? You've come here to make propaganda. But if you're afraid of the kulaks you can have a pistol, only don't dare to wear it outside your jacket. You're a clever lad! You've got a gun, haven't you! You're like a little child! Swaggering around wearing your pistol so that everybody can see it! Put it in your pocket at once, so that the kulaks' supporters won't be able to say of you: "Strange ways they've got of making propaganda, with pistols!"' And through his teeth he added: 'You fool!'

As he clambered into his sledge he called Davidov to him, and said as he twisted the button on his coat:

'I've given my boys a thorough drilling! They'll work like devils now. And you do your job well, too, so that everything gets done as quickly as possible. I shall be in Tubyanskoe, and if anything happens let me know. We've got to give a show when we arrive there, perhaps this very evening. You should see me playing the kulak! I'm such a size that I can act the part to the life! Ah, what old Kondratko has come down to in his old age! And don't worry about the oats, I don't bear any grudge against you for that.' He smiled as he threw his broad shoulders against the back of the sledge.

'What a great block of a head, what shoulders, what legs under him! He's as massive as a tractor,' Razmiotnov laughed. 'Harness him up by himself to a plough and he'd pull it, and you'd save three yoke of oxen. I can't help wondering where such folk get it all from. What do you think, Makar?'

'You're getting to be as big a magpie as old Shchukar,' Makar testily answered.

Chapter 23

A Wrecker at Work

WHILE living with Yakov Lukich, captain Polovtsiev was making active preparations for the spring and the rising. At night he sat till cock-crow in his little room, writing, sketching maps with a copying-ink pencil, or reading. Sometimes Yakov would look in, and would see the captain with his great forehead bent over the little table, soundlessly moving his firm lips as he read. But occasionally he found him in a state of profound thought. At such times he usually sat resting his head on his hands, his fingers thrust into the sparse, long locks of his fair hair. His stern jaws worked as though they were chewing something unyieldingly hard, his eyes were half closed. Only after Yakov had called him several times would he raise his head, and then his anger would flame up in his tiny, terribly immobile pupils. 'Well, what do you want?' his bass voice would bark. At such moments Yakov Lukich felt even greater fear and involuntary respect for him.

It was part of Ostrovnov's duty to inform Polovtsiev daily of all that was happening in the village and the collective farm. He reported conscientiously, but every day brought Polovtsiev fresh bitterness, and deepened the lines in his cheeks.

The night after the kulaks were expelled from Gremyachy the captain did not sleep a wink. His heavy but quiet tread was heard continually until dawn, and Yakov Lukich, who went on tiptoe to the door of the little room, heard him grinding his teeth and muttering: 'They're cutting the ground from under my feet. Robbing us of a basis. They must be cut down, cut down without mercy!' Then he was silent, and he would walk up and down again, treading quietly in his felt boots, and scraping his fingers over his body, scratching his chest as was his habit. Then he would begin to mutter: 'Cut them down, cut them down!' And more quietly, with a muffled scream in his voice: 'Merciful God, almighty and just! Help us! When will the hour come? Lord, hasten the day of thy vengeance!'

At dawn the anxious Yakov Lukich went once more to the room door, and set his ear to the keyhole. Polovtsiev was muttering a prayer: with a groan he dropped to his knees, and bowed his head to the floor. Then he put out the light and lay down, but even as he was half-asleep he once again distinctly whispered: 'Cut them down . . . to the last man!' And he groaned.

Some nights later, Yakov Lukich heard a knock at the window shutter, and he went out into the porch.

'Who's there?' he asked.

'Open, master!'

'Who is it?'

'I want to see Alexander Anisimovich,' came in a whisper from the other side of the door.

'Want to see who? There's nobody of that name here.'

'Tell him I'm from Chorny, with a packet.'

After a momentary hesitation Lukich opened the door. 'Let come what may,' he thought. A stocky man with his head enveloped in a hood entered. Polovtsiev led him into his room, and closed the door fast. For an hour and a half the muffled sound of hurried talk was audible. Meantime Yakov's son gave the new arrival's horse some hay, loosened the saddle-girths, and removed the bit from its mouth.

From that time horse couriers began to arrive almost every day, not at midnight, but towards the dawn, usually about three or four o'clock in the morning. Evidently they had to travel farther than the first man had come.

A strangely dual existence Yakov Lukich lived during those days. Each morning he went to the collective farm office, talked with Davidov, with the carpenters, and with the brigade leaders. His cares for the building of yards for the cattle, the treatment of the grain, and repair of the implements left him not a minute for other thoughts. Unexpectedly to himself the energetic Yakov Lukich found himself in a very pleasant state of active bustle and unceasing cares, the only essential difference from his old life being that now he rode around the village not on business for his own profit, but on work for the collective farm. But he was glad, only too glad to avoid his sombre thoughts, to avoid thinking at all. He was attracted by his work, he wished to do well at it, and his mind was occupied with planning all kinds of schemes. He vigorously set about the task of strengthening the cattle-yards, and the construction of a large stable. He directed the removal of certain granaries, and the construction of a new and bigger one. But in the evening, as soon as the bustle of the day had died away and it was time for him to go home, at the very thought that Polovtsiev, gloomy and terrible in his loneliness, was sitting in his little room like a carrion vulture on a burial mound, he felt weak in the pit of his stomach, his movements grew languid, and his body felt indescribably weary. When he returned home, before having his supper he would go in to see Polovtsiev.

'Tell me the news,' the captain would order, rolling a cigarette and preparing to listen intently. And Yakov Lukich would tell of his day spent in collective farm activities. Usually Polovtsiev listened in silence, and only once, when Yakov was informing him of the distribution of kulak clothing and boots among the poor cossacks, did he interrupt with:

'In the spring we'll tear the throats out of every man who took anything. All of them ... Make a list of all those swine. D'you hear?'

'I've got a list, Alexander Anisimovich.'

'Have you got it here?'

'Yes.'

'Give it to me.'

Polovtsiev took the list and made a careful copy of it, writing down Christian names, patronymics, and surnames, the articles each had received, and setting a cross against the name of everyone who had had clothes or boots.

When he had finished talking to Polovtsiev Yakov Lukich would go to have his supper. But before going to bed he would return and receive his instructions for the following day.

It was at Polovtsiev's instigation that on 8 February Yakov Lukich ordered the leader of the second brigade to send four sledges and men to cart river sand to the bullock yards. The sand was brought. Lukich gave orders for the earthen floors of the bullockyards to be thoroughly cleaned, then spread with sand. The work was nearly finished when Davidov entered the yard assigned to the second brigade.

'What are you doing with that sand?' he asked Diemid, who had been appointed brigade bullock-yardsman.

'We're spreading it over the yard,' Diemid answered.

'What for?'

No answer.

'What for, I asked you?'

'I don't know.'

'Who gave orders for it to be done?'

'The manager.'

'And what did he say?'

'He said it was to keep the place clean. He's making up jobs for us to do, the son of a bitch!'

'That's a fine idea! Fact! The place certainly will be clean, and the dung lying around might poison the oxen. They've got to be kept clean, too, so the veterinary surgeons say. Fact! And it's no good your ... getting dissatisfied. Why, the oxen yard's good to look at now, it's so clean with this sand. Isn't it? Don't you think so?'

But Davidov could not get Diemid to talk; the silent one went off to the chaffshed, and Davidov, mentally approving his manager's initiative, went home to have his dinner.

In the early evening Liubishkin came running to him, and indignantly demanded:

'So we've got to put down sand instead of straw to the oxen from now on, have we?'

'Yes, that's right.'

'And it's your Ostrovnov that's given the order, isn't it? Is he mad? Whoever heard of that before? And how about you, comrade Davidov? Surely you don't agree with such an idiotic trick?'

'Don't get agitated, Liubishkin. It's all a question of hygiene, and Ostrovnov's quite right. It's safer when it's clean, there won't be any infection hanging around to be caught.'

'What sort of "hyena" do you call this, damn it? What are the oxen to lie on? And with the frosts we're getting now! The bullocks keep warm in the straw, but you try lying on the sand yourself, and see how you like it!'

'Now, please stop making objections. We've got to give up our old methods of looking after cattle. We must have a scientific basis for everything.'

'But what sort of basis d'you call this?' Liubishkin brought his black cap with a smack against the leg of his boot, and rushed off with a face redder than a beetroot.

In the morning twenty-three oxen were unable to rise from the ground of the yards. During the night the frozen sand could not soak up the bullocks' urine, and they had been frozen fast to the damp sand. Some of them struggled to their feet, leaving scraps of their skin behind on the stony sand; four of them broke their frozen tails, the others were all sick.

In carrying out Polovtsiev's instructions Yakov Lukich had over-reached himself. 'We'll get their bullocks frozen for them,' Polovtsiev had said the evening before he arranged for the sand to be spread. 'They're fools, they'll believe that you did it for the sake of cleanliness. But look after the horses, so that they can be ready for service this very day if we want them.' And Lukich had carried out the instruction.

In the morning Davidov sent for him, fastened the door, and, without raising his eyes, demanded:

'What's your game...'

'I made a mistake, dear comrade Davidov. And I ... my God ... I'm ready to tear my hair out...'

'What was your game, you reptile?' Davidov went white, and his eyes filled with tears of rage. He suddenly lifted his head and stared into Yakov's face. 'Going in for wrecking, are you? Didn't you know you mustn't put sand down in the yards? Didn't you know the oxen might freeze to it?'

'I wanted the oxen ... God knows, I didn't know.'

'Shut up ! I don't believe that you, a capable farmer like you, didn't know.'

Yakov Lukich bursts into tears and snuffling through his nose, muttered over and over again:

'I wanted the yards to be kept clean ... I didn't want the dung lying ... I didn't know, I didn't think it would work out like that...'

'Go and hand over your job to Ushakov. We'll have you tried for this.'

'Comrade Davidov...'

'Get out, I tell you !'

After Lukich had gone Davidov thought the incident over more quietly. And it began to appear to him that it was nonsensical to suspect Lukich of wrecking. After all, Ostrovnov was not a kulak. And if anyone had ever called him that, it was purely because of personal enmity. Soon after Ostrovnov had been appointed manager Liubishkin had happened to remark: 'Ostrovnov himself used to be a kulak.' Davidov at once checked up the statement, and found that many years before Yakov Lukich had certainly lived prosperously enough, but then a failure of crops had ruined him and reduced him to the level of the middling peasants. Davidov thought and thought, and came to the conclusion that Lukich was not to be blamed for the unfortunate accident with the bullocks, and that he had given orders for sand to be strewn in the bullockyards out of a desire to have clean liness, and partly, perhaps, through his own continual zeal for the latest methods. 'If he had been a wrecker he wouldn't have worked so hard as he has; and besides, his pair of bullocks suffered, too,' Davidov thought. 'No, Ostrovnov's a devoted collective farm worker, and the accident with the sand is simply an unfortunate mistake. Fact!' He remembered how carefully and intelligently Lukich had had the warm winter yards built, how economically he served out hay, how, on one occasion, when three collective farm horses fell sick, he had spent all night in the stables and had himself administered enemas, pouring hemp oil into them so that the colic should pass. He had been the first to propose that the man responsible for their sickness – Kuzhenkov, the stable-man to the first brigade – who, it transpired, for a whole week had fed the horses only on barley straw, should be turned out of the collective farm. So far as Davidov had observed, Lukich cared for the horses better than anyone else. Remembering all this, he felt ashamed and at fault for his outburst of unjustified wrath. He felt awkward at having shouted so roughly at a good collective farm worker, a management committee member who had the respect of his fellow-citizens, and had even suspected him of wrecking because he had been guilty of one piece of carelessness. 'What nonsense!' Davidov tousled his hair, cleared his throat vigorously in his annoyance with himself, and went out.

He found Yakov Lukich talking to the book-keeper, holding a bunch of keys in his hand, his lips quivering with resentment.

'Look here, Ostrovnov,' Davidov said. 'Don't hand over your work to Ushakov. You keep on with it. But if it happens again ... I tell you ... Send for the district veterinary surgeon, and tell the brigade leaders to let the frozen oxen rest.'

Ostrovnov's first attempt to damage the collective farm passed off well enough for him. Polovtsiev temporarily released him from further tasks, as the captain was occupied with other matters: another man had come to visit him, at night as usual. As soon as he entered the hut Polovtsiev took him into his little room, and gave orders that no one was to enter. They talked together until the early morning, and the next day Polovtsiev, in much more cheerful mood, called Yakov Lukich into his room.

'This man's a member of our Alliance, my dear Yakov Lukich,' he explained; 'a companion-in-arms, so to speak: lieutenant Vatslav Avgustovich Lyatievsky. Look after him well. And this is my host,' he turned to the newcomer, 'a cossack of the old breed, but at the moment the manager of the collective farm. A Soviet employee, one may say.'

The lieutenant rose from the bed, and stretched his broad white hand out to Yakov Lukich. He looked about thirty, and was gaunt and yellow of face. His wavy black hair was combed back, and cascaded down to the stiff collar of his black satin shirt. A thin moustache curled over his smiling lips. His left eye was perpetually screwed up, evidently as the result of a wound; under it the skin was puckered into lifeless folds, and was as dry and dead as an autumn leaf. But the screwed-up eye did not contradict, but rather emphasized the humorous expression of the former lieutenant's face. The hazel eye seemed about to wink maliciously, the skin to smooth out and spread in a radiation of wrinkles to the temple, and the high-spirited lieutenant to give vent to youthful and infectious laughter. The apparent bagginess of his clothes was intentional; it did not constrain the wearer's swift movements and did not conceal his spruce bearing.

That day Polovtsiev was unusually cheerful, and was even gracious to Yakov Lukich. He quickly brought the meaningless talk to an end, and, turning to Yakov, informed him :

'Lieutenant Lyatievsky will be staying with you for a couple of weeks, but I'm going away as soon as it's dark. Supply Vatslav Avgustovich with everything he needs; all his orders are my orders, you understand? Well then, Yakov my dear Lukich !' he added with considerable emphasis, laying his swollen-veined hand on Yakov's knee, 'we'll be beginning soon now. We've only got a little longer to wait. Tell that to our cossacks, let them keep their spirits up. And now you can go; we've got to finish our talk.'

Something extraordinary must have happened to compel Polovtsiev to leave Gremyachy Log for a couple of weeks. Yakov Lukich burned with curiosity to know what it was. In the hope of finding out, he went into the hall where Polovtsiev had listened to his conversation with Davidov, and set his ear against the thin partition. He could just catch fragments of the conversation going on in the room on the other side.

'Unquestionably you must make contact with Bikadorov,' he heard Lyatievsky say. 'Of course at your meeting His Excellency will inform you that the plans ... a favourable situation ... It's splendid ... In Salsk region ... armoured train ... in the event of defeat...'

'Shsh !' said Polovtsiev.

'Nobody can overhear us, I hope?'

'But all the same... conspiratorial methods always...'

Lyatievsky spoke still more quietly, so that Yakov Lukich involuntarily lost the thread of his remarks. 'Defeat ... of course ... Afghanistan ... With their help we can get through to ...'

'But the means ... the G.P.U. ...' The rest of Polovtsiev's remarks was one confused jumble.

'There is a variant: to cross the frontier ... Minsk ... avoiding ... I assure you that ... the frontier guard ... the general staff departments will unquestionably receive ... A colonel, I know his name ... conditional appearance ... and that's a tremendous help ! Such patronage... It's not so much the subsidy...'

'And *his* opinion?'

'He's sure the general will repeat ... much. I've been told verbally that ... extremely tense ... exploiting ... not to lose a moment...'

The voices dropped into a low whisper, and Yakov Lukich, who had understood nothing of this disconnected conversation, sighed and went off to the collective farm office. He approached the hut which formerly had belonged to Titok, and, as was his habit, ran his eyes over the white board nailed above the gate, on which was the inscription: 'Administration of the Gremyachy Collective Farm "Stalin".' And once more he had his customary feeling of being pulled in two opposite directions. But then he remembered lieutenant Lyatievsky, and Polovtsiev's confident words: 'We'll be beginning soon, now,' and with malignant joy, with anger at himself he thought: 'The sooner the better ! Otherwise between them and the collective farm I'll be torn in two like a bullock on a slippery road.'

That night Polovtsiev saddled his horse, put all his documents into his saddle-bags, took some provisions for the journey, and said good-bye. Yakov Lukich heard the captain's horse dance with a dry clippety-clop of hoofs past the window.

The newcomer proved to be no man for sitting still, and he was militarily unceremonious. For whole days he roamed about the hut, gay and smiling, joking with the women, giving no rest to Yakov's old mother, who mortally hated tobacco smoke. He went about as though he had no fear of outsiders dropping into the hut, so much so that Yakov had to go so far as to hint to him :

'You should be more careful ... You never know when somebody might come in and find you here, Your Excellency.'

'And is it written on my forehead that I am "Your Excellency"?'

'No, but they might ask who you are and where you've come from.'

'My pockets are full of documents, my friend, and if things turn difficult and they don't believe them, I'll present them with this mandate here. With it one can pass everywhere !' From his breast he drew out a black, dull-gleaming Mauser, smiling as he did so, his immobile eye, half-hidden beneath the swelling fold of skin, staring challengingly.

The dashing lieutenant's gaiety was not at all to Ostrovnov's taste, especially after an incident which occurred when he arrived home one evening from the office. He heard muffled voices, a stifled laugh and a noise in the porch. Striking a match, he saw the lieutenant with his single glittering eye, in one corner behind a box of bran, while Yakov's daughter-in-law was at his side, as crimson as red bunting, disconcertedly pulling down her skirt and adjusting the kerchief which had slipped to the back of her head. Without a word, Yakov Lukich was about to pass through into the kitchen, but Lyatievsky overtook him at the threshold, clapped him on the back, and whispered :

'You keep your tongue quiet, daddy ! Don't upset your little son ! You know what we soldiers are like ! Speed and audacity ! Where's the man who hasn't sown his wild oats in his young days? Here's a cigarette, have a smoke. You've had a fling with your daughter-in-law yourself, I expect. Ah, you old rogue !'

Yakov Lukich was so dumbfounded that he took the cigarette, and went into the kitchen only after he had lit it from Lyatievsky's match. As the lieutenant held the match for his host he said in a moralizing tone, stifling a yawn:

'When anyone does you a service, strikes a match for you for example, you should say "thank you". You've got bad manners. And you're manager of the collective farm, too! In the old days I wouldn't have taken you on as my batman!'

'The devil's hung a fine lodger around my neck!' thought Yakov Lukich.

Lyatievsky's insolence had a depressing effect on Lukich. His son was not at home, but had gone to the district to fetch the veterinary surgeon. Yakov decided to say nothing about the incident to him, but called his daughter-in-law into the granary, and there quietly gave her a lesson, administering a good beating with a saddle-girth. He did not strike her on the face, but on her back and buttocks, so that no marks of the beating were visible. And even Siemion did not notice anything when he returned. He reached home after dark, and his wife got his supper ready. When she sat down on the very edge of the bench Siemion simple-mindedly exclaimed:

'What are you sitting like that for, as if you were a guest?'

'I've got a boil,' she flared up and rose from her seat.

'You should chew some bread and onion and make a poultice of it; it'll draw the boil at once,' Yakov Lukich compassionately advised her as he sat by the stove twisting a waxed thread. His daughter-in-law flashed her eyes at him, but she meekly answered:

'Thank you, father; it'll get better of itself.'

Occasionally couriers brought packets for Lyatievsky. After reading the contents he at once burned them in the stove. Then he began to drink at night, no longer played about with Yakov's daughter-in-law, grew morose, and more and more frequently asked Yakov or Siemion to get him a 'half-litre', thrusting new crackling chervonietz notes into their hands. When he was drunk he was willing to talk about politics, being disposed to express broad generalizations and to explain his own objective estimate of the situation. One day he completely discomposed Yakov Lukich. He called him into his room, treated him to vodka, and asked with a cynical wink:

'Are you disorganizing the collective farm?'

'No, why should I?' Yakov Lukich pretended to be astonished.

'Then what methods are you using?'

'What do you mean?'

'What work are you carrying on? You're a wrecker, you know. So what are you doing there? Are you poisoning the horses with strychnine, are you doing damage to the implements, or what?'

'I've not been ordered to touch the horses; on the contrary, in fact,' Yakov admitted. Of late he had hardly touched drink, so the glass of vodka had considerable effect on him, and opened his mouth. He was about to complain of how much he suffered through having simultaneously to build up and break down the socialized village agriculture, but Lyatievsky would not let him talk. Drinking down his own vodka and not pouring out any more for Lukich, the lieutenant asked:

'But why did you join in with us, you block-headed fool? I ask you, why did you? What the devil for? There's nothing else Polovtsiev and I can do; we're going to our death. Yes, to our death! We may win, although, Hamlet, there's shamefully little chance of that, you know ... One per cent, not more! But we've got nothing to lose but our chains, as the communists say. But how about you? In my opinion you're simply an evening sacrifice. There's no reason why you shouldn't go on living, living like the fool you are. I don't believe Hamlets like you can build socialism, but all the same, you could stir up the water in the mud of the world. But now there'll be a rising, and they'll bowl you over, you grey-headed devil, or they'll simply take you prisoner and send you to Archangel province as an unwitting class enemy. And there you'll chop down pines until Communism's second Advent. Ah, you donkey! I realize why we've got to have a rising, for I'm a noble. My father had some five thousand hectares of arable land and almost eight hundred of forest. It was a mortal shame for me and such as me to leave our country and to have to earn our daily bread somewhere in exile, in the sweat of our brow, as they say. But you? Who are you? A grower of grain and an eater of grain. A dung beetle! They didn't shoot enough of you cossack sons of bitches during the civil war!'

'But we can't go on living as we are,' Yakov Lukich objected. 'They've choked us with taxes, they're taking away our property. There's no life left for the individual farmer to live. If it hadn't been for that we wouldn't need you nobles and your likes. Not for anything would I have taken such a road otherwise.'

'Taxes! You stop to think! As if the peasants of other countries don't pay taxes. They pay more than you do!'

'That can't be.'

'I assure you it's true.'

'But how do you know how they live and what they pay?'

'I've lived there, that's how I know.'

'So you've come from abroad?'

'And what's that to do with you?'

'I'm only interested.'

'If you know too much you'll grow old too quick! Go and get me some more vodka.'

Yakov Lukich sent his son Siemion for the vodka, and, feeling that he wanted to be alone, went to the threshing floor and sat for a couple of hours at the foot of a stack of straw. 'Damned ugly-mug! He talked at me until my head swelled. Perhaps he was seeing what I'd say and whether I'll turn against them, and then when Alexander Anisimovich comes back he'll tell him, and they'll kill me as he killed Khoprov. Or maybe that's what he really thinks? The drunkard says what the sober man thinks. Perhaps I shouldn't have got tangled up with Polovtsiev; I ought to have put up with life in the collective farm for a year or two. Maybe the government will break up the farms within a twelve-month, when they see how badly things are going with them. And then I'd begin to live like a man again. Ah, my God, my God! What am I to do now? My head won't stand it ... it's all one now ... Knock the owl against the stump or the stump against the owl, it's all one to the owl, he won't live.'

A wind tore through the wattle-fence and strode across the threshing floor. It swept up the straw scattered by the gate and carried it to the stack, beat it into the holes left by the dogs, combed the ragged corners of the stack, and swept the dry snow from the top. The wind was strong and cold. Yakov Lukich spent a long time trying to decide which way it was blowing, but without success. It seemed to be blowing all around the stack, and from all sides in turn. Disturbed by the wind, the mice scurried about in the straw. They ran squeaking along their secret burrows, sometimes quite close to Yakov's back as he leaned against the stack. Listening to the wind, to the rustling of the straw, the squeaking of the mice and the scraping of the crane at the well, Yakov Lukich must have dozed, for all the nocturnal sounds seemed like a distant, mournful music. With half-closed, tear-filled eyes he gazed at the starry sky; he breathed in the scent of the straw and the steppe wind; everything around him seemed beautiful and simple.

But at midnight a mounted courier arrived from Polovtsiev, who was at Voiskovoi. Lyatievsky read the letter, which was marked 'urgent', and awoke Lukich, who was sleeping in the kitchen.

'Here, read this!' he said.

Rubbing his eyes, Yakov took the letter. The writing was in copying-ink pencil on a leaf taken from a notebook, and in a clear hand, using the obsolete letters of Tsarist days.

'Lieutenant:

'We have received reliable information that the Central Committee of the Bolsheviks is collecting grain from the agricultural population, ostensibly for collective farm sowing. But in fact the grain is going to be sold abroad, and the peasants, including the collective farmers, will be destined to ruthless starvation. In presentiment of its inevitable and imminent end, the Soviet government is selling the last grain and completing the ruin of Russia. I order you immediately to develop among the people of Gremyachy Log, where you are at present representative of our Alliance, an agitation against the collection of so-called sowing grain. Let Y.L. know the contents of this letter, and instruct him to begin explanatory activities at once. It is highly necessary to hinder the collection of grain at all costs.'

Next morning, instead of going to the collective farm office, Yakov Lukich visited Bannik and the other individual farmers whom he had enrolled in the 'Alliance for the Liberation of the Don'.

Chapter 24

Going too Far

THE brigade of three men left behind by Kondratko, the propaganda column commander, set to work to collect the seed grain fund. One of the huts vacated by the kulaks was assigned to them as headquarters. Here one of them, the young agricultural expert Vietutniev, spent most of the day working out the details of the plan for spring sowing, and supplying cossacks with information on agricultural problems. The rest of the time he supervised the cleaning and treatment of the seed grain as it came in, or occasionally went to attend a sick cow or sheep. For a 'visit' he usually received payment in kind, having his dinner with the owner of the animal, and sometimes bringing back an earthenware jug of milk or a pot of boiled potatoes. The other two men, Lubno, a worker at the State flour mill in the district town, and Ivan Naidionov, a young Communist who worked in the vegetable oil mill, summoned the Gremyachy farmers to their 'staff headquarters', checked up each citizen's supply of seed grain against the list provided by the foreman at the granary, and carried on an incessant propaganda to get in the grain.

From the very beginning of their activities it was obvious that it was going to be very difficult to get the grain fund collected in the period fixed. All the measures undertaken by the brigade and the local nucleus for the purpose of accelerating its collection met with tremendous opposition from the majority of the collective farm members and the individual farmers. Rumours spread through the village that the grain was being collected to send abroad, there would not be any sowing done that year, and war was to be expected hourly. Nagulnov called daily meetings, and with the help of the brigade explained the situation, refuted the absurd rumours, threatened with the harshest of punishment those caught in 'anti-Soviet propaganda'. But the grain continued to come in extremely slowly. The cossacks found excuses for going off somewhere away from home early in the morning. They went to the forest for wood, or gathered brushwood. Or they went off with their neighbours to spend the anxious day in some secluded spot, in order to avoid having to answer a summons to the village Soviet or the brigade staff. The women completely gave up going to meetings, and when a delegate from the village Soviet called on them they got rid of him with the curt remark: 'My husband isn't at home, and I don't know anything about it.'

It was as though some powerful hand were holding back the grain.

Every day conversations like the following were to be heard in the brigade headquarters.

'Brought in your seed grain?'

'No.'

'Why not?'

'I haven't got any grain.'

'What do you mean, "haven't got any"?'

'What I say; it's very simple ... I thought of saving it for sowing, but then I gave up all my surplus for the grain collection and I had nothing left to eat. So I ate the seed grain.'

'And so you weren't thinking of sowing this year?'

'I was thinking of it, but I haven't got anything to sow with.'

Many relied on the statement that they had given up seed grain for the food grain collection. Davidov in the office, and Naidionov in the brigade headquarters, rummaged through the lists and the receipts for grain collections, checked up the statements, and convicted the obstinate of giving inaccurate information, for it appeared that grain had been left for seed. Sometimes in order to achieve this it was necessary to calculate the approximate quantity of grain threshed the previous autumn, to reckon up the total quantity handed over for the food grain fund, and to calculate the difference between the two amounts. But even when it was proved that grain was left, the cossacks stubbornly refused to yield.

'We had some grain left over, of course. But you know how it is on a farm, comrades. We're used to eating grain without weighing it, and using it without measuring it out. They left me with a pood a month for each of us, but I, for instance, eat three or four pounds a day. And that's nearly three poods. I eat so much bread because there's little else for us to eat. And so we've used it all up. We haven't got any grain; you can search for it if you like.'

At the nucleus meetings Nagulnov proposed that wherever the richer inhabitants of the village had not brought in grain, a search should be instituted. But Davidov and the others were against the proposal. Moreover the District Committee's instructions on collecting seed grain strictly prohibited resort to search.

During three days' hard work only 480 poods of seed grain were collected from collective farmers, and 35 poods from individual peasants. The active members of the collective farm handed over their share in full on the very first day. The following morning Yakov Lukich and his son Siemion drove up to the communal granary on two sledges. Lukich went immediately to the office, and Siemion began to carry the sacks of grain from the sledges to the granary. Diemka Ushakov received and weighed them. Four sacks Siemion poured out, but as he was untying the knot of the fifth, Ushakov flew at him like a hawk.

'Is this the grain your father was going to sow?' he demanded, thrusting a handful of seed under Siemion's nose.

'What's the matter with it?' Siemion flared up. 'With your squint you seem to have taken wheat for maize!'

'No I haven't. I may squint, but I can see better than you, you crook! You and your father are a fine pair, we know! What's this? Seed grain? Don't turn your nose up! What have you poured into my clean grain, you reptile's mug?'

Diemka thrust his palm right against Siemion's face; on the palm lay a handful of dirty grain mixed with earth and tares.

'I'll call everybody to see it!' he threatened.

'Don't get excited!' Siemion took alarm. 'I must have picked up the wrong sack. I'll take it back and change it at once. It's strange, by God it is! What are you flaring up like a horse for? I've said I'll change it; there's a mistake somewhere.'

Diemka rejected six sacks out of Siemion's fourteen. And when Siemion asked him to help lift one of the sacks of rejected grain on to his shoulders, Diemka turned to the scales as though he had not heard.

'So you won't help?' Siemion asked, his voice quivering.

'What do you think? You lifted them at home, and they were light enough there, and now they've suddenly grown heavy! Lift them yourself, you devil!'

Crimson with the effort, Siemion lifted the sack and carried it back to the sledge.

During the two following days almost no grain was brought in. At the nucleus meeting it was decided to visit the huts. The previous evening Davidov had driven to a seed-selection farm in the neighbouring district, in order to obtain some drought-resisting spring grain with which to sow at least a few hectares. The previous year the grain had yielded a splendid crop on the farm's experimental fields. Both Yakov Lukich and the brigade leader Agafon Dubtsiev had talked a good deal about this new sort of wheat, which had been obtained at the selection farm by crossing imported Californian with the local white-grained wheat. And Davidov, who recently had been spending his nights studying agricultural journals, decided to drive to the farm to obtain some of the new grain.

He returned from the trip on 4 March, but the day before his arrival Makar Nagulnov was involved in an unfortunate incident. In the morning Makar, who was attached to the second brigade, went with Liubishkin to visit some thirty farms, and in the evening, when Razmiotnov and the secretary had left the village Soviet, he summoned there those cossacks whom he had not been able to visit during the day. He saw four men without obtaining any positive results. 'We haven't got any grain for seed.' 'Let the State supply it,' they said. At first Nagulnov tried the method of calm persuasion, but after a while he began to hammer with his fist.

'How can you say you've got no grain?' he demanded. 'You, for instance, Konstantin Gavrilovich, you threshed three hundred poods last autumn.'

'And how much did you give the State for me?'

'How much did you hand over?' Nagulnov asked.

'Well, a hundred and thirty poods.'

'Where's the rest?'

'Don't you know where? Eaten !'

'You're lying ! You'd burst if you ate so much grain ! You've only got six in your family to eat all that ! Bring it in without further argument, or we'll kick you straight out of the collective farm.'

'Put me out of the farm ! Do what you like, but I haven't got any grain, by Christ ! Let the government give the grain against interest...'

'You've got into the habit of sucking at the government. Did you return the money you borrowed from the credit association to buy a sower and reaper? That's just it ! You've spent that money, and now you want to live on the grain, don't you?'

'All the same the reaper and sower are the collective farm's now. I never had the chance of using them, so don't fling that up against me !'

'You bring in the grain, or it'll be the worse for you. You're a hardened grumbler. Shame on you !'

'I'd hand over the grain and be only too glad, if I had it.'

No matter how Nagulnov argued and threatened, he had to let them go without getting any promise of grain. They went out, stopped for a moment to talk in the porch, then the steps creaked. A little later the individual farmer Gregor Bannik came in. In all probability he knew how matters had gone with the collective farmers whom Nagulnov had just dismissed, for a self-confident, challenging smile lurked in the corners of his lips. With trembling hands Nagulnov fidgeted with the list on the table, and said in a thick voice:

'Sit down, Gregor Matveich !'

'Thanks for the invitation.' Bannik sat down, planting his legs wide apart.

'Why haven't you brought in your seed grain, Gregor Matveich?'

'What have I got to bring it in for?'

'That was the decision of the general meeting. Both collective and individual farmers have got to bring in seed grain. Have you got any?'

'Of course I have.'

Nagulnov glanced at the list; against Bannik's name, in the column 'proposed area for spring 1930 sowing', was the figure six.

'So you intended to sow six hectares with wheat this spring?' he asked.

'That's right.'

'That means you've got forty-two poods of seed grain?'

'I've got it in full, sifted and cleaned grain as good as gold.'

'Well, you're a hero!' Nagulnov praised him, sighing with relief. 'Bring it to the communal granary tomorrow. You can leave it in your own sacks. We'll accept it from individual farmers in their own sacks if they don't want the grain mixed. Bring it in and have it weighed by the foreman. He'll seal up your sacks, hand you a receipt, and in the spring you'll get back the whole of your grain. But there are lots who complain that they haven't kept their grain, they've eaten it. It'll be kept safer in the granary.'

'You can give up that idea, comrade Nagulnov!' Bannik smiled jauntily, and stroked his fair whiskers. 'That game doesn't come off. I won't give you my grain.'

'Why not, if I may ask?'

'Because it will be safer with me. If I give it to you, in the spring I shan't even get back the empty sacks. We've grown wiser now, you don't get over us that way.'

Nagulnov raised his eyebrows, and his face paled a little. 'How dare you distrust the Soviet government!' he demanded. 'So you don't believe what I say?'

'Well, that's right. I don't believe it. We've heard that sort of yarn before.'

'Who's told you yarns? And what about?' Nagulnov turned more noticeably pale, and slowly rose to his feet.

But, as though he had not noticed anything, Bannik continued to smile quietly, revealing his few, firm teeth. Only his voice quivered with a note of grievance and burning anger as he said:

'You'll collect the grain, and then you'll load it into trains and send it to foreign parts. You'll buy motors so that partymen can ride around with their bobbed-hair women. We know what you want our grain for! We've lived to see equality all right!'

'Have you gone mad, you devil? What are you babbling?'

'You'll go mad all right if they take you by the throat! A hundred and sixteen poods I brought in for the grain collection! And now you want our last seed grain . . . so that my children . . . may starve . . .'

'Hold your tongue! You're lying, you reptile!' Nagulnov thundered his fists on the table.

The abacus fell to the floor, the ink-bottle overturned. A thick, glittering violet stream crawled over the paper, and fell on to the edge of Bannik's sheepskin jacket. He brushed off the ink with his palm, and rose. His eyes narrowed, flecks of white showed in the corners of his lips, and with suppressed fury he hoarsely shouted:

'Don't tell me to shut up! You raise your fist to your wife Lukeria, but I'm not your wife! This isn't 1920! Understand? And I won't give you my grain! You can go to the devil!'

'What's that? . . . Whose words are those? What are you saying to me, you counter-revolutionary? Laughing at socialism, you reptile? But now . . .' Makar could not find words, and he panted. But, somehow mastering himself, wiping the beads of sweat from his face with the back of his hand, he said:

'Write me a note at once that tomorrow you'll bring in the grain, and then tomorrow I'll see that you'll go to the right place. They'll find out there where you learned to make such speeches.'

'You can arrest me, but I won't sign a note and I won't give up my grain!'

'Write, I say!'

'You wait a bit . . .'

'For your own good I ask you . . .'

Bannik went towards the door, but his anger flared up so furiously in him that he could not restrain himself. Seizing the door handle, he shouted:

'I'll go at once and give the grain to the pigs! Better they should have it than you, you parasites!'

'To the pigs? Seed grain?' In two bounds Nagulnov reached the door, pulled his pistol from his pocket, and struck Bannik on the temple with the butt. Bannik swayed, leaned against the wall, rubbing the whitewash with his back, then began to crumple to the floor. He fell. The dark blood oozed out of the wound on his temple, wetting his hair. Beside himself with rage, with his foot

Nagulnov kicked Bannik several times as he lay, then drew back. Like a fish on dry land, Bannik yawned once or twice, then, clinging to the wall, began to lift himself up. Hardly had he risen to his feet when the blood began to flow more copiously. He silently wiped it away with his sleeve; a chalky dust sprinkled from his back. Nagulnov drank some unpleasantly lukewarm water straight from the carafe; his teeth clinked against the edge. Glancing sidelong at Bannik as he struggled to his feet, he went up to him, seized him by the elbow as though in a vice, pushed him towards the table, and thrust a pencil into his hand.

'Write!' he ordered.

'I'll write, but the public prosecutor will know about it. I'll write anything you like at the pistol point. Under the Soviet government beating up isn't allowed. It ... the party ... won't respect you for this, either!' Bannik hoarsely muttered, helplessly sitting down on a stool.

Nagulnov stood opposite him and cocked his pistol.

'Aha, counter-revolutionary! And you dare to talk about the Soviet government and the party! It won't be the people's judge that will try you, but I, now and with my own court. If you don't write I'll shoot you as a dangerous reptile, and afterwards I'll go to prison and do ten years for you if necessary. I won't allow you to dishonour the Soviet regime! Write: "Statement". Written that? Now write: "I, a former active White guard, who fought with arms in hand against the Red army, take back my words ..." Written that? "... my words, impossibly insulting to the All-Union Communist Party ..." Write those words in capital letters. "... and the Soviet regime. I ask their forgiveness and promise in future, although I am a secret counter-revolutionary ..."'

'I won't write that! What are you forcing me to do?'

'Yes, you will! What did you think? That I, wounded by the Whites, disfigured by them, would let you off? You jeered at the Soviet regime to my face, and have I got to be silent? Write, or I'll let the soul out of you.'

Bannik bent over the table, and once more the pencil in his hand crawled painfully over the sheet of paper. Keeping his finger on the trigger of his pistol, Nagulnov dictated slowly and distinctly:

' "Although I am a secret counter-revolutionary, I shan't injure the Soviet government, which is dear to all toilers and has been set up by the blood of the toiling people, neither by word, writing or deed. I shall not curse or hinder it, but shall patiently wait to see the world revolution, which will put an end to all of us, its enemies, on a world scale. And I also promise not to lie across the path of the Soviet government and not to undermine the sowing plan, and tomorrow, 4 March 1930, to bring to the communal granary ... " '

At that moment a Soviet delegate and three collective farm workers entered the room.

'Wait a bit in the porch,' Nagulnov called to them, and, turning to Bannik, he went on:

' "... forty-two poods of seed grain in wheat. To which I set my hand." Sign it !'

His face heavily flushed, Bannik signed and rose to his feet.

'You'll answer for this, Makar Nagulnov ...'

'We each have to answer for our own deeds, but if you don't bring that grain tomorrow, I'll kill you !' Nagulnov folded up the statement and put it into the breast pocket of his khaki shirt, threw the pistol on the table, and saw Bannik to the door. He remained in the village Soviet until midnight. He ordered the militia-man not to go away, and with his help he brought in and locked up three other collective farm members who had refused to hand over the grain. Only after midnight, broken with weariness and the nervous tension at which he had been living during the past few hours, he fell asleep, sitting at the Soviet table, his dishevelled head resting on his long hands. All night he had dreams of enormous crowds of people dressed in holiday clothes, incessantly marching, covering the steppe like a spring flood. In the gaps between the people rode horsemen. The varicoloured horses trod the soft steppe earth with their hoofs, but the thunderous rumble of the hoofs was hollow and echoing, as though the squadrons were marching over sheets of iron. Suddenly, quite close to Makar, the silver trumpets of an orchestra began to play the 'International,' and Makar felt, as he always felt when awake, a pinching agitation, a fiery spasm in the throat. At the end of the marching squadrons he saw his dead friend Mitka Lobach, who had been cut down by Wrangel's men in 1920. But he was not surprised, only gladdened, and, pushing through the people, threw himself towards the passing squadron. 'Mitka, Mitka! Stop!' he called, not hearing his own voice. Mitka turned in the saddle, stared at Makar indifferently, as though at a stranger, and rode on at a trot. Then Makar noticed his former orderly, Tiulim, who had been killed by a Polish bullet near Broda in the same year 1920, riding towards him. Tiulim galloped past smiling, holding the reins of Makar's horse in his right hand. And the horse, the same white-stockinged and lean-headed animal it had been in those days, went riderless, its head raised high and proudly, arching its neck.

The creaking of the window-shutters, swung continuously all night by the wind, passed into Makar's dream as music; the rumbling clatter of the iron roof became the drumming of horses' hoofs. When Razmiotnov came into the Soviet at six o'clock next morning, he found Nagulnov still asleep. On Makar's yellow cheek, lit by the lilac dawn of the March morning, a tense and expectant smile was frozen; his eyebrows were quivering with torturous intensity. Razmiotnov jostled him, and swore:

'You've stirred up a nice kettle of fish, and now you're sleeping? Having happy dreams, aren't you, grinning like that! What did you beat up Bannik for? At dawn he brought in his seed grain, handed it over, and at once drove off hard to the district. Liubishkin came running to me and told me Bannik had gone to make a complaint to the militia about you. You've done it this time, haven't you? What will Davidov say when he comes back? Ah, Makar!'

With his palms Nagulnov rubbed his face, which was swollen with his awkward sleep, and smiled meditatively.

'Andrei!' he said, 'What a fine dream I've just had! A splendid dream!'

'Never mind telling me about your dreams! Tell me what you did to Bannik.'

'I don't want to talk about such a poisonous reptile! You say he brought in the grain? Well, it worked, then! Forty-two poods of seed grain: that's not to be sneezed at. If every counter-revolutionary was to hand over forty-two poods after one blow from a pistol, I'd spend all my life going around hitting them! After what he said he deserved more than he got. He ought to be glad I didn't tear his legs from his arse!' And, with glittering eyes, he ended furiously: 'That scum was with general Mamon-tov's band. He fought against us until we made him bathe in the Black Sea, and even now he's trying to lie across our road, to harm the world revolution. And you should have heard what he said to me about the Soviet regime and the party. My hair stood on end with shame.'

'That wouldn't be much! But you oughtn't to have struck him, it would have been better to have arrested him.'

'No, he ought to be killed, not arrested!' Nagulnov threw out his hands in a hopeless gesture. 'And why didn't I kill him? I can't make out why I didn't. That's what I'm sorry about now!'

'If I call you a fool you'll get annoyed; but there's no limits to the fool in you. When Davidov comes back he'll give you a lesson for this business.'

'When he comes he'll be pleased with what I have done. He's not an old stick-in-the-mud like you.'

With a laugh Razmiotnov knocked a bent finger against the table, then against Makar's forehead, and declared: 'The same sound exactly.' But Makar angrily pushed his hand away, and began to put on his sheepskin jacket. As he grasped the door handle he turned his head and barked:

'Oh, you're clever, aren't you! Let the petty bourgeoisie out of the empty room, and tell them they've got to bring in the grain this very day. I'm going to have a wash, and when I come back I'll have them arrested again.'

In his amazement Razmiotnov's eyes started out of his head. He ran to the spare room where the village Soviet archives were kept together with specimen ears of corn from the previous year's district agricultural exhibition. Opening the door, he discovered three collective farm members. They had spent the night com-fortably on old newspapers spread over the floor, and rose when Razmiotnov appeared.

'Citizens, I must . . .' Andrei began. But the old cossack Krasnokutov energetically interrupted him:

'What's there to talk about, Andrei Stepanich? We're at fault, there's no other word for it. Let us go, and we'll bring the grain in at once. We had a little talk among ourselves during the night, and we've decided to hand over the grain. There's no point in hiding the truth: we wanted to keep our wheat . . .'

Razmiotnov, who had been on the point of apologizing for Nagulnov's unpremeditated conduct, realized the position and at once changed his tactic.

'You should have brought it in long before!' he declared. 'And you're collective farmers, too! You ought to be ashamed to keep the grain back.'

'Let us go, please, and we'll forget the past . . .' Antip Grach smiled shamefacedly into his jet black beard.

Throwing the door wide open, Razmiotnov went to the table. And it has to be admitted that as he did so the thought crossed his mind:

'But maybe Makar's right after all. Perhaps we should squeeze them tighter, and then they'd hand over all the grain in a day!

Chapter 25

Youth Shows the Way

CHEERFUL of mood, and satisfied with his success, Davidov returned from the selection farm with twelve poods of wheat. While she was getting his supper the mistress of the hut told him that during his absence Nagulnov had beaten up Gregor Bannik, and had locked three collective farmers in the Soviet for the night. Evidently the rumour had already been spread widely through the village. Davidov hurriedly ate his supper, and anxiously went to the collective farm office. There the story was confirmed, and supplemented with details. Opinions varied as to Nagulnov's conduct: some approved of it, others condemned, and

some were discreetly silent. Liubishkin, for instance, wholeheart-
edly took Nagulnov's part, whereas Yakov Lukich pursed up his
lips and wore an injured look, as though he himself had had a
taste of Nagulnov's reprimands. Shortly afterwards Makar himself came into the office. He seemed sterner than usual, and
greeted Davidov reservedly, but looked at him with secret anxiety
and expectation. When they were left alone Davidov, unable to
restrain himself, sharply demanded:

'What's this latest game you've been up to?'

'You've heard; what are you asking for?'

'Is that the kind of propaganda you're beginning to use to get
in seed grain?'

'Then don't let him say such filthy things to me! I've never
pledged myself to stand the jeers of an enemy, a White reptile!'

'But did you stop to think what reaction it would have on
others, how it would look from the political aspect?'

'There wasn't any time to think.'

'That's no answer. Fact! You should have arrested him for
abusing the government, but you shouldn't have struck him.
That's a disgraceful action for a communist. Fact! And we shall
raise the question today at the nucleus. Look at the harm you've
done us by your conduct! We must censure it. I shall talk about
it at the collective farm meeting, too, without waiting for the
decision of the District Committee, I tell you! If we say nothing
about it the collective farm workers will think we see eye to eye
with you, and that we tolerate your conduct. No, brother! We
shall dissociate ourselves from you and censure you. You're a
communist, and you behaved like a gendarme. It's a disgrace. The
devil take the incident, and you with it!'

But Nagulnov was as obstinate as an ox; to all Davidov's attempts to convince him that such conduct was politically injurious, impermissible to a communist, he replied:

'I did right in beating him! And I didn't even beat him. I
only hit him once, and I should have given him more! Leave
me alone! It's too late to re-educate me, I'm a partisan, and I
know well enough how to defend my party from the attacks of
such scum.'

'But I don't say that Bannik is one of us, damn his eyes! What

I say is that you shouldn't have struck him. You could have found other methods to defend the party from insult. Fact ! You go and cool down a little and think it over, then you'll come to the nucleus this evening and say I was right. Fact !'

As soon as Makar, his brows knitted entered the room before the beginning of the nucleus meeting that evening, Davidov asked him :

'Thought it over?'

'I have.'

'Well?'

'I didn't give him enough, the son of a bitch ! I ought to have killed him !'

The propaganda column brigade was entirely on Davidov's side, and voted in favour of Nagulnov being sternly reprimanded. Andrei Razmiotnov did not vote, nor did he speak at all during the discussion. But when, as Makar was leaving the meeting, he barked out, 'I stand by my own right opinion,' Razmiotnov jumped to his feet and ran out of the room, furiously spitting and cursing.

As they stopped in the dark porch to light cigarettes, by the match flame Davidov examined Nagulnov's sullen face, and said in a conciliatory tone :

'It's no use your being offended with us, Makar. Fact !'

'I'm not offended.'

'You're using the old partisan methods, but the days are different now, and it's not raids, but trench warfare we need. We've all been sick with the partisan spirit, especially our men in the fleet, and that includes me, of course. Although you do suffer with your nerves, you must, my dear Makar, you simply must get more control of yourself, mustn't you? You look at the men coming on to take our places; look at the miracles our Young Communist of the propaganda column, Vania Naidionov, is working. He's got in more seed grain from his section than any of us; he's got in almost all of it. He's not very lively to look at, he's small and he's smothered with freckles, but he works better than all the rest of us put together. He goes around the huts talking, the devil, and they say he tells the peasants marvellous stories. And they bring in the grain for him without any smashing of

212

snouts and without any sitting in cold cells. Fact!' A smile and a warm note crept into Davidov's voice as he spoke of Naidionov, and Nagulnov felt a feeling akin to jealousy of the efficient Young Communist. 'Out of curiosity you go along with him tomorrow and see how he does it,' Davidov continued. 'There's nothing insulting to you in suggesting that, by God there isn't! Sometimes we can learn things even from the youngsters. Fact! They're growing up different from us, they seem to be better adapted ...'

Nagulnov held his peace, but early the next morning he sought out Vania Naidionov, and, as though casually, told him:

'I've got nothing to do today, I'd like to go round with you and give you a hand. How much more grain have you got to get in?'

'Hardly any, comrade Nagulnov. Come along by all means; we'll have more fun with two of us.'

They set off. His body swaying unsteadily like a duck's, Naidionov walked along at a speed to which Nagulnov was unaccustomed. His leather jerkin was flung open, and smelt strongly of sunflower seed oil; his check cap was pulled down over his eyebrows. With sidelong glances Nagulnov inquisitively scrutinized the undistinguished, childishly freckled face of this Young Communist, about whom Davidov had spoken with such unusual tenderness the previous evening. The expression of the face was strangely friendly and attractive, and prepossessing, either because of the open, speckled grey eyes, or the resolutely lifted, youthfully rounded chin.

They arrived at the hut of the former 'hen-feeler', Akim Beskhlebnov, just as the entire family was having breakfast. The old man himself was sitting at the farther end of the table under the ikons; at his side was his son Akim, a man of some forty years of age, and called 'the younger' to distinguish him from his father. The younger Akim's wife and ancient widowed mother-in-law were on his right hand, two grown-up daughters were perched at the other end, while the two sides were plastered with children like flies on a wall.

'Good day, my masters!' Naidionov drew off his greasy cap, and smoothed down his bristling forelock.

'Good day, so long as you're not joking,' Akim the younger,

always simple and jovial in his relationships, answered with a hardly perceptible smile.

In reply to this jesting welcome Nagulnov would have raised his eyebrows, and, with overweening severity, would have said: 'We've got no time for joking. Why haven't you brought in your grain?' But Naidionov smiled, and remarked as though he had not noticed the chilly restraint in their faces:

'Good appetite!'

Akim the younger had no time to open his mouth and, without inviting the visitors to sit down at the table, to utter a miserly 'Thank you' or dismiss them with the rough jest: 'We're at breakfast, but it's our own, and you can wait until we've finished.' For Naidionov hurriedly went straight on:

'But don't bother to get up for us. There's no need. For that matter we don't mind sitting down and having a bit of breakfast with you. I must say I haven't eaten yet today. Comrade Nagulnov's a local man, and of course he's given himself a good foundation. But we eat at the end of the day, like the "birds of the air".'

'So you neither sow nor reap, but you get your bellyful,' the younger Akim laughed.

'Whether our bellies are full or not, we're always ready to laugh.' With these words, to Nagulnov's astonishment Naidionov flung off his jerkin and sat down at the table in a trice. Old Akim grunted at such an unceremonious guest; but Akim the younger roared with laughter.

'Well, that's true soldier fashion!' he exclaimed. 'You're lucky to have got your word in before me, my lad, for I was just about to reply to your "Good appetite" with: "What we're eating's our own, and you can wait till we're finished." Girls, give him a spoon!'

One of the girls jumped up and, giggling into her apron, went to the stove shelf for a spoon. But she handed it to Naidionov with a curtsey, with all the respect due to a man. The company grew lively and merry. Akim the younger invited Nagulnov also to eat with them, but he refused and sat down on the chest. With a smile Akim's white-eyebrowed wife handed the guest a piece of bread, and the girl who had fetched the spoon ran to the best room and brought back a clean towel to lay across Naidionov's knees. With unconcealed approval the younger Akim stared inquisitively at the freckled face of this youngster who was so much bolder than any of the village lads, and remarked:

'As you see, comrade, my daughter's taken a fancy to you. She's never handed her father a clean towel in all her life, but you get one before you've managed to make yourself comfortable at the table. If you want her we'll give her to you at once.'

The girl flamed up at her father's joke, covered her face with her hand, and rose from the table. But Naidionov added to the gaiety by jesting back:

'She'll never take up with a freckle-face. I can only get betrothed after dark, but then I'm handsome and the girls find me attractive.'

A dish of stewed fruit was put on the table. All conversation ceased. The only sounds to be heard were the champing of jaws and the scraping of wooden spoons on the bottom of the dish. The silence was broken only when one of the younger boys began to describe circles with his spoon inside the dish in search of stewed pear. As soon as that happened old Akim licked his spoon and gave the offender a loud crack on the forehead with it, admonishing him:

'Don't fish for the best bits!'

'It's as quiet as a church here,' the mistress remarked.

'And it isn't always quiet in church!' Vania said, as he attacked his buckwheat hash and fruit in great style. 'I remember something that happened in our town just before Easter – you'd have split your sides with laughing.'

The mistress stopped clearing the table, Akim the younger rolled a cigarette, sat down on the bench and prepared to listen, and even old Akim, belching and crossing himself, pricked up his ears at Naidionov's words. Nagulnov began to manifest open signs of impatience, and thought: 'But when is he going to talk about the grain? It's quite clear there's little hope for us here. Neither of the Akims can be turned in a hurry, they're the most obstinate devils in all Gremyachy. And you're not going to do it by frightening them, when the younger Akim served in the Red Army, and is wholly and entirely on our side. Yet he won't bring in his grain because he's too mean and clings too tight to his property He wouldn't give you snow in winter no matter how much you begged! I know him!'

Meantime, Naidionov waited a moment, then went on:

'I was born in Tatsinsk district, and one Easter service was being held, the religious people were all gathered in the church, and it was stifling with the crowd. The priest and the deacon were singing and reading, of course, and the lads were playing around in the churchyard. In the village there was a yearling calf so fond of butting that you had only to touch it and it would lash out like a pike and try to gore you with its horns. This calf was grazing peacefully outside the churchyard, but the boys teased and teased it until it chased after one of them and all but caught him. The lad dashed through the churchyard, the calf after him. The lad dashed into the porch, the calf after him. The people were packed tight in the porch, but the calf sent them scattering, and helped the boy on with a great butt at his bottom. He went flying, and landed under the feet of some old woman. She fell over, knocked the back of her head against the floor, and began to bawl: "Save me, good people! Oh, evil has come on me!" And the old woman's husband gave the lad a whack on the back with his stick, with a "May you burn in hell fire, you limb of Satan!" But the calf bellowed and put its horns down at the old man. And then you should have seen the panic there was! Those who were standing near the altar couldn't understand what was the matter; but they could hear a noise at the door, and they all stopped praying, getting more and more agitated and asking one another what all the noise was about.' In the inspiration of his story-telling Vania conveyed so realistically in his own features how his frightened fellow-villagers whispered to one another, that the younger Akim could not resist bursting into a roar of laughter. 'That calf caused an upset, all right!' he remarked.

Baring his white teeth in a smile, Vania went on:

'One fellow jokingly said to his neighbour: "Perhaps a dog's run into the church, it ought to be driven out!" At the side of him was a woman in the family way, and she got frightened and screamed all through the church: "Oh, my own mother! It'll bite us all!" Those behind pressed up against those in front, the candlesticks got overturned, and then there was a smell of burning. And the church went dark. Then of course someone roared: "We're on fire!" And that did it! "Mad dog!" "Fire, fire!" "What's all the row about?" "It's the end of the world!" "What? The end of the world? Wife, come on home!" They poured towards the side doors, and there they got jammed so that nobody could get out. The candle-stall was knocked over, the five-kopek pieces were scattered all over the place, and the churchwarden fell down and shouted "Thieves!" The women rushed like a lot of sheep to the altar, but the deacon struck them on their heads with a censer, and shouted: "Pfooh! You sinners, where are you going? Unclean that you are, don't you know that women aren't allowed at the altar?" And the head of the village – he was a fat man with a chain across his belly – he crawled to the door and pushed the people aside, roaring: "Let me out! Let me out, damn you! It's me, it's the head of the village!" But how could they let him out when it was "the end of the world"?'

Amid roars of laughter Vania ended his story:

'There was a horse-stealer named Arkhip Chokhov lived in our village. He stole horses every week, but nobody could ever catch him at it. And Arkhip was in the church praying away his sins. When they began to shout: "The end of the world!" "We'll perish, brothers!" Arkhip threw himself towards a window, broke it, and tried to get through. But the window was barred outside. All the people were choking at the door, and Arkhip ran up and down the church, then came to a halt, swung his arms around and said: "Oh, I'm caught at last! I'm caught, I'm caught at last!"'

Akim the younger, his wife and the two girls laughed until the tears rolled down their cheeks, and they were seized with hiccoughing. Old Akim also noiselessly bared his empty gums. And only the old wife, who had not heard half the story and could not understand the rest because she was deaf, began to cry for no apparent reason, and, wiping her red, tear-filled eyes, mumbled:

'So he got caught, the poor wretch! Queen of heaven! And what did they do to him?'

'To who, old lady?'

'Why, to this holy man?'

'What holy man, old girl?'

'The one you were talking about, the pilgrim.'

'But what pilgrim?'

'I don't know. I'm a bit hard of hearing, my boy. I don't catch everything . . .'

There was another explosion of laughter. And, as he wiped the tears from his eyes, the younger Akim asked five times in succession:

'What was it he said, that thief of yours? "Now I'm caught at last?" Well, my lad, it's a wildly funny story you've told us!' he exclaimed with naive rapture, clapping Vania on the back. But Naidionov swiftly changed to a serious mood, and sighed:

'Yes, it's a funny story all right, but there are things happening these days that aren't to be laughed at. There was something I read in the paper today that made my heart sink . . .'

'Sink?' Akim asked, still expecting a further funny story.

'Yes. It sank to read of the way men are being tortured and brutally treated in capitalist countries. I read that in Romania two Young Communists were opening the peasants' eyes, and telling them they ought to take the land from the landowners and divide it up among themselves. The farmers have a very poor time of it in Romania.'

'I know that's true, for I saw it for myself when I was with my regiment on the Romanian front in 1917,' Akim confirmed.

'So these two communists were carrying on propaganda to overthrow capitalism and to get a Soviet regime set up in Romania. But the savage gendarmes caught them and beat one to death, and began to torture the other. They dug out his eyes, and tore all the hair off his head. Then they heated red-hot a thin iron bar and began to push it under his nails . . .'

'The devils!' Akim's wife groaned and wrung her hands. 'Under his nails?'

'Under his nails. And they asked him: "Tell us the other members of your nucleus, and give up being a Young Communist." "I won't tell you, you vampires, and I won't give up my communism!" the youngster firmly replied. Then the gendarmes began to cut off his ears with their sabres, and sliced off his nose. "Will you tell?" they demanded. "No," he said, "I'll die at your bloody hands, but I won't tell! Hurrah for communism!" Then they tied him up to the ceiling by his hands, and lit a fire under him ...'

'Curse them, what butchers there are alive! What a shame!' the younger Akim waxed indignant.

'They burned him with fire, but he only wept bloody tears. He wouldn't betray any of his comrades, and only declared: "Hurrah for the proletarian revolution and communism!"'

'Brave lad not to give away his comrades. That's the spirit! Die honestly, but don't give away your friends! The scriptures say: "Lay down your life for your friend."' Old Akim banged with his fist and urged Naidionov on.

'They tortured him and tried him in all sorts of ways, but he would not speak. So it went on from morning till evening. He fainted, but the gendarmes poured water over him and set about their work again. When they saw they wouldn't get anything out of him that way, they went and arrested his mother and brought her into their office. "Look how we are dealing with your son," they told her. "Tell him to submit, or we'll kill him and throw his meat to the dogs!" His mother fell down in a faint, but when she came round she threw herself on her child, embraced him, and kissed his bloody hands.' Pale of face, Vania lapsed into silence, and gazed with dilated eyes around his audience. The girls' gaping mouths had gone dark, and tears were standing in their eyes. Akim's wife sniffed into her apron, whispering through her sobs: 'Putting his mother on to her child! Lord!' The younger Akim suddenly groaned, and, seizing his tobacco pouch, hurriedly began to roll a cigarette. Only Nagulnov, sitting on the chest, retained his outward composure, but during the pause his cheek began to twitch suspiciously and his lips writhed.

'"My own son! For my sake, for your mother's sake, submit to them, the devils!" she said to him. But he heard her voice and replied: "No, my mother, I won't give away my comrades. I'll die for my ideals. And you'd better kiss me before my end, then it will be easier for me to die ..."'

With a quivering voice Vania finished his story of how the young Romanian communist had died, tortured by the gendarme executioners. Then there was silence for a minute, until Akim's wife asked with tears running down her cheeks:

'How old was he, the martyr?'

'Seventeen,' Vania answered without hesitation, clapping on his check cap immediately afterwards. 'Yes, the working-class hero died ... our dear young Romanian communist comrade. He died that the toilers might have a better life. And it's our job to help them overthrow capitalism, to set up a workers' and peasants' government. In order to do that we must build up collective farms, and strengthen the collective farm economy. But there are farmers among us who, because they don't know any better, are assisting the gendarmes and hindering the work of constructing collective farms ... They refuse to hand over their seed grain. Well, thank you for the breakfast. Now to the business we've called about. You must bring in your seed grain at once, you know. Your farm has to supply exactly seventy-seven poods. Come on, bring it in!'

'Well, I don't know ... We've got hardly any grain left,' the younger Akim began irresolutely, dumbfounded by the unexpected attack. But his wife gave him an indignant look and interrupted:

'What are you humming and ha-ing for? Go and sack it up and carry it in.'

'We haven't got seventy poods. And besides, it hasn't been sifted,' Akim feebly objected.

'Carry it in, Akim. We've got to hand it over, what are you refusing for?' old Akim supported his daughter-in-law.

'We're not proud; we'll give a hand to sieve it,' Vania readily declared. 'Have you got a sieve?'

'Yes ... But it wants a little repairing.'

'What a pity! But we'll mend it. Hurry up, master. We've already spent a long time talking ...'

Within half an hour the younger Akim was fetching two oxen sledges from the collective farmyard, while Vania, his face covered with little beads of sweat like freckles, was dragging sacks of sifted wheat, firm and healthy grain as ruddy as pure gold, from the chaffshed to the granary steps.

'What did you keep your grain in the chaffshed for?' with a sly wink Vania asked one of Akim's daughters. 'You've got a fine large granary, and you let the grain lie like that to be spoilt!'

'Father arranged it like that,' she replied in embarrassment.

Beskhlebnov carried his seventy-seven poods to the communal granary, and Makar and Vania took their leave. As they were going on to the next farm, Nagulnov, glancing at Vania's tired face, asked in joyously agitated tones:

'Did you make up that story about the Young Communist?'

'No,' he replied abstractedly. 'I read about the case in a paper some time ago.'

'But you said you read it today.'

'What does that matter? The main thing is that there was such a case; that's the pity of it, comrade Nagulnov.'

'Yes, but you ... did you add to the story to make it sound more pitiful?' Nagulnov persistently questioned.

'That's not the point.' Vania irritably avoided the question, and, bristling with the cold, he buttoned up his leather jerkin as he declared:

'The point is that the people must be brought to hate the executioners and the capitalist system, and sympathize with our fighters. The point is that they've carried in the grain, and that's all that matters. And I added hardly anything, in any case. That stewed fruit was as sweet as honey. You were a fool to refuse, comrade Nagulnov.'

Chapter 26

A Well-Earned Reward

DURING the evening of 10 March a mist fell like a blanket over Gremyachy. All night the water was thawing and bickering from the roofs of the huts; a warm, wet wind hurried from the range of hills to the south. The first night of oncoming spring hung over Gremyachy, veiled in the black silks of flowing mists and silence, fanned by spring breezes. Late in the morning the rosy-hued mists were swept away, revealing the sky and the sun; from the south the wind came rushing powerfully, dripping with dampness; with a rumbling and roaring the large-grained snow began to settle, the roofs turned brown, the roads were covered with black patches. And towards noonday the hill water, as sparkling as tears, was pouring down the ravines and valleys, and rushing by innumerable streams into the gulleys, into the meadows and gardens, washing the bitter roots of the cherry trees, flooding over the riverside reeds.

Within three days the hills, exposed to every wind, were laid bare; their saturated slopes glistened with damp clay, the hill waters grew turbid, and their seething, shaggy waves carried along yellow caps of exuberantly frothy foam, washed-up corn roots, dry refuse from the ploughed lands, and uprooted bushy hemp-nettle.

Close to Gremyachy Log the river overflowed its banks. From somewhere in its upper reaches azure plates of ice, melted away by the sun, came floating down. At the bends of the river they were flung out of the main stream, and whirled and grated like great fish in a wattle-net. Sometimes the current dashed them on to the steep bank, and sometimes the ice, dragged along by a torrent falling into the stream, was carried into the orchards and floated among the trees, scraping against the trunks, smashing the young saplings, damaging the apple trees, and bending down the young shoots of the cherries.

Outside the village the snow-freed fallow land blackened challengingly. The layers of sticky black earth left upturned by the ploughshares began to steam with the sun's warmth. A great, blessed silence hung over the steppe at the noon hour. Above the ploughed lands were the sun, a milky-white mist, the agitating song of the early skylark, and the beckoning cries of the cranes piercing the dense azure of the cloudless sky with the breast of their triangular flight. Above the mounds a heat mirage quivered and flowed. Thrusting aside the dead, last-year's stalks, the sharp green stings of the grass-blades struggled towards the sun. Dried by the wind, the winter rye rose as though on tiptoe, stretching out its leaves to meet the light-bearing rays. But there was still not much life in the steppe; the marmots had not awakened from their winter sleep, the beasts of the field had fled to the forests and ravines; only occasionally a field mouse would scurry across the ancient steppe scrub, and the mated partridges would fly to their winter quarters.

By 15 March the seed grain fund had been collected in full in Gremyachy Log. The peasants still individually working their own lands deposited their grain in a separate granary, the key to which was kept in the collective farm office. The collective farmers filled six communal granaries to their roofs. The cleaning of the grain went on day and night, three lamps being used during the hours of darkness. In Ippolit Shaly's forge the broad throat of the smithy bellows panted all day, the golden grains of fire scattered from under the hammer, the anvil rang musically. Shaly worked hard, and by 15 March he had repaired all the harrows, shares, sowers and ploughs brought to him. On the evening of the 16th, in the presence of a large crowd of collective farm workers, Davidov rewarded the smith with the tools he had brought from Leningrad. Freshly shaved for the occasion, wearing a clean jersey, he picked up the tools, which had been set out on a piece of red satin, while Andrei Razmiotnov pushed the crimson Ippolit on to the platform. Turning to the smith, Davidov said:

'To our dear smith, Ippolit Sidorovich Shaly, for his genuine shock labour, which should be copied by all the other collective farmers, we, the management of the collective farm, present these tools.

'Down to today comrade Shaly has repaired the implements to a full 100 per cent. Fact, citizens! He has mended 54 shares, put twelve sowers of various kinds into working order, and many other machines too. Fact! Dear comrade, accept our fraternal gift as a reward, and we hope that in the future you will work just as hard, damn you, so that all our implements in the collective farm will always be in good order. And the rest of you citizens must work just as hard in the fields. Only then shall we justify the name of our collective farm, otherwise we shall be brought to shame and contempt in the eyes of all the Soviet Union. Fact!'

Davidov wrapped the reward in the three-metre length of red satin and handed it to Shaly. The Gremyachy inhabitants had not yet learned to express their approval by clapping their hands, and when Shaly took the red bundle in his trembling fists a hubbub arose in the school:

'He deserves it. He's worked hard.'

'He's turned useless implements into useful ones.'

'He's got the tools, and his wife a piece of satin for a dress!'

'Ippolit, how about drinks all round, you black bull!'

'Up in the air with him!'

'Don't be mad! He's had enough swinging over the anvil!'

The shouts passed into a general roar, but old Shchukar managed to pierce through the tumult with his shrill, falsetto voice:

'What are you standing dumb for? Speak up! You've got to answer. His parents were a log and a block!'

Shchukar was supported by others, and both seriously and in jest the shouts arose:

'Let Diemid the Silent speak in his place!'

'Ippolit! Hurry up or you'll fall down!'

'Look, his knees are really shaking under him!'

'He's swallowed his tongue in his joy.'

'It's not like using a hammer.'

But Andrei Razmiotnov, who was fond of celebrations of all kinds, and who was directing the ceremonies for the evening, mastered the uproar and calmed the excited gathering.

'Cool down a little, can't you?' he exclaimed. 'What are you bawling away like that for? Smelt the spring? Clap your hands like civilized beings, and don't shout! Silence, please, and let a man reply!' He turned to Ippolit and imperceptibly jostled him with his elbow, whispering: 'Get a lot of air into your lungs and talk! Make a long speech like an educated man. You're the hero of the celebrations, and you must make a speech according to all the rules, a long one...'

But, distracted by so much attention, Ippolit Shaly, who in all his life had never made a long speech, and who formerly had only received miserable treats of vodka in payment for his work, was completely overwhelmed. As the result of the reward and the circumstance of its solemn presentation he had lost all his customary poise. His hands trembled as they pressed the red bundle firmly against his chest; even his legs, which in the smithy always stood so firmly and widely planted, trembled also. Clinging tightly to the bundle, with his sleeve he wiped away a tear and polished his face, scrubbed crimson for the occasion, then hoarsely declared:

'Of course we need the tools. We're thankful ... And to the management, for their ... Thank you and again thank you. And I, once I'm born a smith and I can ... With all my heart I'll always be a collective farm worker as I am today ... And of course my wife will like the satin ...' His eyes wandered helplessly over the packed classroom, as he looked for his wife and secretly hoped she would help him out. But he could not see her, and he sighed and ended his far from long speech : 'And for the tools ... and the satin ... and for our work, thank you, comrade Davidov and the collective farm.'

Seeing that Shaly's agitated speech was coming to an end, Razmiotnov vainly made desperate signs to the sweating smith. But Shaly had no intention of seeing them, and, bowing, he left the platform, carrying the bundle in outstretched arms as though it were a sleeping baby.

Nagulnov hurriedly tore off his cap and waved his hand. The orchestra, consisting of two balalaikas and a violin, struck up the 'International'.

Every day the brigade leaders Dubtsiev, Liubishkin and Ushakov rode out into the steppe to see whether the virgin and fallow land were ready for ploughing and sowing. The spring was passing over the steppe in the dry breath of the winds. The weather turned fine, and the first brigade made ready to plough the grey sandy soil which had been allotted to them.

The propaganda column members were summoned to rejoin the main body at the village of Voiskovoi, but at Nagulnov's request Vania Naidionov was left behind in Gremyachy for the sowing period.

The day after Shaly received his reward Nagulnov separated from his wife Lukeria. She went to live with her aunt, who had a hut a little apart from the rest of the village, and was not seen about for a couple of days. Then she happened to meet Davidov close to the collective farm office, and she stopped him.

'How am I to live now, comrade Davidov? Give me your advice,' she asked.

'Easier asked than answered ! But we're thinking of organizing a crèche, give a hand with that.'

'No, thank you! I've had no children of my own, and am I to nurse other people's at my age? That's a fine idea!'

'Well, go and work in a brigade.'

'I'm not a working woman. My head swims when I do field work.'

'Well, aren't you tender! Then you can go and do what you like, but you'll get nothing to eat. With us it's a case of "He who won't work shan't eat".'

Lukeria sighed and, digging the pointed toe of her shoe into the damp sand, she drooped her head.

'My friend Timofei has sent me a letter from the town of Kotlas in the Northern Province. He promises me he'll come back soon,' she informed him.

'Well, that's the last word!' Davidov smiled. 'But if he does, we shall send him still further.'

'So there's to be no pardon for him?'

'No! Don't expect it. And don't be lazy. You must work. Fact!' Davidov sternly replied, and was about to go on. But Lukeria, a little embarrassed, held him back. A laughing and challenging note sounded in her voice as she slowly asked:

'But maybe you could find me a cast-off husband of some sort?'

'I'm not in that line of business! Good-bye!'

'Wait a bit! One other question.'

'Well?'

'Wouldn't you take me as your wife?' A direct challenge and mockery marked the tone of her voice.

It was Davidov's turn to be embarrassed. He flushed to the roots of his hair, and his lips worked silently.

'You take a look at me, comrade Davidov,' she continued with affected humility. 'I'm a beautiful woman, and I'm very good for love. Take a good look: my eyes are good, my eyebrows, my legs under me, and as for all the rest ...' With her fingertips she slightly raised the hem of her green woollen skirt, and setting her arms akimbo, she turned herself round in front of the dumb-founded Davidov. 'Am I bad to look at? Say right out what you think ...'

With a hopeless gesture Davidov pushed his cap on to the back of his head.

'You're a fine girl,' he said, 'there's no other word for it. And the legs under you are beautiful, only ... only you don't use them to walk where you ought to go. That's a fact!'

'I go where I want to. So I can't live in hopes of you?'

'You'd better not!'

'Don't think I'm pining for you or wanting to hitch myself on to you. I simply feel sorry for you. I've been thinking: "There's a young man, unmarried, single, not interested in women." And I was sorry for you when you looked into my eyes, and there was hunger in your eyes.'

'You ... You're a she-devil ...! Well, good-bye! I haven't got time to waste on you!' And he jestingly added: 'When we've finished sowing then you can set your cap at the old sailor; only you must get Makar's permission first. Fact!'

She burst into a peal of laughter, and called after him as he walked away: ...

'Makar always defended himself from me behind the world revolution, but you hide behind the sowing! But there'll be no more of that! I don't need such as you. I need a fiery love, and what have you got? Your blood's gone rusty with work, and the heart freezes in a poor body.'

Davidov went into the office with an embarrassed smile on his lips. At first he thought: 'We must fix her up with some work somehow, or the woman will go wrong. A week-day, and she's got herself up like that and starts talking in that fashion ...!' But then he mentally washed his hands of her: 'Oh, let her go! She's not a child, she ought to understand. What am I in reality, a bourgeois lady doling out charity? I offered her work and she didn't want it, so let her go where she likes.'

He curtly asked Nagulnov:

'Left your wife?'

'None of your cross-examinations, please!' Makar muttered, studying the nails of his long fingers with unnecessary attention.

'But I only ...'

'Well, and I only ...!'

'Oh, damn you! I can't even ask now. Fact!'

'It's time the first brigade started, and they're finding excuses for delay.'

'You should put Lukeria on the right road. She's got the wind in her tail now, and she'll go wrong.'

'Am I her priest, or what? Drop it! I said the first brigade ought to be going out tomorrow . . .'

'And it will be going out tomorrow. But do you think it's so simple? You've separated, and that's all there is to it? Why didn't you educate the woman on communist lines? You're always causing misfortune. Fact!'

'I'll go out to the fields with the first brigade myself tomorrow. What are you sticking to me like a burr for? "Educate, educate!" How the devil could I educate her when I was quite uneducated myself? Well, we've separated, and what then? You eat away like a boil. There's the trouble with that Bannik, damn him! I've got enough on my hands, and you go on at me about my former wife!'

Davidov was about to answer, but a motor horn sounded in the yard. Swaying, and splashing up the thaw-water in the puddles, the District Executive Committee's Ford arrived. Samokhin, the chairman of the District Control Commission, threw open the door and got out.

'He's come about my business,' Nagulnov frowned and stared angrily at Davidov. 'Look here, don't let out about the woman to him, or you'll drive me into a monastery! You don't know what Samokhin's like, do you? It'll be: "Why have you separated from your wife, and for what reason?" It's like a sharp sword in his side to him when a communist leaves his wife. He's a priest, and not the head of the Workers' and Peasants' Inspection! I can't stand him, the big-headed devil! Oh, that Bannik . . . I could kill the reptile, and . . .'

Clinging tightly to his canvas document case, Samokhin entered the room and, without a word of greeting, half-jestingly remarked:

'Well, Nagulnov, you've done something now, haven't you? And I've had to drive over in a terrible hurry because of you. Who is this comrade? Davidov, is it? Good morning.' He shook Nagulnov's and Davidov's hands, and sat down at the table. 'Leave us for half an hour or so, comrade Davidov; I've got to have a talk with this queer lad,' he said with a gesture in Nagulnov's direction.

'Lay on, get down to it!' Davidov remarked. As he rose he was astonished to hear Nagulnov, who evidently had decided that he might as well be hanged for a sheep as for a lamb, blurt out:

'I've beaten up a counter-revolutionary, that's true enough. And now there's something more, Samokhin...'

'Well, what else is there now?'

'I've turned my wife out.'

'You don't mean to say?' the lofty-browed, gaunt Samokhin slowly remarked in an alarmed tone. Then he snorted horribly, and rummaged in his document case, rustling the papers without saying another word.

Chapter 27

The Conspiracy Fails

LATE one night, through his sleep Yakov Lukich heard footsteps and someone at the gate. But he could not wake up. When he did struggle out of his sleep he clearly heard a board of the fence creaking under the weight of a body, and a metallic clatter. Hurriedly going to the window, he pressed his face against the pane and gazed out. In the deep blue shadows of the twilight he saw someone big and heavy jump over the fence, and heard the dull thud of the take-off. By the fur cap gleaming white in the night he guessed it was Polovtsiev. He threw on his jacket, took his felt boots down from the stove, and went out. Polovtsiev had already led his horse through the wicket gate, and had bolted up the main gate. Yakov Lukich took the reins from his hand. The horse was wet to its withers, it swayed, and internally rumbled. Without replying to Yakov's greeting, Polovtsiev asked in a hoarse whisper:

'Is he ... is Lyatievsky here?'

'He's asleep. He's given us a good deal of trouble. He's done nothing but drink vodka all the time...'

'Damn him! The swine! I've over-ridden my horse, I'm afraid.'

Polovtsiev's voice was unrecognizably quiet, and Yakov Lukich thought he detected overstrain, great anxiety and weariness in its tones.

In the little room Polovtsiev removed his boots, took out blue, striped cossack trousers from his saddle-bag, drew them on, and hung those he had been wearing, which were wet to the high, backstitched belt, over the stove to dry. Yakov Lukich stood by the door, watching his chief's unhurried movements. The captain sat down on the sleeping-place at the back of the stove, embraced his knees with his arms, and warmed the bare soles of his feet. He momentarily dozed off. Evidently he mortally wanted to sleep, but he forced his eyes open, stared at Lyatievsky, who was sleeping the inviolable sleep of the drunkard, and asked:

'Has he been drinking a long time?'

'Ever since he arrived. He drinks too much. It got awkward for me in front of other people when I had to get hold of vodka every day. They might get suspicious.'

'The swine!' Polovtsiev hissed in a tone of terrible contempt through his clenched teeth. He dozed off again where he sat, nodding his great, grizzled head. But after a few minutes of gloomy, inflowing sleep he shuddered, let his legs hang down from the sleeping-place, and opened his eyes.

'I haven't slept for three days ... the rivers are in flood. I had to swim across your Gremyachy river.'

'You should lie down and rest, Alexander Anisimovich.'

'I shall. Give me some tobacco. I've got mine wet.'

After a couple of avid puffs Polovtsiev revived a little. The sleep disappeared from his eyes, and his voice grew stronger.

'Well, how are things going here?' he asked.

Yakov Lukich briefly reported on the situation, then asked in his turn:

'And how are your successes? Will it be soon now?'

'During the next few days or ... not at all. Tomorrow night you and I are going to Voiskovoi. We must start from there. It's nearer to the district town. They've got a propaganda column there at the moment, and we'll try out on them. I shall need you on this trip. The cossacks there know you, your words will have effect on them.' Polovtsiev was silent, while with his large palm he long and gently stroked the black cat which had jumped on to his knees. Then he whispered, and there was an unusual warmth and tenderness in his voice:

'Puss, puss! Little pussy! How black you are! I'm fond of cats, Lukich. The horse and the cat are the cleanest of all the animals. I had a Siberian cat at home, it was a huge fluffy one. It always slept with me ... Its colour was ...' Polovtsiev thoughtfully screwed up his eyes, smiled, and gently moved his fingers. 'It was a smoky grey with white patches. It was a remarkable cat. But you don't like cats, do you, Lukich? And I don't like dogs. I hate dogs. You know, when I was a child, I suppose I must have been about eight, we had quite a small puppy, and I was playing with him one day and must have hurt him. He seized hold of my finger and bit until the blood came. I flew into a temper, picked up a stick and began to beat him. He ran away, and I ran after him and beat him ... with the utmost satisfaction! He ran under the granary, and I went after him. He got under the porch, but I drove him out and went on beating him. I beat him so much that he was all wet with his piss, and didn't howl any more, only panted and whimpered. And then I picked him up.' Polovtsiev smiled a little guiltily, shamefacedly, on only one side of his mouth. 'I picked him up and sobbed so much out of pity for him that my heart almost burst. I couldn't stop trembling. My mother ran out, but I lay down on the ground at the side of the puppy close to the coach house, and kicked out my legs. Ever since then I haven't been able to stand a dog. But I'm devilishly fond of cats. And children. Little ones. I'm very fond of them, almost so that it hurts. I can't stand children's tears, they turn me all over inside. But do you like cats or not, old man?'

Yakov Lukich was astonished beyond words at his chief's unusual conversation and demonstration of such simple, human feelings. For he knew Polovtsiev as an elderly, hard-bitten officer, renowned even during the German war for his harshness in handling the cossacks. He shook his head. Polovtsiev was silent; his face grew stern, and in a dry, business-like voice he asked:

'Has there been a post recently?'

'There are floods everywhere; all the valleys are flooded, and there are no roads. We haven't had a post for ten days.'

'Hasn't there been any news in the village about Stalin's article?'

'What article?'

'There was an article of his on the collective farms printed in the papers.'

'No, we haven't heard about it. We couldn't have received those papers yet. But what did the article say, Alexander Anisimovich?'

'Oh, nothing ... It won't interest you. Well, go and get some sleep. Give the horse a drink after about three hours. Tomorrow night get hold of a pair of collective farm horses, and as soon as it's dark we'll ride to Voiskovoi. It isn't far.'

Next morning Polovtsiev had a long talk with the sobered Lyatievsky. After the talk the lieutenant came out into the kitchen, looking pale and angry.

'Perhaps you'd like a drink?' Yakov Lukich anticipatorily asked. But Lyatievsky stared somewhere above his head, and emphatically replied:

'I don't want anything now.' And he went back into his room.

That night Ivan Batalshchikov, one of the cossacks Lukich had persuaded to join the 'Alliance for Emancipation of the Don', was on duty in the collective farm stables. But Yakov Lukich did not tell him where and for what purpose he was going. 'I've got to go a short journey on our affair,' he evasively replied to Ivan's question. And without hesitation Ivan untied a couple of the best horses. Lukich led them out behind the threshing floors, tied them up among the waterside trees, then went to fetch Polovtsiev. As he was approaching the door of the captain's room he heard Lyatievsky shout: 'But that also involves our defeat, don't you realize that?' Polovtsiev harshly replied in his deep bass voice, and, overwhelmed by a presentiment of misfortune, Yakov Lukich quietly knocked.

Polovtsiev carried out his own saddle. They went to the horses, and set off at once. They forded the little river when they got outside the village. Polovtsiev was silent throughout the ride. He forbade smoking, and insisted on riding not along the road, but some twenty yards to one side.

They were expected in Voiskovoi. In the kitchen of a cossack acquaintance of Yakov's some twenty villagers were gathered. The majority were old men. Polovtsiev shook hands with them all, then went with one of them to the window, and talked in undertones for some five minutes. The others silently stared first at Polovtsiev, then at Yakov Lukich. And Yakov, who had seated himself close to the door, felt lost and awkward among these cossacks who were strangers or the barest acquaintances.

The window was closely covered on the inside with sacking, the shutters were fastened, and the master's son-in-law kept watch in the yard. But, despite all these precautions, Polovtsiev spoke in whispers.

'Well, cossacks,' he said, 'the hour is at hand. The days of our slavery are drawing to an end, it's time to act. Our fighting organization is ready. We shall act the night after tomorrow. Half a company of horsemen will ride into Voiskovoi, and at the first shot you must run and seize these propaganda columnists in their quarters. Let not one of them escape alive! I'm putting Cornet Marin in command of your group. I advise you to sew white ribbons on your caps before you begin, so as not to be confused with the enemy in the dark. Every man must have ready his horse and such arms as he possesses, sword, rifle or fowling piece and three days' victuals. After you've settled with the propaganda column and your local communists, your group will join forces with the half-company sent to your assistance; the command will then pass into the hands of the commander of the half-company. Under his orders you will ride where he leads you.'

Polovtsiev sighed deeply, drew the fingers of his left hand out of the belt of his shirt, wiped the sweat from his brow with the back of his hand, and continued in a louder tone :

'I've brought with me from Gremyachy Log a cossack you all know, my old regimental comrade Yakov Lukich. He will confirm that the majority of the Gremyachy cossacks are ready to act with us in the great task of liberating the Don from the yoke of the communists. Now, Ostrovnov !'

Polovtsiev's weighty glance brought Yakov Lukich up from his stool. He promptly rose to his feet, feeling an unusual heaviness in his body, and a burning in his dry throat. But he had no chance to speak, for he was forestalled by a cossack who appeared to be the oldest man present, a member of the local church council, who until the war had been a permanent guardian of the Voiskovoi church day-school. He rose together with Lukich, and gave him no opportunity to say a word.

'But have you heard, your Excellency, captain,' he asked, 'that ... Before you arrived we'd been talking things over among ourselves ... We've received a very interesting newspaper ...'

'What? What are you saying, grand-dad?' Polovtsiev slowly demanded in a hoarse tone.

'I said a newspaper's come from Moscow, and in it is printed a letter from the chairman of all the party ...'

'The secretary,' one of the others corrected him.

'Well then, the secretary of all the party, comrade Stalin. Here's the paper, dated the fourth of this month,' the old man unhurryingly replied in his aged tenor voice. Out of the inside pocket of his jacket he drew a newspaper carefully folded into four. 'We read it aloud among ourselves a little while before you arrived, and ... it works out that this paper's separated us from you. It's clear now that we, the peasants that is, have got another road to take in life. We heard about this paper yesterday, and this morning I got on my horse and, despite my age. I rode to the district town. I had to swim the horse across one ravine; with tears in my eyes I rode, but I got across. I pleaded with a man I know to let me have it for the love of Christ; I bought it from him and paid for it. Fifteen roubles I paid ! And afterwards I looked at it and the price marked on it is five kopeks. But they're getting the money for me from the group, ten kopeks from each yard; that's what we've decided. But the paper was worth it all, and I think even more ...'

'What are you talking about, grand-dad? What is it you're bringing us from beyond the Don and across the seas? Have you lost your senses in your old age? Who gave you authority to speak in the name of all the men present?' Polovtsiev demanded with an angry quiver in his voice.

A stocky cossack came forward. Judging by his looks he was some forty years of age, with cropped, golden whiskers and a squashed nose. He stepped out from a crowd standing along the wall, and spoke challengingly and angrily.

'Don't you shout at our old men, comrade former officer, you did enough shouting at them in the old days. There's been enough lording it, and now you must talk without using rough language. Under the Soviet regime we've got unused to such treatment, don't you see? And our old man said truly that we've been talking it over, and owing to this article in *Pravda* we've decided not to revolt. Your road and ours have completely separated now. Our village authorities have been stupid; they've driven some of us into the collective farm, they've unfairly treated many middling peasants as kulaks, and our government didn't understand that you can only frighten girls, but you can't treat all the people like that. The chairman of our Soviet tried to muzzle us so much that we weren't allowed to say a word against him at a meeting. They tightened up the girths so well that we couldn't breathe; but a good master loosens the girths round his horse when going over sand or along a heavy road, and tries to make it easier for her. Well, we did think, of course, that the order had come from the central authorities to squeeze the fat out of us and we understood that this propaganda had been started by the Central Committee of the Communists, and we said the windmill sails don't turn without wind. And so you see, that's why we decided to rise and join your Alliance. But now it comes out that Stalin's going to remove from their positions all those local communists who drove the people forcibly into the collective farms, and closed down the churches for no reason whatever without being asked. And it appears the peasant's going to have an easier time; they've loosened his saddle-girths. If you want to you can join the collective farm, but if you want to you can remain an individual peasant. And so that's how we've decided. Give us back the documents we were stupid enough to sign and give you, and go where you will. We shan't do you any harm because we're tarred with the same brush . . .'

Polovtsiev walked across to the window, leaned his back against the jamb, and turned so pale that all noticed it. But his voice sounded firm and dry of tone, when, looking around them all, he asked:

'What is this, cossacks? Treachery?'

'Call it what you like,' another old man replied. 'What you like, but you and us are not going the same road now. Once the master himself has come to our defence, why should we crawl off to others? They took my vote away from me for no reason whatever, and wanted to exile me. But I've got a son in the Red Army, and so I shall get back my right to vote. We're not against the Soviet government, but against our own village disorders. But you wanted to turn us against the government. No, that won't do! Give us back our papers, we ask in good will . . .'

One other elderly cossack spoke, slowly stroking his curly little beard with his left hand.

'We've missed the mark, comrade Polovtsiev . . . God knows we've missed the mark. We were wrong in linking ourselves up with you. Well, there's no harm done in asking, and now we shall walk without wobbling. The last time we listened to you you promised us the golden mountains. And we were surprised: you were promising a little too much! You said that if there was a rising our allies would at once send arms and all military necessities. All we had to do was to shoot the communists. But afterwards we thought it over, and where did we get to? They'll bring arms, they're cheap enough; but will they come themselves to our land? And even if they do, we shall never get rid of them afterwards. We might have to drive them, too, off the Russian earth with pikes. The communists are our own people, they're Russians like us. But those others, the devil knows what language they talk. They're all stuck-up, they won't give you snow in mid-winter no matter how hard you plead, and if you get in their way, then don't expect any mercy. I was abroad in 1920; I tasted the French bread in Gallipoli and never hoped to drag my legs back home again. Their bread is too bitter for me! And I saw many nations, and I will say that there's no better or kinder-hearted nation than the Russian people. I worked in the ports at Constantinople and Athens, and had a good look at the English and French. Some well-ironed reptile would walk past you and make a face because you were unshaven, dirty as mud, and so you smelt; and he would look at you as if he could kill you. He would be like an officer's nag, washed and scraped down to his crupper, and he'd be proud of it and look down on you. In the public-houses their sailors would jeer at us, and if we said anything they landed out with their fists. But our Don and Kuban cossacks got a little used to foreign countries, and began to weigh it out to them.' The cossack smiled, and his teeth gleamed like a bluish blade in his beard. 'One of us landed out in the Russian fashion at some Englishman, and he was knocked off his feet, and lay holding his head and snorting. They're tender to the Russian fist, and though they feed well they're flabby. We've had a taste of these allies! No, we'll make our peace somehow with our own government, but we're not going to wash our dirty linen in public. Please to give us our papers back.'

'He'll be jumping through the window directly, and I'll be left like a fish in the shallows,' Yakov Lukich thought. 'A fine mess I've got into! Oh, mother, you bore me in an evil hour. I've linked myself up with a devil! The unclean spirit has led me astray.' He fidgeted on the bench and did not remove his eyes from Polovtsiev. But the captain stood calmly at the window, and his cheek was no longer pale, but flushed with the dark crimson of anger and resolution. Two swollen veins stood out on his forehead; his hands were firmly gripping the window-sill.

'Well, cossacks, it's your will! If you don't want to come in with us, we shan't ask you to. We're not going down on our knees to you. I won't return the papers. I haven't got them with me, they're at the staff. But you've got no reason to fear, I shan't go to the G.P.U. and inform against you ...'

'That's true,' one of the old men agreed.

'And it isn't the G.P.U. you have to fear.' Polovtsiev, who hitherto had spoken slowly and quietly, suddenly began to shout at the top of his voice. 'It's us you've got to be afraid of! We shall shoot you as traitors. Well, out of the road! Stand aside! Over to the walls!' Drawing his revolver, and holding it in his outstretched hand, he went towards the door.

The cossacks rushed to make way for him, while Yakov Lukich

went in front of Polovtsiev, sent the door flying open with his shoulder, and flew out into the porch like a stone flung from a catapult.

In the darkness they untied the horses and rode off at a trot. A hum of agitated voices came from the hut. But nobody came out, not one of the cossacks attempted to detain them.

They galloped back to Gremyachy Log, and Yakov Lukich took the steaming horses to the collective farm stables. When Polovtsiev entered the hut he did not remove his sheepskin jacket or his fur cap, but at once ordered Lyatievsky to get ready to leave, read a letter arrived by horse courier during his absence, burnt it in the stove and began to pack his things in his saddle-bags.

When Yakov Lukich returned from the stables Polovtsiev called him into his room. He found the captain sitting at the table. His eyes glittering, Lyatievsky was cleaning a revolver, putting the well-greased parts together with swift, exact movements. At the creak of the door Polovtsiev removed his hand from his brow, and turned to face Lukich. Yakov noticed that tears were running down the captain's deeply sunken, bloodshot eyes, and gleaming on the broad bridge of his nose.

'I'm crying because we've failed ... for this time,' Polovtsiev said in ringing tones. With a sweeping gesture he removed his white lambswool cap and dried his eyes with it. 'The Don has grown poor in true cossacks, and rich in swine: in traitors and villains. We're leaving in a few minutes, Lukich, but we shall come back! I've just received this letter ... The cossacks have refused to revolt in Tubyanskoe and in my own district, too. Stalin has won them over with his article. There's the man I'd like to lay my hands on now, I'd ...' There was a gurgling sound in Polovtsiev's throat, the muscles worked beneath his cheekbones, and the fingers of his sinewy hands crooked and pressed into the the palms until the joints stood out. Sighing deeply and hoarsely he slowly extended his fingers and smiled on one side of his mouth. 'What a people! Scum! Fools, bearing God's curse! They don't realize that this article is a shameful fraud, a manoeuvre. And they believe it like children. Oh, damn them! They're the scum of the earth! For the sake of high politics the fools are played like a fish on a hook, the reins are slackened so that they shan't be choked to death, and they take it all in good faith. Well, all right! They'll understand and be sorry, but then it'll be too late. We're going off, Yakov Lukich. Christ save you for your hospitality, for everything you've done. And this is my order to you: don't withdraw from the collective farm, but do what harm you can to it. And tell those in our "Alliance" my resolute word: we're retreating for the time being, but we're not shattered. We shall come back, and then woe to those who have left us, have betrayed us and the cause ... the great cause of saving the Fatherland and the Don from the government of international Jews! Death at a cossack's sabre shall be their payment, tell them!'

'I'll tell them!' Yakov Lukich whispered.

Polovtsiev's speech and tears deeply affected Lukich, but in spirit he was terribly glad that he was getting free of his dangerous guests, that everything had ended so that in future there would be no need to risk his possessions and his skin.

'I'll tell them,' he repeated, and ventured to ask:

'But where are you going, Alexander Anisimovich?'

'What do you want to know for?' Polovtsiev cautiously asked.

'It may be needed, or someone may come for you.'

Polovtsiev shook his head and rose.

'No,' he said. 'That I can't tell you. But you can expect to see me again within three weeks. Good-bye.' He held out his cold hand to Lukich.

He himself saddled his horse, carefully smoothed the folds out of the saddle-cloth, and tightened the girths. Lyatievsky waited until he was in the yard before he said good-bye to Lukich, then thrust a couple of notes into his hand.

'Are you going on foot?' Yakov asked him.

'I'm only leaving your yard on foot; my own motor is waiting for me in the street,' the irrepressible lieutenant jested. Waiting until Polovtsiev had seated himself in the saddle, he took hold of the stirrup strap. 'Well, gallop, prince, to the enemy's camp, and I on foot will keep pace with you,' he declaimed.

Yakov Lukich saw them out of the yard, then, with a feeling of tremendous relief, he bolted the gate and crossed himself. Anxiously pulling out of his pocket the notes Lyatievsky had given him, he tried hard in the glooms of the early morning to make out their value, and to decide by their feel whether they were false or not.

Chapter 28

The Party Line

THE newspaper containing Stalin's article 'Dizzy with Successes', which had been held up by the floods, was brought to Gremyachy Log by the postman on the morning of 20 March. The three copies of *Molot* dated 4 March went the round of all the huts, and by the evening were transformed into damp, greasy, ragged fragments. Never during all Gremyachy Log's existence had a newspaper gathered so many readers and listeners around it as on that day. They collected into groups in huts, at street corners, at the backs of yards, by the entrances to granaries. One read aloud while the others listened, afraid of losing one word, keeping silence by all means. The article caused great argument everywhere. Each man interpreted it in his own fashion, and in the majority of cases in accordance with his own wishes. Almost everywhere, if Nagulnov or Davidov appeared the paper was, for some unknown reason, passed hurriedly from hand to hand, flying like a white bird across the crowd, until it disappeared into someone's capacious pocket.

'Well, now the collective farms will burst at the seams like rotten clothes,' the exultant Bannik was the first to express an opinion aloud.

'The rubbish will be washed away, but the heavier stuff will remain,' Diemka Ushakov replied to him.

'You look out that the opposite doesn't happen,' Bannik spitefully remarked, before he hurried off to find more reliable cossacks to whom to whisper : 'Grumble and get out of the collective farm, while they've announced that the serfs are free !'

'The middling peasant's gone bandy! He's got one foot in the collective farm, but he's lifted the other and is shaking it free, already trying to see how he can step back out of the collective farm into his own,' Pavel Liubishkin said to Arkady. He pointed to a group of cossacks, middling peasants who had joined the farm, who were standing talking excitedly.

The women, who understood very little of the matter at all, occupied themselves in their feminine fashion with guesses and surmises. And the rumours spread through the village:

'The collective farms are being broken up!'

'Moscow has ordered the cows to be given back!'

'The kulaks are coming home and are going to join the collective farms.'

'Those who've lost their votes are to have them back.'

'They're opening the church at Tubyanskoe, and the seed grain which was stored in it is being distributed to the collective farmers for food.'

Great events were impending. Everybody felt that. In the evening, at a private meeting of the party nucleus Davidov spoke with obvious nervousness:

'Comrade Stalin's article is very timely indeed. For instance, it gives Makar one not between the eyes, but right in the eye. Makar's head had got dizzy with successes, and our heads, too, had swum a little. I'd be glad of suggestions, comrades, as to what part of our policy we've got to correct. We've already given back the fowls, we saw the need for that in good time. But what are we to do about the sheep and cows? What are we to do with them, I ask you? If we don't act politically in the matter we shall get . . . we shall get a sort of signal flying: "Save yourself who can!" "Run from the collective farms!" Fact! And they'll run, taking all the cattle with them. And all we shall be left with will be a broken cattle-trough, that's very certain!'

Nagulnov, who had been the last to arrive at the meeting, rose to his feet, and fixed his watery bloodshot eyes stubbornly on Davidov. As he began to speak Davidov smelt the pungent scent of vodka coming from him.

'So you say that article hits me in the eye?' he demanded. 'But you're wrong; it's not in my eye, but right in my heart. Right through and out at the back! And my head went dizzy not when we set up the collective farm, but just now, after reading this article . . .'

'After a bottle of vodka,' Vania Naidionov quietly interposed.

Razmiotnov smiled and winked sympathetically, while Davidov bent his head over the table. But Makar dilated his nostrils, and a frenzy glittered in his filmy eyes as he cried:

'You're young to teach me and give me lessons! Your navel wasn't dry when I was fighting for the Soviet regime and joined the Party. And that's that! But as our Davidov would say, it's a fact that I've been drinking today. And not one bottle, but two!'

'You've found something to boast about! That's why you're talking nonsense,' Razmiotnov glumly remarked.

Makar only gave him a sidelong glance, but he went on more quietly, and, instead of waving his hand meaninglessly, he pressed it firmly to his breast. So he remained standing until the end of his disconnected fiery speech.

'I'm not talking nonsense now, you're lying, Andrei! I've been drinking because this article of Stalin's has pierced me through and through like a bullet, and the hot blood is boiling in me!' Makar's voice quivered and sank to even lower tones. 'I'm the secretary of the nucleus here, that's correct, isn't it? I came to the people and to you, you devils, in order to drive the chickens and geese into the collective farm, didn't I? How did I make propaganda for the collective farm? Like this: Although they were reckoned as middling peasants, I told some of our villains straight out: "So you won't join the collective farm? So you're against the Soviet government? You fought against us and opposed us in 1919, and you're still against us? Well, then don't expect any peace from me! I'll send you to the grave so messed up that all the devils will be sick at the sight of you!" Did I talk like that? I did, and I even banged my pistol on the table. I don't deny it! True I didn't say it to everybody, but only to those who are especially against us in their hearts. And I'm not drunk now, so none of your silly remarks, thank you! I couldn't stand that article, and because of it I went and drank for the first time in six months. What is that article? It's one that our comrade Stalin wrote, and it hits me, Makar Nagulnov that is, smack! And there I am

242

lying face downward in, the mud, ground down, knocked off my feet ... And how is that? Comrades! I agree that I deviated to the left over the chickens and the other livestock. But brothers, brothers, why did I deviate? And why do you hang Trotsky round my neck, yoking me up to him? You, Davidov, you're everlastingly flinging it in my face that I'm a left-wing Trotskyist. But I don't know my letters like Trotsky and I'm not like him ... I didn't graft myself on to the Party like a learned bit of gristle, but with my heart and with the blood I've poured out for the Party.'

'Talk to the point, Makar! What are you blowing the bagpipes for, when time's so precious? Time won't wait; make some proposal how we're to correct our general mistakes, for now you're talking just like Trotsky: "I'm in the Party, I and the Party ..." '

'Let me speak!' Makar began to roar, flaring up and pressing his right hand still more firmly to his chest. 'I spurn Trotsky! It's a disgrace for me to stand on the same footing as him now. I'm no traitor, and I warn you beforehand: anyone who calls me a Trotskyist will get his snout smashed! I'll beat it into pulp! And I went "left" over the chickens not because of Trotsky, but because I was in a hurry for the world revolution. Because of that I wanted to do everything quicker and quicker, and tie up the property owner, the petty bourgeoisie, tighter and tighter! Everything was to be a step nearer to dealing with world capitalism! Well? What are you silent for? And now it works out like this: Who am I according to comrade Stalin's article? This is what is written in the middle of it.' Makar drew the *Pravda* out of his sheepskin jacket, opened it, and slowly began to read: ' "To whose benefit are these distortions, this bureaucratic decreeing of a collective farm movement, these unworthy threats against the peasants? To nobody but our enemies! What may they lead to, these distortions? To the strengthening of our enemies and the discrediting of the collective farm movement idea. Is it not clear that the authors of these distortions, who think they are left-wingers, are in reality supplying water to the mill of right-wing opportunism?" So it comes out that I'm a decreeing bureaucrat and author, that I've discredited the collective farms, and supplied water for the right-wing opportunists to get their mill to work. And all this because of a few sheep and chickens, damn them! And because I've frightened a few Whites who came into the collective farm to put the brakes on! It isn't sound! We set up the collective farm, and now that article beats the retreat. I led the squadron against the Poles and against Wrangel, and I know that once you've started to attack you mustn't turn back half-way.'

'Now you've galloped ahead of your squadron like a captain!' Razmiotnov, who had become a firm supporter of Davidov, said with a frown. 'And please finish your speech, Makar, we've got to get down to business! When you're elected Secretary of the Party Central Committee you can throw yourself headlong into the attack. But you're a rank and file soldier now, and you keep to the rank, or we'll soon pull you up!'

'Don't you interrupt, Andrei! I'll submit to any order of the Party, but now I want to speak not because I'm intending to oppose my own party, but because I wish its good. Comrade Stalin wrote that it was necessary to work taking local conditions into account, didn't he? Then why do you do, Davidov, say that the article hits me in the eye? It doesn't say in so many words that Makar Nagulnov is an author and a bureaucrat, does it? And maybe those words don't refer to me at all. If comrade Stalin was to come to Gremyachy Log I'd say to him: "Dear Osip Vissariono-vich! So you're against giving our middling peasants the spur? You want to invite them in and try to persuade them by kindness? But supposing a middling peasant was one of the White cossacks in the old days, and is still attached beyond all belief to his prop-erty? Then how am I to fawn on him so that he joins the collective farm and goes patiently towards the world revolution? Supposing this middling peasant joins the collective farm, he still can't give up his property, and all the time he tries to feed his own animals better. That's what he's like!" Well, but supposing, after taking a look at that sort of person, comrade Stalin still insisted that I'd caused a distortion and had discredited the collective farmers, then I'd say to him straight out: "Let the devil credit them, comrade Stalin, but I can't any longer because of the state of my health, which was ruined at the fronts. Let me go to the Chinese frontier, I could be of great help to the party there. And let Andrei Raz-miotnov collectivize Gremyachy. He's got a back that will bend,

he can bow beautifully to the former Whites, and shed tears ...
He can do that, too.'"

'Leave me out of it, or I can give you a dose, too ...'

'Oh, well, that's enough, quite enough for today.' Davidov
rose, went right up to Makar and with unusual chilliness in his
voice asked him : 'Comrade Stalin's article, comrade Nagulnov, is
the line of the Central Committee. Do you mean to say that you
don't agree with the article?'

'No, I don't agree with it.'

'But do you admit your mistakes? I admit mine, for instance.
You can't fight facts and you can't jump over your own head. I not
only admit that we put too much salt in the porridge, by socializing the smaller animals and the calves, but I shall correct my
mistakes. We've been too interested in the percentage of collectivization, although that's the District Committee's fault too, and
we've worked too little on making the collective farm itself a
success. Do you admit that, comrade Nagulnov?'

'I do.'

'Then what is your point?'

'The article is unsound ...'

For a minute Davidov smoothed the dirty French cloth on the
table with his palm, and unnecessarily turned up the wick of the
steadily burning lamp. Evidently he was trying to control his
agitation. But he could not.

'You're a block of oak, you devil ! In other places they'd have
sent you flying out of the party for those words ! Fact ! Have you
gone out of your mind? Either you stop your ... opposition at
once, or we'll give you ... Fact ! We've stood enough of your dec-
larations, and if you hold to them seriously, right-ho ! We shall
officially inform the District Committee of your attack on the
party line.'

'Inform them, then ! I'll inform them myself. I'll answer for
Bannik and everything else all together.'

Davidov calmed down a little as he listened to Makar's strangled
voice, but, shrugging his shoulders with unappeased indignation,
he said :

'Do you know what, Makar? Go and sleep it off and then we'll
have a serious talk with you. At present we're like in the story

of the white bull: "Did you and I go together?" "We did." "Did we find a sheepskin?" "We did." "Well, let's divide the sheepskin according to the agreement." "What sheepskin?" "But did you and I go together?" "We did ..." and so on without end! One minute you say you admit your mistakes, and the next you declare that the article's unsound. What mistakes do you admit, if in your view the article is unsound? You've got all mixed up! Fact! And another thing. Since when has any secretary of a party nucleus begun to come drunk to a nucleus meeting? Do you know what that is, Nagulnov? It's a party crime! You're an old member of the party, a Red Partisan, a member of the Order of the Red Banner, and you suddenly turn up like that ... Here's Naidionov our Young Communist; what must he think of your state? And if it gets to the ears of the Control Commission that you're drinking, and at such a serious time, and that you've not only frightened middling peasants with arms in your hands, but have taken up a non-Bolshevik attitude to your distortions and are even attacking the party line, there'll be miserable consequences for you, Nagulnov! Not only will you no longer be secretary of the nucleus, but you won't even be a member of the party, understand that! I tell you that is a fact!' He rumpled his hair, and was silent, feeling that he had touched Makar to the quick. Then he continued: 'There's no point in arranging a discussion about the article. You won't bring the party to your point of view; it's broken the horn of better men than you and made them submit. Don't you realize that?'

'Don't waste any more time on him! He's occupied a good hour with his talk and there was nothing to listen to! Let him go and sleep. Go on, Makar! Shame on you! Look at yourself in the glass and you'll be horrified: your face all swollen, your eyes like a mad dog's. What did you want to turn up like that for? Clear off!' Razmiotnov jumped up and shook Makar furiously by the shoulder. But with a languid, lifeless movement Makar removed his hand, and huddled into himself more than ever.

In the oppressive silence that followed, Davidov drummed on the table with his fingers. Vania Naidionov, who had sat staring at Nagulnov all the time with a perplexed smile on his face, requested:

'Let's get on, comrade Davidov.'

'Well, then, comrades,' Davidov said rather more cheerfully, 'I propose that we return the smaller animals and cows to the collective farmers, but where they handed over two cows we must try to persuade them to leave one in the collective farm socialized herd. The first thing tomorrow morning we must call a meeting and explain the position. We must put all our efforts into explanations at the moment. I'm afraid we shall be getting a general exodus from the collective farm, and we ought to be going out to the fields any day now. That's where you want to show your mettle, Makar! Persuade them, and without using a pistol, not to leave the collective farm, and that will be something worth doing. Well then, shall we vote on my proposal? Who's in favour? Aren't you voting, Makar? Well, note in the minutes that there was one abstention.'

Razmiotnov proposed that war should be waged on the marmots, beginning the very next day. For this task it was decided to mobilize some of the collective farmers, choosing men who would not be occupied in field work, and allotting them several pairs of bullocks for carting water. Also the schoolmaster was to be asked to go out into the fields with his scholars, for the children to help in drowning the animals.

For the time being Davidov was uncertain whether to bring pressure to bear on Nagulnov or not. Should he raise the matter by calling on him to answer to the party for his attack on Stalin's article, for his reluctance to correct the left-wing mistakes he had committed when the collective farm was being established? But towards the end of the meeting he glanced at Makar's sweating, deathly pale face, at the veins standing out on his temples, and decided: 'No, better not! He'll understand of his own accord. Let him admit he's wrong without any pressure being brought on him. He's gone wrong, but it's terrible, after all he's one of us. And then there's his illness, his fits. No, we'll keep the matter quiet.'

But Makar sat silent until the meeting was finished, showing no signs of his agitation. Only once, as Davidov glanced at him he noticed that Makar's hands were trembling terribly as they lay helplessly on his knees.

'Take Nagulnov home with you for the night, and see that he doesn't drink,' Davidov whispered to Razmiotnov. Andrei nodded his head in assent.

Davidov returned home alone. He passed a group of cossacks sitting on a fallen fence outside a yard, talking animatedly. Davidov was walking on the opposite side of the road, and as he drew level, in the darkness he heard an unknown voice say confidently, with a smile in its deep tones:

'... no matter how much you give, how much you pay, it's always too little for them.'

Another low voice added:

'The Soviet regime has grown two wings now, a right and a left. When will it fly away from us to the devil?'

There was an outburst of laughter from several throats, then it died away with unexpected suddenness. 'S-sh!' came an anxious whisper. Immediately the same bass voice drawled, without the least hint of humour, in an assumed, business-like tone:

'Yes! So long as rain doesn't fall we'll soon get the sowing done. The earth's drying as I've never seen it before. Well, brothers, time for bed, I think. Good night, all of you.'

A cough, and footsteps ...

Chapter 29

Deserting the Farm

THE following day twenty-three cossacks handed in notices of withdrawal from the collective farm. The majority were middling peasants who had been among the last to join, usually sat silent at the meetings, were continually arguing with the foremen, and were reluctant to work. It was of them that Nagulnov had said: 'D'you call them collective farmers? They're neither fish nor flesh!' Those who left had been essentially dead ballast, who had joined either through fear of falling into disfavour with the government, or had been carried away by the powerful social drive into the collective farm during the early days.

When Davidov received the notices he attempted to argue with them, advised them to think it over, to wait a little. But they stood to their guns, and at last he waved his hand:

'All right, citizens; but remember that when you ask to be taken back into the collective farm we shall think twice whether to accept you or not.'

'We're not likely to ask to be taken back! We hope to manage to live without the collective farm again. You see, Davidov, we managed somehow to live without it before, we didn't swell with hunger, we were masters of our own goods, strangers didn't show us how to plough, how to sow, we were never under slave-drivers, and we think we shall live without the collective farm and not regret it.' So Ivan Batalshchikov answered for them all, smiling into his twisted chestnut whiskers.

'And we shall manage to get on without you somehow! We shan't cry and go thin over it! Fact! It's easier for the horse when the woman's off the cart,' Davidov retorted.

'And it's better we should part friends. Glass against glass, and separate with no offence done. May we collect our cattle from the brigade?'

'No. We shall raise that question at the management committee. Wait till tomorrow.'

'We haven't got time to wait. You in the collective farm can start sowing after Whitsun, maybe, but we must go out to the fields. We'll wait till tomorrow, but if you keep our cattle a day longer we shall take them ourselves.'

There was a direct threat in the tone of Batalshchikov's voice, and Davidov flushed a little with anger as he replied:

'I shall see how you'll manage to take anything from the collective farm stables without the management knowing! In the first place we shan't hand them over, and in the second, if you take them you'll answer for it in court.'

'For our own cattle?'

'At the moment they're collective farm cattle.'

Davidov felt not the least regret at letting these men go, but

Diemid the Silent's notice of withdrawal affected him unpleasantly. Diemid came along in the early evening, badly drunk, yet as taciturn as ever. Without a word of greeting he held out a piece of newspaper with the words written across the text: 'Let me leave the collective farm.'

Davidov turned over the laconic application in his hands, and with some surprise and dissatisfaction in his voice he asked:

'What does this mean from you?'

'I'm going away,' Diemid bellowed.

'Where to? What for?'

'Out of the collective farm, that's where.'

'But what are you leaving for? Where are you going?'

Diemid was silent, and he stretched his arms out wide.

'D'you want to go to all the four corners of the earth?' Razmiotnov interpreted his gesture.

'That's it!'

'But why are you leaving?' Davidov insisted, flabbergasted by the withdrawal of a poor peasant and active worker.

'Other people are leaving . . . And I'm following them.'

'But if the other people throw themselves head first over a cliff, will you do the same?' the quietly smiling Razmiotnov asked.

'Well, hardly, brother!' Diemid burst into a hollow guffaw. His laugh was astonishingly like the rumble of an empty barrel.

'All right then, drop out,' Davidov sighed. 'You can take your cow. As you're a poor peasant we'll hand it back to you without any argument. Fact! We'll give it back, shan't we, Razmiotnov?'

'We must,' Razmiotnov agreed. But Diemid again guffawed thunderously, and barked:

'I've got no use for the cow. I give it to the collective farm. I'll have to work for my son-in-law. What d'you think of that? You're not surprised, are you?' He went out without saying good-bye.

Davidov glanced out of the window, and saw Diemid standing motionless by the porch. The crimson setting sun streamed over his bearish back, his brown, powerful neck, the curly golden hair growing down to his collar. The collective farmyard was flooded with thaw-water. An enormous puddle stretched from the porch to the granary. From the steps a path trodden out in the crumbling snow ran past the wattle fence. In order to avoid the puddle people usually walked along right against the fence, holding on to the stakes. Diemid stood in a dull, heavy contemplation. Then he swayed, and suddenly, with drunken indifference, walked straight into the water and made his way to the granary, reeling slowly and unsteadily.

As he interestedly watched him, Davidov saw Diemid pick up a scrap of iron lying by the granary steps, then go towards the gate.

'He hasn't made up his mind to smash us up, has he, the devil?' Razmiotnov, who had come to the window, asked with a laugh. He had always had a warm and friendly feeling for Diemid, and a secret invincible respect for the man's physical strength.

Diemid half-opened the gate, and threw the scrap of iron with such force against a frozen snowdrift that he knocked off an enormous lump of ice weighing some three poods. The icy fragments rattled like hail against the gate, and through the channel made by the iron the water silently ebbed away from the yard.

'Well, he'll come back to the collective farm!' Razmiotnov said, seizing Davidov by the shoulder and pointing after Diemid. 'He saw something wrong, put it right and went off. That means he's left his spirit behind him in the farm. Don't you think so?'

Shortly after the newspapers containing Stalin's article arrived in the district, the District Committee sent the Gremyachy Party nucleus a lengthy letter of instruction on the subject. But it dealt only vaguely and unintelligibly with the problem of eradicating the effects of forced collectivization. It was obvious that there was complete bewilderment in the District Committee, and nobody from the district authorities showed his face in any of the collective farms. When the local workers wrote asking what was to happen to the property of those who left the collective farms, neither the Committee nor the District Agricultural Union made any reply. Only after the Central Committee's resolution 'On the Struggle against Distortions of the Party Line in the Collective Farm Movement' had been issued did the District Committee bestir itself. Then Gremyachy Log was overwhelmed with instructions to supply urgently lists of evicted kulaks, to return the small cattle and fowls to their former owners, and to revise the lists of those deprived of voting rights. At the same time an official instruction was received requiring Nagulnov to attend a joint meeting of the District Committee Bureau and the District Control Commission at 10 a.m. of 28 March.

Chapter 30

Two Lovers Part

IN the course of a week about a hundred farms were withdrawn from the collective farm in Gremyachy Log. There was a particularly strong withdrawal from the second brigade, which was left with only nineteen farms. Even among these nineteen there were several cossacks who were 'due for flight', as the brigade leader Liubishkin expressed it.

The village was shaken with events. Every day brought Davidov fresh unpleasantness. In reply to his repeated inquiry whether the draught cattle and agricultural implements were to be returned to the former members immediately, or after the sowing period, the District Agricultural Union and Party Committee replied with a thunderous instruction, of which the purport was that by all means and with all their power the Gremyachy workers were to avert the break-up of the collective farm, were to restrain as large a number of members as possible from resigning, and were to delay all settlements with former members, including the return of their property, until the autumn.

A day or two later Bieglikh, the head of the District Agricultural Department and a member of the District Committee Bureau, arrived at Gremyachy. Hurriedly, for he had several village soviets to visit in the course of that one day, he acquainted himself with the local situation, and then declared:

'Not in any circumstances are you to hand back the cattle and implements to the members who have resigned. Leave it till the autumn, and then we shall see.'

'But they're at our throats about it,' Davidov attempted to object. Bieglikh, a firm and resolute man, only smiled.

'Then you go at them in your turn,' he replied. 'Of course by rights we ought to return their property, but the Regional Committee takes the attitude that they are to be given back only in exceptional cases, observing the class principle.'

'Which is?'

'Well, you ought to understand that without any "which is". Give them back to the poor, but promise the middling peasants they'll have theirs in the autumn. Now is it clear?'

'But won't the same thing happen as with hundred per cent collectivization, Bieglikh? The District Committee took the attitude that we were to drive for a hundred per cent at all costs and as soon as possible. And we went dizzy. If we don't give the middling peasants their cattle back, that means that in fact we're putting pressure on them, doesn't it? What will they plough and sow with?'

'It's not for you to worry over that. Your concern is not with the individual peasant, but with your collective farm. What are you going to work with if you hand back the cattle? And besides, it's not our proposal, but the Regional Committee's. And as soldiers of the revolution we have to submit to it without reservation. How do you think you're going to fulfil the plan, if fifty per cent of your cattle goes back to the individual peasants? No talks, and no discussions! Hold on to the cattle tooth and nail! If you don't fulfil the sowing plan you'll lose your head!'

As he was seating himself in his britzka he casually remarked:

'Altogether, things are difficult. We've got to pay for the distortions, brother, and someone will have to be made a scapegoat. That's the system. Our people of the District Committee are ready to tear Nagulnov to bits. What's he been up to here? I hear he beat up some middling peasant, arrested him and threatened him with a pistol. So Samokhin told me. He's got a whole pile of papers on the case. Yes, Nagulnov's turned out to be a "left-winger" on a grand scale. And d'you know what the attitude is now? Punishment right down to exclusion from the Party! Well, good-bye! Hold on to the cattle.'

Bieglikh drove off to Voiskovoi. The wind had not completely dried the marks of his britzka wheels when Agafon Dubtsiev, the leader of the third brigade, came running up in great agitation.

'Comrade Davidov!' he cried. 'They've taken oxen and horses from me – those who've resigned from the collective farm. They took them by force.'

'What d'you mean, "taken them"?' Davidov shouted, turning livid.

'What I say! They've taken them. They locked up the herdsman in the hayloft, untied the bullocks and drove them off into the steppe. Eighteen pairs of bullocks and seven horses. What are we to do about it?'

'Oh, you ... And what did you do? Where were you? Why did you let them? Where the devil did you ... Well?'

Patches of white appeared on Agafon's thickly pockmarked face, and he, too, raised his voice:

'I'm not obliged to sleep in the cattle stables. You needn't shout at me! And if you're so very brave yourself, you go and get the bullocks back! You may get a stake shoved between your shoulders.'

Not until late afternoon were the bullocks recovered from the steppe pasturage to which their former owners had driven them under a strong guard. Liubishkin, Agafon and six members of the third brigade mounted horses and rode off into the steppe. Seeing the bullocks pasturing on the farther slope of a valley, Liubishkin divided his little detachment into two.

'Agafon, you take three men and ride at a fast trot across the valley to get at them from the right flank, and I'll tackle them from the left.' Liubishkin stroked his raven whiskers, and ordered: 'Give your horses the rein! At a trot, after me, forward!'

The matter was not settled without a fight. Liubishkin's cousin Zakhar, who, with three other recent collective farm members, was guarding the bullocks, managed to seize Mishka Ignationok by the leg as he was rounding up the animals. He pulled him off his horse and dragged him over the ground, leaving him badly bruised and with his shirt ripped clean from his back. While Liubishkin, without dismounting, laid about his cousin with a stout long stockwhip, the others drove off the herdsmen, captured the cattle and took them back at a trot to the village.

Davidov gave orders that the cattle-sheds and stables were to be padlocked at night, and pickets to be set from among the collective farm members. But despite all the measures taken to protect the animals, in two days seven pairs of bullocks and three horses were captured by former members. The cattle were driven off to distant valleys in the steppe, and in order that adults should not be missed from the village, lads were sent with them as herdsmen.

A throng of people jostled into the collective farm office and the village Soviet from morning till night. And the management found itself faced with the further threat that the former members would seize the collective farm lands.

'Either allot us land at once, or we shall begin to plough our old fields !' they demanded of Davidov.

'We'll allot you land; don't get agitated, citizens ! We'll begin the allotment tomorrow. Go to Ostrovnov. He'll have this matter in hand, I tell you as a fact !' Davidov tried to appease them.

'But where will the land be and what sort of land will it be?'

'Wherever it's free.'

'And supposing it's free at the far end of the village lands, what then?'

'Don't play the fool, comrade Davidov ! All the lands close to the village have been taken by the collective farm, so our land will be a good way off, won't it? You won't give us our cattle back, so we've got to sow with our own hands or with cows, and then will you give us distant land? That's the sort of just government we've got !'

Davidov argued, and explained that he could not allot them land just wherever they wanted it, for he could not break up the stretch of collective farm land, or cut wedges out of it and so violate the arrangements made in the autumn. The former members went out grumbling, but in a few minutes another crowd had poured in, shouting as they crossed the threshold :

'Give us land ! What d'you call this ? What right have you got to hold back our land ? That means you're not going to let us sow ! And what did comrade Stalin write about us ? We shall write and tell him you're not only refusing to give us back our cattle, but the land, too. You're robbing us of all right to exist. And he won't praise you for this business !'

'Yakov Lukich, allot them land beyond the Rachy pond to-morrow morning,' Davidov ordered.

'Is that virgin land?' they roared at him.

'It's fallow. How d'you call it virgin land? It's been ploughed, only it was a long time ago, some fifteen years back,' Yakov Lukich explained.

And at once a boiling, stormy shout arose:

'We don't want tough land!'

'What are we to plough it with? What they make children with?'

'Give us land easier to work.'

'Give us back our cattle, then we'll work the hard lands!'

'We'll send delegates to Moscow, to see Stalin himself!'

'Are you trying to kill us off?'

The women were furious with rage. They were willingly and vigorously supported by the cossacks. Great force had to be used to suppress the tumult. Usually Davidov lost control of himself towards the end, and shouted:

'And do you want us to give you the best lands? You won't get them! Fact! The Soviet government is giving all the preference to the collective farms, and not to those who go against the farms. Clear out of here and go to the devil!'

Here and there individual cossacks began to plough and work lands which had formerly belonged to them, but had afterwards been taken over by the collective farm. Liubishkin drove them off the fields, and Yakov Lukich went with a wooden measuring rod and spent two days measuring out allotments of land beyond Rachy pond for the individual peasants.

On 25 March Diemka Ushakov's brigade went out to plough the grey, sandy land. Davidov put the most able-bodied members of the collective farm at the disposal of the brigade leaders, and distributed his forces. The majority of the old men willingly went out with the brigades to tend the sowers, ploughs and harrows. It was decided that no sowing was to be done by hand. Even the decrepit old Akim Beskhlebnov, the former 'chicken-feeler', expressed a desire to tend a sower. Davidov appointed Shchukar stableman to the collective farm office. Everything was ready for work. But the sowing was held up by steady rains. For two days it generously soaked the Gremyachy uplands and ploughed lands, which were wrapped in a white blanket of mist in the mornings.

The resignations from the collective farm came to an end. A strong, reliable core of workers was left. The last to resign in Gremyachy was Andrei Razmiotnov's mistress, Marina Poyarkova. Somehow their life together had gone awry. Marina was drawn towards religion, and became devout. She fasted all through Lent, and during the third week went every day to pray in the Tubyanskoe church, confessing herself and taking the sacrament. She bore Andrei's reproaches silently and meekly, made no answer to his curses, and grew more and more taciturn, in order not to 'desecrate the sacrament'. Arriving home late one night, Andrei saw an ikon lamp burning in the best room. Without thinking much about it he went into the room, took down the lamp, poured the vegetable oil into his palm and thoroughly greased his hard leather boots with it. Then he broke the lamp against his heel.

'The fools have been told again and again that all this is opium and a drug on the mind. And it's no good! They go on praying to their wooden idols, burning oil, making wax into candles. Ah, you ought to have a taste of the knout, Marina! There's something behind this sudden church-going of yours!'

There certainly was something behind it! On 26 March Marina handed in her resignation from the collective farm on the ground that it was 'going against God' to be in it.

'But you're sleeping in the same bed as Andrei; isn't that going against God?' Liubishkin asked with a smile. 'Or is that only a "pleasant little weakness"?'

Once more Marina held her tongue.

But Andrei, pale and angry, came running from the village Soviet. Wiping the sweat from his scarred brow with his sleeve, he asked in front of Davidov and Yakov Lukich:

'Marina! My darling! Don't ruin me, don't bring disgrace on me! What are you leaving the collective farm for? Haven't I had pity on you, haven't I loved you, you devil? They've given you back your cow ... what else do you want? And how can I share my love with you after this, if you're longing for individual life? They've let you have your chickens and fowls, your smooth-necked cock ... And your Dutch gander, which you wept such bitter tears over, is in your yard again. What more do you want? Take your resignation back.'

'Never, never !' Marina shouted, angrily narrowing her slanting eyes. 'I don't want to, so you needn't ask me to ! I don't want to be in the collective farm. I don't want to be in your sin ! Give me back my cart and plough and harrow.'

'Marina, think it over ! Otherwise I'll have to give you up !'

'And the devil take you, you flaxen-haired devil ! You lecher, you accursed hound ! So you're blinking, you unclean spirit? Staring your frenzied eyes out? But who was it standing in the by-lane with Malashka Ignatienkova last night? It wasn't you, was it ! Ah, you devil, you son of a bitch ! And give me up ! I'll manage to live without you. You've long been intending to, that I can see.'

'Marina, my berry, where did you get that story from? With what Malashka? I've never stood with her once in all my life. And what's that got to do with the collective farm, anyway?' Andrei clutched his head with his hands, and fell silent, evidently having exhausted his arguments.

'Don't go down on your knees to her, the bitch !' the indignant Liubishkin intervened. 'Don't plead with her; have some respect for your own pride. Remember you're a Red Partisan. What are you pleading with her for, staring at her teeth? Give her one in the face ! Knock out her castanets, she'll quieten down at once !'

˙ Marina, her face patched with a crimson flush, started as though she had been pricked. She sailed towards Liubishkin, her expansive bosom thrust forward. her broad shoulders working and, like any man, she belligerently began to roll up her sleeves.

'What are you poking your nose into other people's business for, you reptile's slough, you gipsy's abortion, you black idol, you fright ! I'd spoil your face for you first ! I'm not afraid because you're a brigade leader ! I've seen such as you before, and flung them across my shoulder !'

'I'd throw you across mine first ! I'd make you lose your fat !' Liubishkin morosely growled, retreating into the corner and preparing for any unpleasant surprise that might befall him. He well remembered how once, at the Tubyanskoe mill, Marina had started to fight a healthy-looking cossack from the farther side of the Don. To the great satisfaction of the onlookers she had thrown him down, and had finally settled him, completely annihilating him with the stinging remark: 'You can't do anything on top of a woman, daddy!' After taking breath she had added: 'With your puny strength and grip all you're good for is to lie under her backside and pant!' And, tidying her hair which in the struggle had escaped from her kerchief, she went off to see the scalesman. Liubishkin remembered how livid were the cossack's cheeks when, smothered with scattered flour and dung, he scrambled to his feet. So Liubishkin held his left arm bent at the elbow, and warned her:

'Don't you come at me, or by God I'll knock the stuffing out of you!'

'Did you ever get a smell of this with your whore?' For a second Marina, almost beside herself with her boiling rage, lifted her skirt high and waved it in front of Liubishkin's nose. Her plumpy rosy knees and the creamy yellow of her body, as strong and solid as a cast, flashed before his eyes. Even Liubishkin, who had seen some sights in his time, was dazzled by the strength and whiteness of her body, and stepped back, muttering flabbergastedly:

'You've gone mad! You devil! You're a stallion, not a woman! Get back, curse you!' He slipped sideways past the furiously screaming Marina, and went out into the porch, spitting and cursing.

Davidov laughed until he collapsed, dropping his head on the table and screwing up his eyes. Razmiotnov ran out hard on Liubishkin's heels, slamming the door behind him with a crash, and Yakov Lukich alone essayed to bring the frenzied sergeant's widow to reason.

'What are you bawling like that for? What a shameless woman! A fine idea, lifting your skirt! You might at least have had more decency than to do that in front of an old man like me!'

'Shut up!' Marina shouted at him, as she turned to the door. 'I know the old man you are! What did you suggest to me last summer, about Trinity Sunday, when we were fetching in the hay? Does that pay you back? You're as bad as the rest of them!'

She swept across the yard like a storm cloud. Yakov Lukich followed her with his eyes, coughing in his embarrassment, and reproachfully shaking his head. Some half-hour later he saw Marina harness herself into the shafts of her cart, and easily carry off the harrow and plough from the first brigade yard. Diemka Ushakov, who had returned from the fields because of the rain, followed some way behind her, probably not daring to approach within shorter and more dangerous distance. He called after her:

'Marina! Hey, citizeness Poyarkova! D'you hear? Marina! I can't give you back your property so long as it's included in my inventory.'

'I think you can!'

'Don't you understand, you fool, that it's socialized? Bring it back, please, and don't play about. Are you a human being or what? What are you stealing it for? You'll be taken to court for such villainy. I can't give anything back without Davidov's signature.'

'I think you can!' Marina replied in monosyllables.

Diemka's eyes squinted disconcertedly, he pressed his hands imploringly to his chest. But Marina, sweating, a burning flush in her cheeks, inexorably dragged the cart along, and the harrow rattled mournfully against its side.

'I ought to take the cart away from her, so that she should learn how to use her tongue. But how am I to get it? You've only got to touch her and you won't enjoy the light of day for a while,' Yakov Lukich thought, and he prudently turned into a side road.

The next day Razmiotnov removed his things, his rifle, cartridge case, and papers, from Marina's hut, and carried them home. He felt deeply the break with her, and avoided being alone. For that reason he went along to Nagulnov's hut to talk, and to 'drive away his yearning'.

Night had fallen over Gremyachy Log. The rain-washed young moon was resting, a bright, gleaming slip, in the western sky. The black March silence, violated only by the hushing whisper of spring watercourses, held the village prisoner. Andrei dragged his feet with a squelch out of the stiffening mud, and walked along quietly, thinking of his own affairs. The agitating scents of spring were already perceptible in the raw air. The earth breathed out a bitter dampness, the threshing floors greeted him with a musty smell, a pungent, wine-like aroma filled the orchards, and the fresh growth of the grass emerging by the wattle-fences smelt sharply intoxicating and youthful.

Andrei avidly breathed in the varied scents of the night, watched as the reflections of the stars in the puddle water disintegrated and scattered in sparks under his feet, thought of Marina, and felt bitter tears of umbrage and yearning scorching his eyes.

Chapter 31

A Misadventurous Life

OLD Shchukar enthusiastically accepted his appointment as permanent coachman to the collective farm office. When he entrusted him with two stallions, formerly kulak property, and now assigned for the official use of the management, Yakov Lukich said:

'Look after them as the apple of your eye! See that they're always in good condition, and don't overdrive them. That grey stallion which used to be Titok's is a blood horse, and the sorrel comes of good Don stock. We don't have much driving around to do, and we'll be putting them to mares soon. You're responsible for them.'

'You don't say!' old Shchukar replied. 'Do you think I don't know how to look after horses? I've seen enough of them in my day! I've had more horses pass through my hands than there are hairs on a man's head!'

But in reality, during all Shchukar's life only two nags altogether had 'passed through his hands'. One of them he had changed for a cow, and as for the other ... Some twenty years previously Shchukar, returning in a state of merry intoxication from Voiskovoi, had bought it from a passing gipsy for thirty roubles. When he looked it over before buying it, the mare was well filled out, of a mousey-grey colour, lop-eared, with a wall-eye, but very fast. Shchukar haggled with the gipsy until noonday. Forty times they clapped hands on the bargain, fell out, and came to agreement again.

'She's pure gold, and not a mare! She gallops so fast that if you close your eyes you can't see the earth under her. She's as swift as thought, as a bird!' the gipsy assured him with oaths, dribbling spittle and seizing the weary Shchukar by the edge of his coat.

'It's hardly got a back tooth left, it's wall-eyed, all its hoofs are broken, it's pot-bellied. Where's the gold? It's bitter tears, not gold!' Shchukar decried the horse, terribly anxious to get the gipsy to abate the last rouble over which they were haggling.

'But what d'you want teeth for? It'll eat less. And she's a young mare. God's truth! She's a filly, not a mare. She lost her teeth owing to a chance illness. And what does it matter to you that she's wall-eyed? She's not wall-eyed anyway, that's a cast, and her hoofs will grow and clean up. She's a grey mare, but she's very beautiful, and you don't want her to sleep with, but to plough with. That's so, isn't it? You look and see why she's pot-bellied: that's because of her strength. When she runs the earth trembles; when she falls down she lies for three days ... Ah, daddy! Clearly what you want for your thirty roubles is a race-horse. You won't buy one alive, and if one dies they'll give you the meat for nothing.'

Happily the gipsy proved to be a decent sort. After chaffering he abated the last rouble, handed Shchukar the bridle-rein, and even hypocritically sobbed, wiping his brown forehead with the sleeve of his bright blue, long-tailed coat.

Hardly had Shchukar taken the rein when the mare lost all her liveliness. Painfully setting forward her clawlike legs, she un-willingly submitted to his extraordinary exertions to get her to follow. And only then did the gipsy laugh, baring his close-set, chalk-white teeth. He shouted after Shchukar:

'Hey, daddy! Don Cossack! Remember my kindness! That horse has been in my service for forty years, and she'll serve you as long again. But only feed her once a week, or there'll be no holding her in. My father came from Romania on her, and he got her from the French when they ran away from Moscow. She's a valuable horse!' He shouted something else after Shchukar as the old man dragged his purchase behind him. Around the tent and between the gipsy's legs his noisy, swarthy children bawled, and the gipsy women whistled and laughed. But old Shchukar walked on, paying no attention to anyone, and good-naturedly thinking: 'I can see for myself what sort of animal I've bought. If I had the money I wouldn't buy one like this. The gipsy's fond of a joke, he's a merry lad like me. Well, I've got a horse. On Sunday I'll drive with the wife to the market in the district town.'

But before he reached Tubyanskoe miracles began to happen to the horse. He chanced to look back, and stood aghast: behind him dragged not the big-bellied, well-fed mare he had bought, but an emaciated old nag with sunken belly and flanks. Within half an hour it had lost half its fatness. Crossing himself and whispering: 'God, God, God!' Shchukar let the rein drop from his fist, and halted, feeling his intoxication pass from him as though removed by a hand. Only when he walked around the mare did he discover the reason for so incredibly swift an emaciation. From under her stringy tail which was quite shamelessly twisted upward and sideways, a foul smell and spatters of liquid dung were bursting with a whistle and hiss. 'So that's it!' groaned Shchukar, clutching his head. Seizing the bridle, with tenfold strength he dragged the mare onward. The volcanic eruption from its inside continued, leaving a shameful track behind it, all the way to Tubyanskoe. Shchukar might have reached Gremyachy without further incident, but he had hardly drawn level with the first hut in Tubyanskoe, where his child's godfather and numerous acquaintances lived, when he decided to mount the horse's back and to ride, even at a walking pace, rather than drag it along by the rein. An unprecedented pride suddenly awakened within him, and with it his inveterate desire to boast, to show that he, Shchukar, had now won his way out of poverty, and was riding his own horse, even though it was a sorry nag. 'Whoa! You devil! You're always wanting to be too playful!' he shouted furiously, as out of the corner of his eye he saw a cossack acquaintance emerging from the hut opposite. As he spoke he pulled on the rein and tried to look dignified. His horse, whose desire for playfulness and bucking had long been left behind with her childhood, had no thought at all of being playful. She stopped with her head drooping gloomily, her hind-legs crossed.

'I ought to ride past my friend and give him a chance to see me,' Shchukar thought. Jumping up, he fell with his belly across the sharp ridge of the horse's backbone. And immediately he suffered a mishap and humiliation which for long afterwards was the talk of the Tubyanskoe cossacks, which has become a legend in the district, and is likely to be handed down to the next generation. Hardly had his feet left the ground when, as he was hanging on the mare, lying across her back and attempting to seat himself astride, the animal swayed. A rumbling sound began inside her, and, throwing out her tail, she crumpled to the ground where she stood. With arms outstretched Shchukar flew across the road and fell full-length on the dusty roadside vegetation. He jumped up in a towering rage, and, noticing that the cossack had seen his disgrace, tried to put a good face on the affair by shouting: 'You devil! You're always bucking!' He landed out at the horse with both feet. The mare got up, and, as though nothing had happened, stretched out her nose to the wilted grass at the roadside.

The cossack who had seen Shchukar's misadventure was a great wag and joker. He jumped across the wattle fence and went over to Shchukar, with a 'Your health, Shchukar! Surely you haven't bought a horse?'

'Yes, I have, but I'm afraid I've tripped up a little, I've got hold of such a restive devil! No sooner do you get on her than she bucks, and you're on the ground. It looks as though she's never been broken in to the saddle.'

Screwing up his eyes, the cossack walked around the mare a couple of times, glanced at her teeth as he passed, and said in quite a serious voice:

'Well, of course she's not been broken in. But she's come of good stock, you can see that. Judging by her teeth she must be about fifty, not a day less; but because she's a blood mare nobody can manage her.'

Noticing the cossack's sympathetic attitude, Shchukar ventured to ask:

'But tell me, Ignaty Porfirich, why has she gone thin so

quickly? She melted away right before my eyes as I led her along. A terrible stink came from her and the dung flew out as though from a gun. She left her traces all along the road.'

'But where did you buy her? Not off the gipsies?'

'Yes, I did. There's a camp of them just outside your village.'

'Well, this is why she's gone thin,' the cossack, who knew both horses and gipsies well, began to explain. 'Before they sold her to you they blew her up. When a horse starts to go thin with age, before they sell her they push a hollow reed up her back passage, and then they all take turns to blow her up until her sides swell and she looks to be well filled out and fat. And when they've blown her up like a bullock's bladder, they pull the reed out and at once push a tarred rag or a stopper of some sort in its place, to keep the air in. You've bought a mare that was blown up like that. The stopper must have fallen out on the road, and your mare began to get thin. You go back and find the stopper, and we'll blow her up again for you in a moment.'

'The devil seize them all!' Shchukar shouted in despair, and he hurried back to find the gipsy encampment. But when he reached the slope of the valley in which he had first met them, he could see neither tents nor covered wagons by the river. The blue smoke of a campfire was still rising from the spot where the camp had been, but in the distance a grey dust was rising from the summer track and winding and dispersing in the wind. The gipsies had disappeared as in a fairy-tale. Shchukar fell to weeping, and turned back again. The kindly Ignaty Porfirich once more came out of his hut. 'I'll put my shoulder under her belly, so that she doesn't fall down again in her temper, and you get on her back,' he proposed. Wet with shame, grief and sweat, Shchukar accepted his services, and somehow managed to mount the animal. But his woes were not yet ended. This time the mare did not fall down, but she proved to have quite an incredible way of bounding along. She threw out her forelegs as though galloping, and kicked her hind-legs about, flinging them above her back. In this manner she carried Shchukar to the first corner. During this furious scamper his cap fell off his head, and the terrible shaking caused something to throb and seem to burst inside him. 'My God, I can't go on riding like this!' he decided, and dismounted while the horse was careering along. He went back for his cap, but, seeing a crowd hurrying along a by-lane towards him, he hastily returned and led out of the village this ill-starred mare which had displayed such an unexpected turn of speed. He was accompanied by a swarm of children as far as the windmill, then they left him. But Shchukar did not dare to mount the gipsy's 'thought' again. He made a wide detour around the village across the hills, but grew tired of pulling on the bridle-rein, and decided to drive the mare in front of him. Then it transpired that the horse he had taken so much trouble to purchase was blind in both eyes. She made straight for the ditches and channels in her path, yet she did not jump across them, but fell down into them. Then, supporting herself on her trembling forelegs, she scrambled up, breathing heavily, and went on. But she went on in an extraordinary manner, in continual circles. Shaken by his latest discovery, Shchukar let her have complete liberty, and stood watching her. She described one circle, then began another, and so on incessantly along an invisible spiral. Then he guessed that his mare had spent all her long and toilsome life at a water-pump, and had gone blind and grown old while working the pump.

Ashamed to enter Gremyachy by daylight, he pastured the mare on the upland slopes until dusk was falling, and only drove her home when night came on. How he was welcomed by his wife, a burly woman who was heavy-handed in meting out punishment, and what the sensitive Shchukar suffered on account of his unfortunate purchase, was 'veiled in the darkness of the unknown', as his friend the cobbler Lokateev observed. All that is known is that a little later the mare caught the mange, peeled completely, and in this unsightly state quietly passed out in the yard one midnight. Assisted by his friend Lokateev, Shchukar drank the proceeds from the sale of the skin.

When he assured Yakov Lukich that he had had not a few horses pass through his hands in his time, old Shchukar must have known that Yakov Lukich could not believe him, for most of his life had been spent under Yakov's eyes. But he had been like that from his birth : he could not help bragging and lying.

In a few words, Shchukar became simultaneously ostler and

coachman. And it has to be said that he carried out his simple duties by no means badly. The sole fault Nagulnov, who liked fast driving, found in him was his frequent halts. Hardly had they driven out of the yard when he would pull on the reins with a 'Whoa, my lads!' 'What have you stopped for?' Nagulnov would inquire. 'The horses needed to,' old Shchukar would answer, and would sit whistling provocatively until Nagulnov pulled the knout from under the driver's seat and gave the stallions a lash across the back. 'These aren't the Tsarist days,' Shchukar would brag to the cossacks, 'when the coachman sat on the driver's seat, and the passengers swung along behind him on a soft cushion. I'm a coachman now, but I sit at comrade Davidov's side. And when I want to smoke I ask him to hold the reins while I roll myself a cigarette. "With the greatest of pleasure," he answers. He takes the reins and may drive for an hour, while I sit importantly and look at nature.' He certainly acquired an important air, and even grew less talkative. Despite the spring frosts he went to sleep in the stables to be closer to the stallions. But after a week of this his old wife installed him back at home, cruelly beating him and cursing him up hill and down dale because, she said, young women had been visiting him at night. Some youngsters had pulled her leg, telling her this abominable slander about him. He did not contradict her, but returned home and, convoyed by his jealous spouse, went to see the stallions a couple of times every night.

He learned to harness the horses so swiftly that he rivalled the speed of the Gremyachy fire brigade, and when he led them out to harness them into the shafts he would soothe the restive and snorting stallions with the continual hoarse shout: 'Whoa! Whoa, now! Neighing like that, you devils! That's not a mare, but a horse the same as you!' When he had finished harnessing the horses and had taken his seat, he would complacently remark: 'Well, we're off, and I shall earn my day's reckoning. I'm beginning to enjoy this life, brothers!'

On 27 March Davidov decided to drive out to the fields where the first brigade was at work, to see whether, despite his instructions, it was harrowing along instead of across the furrows. The smith Ippolit Shaly had been out to mend a sower, and immediately he returned to the village he went to the collective farm office. Squeezing Davidov's hand, he grimly told him:

'The first brigade's harrowing along the furrows. That kind of harrowing won't be good for anything. Go and see for yourself, and order them to work properly. I pointed it out to them, but that boss-eyed devil Ushakov told me: "Your job is to strike the anvil and blow the bellows. Don't push your nose in here, or we'll cut it off with a plough!" To which I answered: "Before I ride off to blow the bellows I'll blow you up, you boss-eye!" And we all but came to using our fists.'

Davidov called Shchukar and told him to harness a stallion into the drozhki. But he could not wait, and ran himself to give a hand. They drove off. The cloudy day and a humid wind from the south-west promised rain. The first brigade was working in the most distant section of the grey sandy lands. It was some ten kilometres from the village, close to a pond beyond the hills. The brigade was ploughing and preparing the land for a sowing of corn, and it was extremely important that the furrows should be carefully harrowed, in order to retain the rain moisture on a smoothly worked tilth. Otherwise it would soak deeply into the furrows.

'Hurry, hurry, daddy!' Davidov asked, glancing at the heavy barrier of massive clouds.

'I am hurrying. The grey is soaping with sweat already.'

On a slope not far from the summer track the schoolchildren, led by their elderly teacher, were walking in single file. Behind them followed four carts carrying barrels of water.

'There's the children going out after marmots,' Shchukar pointed with his knout.

A restrained smile on his lips, Davidov gazed at the children. When the drozhki drew level with them he asked Shchukar to stop, and, fixing his eyes on a white-headed, barefooted lad about seven years of age, he called to him:

'Come here!'

'What have I got to come for?' the lad asked in an independent tone, thrusting his father's cap, with its crimson band and the faded trace of a badge above the peak, on to the back of his head.

'How many marmots have you killed?'

'Fourteen.'

'What's your name?'

'Fiodot Demidich Ushakov.'

'Well, get in with us, Fiodot Demidich, and we'll give you a ride. And you get in, too.' Davidov pointed to a girl wearing a kerchief. Seating them in the drozhki, he ordered Shchukar to drive on, then asked the lad:

'What class are you in?'

'The first.'

'The first? Then you ought to knock the snot off your nose. Fact!'

'I can't. I've got a cold.'

'Why can't you? Give me your nose over here!' Davidov carefully wiped his fingers on his trousers, and sighed. 'You come and see me in the collective farm office some time, and I'll give you a chocolate. Ever tasted chocolate?'

'No.'

'Well, you come to the office, and I'll treat you to some.'

'But I don't want any of your chocolate.'

'You don't? But why not, Fiodot Diemidich?'

'My teeth are breaking to bits, and the lower ones have already fallen out. Have a look!' The lad opened his crimson mouth, and revealed that he had lost two of his lower teeth.

'So in other words, you're gap-toothed, Fiodot Diemidich?'

'You're gap-toothed yourself!'

'Hm! You imp! So you've noticed that, have you?'

'Mine'll grow again, but I don't suppose yours will! Aha!'

'Well, now you're being mischievous, my lad! Mine'll grow, too. Fact!'

'You can tell lies all right! They don't grow again with grown-ups. And I can bite with my upper teeth; by Christ I can!'

'How can you do that?'

'Don't you believe me? Let me bite your finger.'

Smiling, Davidov stretched out his forefinger. But he pulled it back with an 'Oh!' The blue marks of the bite were indented on the top joint.

'Well, Fiodot, now let me bite your finger,' he proposed. But after some hesitation the lad suddenly jumped from the drozhki as it was moving, and, hopping on one leg like a great grey grasshopper, he shouted:

'You'd like to have a bite, wouldn't you! But you're not going to this time!'

Davidov burst into a roar of laughter, helped the little girl out of the drozhki, and stood staring for some time after the red band of Fiodot's cap in the distance. He smiled, and felt a rare warmth around his heart and a moisture in his eyes. 'We'll build a good life for them. Fact!' he was thinking. 'There's Fiodot running along in his father's cossack cap, but in some twenty years' time he'll probably be ploughing up this very earth with an electric plough. I don't suppose he'll ever have to do what I had to do after mother died: wash my sisters' clothes, and darn and cook, and work in the factory. The Fiodots will be happy. Fact!' He swept the boundless, tenderly green steppe with his eyes. For a moment he stood listening to the singing whistle of the larks, and gazed at a ploughman bent over his plough in the distance, while the driver went at the side of the bullocks, stumbling over the furrows. He sighed from the bottom of his heart. 'Machinery will do all the heavy work for man. The people of those days will have forgotten the smell of sweat, I suppose. I'd like to live till then, by all the devils! If only to see what it was like! But you'll die, and there'll be no Fiodot to remember you! You'll die, brother Davidov, as sure as you're alive! Instead of descendants you'll leave behind the Gremyachy collective farm. The farm will become a commune, and then, you see, they'll call it by the name of the Putilov locksmith Siemion Davidov ...' He smiled at the humorous turn his thoughts had taken, and asked Shchukar:

'Shall we be there soon now?'

'The third slope across.'

'Look at the land you've had lying unused. It's a great shame! Within a couple of five-year plans we shall be building factories here. Everything belongs to us, everything is in our hands. Fact! Puff yourself up and live another ten years, and instead of reins you'll be holding a steering-wheel. You'll go along on gas; there's no help for you!'

Shchukar sighed and replied:

'It's a little bit late! If I'd been made a worker forty years ago I might have been a different man! I've never been successful as a peasant. Ever since I was a boy right down to the present my life has gone all awry. I'm afraid it's been blown about by the wind, and the wind's twisted me and buffeted me, and sometimes bowled me right over.'

'But why has it?' Davidov inquired.

'Wait, and I'll tell you down to the last thread. Let the stallions go at their own pace, and I'll tell you all my woes! You're a glum sort, but you ought to understand and show some fellow-feeling. Several times serious things have happened in my life. Right at the beginning, when I was born the midwife at once told my mother: "Your son will be a general when he grows up. By all the signs he's going to be a general: he's got a narrow brow, and a head like a pumpkin, he's pot-bellied, and he's got a deep voice. Cheer up, Katrena!" But within a fortnight everything went contrary to what the woman had said. I was born on St Yevdokia's day, but on that day not only was everything so frozen up that there wasn't enough water for a chick to drink, but even the sparrows froze as they flew, so my mother said. And they took me to Tubyanskoe to be christened. But think for yourself: was it sensible to dip a baby into a font in such cold? They began to warm the water, but the deacon and the priest were both as drunk as they could be. One poured boiling water into the font, and the other didn't try it, but began to chant: "Lord Jesus, we baptize this slave of God ..." and plunged me right over my head into the boiling water. It took all my skin off. They carried me home, and I was all covered with blisters. Well, of course I got a ruptured navel as the result, through crying with the pain and blowing myself up too much. After that I was always falling ill. And all because I was born to the life of a peasant. By the time I was nine the dogs had worried me, and the geese hissed at me beyond all bearing, and a foal had kicked me so hard that I was picked up for dead. And from the time I was nine more and more serious things began to happen to me. I was just gone nine when I got caught on a hook ...'

'What sort of hook?' Davidov asked in surprise, as he listened not inattentively to Shchukar's story.

'Just an ordinary hook, the kind they catch fish with. At that time there was a deaf and hoary old man called Kupir living in Gremyachy. In the winter he caught partridges with snares and lived in a tent, and in the summer he spent all his time fishing with hooks in the river. In those days our river was deeper, and even Lapshinov's little mill stood on its bank. Carp and enormous pike lived under the mill-dam, and so the old man would sit with his hooks close to a willow bush. He'd fish with seven hooks, putting worms on some, and dough on others, and on some he'd put small fish to catch the pike. And we boys used to try to bite off his hooks. The old man was as deaf as a stone, you could have pissed in his ear and he wouldn't have heard you. We would gather by the river and undress behind a bush close to him, then one of us would slip quietly into the water so as not to make any waves, dive under the old man's hooks, get the line between his teeth and bite it through, then get out under the bush again. And the old man would pull up his rod and tremble all over, mumbling: "Another bitten off, curse them! Ah, Holy Mother!" You see, he thought a pike had done it, and naturally he got angry because he'd lost a hook. He bought his hooks from the shop, but we hadn't any money to buy hooks with, so we traded off the old man! One day I had captured a hook, and thought I'd try for another. I saw he was busily baiting a hook, so in I dived. I had only just managed quietly to get hold of the line and put my mouth to it, when he gave a tremendous pull on the rod. The line slipped through my fingers and the hook went into my upper lip. I shouted out, but the water poured into my mouth. And the old man went on pulling at the rod, trying to hoist me out. Of course the pain made me kick out with my legs, I was dragged along by the hook, and felt him thrust his bailer into the water under me. Well, of course, I came to the top and bellowed for all I was worth. The old man was frozen stiff; he tried to cross himself and couldn't, and his face went blacker than a saucepan with fright. And he had good reason to be frightened! He had caught a pike and dragged up a boy! He stood and stood, and then you should have seen him run! His boots almost fell off his feet! I got back home with the hook still in my lip. My father cut it out, and then he walloped me until I was senseless. But I ask you, what good did that do? My lip healed up, but that's how I got the name of Shchukar, after a pike. The silly nickname has stuck to me ever since.

'The next spring I was driving the geese out to pasturage by the windmill. The windmill was working, my geese were feeding close to it, and above them a kite began to hover. The geese were yellow and attractive, and the kite wanted to seize one of them. But naturally I was watching, and kept hissing and making noises to keep it off. Some boy friends of mine came along, and we began to ride on the windmill sails. We would grab hold of one of the sails and let it raise us a couple of yards off the ground, then we would let go and fall, lying still, otherwise the next sail would have hit us. But those boys were real devils! They thought of the game of seeing who would go the highest on the sail; he was to be Tsar and was to be given a ride on the others' backs from the windmill to the threshing floor. Well, we all want to be a Tsar. And I thought I'd go the highest of all, and forgot all about the geese. The sail lifted me up, but I happened to look, and there was the kite just going to carry off a goose. I got frightened, for I knew I'd get a good hiding if I lost a goose. "Boys!" I shouted, "the kite! Drive off that kite!" And for a moment I forgot I was on the windmill sail. When I thought of it again, I'd got the devil knows how far from the ground! It was too terrifying to jump down, and still more frightening to go on riding upward. But where else was I to go? While I was dreaming of what would happen to me the sail reached the top, and there I was stuck on it feet uppermost. But as it began to come down towards the earth again I let go. I don't know how long it took me to reach the ground, I only know it seemed far too long to me. But I reached it at last, and, naturally, I struck it a whack! I jumped up at once, looked at my hand and saw the bones had come through the skin by my wrist. And the pain got so horrible, I lost all interest in everything. The kite got the goose all the same, but I wasn't in the least interested in it. The bone-setter put my bones back in their place, but what was the sense of that? They only came out again the next year, and I was all but cut to pieces by a reaper. Just after St Peter's day I and my elder brother went out to reap the rye. I was driving the horses, and my brother was tossing the swathes off the platform. I sat driving, and there were gadflies hovering above the horses, a white sun in the sky, and such a heat that I began to think I'd fall off the seat in my doze. As we were going along I stared my eyes out to see an enormous bearded bustard stretched like a whip along the furrows at my side. I stopped the horses, and my brother said he would go for it with the pitchfork. But I said: "Let me jump at him and I'll catch him alive." "All right," he said. Well, I jumped and seized the idiot around his middle. And how he tried to get away! He stretched out his wings and beat me on the head with them (he must have been terribly frightened), he smothered me with liquid droppings, and dragged me along behind him like a restive horse dragging a harrow. Why he thought of turning back I don't know. But he did, and he flung himself under the horses' hoofs and then to one side. And the horses were startled. They jumped across me, snorted and galloped off. And I found myself under the reaper. My brother at once pulled the lever and raised the knives. I was knocked under the platform and dragged along beneath it. One of the horses had its leg cut to the bone and its sinews severed, and I was cut about beyond recognition. My brother managed somehow to stop the horses, unharnessed one of them, lay me across its back and rode with me into the village. And I was unconscious and all smothered with droppings and earth, while the scoundrel of a bustard had flown off. I was ill a long time that time. Less than six months later I was coming away from a neighbour's yard, and the village bull cut off my road. I went to walk round him, but he swung his tail like a savage tiger and came at me with his head lowered. D'you think I was greatly interested in having my soul let out by his horns? I turned to run, but he caught me up, got a horn under my bottom rib and threw me across the fence. And the rib was smashed to pieces. If I'd had a hundred ribs it wouldn't have mattered, but it's a pity to lose a rib for no reason at all. And so when I was called up for service I was rejected. And there's no counting the things that have happened to me through other animals! You'd say I was marked down by the devil! If a dog had broken from its chain, no matter where it ran off to it would come running at me, or I'd quite unknowingly come across it.

And it would tear my clothes, or bite my pants. And what was the good of that to me? I was chased by polecats for miles, and wild swine attacked me in the steppe. Once I was knocked about and lost my boots because of the bull. I was going through the village one night, and close to Donietskov's hut I ran into the bull again. It bellowed, and lashed with its tail. "No," I thought, "you be damned! I've learned not to have anything to do with your sort." I kept close to the hut, the bull after me. I started to run, and he snorted just behind my back. The hut window was open to the street, and I flew through it like a bat. I looked around me, and there was nobody in the room. I thought I wouldn't alarm anybody, but would go out by the window again. The bull had bellowed terribly, dug at the ledge of the wall with his horns, and then gone off. I was just climbing out of the window into the street when I felt a hand seize me by the arm, and something hard on my head. It was the master, old Donietskov, who had heard the noise and caught me. "What are you doing in here, young man?" he asked. "I was saving myself from the bull," I told him. "No, you weren't," he said; "we know you bulls! You were crawling in to my daughter-in-law, to our Olya." And he began to beat me, at first half in fun and then harder and harder. He was a strong old man and had made up to his daughter-in-law himself, and so he knocked out my front tooth for me. Then he said: "Will you go after our Olya any more?" "No," I said, "I shan't! You can hang your Olya around your neck instead of a cross." "Well, take your boots off," he said, "or I'll give you some more." And it was no joke losing my last pair of boots. I was angry with that Olya for five years after, but what was the sense of that? And so on everlastingly. Just as an example: when you and I cleared Titok out of his farm as a kulak, why, I ask you, did his hound tear up my sheepskin and not anybody else's? It could have flung itself on Makar or Liubishkin, but no, the devil sent it running all round the yard and drove it on to me. It was a good job it didn't get me by the throat, or it'd have bitten a couple of times and you'd have had to give me a place in your memory. We know these things. Of course it ended like that because I hadn't got a revolver. If I'd had one, what would have happened? A mass murder. I'm desperate when I'm roused. At that moment I might have settled the life of the dog, and Titok's wife, and sent all the rest of the bullets straight down Titok's throat. That would have been murder and Shchukar would have been put into prison. And I've got no desire to sit in prison; I've got my own affairs to look after. Yes ... And that's the sort of general I became. If that midwife was still alive I'd eat her raw. Don't stir up a hornet's nest, say I. Don't upset the children. Well, there's the brigade. We've arrived.'

Chapter 32

Expelled from the Party

As Razmiotnov stood on the porch, cleaning the sticky clumps of mud from his boots with the wet besom, he could see a slanting band of light streaming through the chink of the door from Nagulnov's room. 'So he's not asleep; why isn't he, though?' Andrei thought, as he noiselessly opened the door.

The little lamp, covered by a scorched newspaper lampshade, dimly lit up the table in the corner, and an open book lying on it. Makar's bristly head was bent concentratedly over the table. His right hand was supporting his cheek, the fingers of his left were ruthlessly twined into his forelock.

'Hallo, Makar! What are you still up for?' Razmiotnov asked. Nagulnov raised his head, and looked at Andrei discontentedly.

'What do you want?' he demanded.

'I just dropped in for a talk. Am I in the way?'

'Maybe you are. But sit down, I shan't kick you out.'

'What are you reading?'

'I've found something to do.' Makar covered the book with his hand, and stared challengingly at Andrei.

'I've left Marina. For good ...' Andrei sighed and dropped heavily on to a stool.

'You ought to have done it long before.'

'Why?'

'She held you back, and just at present life is such that we must get rid of all unnecessary baggage. This isn't the time for us communists to amuse ourselves with all sorts of outside matters.'

'How d'you call this an outside matter, when we loved each other?'

'What sort of love was it? It was a millstone around your neck, and not love. You would chair a meeting, and she wouldn't take her eyes off you, but sit jealous. That's not love, brother, but a punishment.'

'So in your view communists ought not to have any truck with women? Should they tie themselves up with cotton and go about like gelded bullocks, or what?'

'And do you think it's impossible, then? Those who'd made fools of themselves and got married I'd let live with their wives, but I'd pass a decree forbidding the youngsters to get married. What sort of revolutionaries will they make if they get used to hanging on to women's skirts? A woman is to us what honey is to a greedy fly. We get stuck at once. I've seen it in my own case, and I know only too well! I'd sit down of an evening to read, to develop myself, and my wife would lie down to sleep. I'd read a little and then lie down, too, and she'd turn her arse towards me. Then I'd feel insulted by her position, and I'd either begin to swear at her or I'd light a cigarette, fuming at her insolence, and unable to get off to sleep. So I wouldn't get enough sleep, and in the morning I'd have a heavy head and would make some political mistake. I've had some! And as for those who have children, they're completely lost to the party. In a jiffy they've learnt how to look after their babies, got used to their milky smell, and then they're done for! They make bad fighters and hopeless workers. In the Tsarist days I used to instruct the young cossack recruits, and I saw that the single youngsters had cheerful faces and looked intelligent. But when they'd left their young wives to join the regiment they'd go wooden with yearning, and become blockheads. You'd only get confusion from them, and you couldn't teach them a thing. You'd be talking to them about the service regulations, and their eyes would be like buttons. The swines would be looking at you, but in reality their eyes would be turned inward, and the reptiles would be seeing their dear little wives. And is that good? No, dear comrade, formerly you could live as you like. But now you're in the party you must leave all stupidities behind. After the world revolution you can die on a woman for all I care, but now you must be entirely concentrated on work for that revolution.'

Makar rose, stretched himself, straightening his broad, handsome back, clapped Razmiotnov on the shoulder, and smiled almost imperceptibly. 'And I suppose you came along to complain to me and get my sympathy! For me to say: "Yes, you're in a bad way, Andrei. It'll be difficult for you without a wife. How will you stand it and get over that difficulty?" Isn't that so? But no, Andrei, anything else, but you'll never hear that from me. I'm only too glad you've separated from your sergeant's widow! She ought to have had a good whacking on her fat arse with a mixing spoon long ago. I've given up Lukeria, for instance, and I know that I'm feeling grand. No one interferes with me, I'm like a sharp bayonet with the point directed into the struggle against the kulaks and the enemies of communism. And I'm even able to learn and educate myself.'

'What are you studying? One of the sciences?' Razmiotnov asked venomously and coldly. He was deeply offended by Makar's words, and by the fact that he had not only refused to sympathize with his trouble but had even rejoiced in it, and had, in Andrei's opinion, expressed unworldly nonsense on the subject of marriage. As he listened to Makar's serious, sincere words, at one moment he had thought a little fearfully: 'It's a good job a big-bellied cow's got no horns, for if Makar were to be given the government what wouldn't he do? With his views he'll turn all life upside down. More, he'd decide to castrate all the males so that they shouldn't be turned away from socialism.'

'What am I studying?' Makar cross-questioned, shutting his book with a bang. 'English.'

'What?'

'English. This book's a self-tutor.' Nagulnov gave Andrei a keen glance, afraid of seeing a sneer on his face. But Andrei was so overwhelmed by the unexpected news that there was nothing but astonishment to be read in his ill-tempered, widely-opened eyes.

'What ... can you already read or talk in that language?' Andrei asked.

With a feeling of secret pride Nagulnov replied:

'No, I can't talk yet. That doesn't come all at once. But, to begin with, I'm getting to understand their print. I've been learning for four months.'

'Is it a difficult job?' Andrei asked, swallowing down his spittle, and looking with involuntary respect from Makar to the book.

Seeing that Razmiotnov was displaying a lively interest in his studies, Makar abandoned his caution, and willingly answered:

'Difficult beyond belief! During these four months I've only learned four words by heart. But the language itself is rather like ours. They've got lots of words taken from ours, only they've put their own endings on to them. For instance, we say "proletariat", and "revolution", and "communism", and so do they. They add a sort of hissing sound to the ends of some of their words, as though they were angry with them, but you can't get away from those words. They've got their roots into all the world, and whether you like it or not, you've got to say them.'

'So you're studying, are you? But what do you want that particular language for, Makar?' Razmiotnov finally asked.

With a condescending smile Makar replied:

'You do ask strange questions, Andrei! You surprise me by your lack of understanding. I'm a communist, aren't I? And there'll be a Soviet government in England, too, won't there? You nod your head, so you evidently think there will. And how many Russian communists can speak English? That's just it, only a few. But the English bourgeoisie have conquered India and almost half the world, and oppressing the blackskins and the darkskins. What sort of order d'you call that? There'll be a Soviet government in England, but many English communists won't know what the class enemy in his pure form is like, and because they're not used to them they won't be able to deal with them as they ought. And then I'll ask to go to them, to teach them. And as I shall know their language, I shall arrive and get down to the job at once. "You've had a revolution?" I shall ask. "A communist one? Then take the capitalists and generals and put them between your nails, my lads. In 1917 we in Russia were innocent enough to let them go, the reptiles, and afterwards they began to cut our veins. Put them between your nails so that you can't make any mistakes, so that everything's alright'." ' Makar dilated his nostrils and winked at Andrei. 'And that's why I'm learning their language, don't you see? I shan't sleep a wink all night, I'll use my last bit of health, but ...' Grinding his close-set, little teeth, he ended: '... but I'll learn that language! I'll talk in English without any tender words to the world counter-revolutionaries! Let the reptiles tremble while they can! They'll find out that Makar Nagulnov's Makar Nagulnov, and not anyone else. There'll be no mercy from him! "So you've drunk the blood of your English working classes, of the Indians and other oppressed nations? So you've exploited other men's labour? Stand up against the wall, you bloody reptile." That's all the conversation I shall have with them. They'll be the first words I shall learn! So that I can out with them without hesitating.'

For another half-hour they talked of various matters, then Andrei went home, and Nagulnov buried himself in his self-tutor. Slowly moving his lips, sweating, knitting his brows with the intensity of the effort, he sat up learning English until half-past two.

The next day he was up early, drank two glasses of milk, then went to the collective farm stables.

'Let me have a horse – a fairly spirited one,' he asked the man on duty.

The man led out a dun, limber-flanked pony noted for its spirit and staying power, and asked:

'Going far?'

'To the district. Tell Davidov I'll be back tonight.'

'Are you riding?'

'Yes. Bring out a saddle.'

Makar saddled the horse, removed the halter, put on a smart-looking bridle which had formerly belonged to Titok, and expertly set his foot in the serrated stirrup. The pony set off at a dancing trot. But as she was leaving the gate she suddenly stumbled, touched the ground with her knees, all but fell, and, somehow recovering herself, nimbly scrambled to her feet.

'Can't you feel the ground under you, you mangy devil?' Makar angrily shouted, lashing the horse with his whip.

'Turn back, comrade Nagulnov; that's a bad sign,' old Shchukar, who was approaching the gate, called as he stepped out of Makar's path.

Without replying, Nagulnov trotted through the village into the main street. By the village Soviet a score of women were jabbering noisily and agitatedly about something.

'Out of the road, magpies, or I'll ride my horse over you,' Makar jokingly shouted.

The women silently stepped aside. When he had passed them he heard a voice hoarse with anger behind him say:

'Mind you don't get trodden on yourself, damn you! Look out, or you'll ride past yourself!'

The meeting of the District Bureau began at eleven. The agenda included a report by Bieglikh, the head of the District Agricultural Department, on the progress of the sowing during the first five days. In addition to the members of the Bureau, the chairman of the District Control Commission Samokhin and the District Prosecutor were also present.

'Don't leave the room, your question will be touched on more than once,' Homutov, the head of the Organization Department, warned Nagulnov.

Bieglikh's report lasted half an hour, and was listened to in a tense, oppressive silence. In some parts of the district sowing had not yet begun, although the soil was already prepared; certain village Soviets had not collected the seed grain fund in its entirety; in Voiskovoi former collective farmers had carried off almost all the seed grain collected; in Olkhovatsk the collective farm management committee had itself distributed seed grain to the members who had resigned. The speaker discussed in detail the reasons for the unsatisfactory state of sowing, and ended by saying:

'Undoubtedly, comrades, our backwardness with the sowing, and I would not even say our backwardness, but our marking time in the one spot, is due to the fact that in a number of village Soviets the collective farms have been set up as the result of pressure from the local workers, who went all out after inflated figures of collectivization, and in some places, as you know, even forced membership at the point of the revolver. These unstable collective farms are now breaking up like a mud wall washed away from the bottom. They are suffering from hold-ups because the collective farmers won't go out to the fields, or if they do go, they work with their sleeves down.'

The District Committee secretary warningly knocked his pencil against the glass stopper of the carafe, and said:

'Your time's up!'

'I'll be ended in one moment, comrades. Allow me to dwell on the conclusions to be drawn. As I've already proved to you, according to our information during the first five days only 383 hectares have been sown in our district. I consider it necessary to have all the district active workers mobilized at once and sent out to the collective farms. In my opinion, we must use all means to prevent the collective farm members resigning, and must compel the farm managements and nucleus secretaries to carry out explanatory work every day among the members and to make their main task the extensive enlightening of the collective farmers ... and giving full explanations of the reliefs the State gives to the collective farms, as in a number of places this has not been explained at all. Even now very many collective farmers do not know what credits have been assigned for the farms and so on. In addition, I propose that the cases of those responsible for the distortions which have prevented us from successfully tackling the sowing, and who, in accordance with the Party Central Committee decision of date 15 March have got to be dismissed from their posts, be considered as matters of urgency, and that they be called to strict Party account. That's all I have to say, comrades.'

'Anyone want to speak to Bieglikh's report?' the District Committee secretary asked, running his eyes around the room, but avoiding looking at Nagulnov.

'What is there to speak about? The picture's quite clear,' sighed one of the Bureau members, the head of the district militia, a portly, continually sweating, robust man in military uniform, with numerous scars on his gleaming, shaven head.

'So we take Bieglikh's conclusions as the basis of our decisions, is that agreed?' the secretary asked.

'Agreed.'

'And now for Nagulnov.' For the first time since the meeting had begun the secretary looked at Makar, letting his wandering, hostile eyes rest on him for several seconds. 'You all know that while holding the position of secretary to the Gremyachy Party nucleus he has committed a number of crimes against the Party. Despite the District Committee's instructions he has followed a leftward line during the collectivization period, and in collecting the seed grain fund. He beat an individual middling peasant with his pistol, and locked up collective farmers in an unheated room all night. Comrade Samokhin himself has been to Gremyachy and investigated the affair, and has laid bare Nagulnov's outrageous violations of revolutionary expediency and his injurious distortion of the Party line. Comrade Samokhin will now speak. Inform the Bureau, comrade Samokhin, what you have established in regard to Nagulnov's criminal activities.'

The secretary covered his eyes with his puffy eyelids, and leaned heavily on his elbow.

The moment Nagulnov entered the District Committee room he had realized that he was in for a bad time, and that he could not expect any indulgence. The secretary had welcomed him with unusual restraint, and, evidently anxious to avoid conversation, had turned at once with some question to the chairman of the District Executive Committee.

'How does my affair stand?' Makar had asked him rather timorously.

'The Bureau will decide,' the secretary had reluctantly answered.

All the other members had avoided Makar's pleading eyes, and had dodged him. Undoubtedly his case had been decided in advance among themselves. Only Balabin, the head of the militia, had smiled at him sympathetically, and had said as he gave him a hearty shake of the hand:

'Don't be afraid, Nagulnov! You've gone wrong, got on the wrong road; but after all we're not so well shod politically ourselves. Cleverer men than you have gone wrong, too!' He had shaken his round head, strong and smooth like a river stone, had wiped the sweat from his short, crimson neck, and commiseratingly smacked his lips. Makar had plucked up courage and looked at Balabin's deeply flushed face, smiling as he gratefully realized that this man saw right through him, understood and even sympathized. 'They'll give me a stern reprimand and remove me from the secretaryship,' he had thought, as he looked apprehensively at Samokhin. That little, big-browed man, who could not stand divorces, gave him more cause for anxiety than any of the others. When Samokhin drew a heavy file of papers out of his document case, Nagulnov painfully felt a sharp prick of alarm. His heart beat with a strained ringing, the blood rushed to his head, his temples burned, and a slight, intoxicating nausea rose in his throat. They were the symptoms he always had just before one of his fits. 'Any time but now!' He shivered inwardly as he listened to Samokhin's deliberate remarks.

'On the instruction of the District Committee and the District Control Commission I have personally investigated this case. By questioning Nagulnov himself, as well as the collective farmers and individual peasants who have suffered at his hands, and also on the evidence of witnesses, I have established the following: undoubtedly comrade Nagulnov has not justified the Party's trust and has done it terrible injury by his conduct. For instance, during the collectivization period in February he went from hut to hut, and forced peasants to join the collective farm by threatening them with his pistol. In this way he "drew into" the collective farms even middling peasants. Nagulnov himself makes no attempt to deny this ...'

'They were the whitest of Whites,' Nagulnov said hoarsely, rising from his chair.

'I didn't call on you to speak! Order, please!' the secretary sternly intervened.

'Then, during the collection of the seed grain fund he beat one middling peasant, an individual farmer, with his pistol until the man lost consciousness, and did this in the presence of collective farm members and village Soviet delegates. He beat the man because he refused to bring in his seed grain immediately ...'

'Shame!' the District Prosecutor said in a loud voice.

Nagulnov rubbed his throat with his hand and turned pale, but remained silent.

'The same night, comrades, like any District police chief of the old days he shut up three collective farmers in a cold room and kept them there all night, threatening them with a pistol because they refused to bring in their seed grain at once ...'

'I didn't threaten them!'

'I'm quoting their words, comrade Nagulnov, and I ask you not to interrupt me. Also, on his insistent demand the middling peasant Gayev was treated as a kulak and exiled, although he was not in the least to be regarded as a kulak, so far as possession of property was concerned. But on Nagulnov's demand he was treated as one because he employed someone in 1928. But what sort of a labourer did he employ? Comrades, Gayev hired a girl from Gremyachy Log for a month during the harvesting period, and he hired her only because his son had been called up to the Red Army in the autumn of 1927, and with his many children Gayev could not manage the work by himself. Such exploitation of hired labour was not prohibited by Soviet law. Gayev hired this girl on the basis of a contract with the Labourers' Committee, and paid her wages in full. That fact I have checked. In addition, Nagulnov is living a disorderly sexual life, and that also is of no little significance where the character of a Party member is concerned. Nagulnov has separated from his wife; and hasn't even separated, but has driven her out, driven her out like a dog. And only on the ground that she was supposed to have accepted the attentions of some Gremyachy lad. In a word, he took advantage of the slander and drove her out in order to get his own hands free. What sort of sexual life he is living now I don't know, but all my information goes to show that he's living a dissolute life, comrades. Otherwise why should he want to drive out his wife? The owner of the hut in which Nagulnov lives told me he comes home very late every night. She didn't know where he had been, but we, comrades, know where he might be! We're not children, and we know where a man who has driven out his wife usually spends his time: seeking distraction in one woman after another. We know! That, comrades, is a brief summary of the heroic exploits' (at this stage of his speech for the prosecution Samokhin smiled venomously) 'which this woeful nucleus secretary, Nagulnov, has managed to perform within a brief period. What does all this lead to? And what are the root causes of such conduct? It has to be said straight out that this is not dizziness through successes, as our leader, comrade Stalin, brilliantly expressed it, but a direct jump leftward, an attack on the Party's general line. For instance, Nagulnov was not only clever enough to treat middling peasants as kulaks and drive them into the collective farm, but he carried through a decision to socialize the domestic fowls and all the dairy and small cattle. And, according to certain collective farmers, he also attempted to set up such a discipline in the collective farm as never existed even in the times of Nikholai the Bloody.'

'There was no instruction from the District Committee regarding fowls and cattle,' Nagulnov quietly remarked. He stood and drew himself up to his full height, spasmodically pressing his left hand against his chest.

'But you'll excuse me there!' the secretary flared up. 'The District Committee did give indications. You're not going to put the blame on to other people like that! There are the Labouring Association regulations, and you're not a suckling that you can't draw your conclusions from them.'

'All self-criticism is suppressed in the Gremyachy collective farm,' Samokhin continued. 'Nagulnov has organized a terror, and won't let anyone say a word. Instead of carrying on explanatory work, he shouts at the workers, stamps with his feet, threatens them with firearms. And so there's grumbling going on in the Gremyachy Collective Farm "Stalin". At the present time mass resignations are taking place, they've only just started sowing, and will definitely be unable to manage their task. The District Control Commission, which is appointed to cleanse the Party from all demoralized elements, from the opportunists of all shades who interfere with us in our great construction work, will undoubtedly draw its conclusions concerning Nagulnov.'

'Finished?' the secretary asked.

'Yes.'

'I call on Nagulnov to speak. Let him tell us how he came to live such a life. Speak up, Nagulnov.'

Towards the end of Samokhin's speech Makar had been possessed with a terrible anger. But now it suddenly left him completely, and was replaced by diffidence and fear. 'What are they doing with me? How can they treat me like this? They want to bury me!' he momentarily, distractedly thought, as he went to the table. Nothing was left of all the angry protests he had prepared while Samokhin was speaking. His head was entirely empty, and he could not think of one appropriate word.

'I've been in the Party ever since the revolution, comrades ...' he began. 'I was in the Red Army ...'

'We know all that! Get down to the subject!' the secretary impatiently interrupted him.

'I fought against the Whites on all the fronts ... And I was in the First Cavalry army ... I was given the Order ...'

'But speak to the point!'

'Isn't that to the point?'

'Don't wriggle, Nagulnov! It's no use your trying to rely on past services now,' the chairman of the District Executive Committee broke in.

'Let the comrade speak! What do you keep interrupting him for?' Balabin angrily cried, and the polished crown of his round, pebbly head was momentarily flooded with an apoplectic, purplish hue.

'Let him speak to the point, then!'

Nagulnov remained standing with his left hand pressed to his breast, while his right slowly reached up to his throat, which had gone hard with a prickly dryness. He turned pale, and continued with difficulty:

'Let me speak. I'm not an enemy; why are you treating me like this? I was wounded while I was in the army ... I got a contusion ... from a heavy shell ...' He lapsed into silence, his blackening lips gasping air into his lungs. Balabin hastily poured some water from the carafe, and stretched out the glass to Nagulnov without looking at him.

The secretary glanced at Makar, and hurriedly removed his eyes. Makar's hand trembled uncontrollably as he clutched the glass. In the silence the sound of the glass tinkling against his teeth was distinctly heard.

'Now, don't get agitated; speak up !' Balabin said irritably.

The secretary frowned. Uninvited pity was creeping into his heart, but he took himself in hand. He was firmly convinced that Nagulnov was a danger to the Party, and that he must not only be removed from his position but expelled from the Party. His opinion was shared by everybody present with the exception of Balabin.

Makar drank the glass of water in one gulp, took a breath, and began to speak again :

'I admit all that Samokhin says. It's true that I did all that. But not because I wanted to attack the Party. Samokhin's lying there ! He lied like a dog, and about my "immorality", too. It's all imagination. I'm having nothing to do with women, and I've got no use for them . . .'

'And is that why you drove out your wife?' the head of the Organization Department sneered.

'Yes, that's why,' Makar answered in all seriousness. 'But I did do all that. I desired the well-being of the revolution. Maybe I was wrong . . . I don't know. You're more educated than I am. You've taken courses, you can see things clearer. I'm not trying to make my guilt look smaller than it is. Judge me as you wish. I ask you to understand only one thing . . .' he again lost his breath, broke off in the middle of a sentence, and was silent for a moment. 'Do understand, brothers, that I did all this without any evil intentions against the Party. And I beat up Bannik because he jeered at the Party and wanted to feed seed grain to the pigs . . .'

'So you say !' Samokhin scoffed.

'I'm telling you what happened. I'm still sorry I didn't kill him. I've got nothing more to say.'

The secretary straightened up, and his chair groaned beneath him. All he wanted was to get this unpleasant business ended as soon as possible. Hurriedly he said :

'Well, comrades, it's quite clear then. Nagulnov has admitted it himself. Although he has tried to wriggle, to justify himself on matters of detail, his justification doesn't sound at all convincing. Anyone who finds the screw being put on him tries to relieve himself of part of the guilt, or to put the responsibility on to others. I consider that, because he has maliciously violated the

Party line in regard to the collective farm movement, and as a communist who has degenerated in his personal relationships, Nagulnov must be expelled from the Party. We shall not take his past services into consideration: that stage is over. We must punish him as an example to others. We shall strike ruthlessly at all who try to slander the Party and to draw it to the left or the right. We can't confine ourselves to half-measures in regard to Nagulnov and such as he. We've nursed him long enough as it is. He went left during the organization of the associations for co-operative land labour last year, and I warned him about it at the time. As he hasn't paid any heed, let him foam at himself. Shall we vote? Only members of the Bureau are allowed to vote, of course. Four in favour, is that right? Are you against, comrade Balabin?'

Balabin smashed his palm down against the tabletop. A network of veins stood out on his temples.

'I'm not only against, but I categorically protest,' he exclaimed. 'You're making a fundamentally unsound decision.'

'You can keep to your personal opinion,' the secretary icily remarked.

'No, you allow me to speak!'

'It's too late, Balabin. The decision to expel Nagulnov from the Party has been passed by a majority.'

'That is a bureaucratic attitude to take up to a man! Excuse me, but I'm not going to let it rest there. I shall write to the Regional Committee. To expel an old Party member, and a member of the Order of the Red Banner ... Have you gone mad, comrades? As if there aren't any other methods of punishment but expulsion!'

'There's no point in discussing it now. We've already voted.'

'You ought to have your face smashed for such voting!' Balabin's voice rose to a thin falsetto, his neck swelled so that it looked as though the blood would pour out at the least touch of a finger.

'You'd better not say much about smashing faces!' the head of the Organization Department said insinuatingly and unpleasantly. 'This isn't the District militia office, but the District Party Committee.'

'I know that without your telling me. But why won't you let me speak?'

'Because I consider it superfluous,' the secretary flared up. He went as livid as Balabin, and clutched the arm of his chair. 'I'm the secretary of the District Committee here! I refuse to let you speak, and if you want to speak you can go out on to the porch.'

'Balabin, don't boil over like that! What are you so excited about? By all means write your opinion to the Regional Committee. But we've voted now, and you've started to wave your fists after the fight's over,' the District Executive Committee chairman attempted to bring Balabin to reason. He took the militia-man by the sleeve of his military shirt, drew him into a corner, and talked to him in undertones.

Meantime, irritated by the encounter with Balabin, the secretary raised his angrily glittering eyes to Makar and said with unconcealed hostility:

'The talk's ended, Nagulnov! By the decision of the Bureau you are expelled from our ranks. Such as you aren't wanted by the Party. Hand over your membership card.' He rapped the table with his palm.

Nagulnov turned deathly pale. He was shaken with a fit of trembling, and his voice was almost inaudible as he said:

'I won't give up my Party card.'

'We'll make you give it up!'

'Go to the Regional Committee, Nagulnov,' Balabin shouted from the corner. He broke off his talk with the chairman in the middle of a word, and went out, slamming the door behind him.

'I won't give up my Party card,' Makar repeated. His voice grew stronger; the bluish pallor slowly ebbed from his forehead and bony cheeks. 'And I shall still be needed by the Party ... And I can't live without the Party. I won't submit to you! There's my ticket, in my breast pocket. Try to take it! I'll cut your throats!'

'Now the tragic act begins!' the District Prosecutor shrugged his shoulders. 'Only without hysterics ...'

Taking no heed of his words, Makar stared at the secretary, and spoke slowly, almost dreamily:

'Where am I to go outside the Party? And why am I to go? No, I won't give up my Party card. I've given all my life ... all my life ...' Suddenly he fumbled aimlessly, like a pitiable old man, on the table, and stumbled over his words as he hurriedly and indistinctly muttered:

'If that's the position, it would be better if you ... ordered the boys ... All there is left for me is to be pulverized. There's nothing left ... My life's got no point now, so expel me from that, too ... Well, I was wanted ... But I've grown old ... kick the old dog out of the yard ...'

His face was as rigid as a gypsum mask, only his lips quivered and stirred. But as he spoke the last words, for the first time in all the years of his adolescence the tears poured down in streams from his glassy eyes. They flowed copiously over his cheeks, were caught in the thick growth of his long unshaven beard, and soiled the shirt on his chest with black drops.

'Enough of that! You won't get out of it like that, comrade!' the secretary frowned painfully.

'You're no ... comrade of mine!' Nagulnov began to shout. 'You're a wolf. And all of you here are poisonous reptiles. You've got the power now! You've learned to talk smoothly! What are you baring your teeth like a whore for, Homutov? Laughing at my tears? You ...! D'you remember how you came into the Regional Committee in 1921, when Fomin's band was ranging over the countryside? Do you remember, you bitch's tail? You came and gave up your Party ticket, and said you were going to take up agriculture ... You were afraid of Fomin, and that's why you gave up your ticket! But afterwards you crawled into the Party again, like a slimy slug across the stones! And now you're voting against me? You laugh at my mortal sorrow?'

'That's enough, Nagulnov, please don't shout. We've got other matters yet to discuss,' the handsome, swarthy Homutov, head of the Organization Department, said in a conciliatory tone. He was not in the least embarrassed by Nagulnov's attack, and his smile still lurked beneath his dark whiskers.

'It's enough for you! But I'll find my own rights! I shall go to the Central Committee!'

'That's the spirit! You go! They'll settle everything in a moment there. They've been expecting you a long time now,' Homutov smiled.

Makar quietly turned to the door, knocked his temple against the doorpost, and groaned.

His last outbreak of anger had completely exhausted him. Without thought, without feeling he walked to the yard gate, unfastened his pony from the fence, and for no good reason began to lead it off by the rein. On the outskirts of the town he tried to mount, but could not. Four times he raised his foot to the stirrup, and each time, swaying drunkenly, he had to let go of the saddle-bow.

A virile old man was sitting on the ledge along the wall of the last hut. From under the peeled peak of his cossack cap he watched attentively as Makar tried to mount the horse, and finally smiled encouragingly.

'Fine lad!' he said. 'The sun's still high, and he can't lift his feet! What's the reason for his being drunk so early? Today isn't a holiday, is it?'

'Yes, it is, daddy Fiodot,' his neighbour replied, as he stared across the wattle fence. 'Today's dedicated to "Simon the Idler", when they go on pilgrimages from one tavern to another.'

'So I see,' the old man smiled. 'There's no youngster stronger than wine! Look how it bowls him out of the saddle!'

Makar ground his teeth and, only lightly touching the stirrup with the toe of his boot, he flew like a bird into the saddle.

Chapter 33

A Fight for Grain

THAT same morning twenty-three collective farm carts arrived at Gremyachy Log from the village of Yarsky. As they were passing the windmill Bannik fell in with them. With a bridle hanging across his shoulder, he was going to the steppe to look for his mare. As the first cart drew alongside he greeted the driver, and the black-bearded cossack replied.

'Where are you from?' Bannik inquired.

'Yarsky.'

'Why haven't your horses got any tails? Why have you put them to shame like that?'

'Whoa! The devil! We've cut off her tail, but she's still frisky. Why haven't they got any tails, did you ask? We've cut them off to sell at a good profit! The town women will use the tails to drive away the flies with. You haven't got anything to smoke, have you? Treat us, we're short of tobacco.' The cossack jumped down from his britzka.

The line of carts halted. Bannik felt sorry he had opened the conversation. He reluctantly drew out his pouch, watching as some five or six more men left their carts, tearing up newspapers into cigarette papers as they came.

'You'll use all my tobacco!' the niggardly Bannik croaked.

'It's the collective farm's now, don't you know? Everything's got to be communal,' the bearded cossack said sternly. And he took as big a pinch of the home-grown tobacco as if the pouch were his own.

They lit cigarettes. Bannik hurriedly thrust his pouch into his trouser pocket, and smiled. He looked with fastidious pity at the horses' tails, which were docked almost to the cruppers. A blood-thirsty horsefly was plaguing the horses, settling on their sweaty haunches and collar-chafed necks. In the attempt to drive off the flies the horses swung their tails automatically, but the shameful, hairless stumps were ineffective.

'Where is she pointing to with her tail?' Bannik venomously asked.

'Always into the collective farm. Haven't they cut off your horses' tails yet?'

'Yes, but only for four inches or so.'

'It was our Soviet chairman gave orders for this to be done. He got a prize for it, but when the heat sets in the horses will be lost. Well, we must be getting on. Thanks for the tobacco. We've had a smoke and it's softened our hearts, for all along the road we were wild because we hadn't got any.'

'Where are you driving to?'

'Gremyachy.'

'So you're going to our village. And what for?'

'For seed grain.'

'What ... what do you mean?'

'The District has sent an order for us to get our seed grain fund from you: four hundred and thirty poods of it. Well, gee up!'

'I knew it would happen!' Bannik shouted. Waving the bridle, he ran back to the village.

Before the Yarsky carts reached the collective farm office half the village knew that they had come to take away seed grain. Bannik did not spare his legs, and he poked his nose into hut after hut.

First the women began to gather in the by-lanes, fussing and fluttering like coveys of startled partridges.

'They're carrying off our grain, my dears.'

'We shan't have anything to sow with.'

'The good folk told us it would be better not to put our grain into the communal granary.'

'If only the cossacks had listened to us.'

'We must go and tell them not to hand over the grain.'

'But we'll see to that ourselves! Come on, women, to the granaries. We'll take stakes, and we won't let them get near the padlocks.'

Then the cossacks began to show themselves. Among them the same kind of talk was to be heard. Passing from by-lane to by-lane, from street to street, they gathered into a crowd and moved towards the granaries.

Meantime, Davidov had read the official note brought by the Yarsky men from the chairman of the District Agricultural Union. 'Dear comrade Davidov,' he wrote. 'You've got 73 centners of wheat which were not handed in to the District after the last grain collection. I propose you give this quantity of wheat to the Yarsky collective farm as they haven't sufficient seed grain. I have got the agreement of the Grain Co-operative to this.'

Davidov read the note, and gave orders for the grain to be handed over. The Yarsky men drove from the yard of the collective farm office to the granaries. But around the granaries the street was dammed by the crowd. A couple of hundred women and cossacks surrounded the carts.

'Where are you going?' they demanded.

'Have you come for our grain? The devil's sent you here!'

'Turn back!'

'We won't give it to you!'

Diemka Ushakov hurried to fetch Davidov, who went to the granaries at a run.

'What's the matter, citizens?' he demanded. 'What have you gathered here for?'

'Why are you giving our grain to the Yarsky people? Did we collect it for them?'

'Who gave you such rights, Davidov?'

'What are we going to sow with?'

Davidov scrambled on to the steps of the nearest granary, and calmly explained that, on the instruction of the Agricultural Union, he was giving out not seed grain, but the remainder of the grain tax.

'Don't get alarmed, citizens,' he said. 'Your grain won't be touched. And instead of hanging around idle and chewing sunflower seeds, you ought to be in the fields. Don't forget the brigade leaders keep records of those who don't go out to work. We shall fine those who don't turn up.'

Reassured by Davidov's declaration, some of the cossacks went away, many of them going out to the fields. The storekeeper began to weigh out the grain for the Yarsky men, and Davidov returned to the office. But in less than half an hour a complete change occurred in the attitude of the women who had remained to watch by the granaries. Yakov Lukich was responsible for this, for he whispered to several cossacks: 'Davidov's lying! They're taking seed grain. The collective farm is already sowing, but the grain handed in by the individual peasants is being given to the Yarsky collective farm.'

The women grew more and more agitated. Bannik, Diemid the Silent, old Donietskov, and some thirty other cossacks stood discussing matters for a few minutes, then went across to the scales.

'We're not giving up the grain to Yarsky!' Donietskov announced on behalf of them all.

'You haven't been asked!' Diemka Ushakov snapped back.

A skirmish began between them. The Yarsky men took Diemka's part. The same black-bearded cossack whom Bannik had treated to tobacco drew himself up to his full height on his britzka, cursed furiously for a good five minutes, then shouted:

'What are you disobeying the government for? What are you making us suffer torments for? We've had to drive thirty miles on a hot day, and you're holding back the State grain. The G.P.U. is crying bitter tears for you! You ought to be sent to Solovka concentration camp, you sons of bitches! You're like dogs in a manger; you lie and don't eat anything yourself, but you won't let others eat either. Why aren't you out in your fields? Is it a holiday today?'

'And what do you want?' the younger Akim Beskhlebnov roared. 'Is your beard itching? We'll comb it for you! In one minute!' He rolled up his sleeves and pushed his way to the britzka.

The bearded Yarsky cossack jumped down. He did not roll up the sleeves of his faded brown shirt, but met Akim with such a well-placed, furious blow on the jaw that Akim flew backward some five yards, waving his arms like windmill sails and sending the crowd scattering.

Then a fight began such as Gremyachy had not seen for many a day. The Yarsky men received severe punishment, and, streaming with blood, they dropped the sacks of grain and clambered into their britzkas. Whipping up their horses, they broke through the crowd of screaming women and galloped off.

From that moment Gremyachy Log became a seething whirlpool of excitement. The crowd wanted to relieve Diemka of the keys to the granaries containing the seed grain, but during the fight the intelligent Diemka had slipped out of the crowd and hurried off to the office.

'What shall we do with the keys, comrade Davidov?' he asked. 'Our people are beating up the Yarsky men, and it's certain they'll be coming along to us next.'

'Give them to me,' Davidov calmly said.

He took the keys, put them in his pocket, and went to the granaries. Meantime the women had dragged Andrei Razmiotnov out of the village Soviet, and were persistently shouting:

'Open the meeting!'

'Women! Aunties! Mothers! My darlings! There aren't any meetings being held at present. We've got to sow now, and not hold meetings. What d'you want meetings for? "Meetings" is a soldier's word. Before you can say it you have to sit three years in the trenches! You have to go to war and feed lice, then you can talk about meetings,' Razmiotnov tried to reason with the women.

But they would not listen to him, and, clinging to his trousers, to his sleeves and the end of his shirt below his belt, they dragged the frowning Andrei into the school, and bawled:

'We don't want to sit in the trenches!'

'We don't want to go to war!'

'Open the meeting, or we'll open it ourselves.'

'You son of a bitch, you're lying when you say you can't. You're the chairman, so you can.'

Andrei pushed away the women, stopped his ears with his fingers, and roared in the attempt to out-shout them:

'Shut up, you devils! Stand back a bit! What d'you want a meeting for?'

'About the grain. We want to talk to you about the grain.'

Finally he was compelled to announce:

'I declare the meeting open.'

'Let me speak!' demanded the widow Yekaterina Gulyashchaya.

'Speak up then, and let the devil smell you!'

'None of your devilling, chairman! Or I'll mark you ... By whose permission did you allow our grain to be dragged off? Who gave orders for it to be given to the Yarsky men, and what need was there for the order?' With arms akimbo, she bent forward waiting for his answer.

Andrei waved her off as though she were a persistent fly.

'You were authoritatively informed by comrade Davidov. And I didn't open the meeting for you to talk such nonsense, but in order ...' He sighed. 'Because, dear citizenesses, we ought to go after the marmots with all our strength ...'

But Andrei's manoeuvre was not successful.

'What marmots?' they demanded.

'The marmots are nothing to do with us.'

'Give us grain.'

'A fine speaker you are, may a hedgehog prick you! Go off after the marmots! But what are you going to say about the grain?'

'There's nothing to be said about it.'

'What, nothing? Give us back our grain!'

Gulyashchaya at their head, the women began to advance towards the stage. Andrei stood by the prompter's sheet-iron box. He gazed at the women with a smile, but inwardly he felt a little anxious: the cossacks crowding behind the white daisy-field of the women's kerchiefs looked rather too grim.

'You go about in leg-boots winter and summer, but we haven't got anything to buy shoes with,' one woman shouted.

'You've become a commissar!'

'How long is it since you wore out Marina's husband's trousers?'

'Your muzzle's had its fill!'

'Undress him, women!'

The shouts rattled out like irregular rifle-fire. Several dozen women crowded right against the platform. Andrei vainly tried to restore silence: his voice was inaudible in the hubbub.

'Pull his boots off him! Come on, women, all together!'

In a moment innumerable hands were stretched towards the stage. Andrei was seized by his left leg. He clung to the prompter's box, and went pale with anger. But the boot was already torn from his foot and thrown back across the crowd. Hand after hand caught the boot and threw it farther, accompanying it with unfriendly, unpleasant laughter. From the back rows came approving male voices:

'Undress him!'

'Let him go without his trousers.'

'Take the other boot off!'

'Get on with it, women! Throw him down ...'

They tore off Andrei's other boot. He shook his leg-rags and shouted:

'Take the puttees, too! Someone may find them useful for nose-rags!'

him for brawling, and had locked him up for the night in the Soviet shed. 'Smoky' had long nourished a great anger against Razmiotnov, and now he climbed on to the stage in order to settle accounts.

He drew nearer and nearer to Andrei. His knees shook, and it made him look as though he were dancing.

'We'll have those trousers,' he said with a noisy intake of breath. 'Come on, off with them!'

The stage was flooded with women, the many-handed crowd again surrounded Andrei, breathing fierily against his face and the back of his head, enclosing him in an impenetrable ring.

'I'm the Soviet chairman,' he shouted, 'and you're making a mock of me, you're making a mock of the Soviet government. Clear off! I won't allow you to take the grain! I declare the meeting closed.'

'We'll take it ourselves.'

'Ho-ho! He's closed the meeting!'

'We'll open it then!'

'We'll go to Davidov and shake him up, too!'

'Come on, along to the office!'

'We must lock up Razmiotnov first!'

'Beat him up, boys!'

'What are you looking at him for?'

'He's against Stalin!'

'Lock him up!'

One of the women dragged the crimson satin cloth off the chairman's table and threw it over Razmiotnov's head from behind. While he was struggling to tear away the dusty and inky cloth, 'Smoky' gave him a short-arm jab in the pit of his stomach. Freeing his hand, panting with pain and reckless fury, Andrei pulled his pistol from his pocket. The women fled back screaming; but 'Smoky' and three other cossacks on the platform seized his arms and took away the weapon.

'So you were going to shoot at the people! You son of a bitch!' one of them joyfully shouted, raising Razmiotnov's pistol with its completely empty chambers above his head . . .

Davidov involuntarily slowed his steps when he heard a single, threatening roar coming from the neighbourhood of the granaries.

A woman's piercing scream flew high above the men's deep voices. It was sharply distinguished from the solid mass of voices, just as, in the forest touched by the first frost, the sobbing, passionate, furiously weeping howl of a hunting bitch following the hot scent of an animal is distinguished from the general tumult of the pack.

'Better send for the second brigade, or they'll share out the grain,' Davidov thought. He decided to return to the office, to hide the granary keys somewhere. He found Diemka Ushakov standing distractedly at the gate.

'I'm going to hide, comrade Davidov,' he said. 'They'll be coming after me for the keys.'

'That's your business. Is Naidionov here?'

'No, he's with the second brigade.'

'Isn't anybody of the second brigade around?'

'Kondrat Maidannikov's here.'

'Where is he? What's he doing here?'

'He's come to get seed grain. There he is!'

Maidannikov hurried up to them. He waved his whip as he approached, and shouted:

'The community's arrested Andrei Razmiotnov. They've put him in a cellar and they're going to the granaries now. You hide somewhere, comrade Davidov, or there may be wrong done ... The people have gone mad.'

'I'm not going to hide! Are you mad? Here are the keys. Gallop back to the brigade, and tell Liubishkin to put some fifteen men on horses and gallop here at once. You can see there's going to be trouble. What did you come in on?'

'On a britzka.'

'Unharness one of the horses and ride it back as fast as it'll go.'

'I'll be there in two ticks.' Maidannikov thrust the keys into his pocket and ran down the by-lane.

Davidov slowly went to the granaries. The crowd quietened down as it waited for him. 'Here comes the enemy!' some woman shouted hysterically, pointing at him. But he did not hurry, and in full view of them all he stopped to light a cigarette, turning his back to the wind and striking a match.

'Come on! Come on! You'll have plenty of time to smoke!'

'You can smoke in the next world!'

'Are you bringing the keys, or aren't you?'

'He's bringing them, I expect. The dog knows the hand that feeds him!'

Puffing out billows of smoke, thrusting his hands into his pocket, Davidov walked up to the front rows of people. His calm, assured bearing had a dual effect on the crowd. Some of them felt that it indicated his consciousness of strength and superiority, others were enraged by it. The shouts rattled out like hail on an iron roof:

'Give us the keys!'

'Break up the collective farm!'

'Clear out of here altogether! Who the devil asked you to come?'

'Give us our seed grain!'

'Why won't you let us sow?'

A gentle breeze played with the ends of the women's kerchiefs, rustled the bunches of reeds on the granary roofs, and brought from the steppe the vapid smell of drying earth and the scent of the young grasses, like unfermented wine. The honey perfume of the buds bursting on the poplars was so cloyingly sweet, that when Davidov began to speak he felt that his lips were sticking together, and even thought he could taste the honey.

'What's all this, citizens?' he demanded. 'What have you refused to obey the instructions of the Soviet government for? Why didn't you let the Yarsky collective farm have the grain? Don't you realize that you'll have to answer in court for this, and for interrupting the spring sowing campaign? It's a fact you will! The Soviet government will not forgive you that!'

'At the moment your Soviet government is under arrest! It's shut up, like a lover, in a cellar!' a short, lame, individual farmer replied.

Someone laughed; but Bannik stepped forward, and angrily shouted:

'The Soviet government doesn't dictate the things you're making up. We won't submit to such a Soviet government as you and Makar Nagulnov have started. Is it right to stop the farmers from sowing? What d'you call that? That's a distortion of the Party!'

'Do you mean to say we're stopping you from sowing?' Davidov asked.

'Well, aren't you?'

'Did you put your seed grain into the communal granary?'

'Yes, I did.'

'And have you got it back again?'

'Yes, I have; but what of it?'

'Then who's stopping you from sowing? What are you hanging around the granaries for?'

Bannik was a little disconcerted by this unexpected turn in the conversation; but he tried to recover his ground:

'I'm not worrying about myself, but about the people, those who've left the collective farm and haven't had their grain back or their property. That's what! And besides, what sort of land have you let me have? Why is it so far off?'

'Clear out of here!' Davidov could not control himself any longer. 'We'll talk with you later! Fact! And don't you shove your nose into the collective farm affairs, or you'll lose it quick! You're working up the people! Clear out, I tell you!'

Muttering threats, Bannik fell back. But the women quickly rushed forward in his place. They all shouted at once and in one voice, not allowing Davidov to say a word. He tried to play for time, in order to give Liubishkin and his men the chance to arrive. But, screaming deafeningly, the women surrounded him, supported by a sympathetic silence among the cossacks.

As he looked around, Davidov noticed Marina Poyarkova. She was standing a little way off, her mighty arms bare to the elbows and crossed on her breast. She was talking animatedly to a group of women, her bluish-black eyebrows frowning until they almost met above her nose. Davidov caught her hostile glance, and almost at the same moment he noticed that close to her was Yakov Lukich. Yakov was agitatedly, expectantly smiling, and whispering something to Diemid the Silent.

'Give us the keys! Give us them for your own good, d'you hear?' One of the women seized Davidov by the shoulder, and thrust her hand into his trouser pocket.

Davidov forcibly shoved her off. The woman stepped away,

fell on her back, and hypocritically howled: 'Oh, he's killed me, killed me! My dears, don't let me perish!'

'What's all this?' someone at the back of the crowd said in a quivering tenor voice. 'So he's beginning to fight? Well then, give it to him so that the juice spurts from his nose!'

Davidov stepped across to pick up the fallen woman, but his cap was sent flying from his head, and he was struck several times on his face and back. They seized his arms. Swinging his shoulders, he threw off the women attacking him. But with a shout they again clung to him, tore the collar of his shirt, and in a few seconds had rummaged through and turned out his pockets.

'He hasn't got the keys!'

'Where are they?'

'Hand them over! Otherwise we'll smash the padlocks.'

Panting and swearing violently, a majestic old lady, the mother of Mishka Ignationok, pushed her way to Davidov and spat in his face.

'That's for you, you Satan! You atheist!'

Davidov turned pale, and exerted all his strength in the attempt to free his arms. But he could not. Evidently some of the cossacks had hurried to the women's aid, for strong, horny fingers had seized and were pressing back his elbows, pressing them back as though with pincers. Then he ceased to struggle. He realized that the matter had gone too far, that none of those around him would come to his help. So he decided to take a different course of action.

'I haven't got the keys to the granaries, citizens. They're kept ...' He stopped short: he was about to say that he did not keep the keys, but he at once realized that if he said that, the crowd would rush to look for Diemka Ushakov and would certainly find him. Then Diemka would have a bad time, and he might be killed. 'I'll say I've got them at home, and I'll go along there and search. Then I'll say I've lost them. They won't dare to kill me, and meantime Liubishkin will have arrived. The devil take the lot of them!' he thought. He was silent while with his shoulder he wiped the blood from his scratched cheek, then he said: 'The keys are kept at my place, but I won't give them to you. And if you smash the padlocks you'll answer for it with all the severity of the law. So now you know. Fact!'

'Take us to your room. We'll find the keys ourselves,' Ignationok's mother persisted. Her flabby cheeks and the great wart on her nose trembled with her agitation, the sweat poured incessantly down her wrinkled face. She was the first to push Davidov, and he readily but slowly walked in the direction of his hut.

'But are the keys there? Maybe you've forgotten,' Bannik's wife Avdotia questioned him.

'Yes, they're there all right, auntie!' Davidov assured her, bending his head to hide a smile.

Four women held him by the arms, a fifth followed behind him with a healthy-looking stake in her hands, on his right hand, shaking continually, old Ignationok walked with a long, masculine stride, and on his left the women hurried in little groups. The cossacks remained at the granaries to wait for the keys.

'Let go of my arms, aunties! I shan't run away!' Davidov asked.

'But who knows, maybe you will after all!'

'No, I shan't!'

'You come with us, it'll be quieter for you!'

They reached his hut, threw down the wattle gate and fence, and poured into the yard.

'Go and fetch the keys. And if you don't bring them we'll call the cossacks and they'll twist your neck lopsided for you!'

'Ah, aunties, you've soon forgotten the Soviet government! But it won't forget you for this business!'

'Seven crimes, only one punishment! It's all the same to us whether we swell with hunger in the autumn because we haven't sown anything, or whether we answer for it now. You go in and get them, go on!'

Davidov went into his room, and, knowing that they were watching him, pretended to make a diligent search. He turned over everything in his suitcase and on the table, shook out all the papers, crawled under the bed and the crooked-legged table.

Going on to the porch, he announced: 'I can't find the keys.'

'Then where are they?'

'I expect Nagulnov's got them . . .' he replied.

'But he's gone off for the day.'

'What's that got to do with it? He's gone himself, but he may have left the keys behind. In fact I'm quite sure he's left them behind, for we were to give out grain for the second brigade today.'

They led him to Nagulnov's quarters. On the way they began to beat him. At first they only cursed and gently jostled him, but, growing enraged because he continually laughed and joked, they began to beat him in earnest.

'Citizenesses! My dear nannies! At any rate don't hit me with sticks!' he pleaded, pinching the nearest women, while he bent his head and forced a smile. But they thrashed him unmercifully on his broad, bowed back. He only grunted, shrugged his shoulders, and, despite the pain, still tried to joke:

'Women! You're near to your graves, and you're laying it on like that! Let me give you a whack or two, eh?'

'You unfeeling idol! You cold stone!' The youthful Nastia Donietskova howled almost tearfully, as she zealously drubbed Davidov's back with her small but strong fists. 'I've broken all my hands open against him, and it seems nothing to him ...'

They split open his ear, his lips and his nose. But he went on smiling with swollen lips, revealing the loss of a single upper tooth, and unhurriedly and gently pushed away the most violent of the women. He was terribly plagued by old Ignationok, the woman with the angrily quivering wart on her nose. She hit him hard in order to hurt, trying to reach the bridge of his nose, or his temple. Unlike the others, she struck him with the knuckles of her clenched fist. Davidov vainly tried to turn his back towards her as he walked along. Panting, she pushed aside the women, ran in front of him and hoarsely screamed:

'I'll hit him on the snout! I'll hit him on the snout!'

'You wait, you she-devil!' Davidov thought in a cold fury, turning away from her blows. 'As soon as Liubishkin arrives I'll give you such a whack that you'll go spinning away from me!'

But there was still no sign of Liubishkin and the other horsemen. Meantime the women dragged him to Nagulnov's quarters. This time the women went with Davidov into the room. They rummaged everywhere, threw aside books, papers, linen, and even searched for the keys in the rooms occupied by the mistress of the hut. Naturally, they did not find them, and they pushed Davidov on to the porch.

'Where are the keys? We'll kill you!' they stormed.

'Ostrovnov's got them,' Davidov replied as he recalled the evilly smiling face of the collective farm manager among the crowd at the granaries.

'You're lying! We've already asked him. He said you ought to have the keys!'

'Citizenesses!' He touched his monstrously swollen nose with his fingers, and quietly smiled. 'Citizenesses! You've beaten me absolutely for nothing! The keys are in the office, in my table. Fact! I remember perfectly now.'

'You're laughing at us!' shrieked Yekaterina Gulyashchaya.

'Take me there; how can there be any question of my laughing? Only without any whacks, please!' Davidov stepped down from the porch. He was tormented with thirst, mastered by an impotent frenzy. It was not the first time he had been beaten, but he had never been beaten by women before, and he was beside himself because of it. 'But I mustn't drop, or they'll go mad and peck me to death, of all things! That would be a silly way of dying! Fact!' he thought, hopefully straining his eyes in the direction of the hills. But there was no sign of dust whirled from the road by horses' hoofs, no sign of a stream of riders. The hill was completely deserted as far as the distant mound on the horizon. And the streets were equally deserted. Everybody had gathered around the granaries, whence arose a dull thunder of innumerable voices.

By the time they reached the office Davidov was beaten so severely that he could hardly keep his feet. He no longer jested, but stumbled again and again without cause, clutched his head more and more frequently, and asked in a hollow voice:

'Enough! Why, you'll kill me! I haven't got the keys! Don't hit me on the head. I'll go on till nightfall, but I haven't got the keys.'

'Go till nightfall?' the infuriated women groaned, and again clung like leeches to the helpless Davidov, scratching, beating, and even biting.

Right outside the office yard he sat down in the road. His canvas shirt was soaked with blood, his short town trousers, fringed with wear at the bottoms, were torn at the knees, his swarthy, tattooed chest was visible through his ragged shirt. He breathed heavily and wheezily, and looked a pitiful sight.

'Get on, you son of a bitch!' old Ignationok thrust at him with her foot.

'And it's for you, you bitches,' he said unexpectedly loud, running his strangely gleaming eyes around them, 'it's for you we're working! And you're killing me! Ah, you bitches! I shan't give you the keys. Understand? I shan't, and that's a fact! Well?'

'Don't worry about him, girls!' shouted a woman who came running up. 'The cossacks have smashed the padlocks and are giving out the grain.'

The women abandoned Davidov by the office gates, and ran off to the granaries. With a tremendous effort he rose and went into the yard. He carried a bucket of water, lukewarm with the heat, on to the porch, and took a long drink. Then he poured the water over his head. Groaning, he washed the blood from his face and neck, wiped himself on a horse-cloth hanging over the balustrade, and sat down on the threshold.

There was not a soul in the yard. Somewhere a chicken was anxiously clucking. On the roof of the starling nest-box a black titlark was twittering with head thrown back. From the steppe came the whistle of marmots. A thin, graded ridge of lilac clouds curtained the sun, yet such an oppressive, exhausting heat hung in the air that even the sparrows which had been bathing on a heap of ashes in the middle of the yard were lying motionless, their little necks stretched out, occasionally fluttering the tiny fans of their open wings.

Hearing a dull, soft trample of hoofs, Davidov raised his head. A saddled, limber-flanked little dun horse came flying through the gate at full gallop. It swung sharply round, dug its hind hoofs into the ground, and circled the yard, snorting as it went and dropping white, fluffy flecks of foam from its haunches on to the hot earth. By the stable door it halted, and snuffed at the step. Its handsome, inlaid silver bridle was broken, the ends of the reins were hanging, the saddle had slipped forward on to its withers, and the broken breast-strap hung to the ground, touching the dark lilac horn of its hoofs. Its sides were heaving, its rosy nostrils were dilated, clumps of brown, last-year's burrs were clinging to its crupper and the tangled strands of its mane.

As Davidov was staring in amazement at the horse, the door to the hayloft creaked noisily, and old Shchukar's head was thrust out. After a moment or two he emerged, opening the door with the greatest caution, and timorously peering in all directions. His sweaty shirt was thickly covered with wisps of hay, and out of his tangled beard stuck the empty ears of quitch, dry blades of grass and leaves, and the yellow pollen of clover. His face was a cherry red, and the impress of immeasurable terror lay on it, while the sweat poured down from his temples over his cheeks and beard.

'Comrade Davidov!' he said in an imploring whisper, tiptoeing to the porch, 'hide yourself, for the love of God! Once they've started to smash us up they'll not stop at murder. How they've mauled you about; I wouldn't know your face. I saved myself in the hay ... It's stifling in there, I'm sweating all over, but you have more peace of mind, by God! Let's wait for this commotion to pass over, and hide together, ah? It's horrible for one to stay ... What's the point of getting killed for you don't know what? Listen how the women are howling like hornets, damn them! And they've done for Nagulnov, that's clear! That's his mare just galloped in. He rode off to the District on her this morning. She stumbled under him at the gate, and I said to him then: "Turn back, Makar; that's a bad sign!" But did he ever listen to anyone who knew? Never in all his life. He's always liked to go his own way, and now they've killed him. But if he had turned back he might have hidden like me.'

'Then he may be at home now,' Davidov queried irresolutely.

'At home? But why has his mare come back riderless, snorting as though she had smelt a corpse? I know those signs only too well! It's quite clear; he returned from the District, saw them taking grain at the granaries, and told them to stop, his hot blood couldn't stand it. And so they killed him!'

Davidov was silent. From the granaries the groan of a myriad-voiced hubbub was still rising; he could hear the creaking of carts

310

and the clattering rattle of wheels. 'They're carrying off the grain,' he thought. 'But what has happened to Makar? Surely they haven't killed him? I'm going to see.'

He rose to his feet. Thinking Davidov had decided to hide with him in the hayloft, Shchukar fussed around him:

'Come on, hurry away from the sin! Or the devil will bring someone else along here, they'll see me and you and do for us! They'll do it in less than no time! And it's really very good in the hayloft. The smell of the hay is easy and pleasant, I'd lie there a month if they brought my food up to me. Only a goat stirred me up a bit. I could have killed the nuisance! I heard the women breaking up the collective farm and saucing you about the grain. "Well," I thought to myself, "you're lost, Shchukar, for a pinch of tobacco!" For every one of these women knows that only me and you, comrade Davidov, have been on the platform from the very first day of the revolution, and that we set up the collective farm in Gremyachy and turned out Titok as a kulak. Who have they got to kill off the very first? That's clear enough: me and you! "Our business is in a bad way," I thought. "I must hide, or they'll kill Davidov and get me, too. And then who will give evidence to the investigator after Davidov's death?" In a moment I plunged into the hay, covered myself with it right over my head, and lay there, breathing heavily and still afraid. Then I heard someone crawling over the hay above me. He crawled, and naturally he sneezed with the dust. "Mother!" I thought, "it must be them looking for me; they must be after my life!" And he crawled and crawled, then he trod on my stomach. I lay still! My soul and body were parting in my fright, but I lay like the damned, because there was nowhere I could go to! And then he stepped right on to my face! I felt with my hand, and found a hoof, and all hairy! The hair of my head stood on end, and my skin all but began to come away from my body. I couldn't breathe for fright. What did I think when I felt that hairy hoof? "It's a devil," I thought. It was terribly dark in the hayloft, and the unclean spirits are fond of the dark. "In a minute he'll begin to beat and worry me to death. I'd rather let the women execute me!" Yes, I was in a fright, there's no denying it! Let anyone else be in my place, a cowardly sort of lad, and he might easily have burst his heart and all his inside out of him. That always happens with sudden fright. But I only turned cold a little, and lay quiet. Then I thought it smelt too much like a goat; and I remembered that Titok's goat lived up in the hayloft, and I'd quite forgotten him, the devil! I peeped out, and it was him sure enough: Titok's goat crawling over the hay, looking for sage, and chewing wormwood. Well, of course, then I got up and gave him what he deserved. I mauled him about as though he was my darling, and pulled his beard and lord knows what else. "Don't crawl over the hay, you bearded devil, when there's a rising in the village! Don't stamp around without reason, you stinking devil!" I shouted. I was so mad that I wanted to put him to death on the spot, just because, although he is an animal, he ought to understand how and when and where he can wander over the hay unnecessarily, and when he ought to hide quietly away and be still ... But where are you going, comrade Davidov?'

Without replying, Davidov went past the entrance to the hayloft and made for the gate.

'Where are you going?' Shchukar whispered fearfully.

Through the half-open wicket gate he saw Davidov walking as though blown along by a gusty wind, going towards the communal granaries with swift, though uncertain steps.

Chapter 34

The Ancient Mound

AT the side of the road stands a burial mound. On its wind-swept summit the bare twigs of last year's wormwood and trefoil rustle mournfully, the brown tufts of cotton-thistles bow moodily to the earth. Over its slopes, from its foot to its summit clumps of yellow, fronded feathergrass are littered. Drearily colourless, faded with the sun and weather, they stretch their hempen stalks over the ancient, weather-beaten ground. Even in springtime, amid the exuberant flowering of the myriad grasses, the mound looks agedly despondent, out-lived. Only towards autumn does it gleam, flooded with a proud, frosty white. And only in the autumn does it seem as though, clothed in a scaly silver chain-mail, the grandly dignified mound is on guard over the steppe.

In the sunset glow of summer evenings a steppe eagle flies from beneath the clouds of the summit. Its wings whistling, it drops to the mound, clumsily hops a couple of steps, and stops, using its hooked beak to clean the brown fan of its outstretched wing, its crop covered with rusty-hued feathers. Then it is drowsily still, its head hanging, its amber, black-encircled eye fixed on the everlastingly azure heaven. Looking like a native stone, the immobile, yellow-brown eagle rests before its evening hunt. Then it lightly breaks from the earth and flies away. Before sunset the grey shadow of its regal wings will be flung again and again over the steppe.

Whither is it borne by the freezing autumnal winds? To the azure foothills of the Caucasus? To the steppe of Mugansk? To Persia or Afghanistan?

But in the winter, when the burial mound is clad in an ermine mantle of snow, through the pearly-grey shadows of the early morning an old, crafty fox makes his way to the summit. Looking as though carved from flaming yellow Carrara marble, he stands long at gaze, his ruddy, teasled brush lying on the lilac snow, his sharp nose, a smoky black around the jaws, pointed into the wind. At that moment only his moist, agate nose is alive in the mighty world of mingled scents, avidly inhaling into his dilated, quivering nostrils the damp, all-enveloping odour of the snow, the undying bitterness of the frost-nipped wormwood, the cheerful, hay-impregnated scent of horse-dung from the nearby track, and the inexpressibly moving, hardly perceptible smell of a brood of partridges at rest in the distant shrubs.

There are so many closely blended qualities in the smell of the partridges that, in order to satiate his scent, the old fox must needs leave the mound and glide some hundred yards, not lifting his paws from the starrily sparkling snow, dragging his icicle-covered, almost weightless body over the tops of the low shrubs. And only then are his black, dilated nostrils lashed by the pungent aroma, the stream of smells: the bitter acid of fresh bird droppings and the intensified scent of a feather. Damp with the snow, and in contact with the grass, the feather links together the bitterness of the wormwood and the acridity of the mugwort at its tip with the smell of warm and salty blood on the blue quill still half-covered with flesh.

The arid eastern winds corrode the dry, crumbling soil of the mound, the midday sun bakes it, the heavy rains wash it, the Epiphany frosts rend it. But the mound still reigns inviolably over the steppe as it did half a thousand years ago, when it arose over the remains of the slain Polovtsian prince who was buried here with martial honours, and over whom it was heaped up by the swarthy, braceleted hands of his wives and the hands of his warriors, kinsmen and slaves.

The mound stands on the range of hills some five miles from Gremyachy Log, and from time immemorial the cossacks have called it the 'Mound of Death', for tradition relates that one day of old a wounded cossack died at its foot.

For some fifteen miles after leaving the District town Nagulnov rode at a gallop, and only halted his dun pony close to the 'Mound of Death'. There he dismounted, and scraped the foam from his horse's neck with his palm.

The warmth was unusually gracious for the beginning of spring. The sun was scorching the earth as in Maytime. A mirage quivered smokily above the rolling horizon. From the distant steppe pond the wind brought the excited calling of geese, the varied quacking of ducks, and the plaintive call of water-hens.

Makar released the bit from the horse's mouth, tied the bridle-rein to one foreleg, and loosened the saddle-girths. The horse greedily stretched down to the young grass, tearing up the burnt brushes of the old couch-grass as it went.

With a dull, fine whistle a flock of wild duck flew across the mound. They dropped down over the pond. Makar aimlessly watched their flight, saw them fall like stones on to the pond, and saw the disturbed water seething around a little reedy island. A flock of startled, timorous barnacle geese at once flew up from the dam.

The steppe was mournfully deserted. Makar lay a long time at the foot of the mound. At first he could hear his horse snorting and moving about, its bit jingling. But then it passed into a valley where the grass was richer, and the steppe was wrapped in a silence such as comes only in the late, stilly autumn, when human beings have finished their work in the fields.

'When I get home I'll say good-bye to Andrei and Davidov, put on the tunic which I wore when I came back from the Polish front, and shoot myself. I've got no other ties in life. And the revolution won't suffer by it. There are plenty of people to work for it. One more or less makes no difference.' So Makar thought as he lay on his stomach and stared fixedly at the tangled stalks of wormwood. 'I suppose Davidov will say over my grave: "Although Nagulnov was expelled from the Party, he was a good Communist. We don't approve of his suicide, that's a fact; but we shall carry on to the end the cause for which he struggled against the world counter-revolution."' And with unusual vividness Makar imagined how the satisfied, smiling Bannik would be in the crowd, stroking his flaxen whiskers and saying: 'That's one stretched himself out, and glory be! A dog's death for a dog!'

'No, you won't, you bloody reptile! I'm not going to shoot myself! I'll settle you and your like first!' Makar said aloud, grinding his teeth. He jumped to his feet as though stung. Thinking of Bannik had completely altered his decision, and, as he looked around for the horse, he was thinking: 'Not a bit of it! I'll bury all of you first, and then I'll be ready to be paid off myself! You're not going to have the chance of glorying over my death. As for the Party secretary, his word isn't final, is it? I'll see the sowing finished, and then I'll go to the Regional Committee. They'll reinstate me. I'll go to the Provincial headquarters, I'll go to Moscow! And if they don't reinstate me, then I'll fight the counter-revolutionary reptiles as a non-Party worker!'

With shining eyes he stared over the world extended around him. Already he was thinking that his situation was by no means so irreparable and hopeless as it had seemed an hour or two before.

He hurried to the valley into which the horse had wandered.

Alarmed by his steps, a wolf bitch rose from the scrub in a hollow. She stood a moment with her long head stretched out, gazing at the man. Then she set back her ears, tucked her tail between her legs and slunk off into the valley. Her black, hanging teats shook flabbily beneath her sunken belly.

As soon as Makar approached the horse she restively threw up her head, and snapped the rein tied to her leg.

'Whoa! Vassia! Whoa!' Makar quietly called, trying to approach the playful mare from behind, and to seize her mane or the stirrup. Shaking her head, the dun hurried her steps and looked askance at her rider. Makar broke into a run, but she would not let him come near, kicked up her heels, and dashed at a furious, thundering gallop across the track and in the direction of the village.

Makar cursed and followed her. For a couple of miles he strode across the fields, making for the ploughed lands lying immediately outside the village. From the long grass rose bustards and mated partridges; farther off, on a slope a great bustard was pacing, guarding the peace of his brooding mate. Possessed by an invincible desire for copulation, he spread fanwise his short, ruddy tail with its rust and flaxen lining, opened his wings, scraping the dry earth with them, and scattered feathers adorned with rosy down at the roots.

A great, fructifying work was being accomplished in the steppe. The grasses were growing exuberantly, the birds and animals were rising. Only the abandoned fallow lands mutely stretched their unsown, steaming fields to the heavens.

In an angry fury Makar strode across the dry, cloddy fallow. He swiftly bent, picked up some earth and crumbled it in his hand. The black earth dust, with its brittle stalks of dead grasses, was dry and hot. The soil had stood idle too long! It called for three or four harrows to be drawn along its friable, turfy surface at once, to tear up the long-lying ground with their teeth, and then for the sowers to be driven along the crumbling furrows, so that the golden grains of wheat might fall the deeper into the earth.

'We're too late! We're ruining the earth!' Makar thought, gazing with griping regret across the black unworked fallows, terrible in their nakedness. 'A day or two more and the fallow will be good for nothing. The earth's like a mare; when she's in heat you must hurry to put the stallion to her, for she won't look at him when her time is past. And so the earth is with a man. Everything except us human beings is clean in this matter. The animals, the trees, and the earth all know the time when they must fructify. But we men are worse and filthier than the foulest beast! They won't come out and sow because their desire for property has made them rear on to their hind legs. Curse them! I'll go and drive them all out into the fields at once! All of them to the last man!' He walked faster and faster, and at times broke into a run. The sweat rolled down from under his cap, the shirt on his back turned darker, his lips dried, and the unhealthy, patchy flush in his cheeks grew brighter and brighter.

Chapter 35

To the Rescue

WHEN Nagulnov entered the village the distribution of the seed grain was already in full swing. Liubishkin and his brigade were still out in the fields. A crowd pressed around the granaries. Sacks of grain were hurriedly being thrown on to the scales, carts drove up incessantly, the cossacks and women were carrying off the grain in sacks, in bags, in their aprons, and scattered grain thickly covered the earth and the granary steps.

Nagulnov at once realized what was happening. Pushing the villagers aside, he made his way to the scales.

The former collective farmer Ivan Batalshchikov was weighing and giving out the grain, and the brown-faced Appollon Pieskovatskov was assisting him. Neither Davidov nor Razmiotnov, nor any of the brigade members was to be seen anywhere near the granaries. Only for a second did he see Yakov Lukich's anxious face in the crowd, and he was at once hidden behind the dense mass of carts.

'Who gave you permission to distribute the grain?' Makar shouted, thrusting Batalshchikov aside.

The crowd was silent.

'Who gave you authority to weigh out the grain?' Makar asked Batalshchikov, not lowering his voice.

'The community . . .'

'Where's Davidov?'

'I'm not his nurse, to run after him!'

'Where's the management? Did they give permission?'

Diemid the Silent, who was standing by the scales, smiled and wiped the sweat away with his sleeve. His thunderous bass voice sounded confidently and artlessly:

'We gave ourselves permission without the management. We're taking it ourselves!'

'Yourselves? So that's the game!' In two bounds Nagulnov was on the steps of the granary. With a blow of his fist he sent flying the lad on the threshold, sharply slammed the door and leaned heavily against it. 'Clear off! I won't let you have the grain! Anyone who tries to come near the granary I proclaim an enemy of the Soviet government!'

'Oho!' 'Smoky' said jestingly, as he helped one of his neighbours to load grain on to a cart.

Nagulnov's arrival was unexpected by the majority of the cossacks. Before he rode off to the District the rumours were assiduously spread through the village that Nagulnov was to be tried for beating up Bannik, that he would be removed from his position, and probably would be put in prison. Bannik, who in the morning had learned of Nagulnov's departure, had declared:

'Nagulnov won't be coming back any more. The Prosecutor told me himself that they would punish him with the utmost severity. Let Makar go and scratch himself! They'll throw him out of the Party, and then he'll know how to beat up a peasant. The old laws don't hold these days.'

For this reason Makar's appearance at the scales was received with a bewildered, uncomprehending silence. But when he threw himself from the scales to the granary and stood shielding the door, the attitude of the majority was at once clarified. 'Smoky's' exclamation was followed by a hail of shouts:

'We've got our own government now!'

'A people's government!'

'Boo him, boys!'

The first to approach the granary was 'Smoky', who swung his shoulders with the jauntiness of youth, and looked back at the crowd with a smile. Several other cossacks irresolutely stepped after him. One of them picked up a stone as he went.

Nagulnov unhurriedly drew his pistol out of his trouser pocket, and cocked the hammer. 'Smoky' halted, uncertainly hesitating. The others also stopped. They all knew that once Nagulnov cocked a pistol he would not think twice about pulling the trigger if necessary. And Makar confirmed their opinion without delay:

'I'll kill seven reptiles, and then you can get to the granary. Well, who's the first? Come on?'

But there were no volunteers. For a minute there was a general confusion. 'Smoky' stood thinking, not daring to approach any nearer. Lowering his pistol, Nagulnov again shouted:

'Clear away! Clear away at once, or I'll start firing!'

He had hardly finished the sentence when an iron bolt crashed against the door above his head. 'Smoky's' friend Yefim Trubachov had flung it, aiming at Makar's head. But, seeing he had missed, he promptly sat down behind a cart. Nagulnov took as quick a decision as in war-time: dodging a stone flung from out of the crowd, he fired into the air and at once ran down from the steps. The crowd broke away. Sending one another flying, the foremost turned to flee, the shafts of britzkas and carts began to crack, and a woman knocked down by the cossacks howled with fright.

'Don't run! He's only got six bullets left,' Bannik, who had turned up from somewhere, encouraged and halted the crowd.

Makar went back to the granary. He did not return to the steps, but stood by the wall in order to keep all the granaries within range of his vision.

'Don't come any closer!' he shouted to 'Smoky', Trubachov and others who were again approaching the scales. 'No nearer, I tell you! Or I'll shoot!'

The crowd had drawn up about a hundred paces from the granaries. Deciding to resort to cunning, Ivan Batalshchikov,

Atamanchukov, and three others who had resigned from the collective farm stepped forward. They drew nearer by some thirty paces. Batalshchikov anticipatorily raised his hand.

'Comrade Nagulnov!' he called. 'Wait a moment, don't raise your pistol.'

'What do you want? Clear off, I say!'

'We'll be going in a minute, but there's no point in your raging like that. We're taking the grain by permission...'

'Whose permission?'

'Someone arrived from the Region ... from the Regional Executive Committee, and he allowed us to take it.'

'But where is this man? And where's Davidov? And Razmiotnov?'

'They're at the office.'

'You're lying, you carrion! Get back from the scales, I tell you! Well?' Nagulnov bent his left arm at the elbow, and laid the pistol, greying with age, in the crook.

Batalshchikov fearlessly continued:

'If you don't believe us, go and see for yourself; and if you won't, we'll bring them here ourselves at once. Stop threatening us with your weapon, comrade Nagulnov, or it'll be the worse for you! Who are you going against? Against the people! Against the whole village!'

'Don't come any closer! Not a step farther! Don't call me comrade! Once you've started stealing the State grain you're a counter-revolutionary. I won't let you tread the Soviet government underfoot!'

Batalshchikov was about to say something more. But at that moment Davidov came round the corner of the granary. Terribly beaten, covered with bruises, scratches, and congealed blood, he walked with an uncertain, stumbling gait. Nagulnov took one glance at him, then threw himself towards Batalshchikov with a hoarse shout: 'Ah! You reptile! Trying to trick me? You'll beat us up, will you?'

Batalshchikov and Atamanchukov fled. Twice Nagulnov fired after them, but missed. On one side 'Smoky' broke a stake out of a fence, the others grumbled sullenly, but did not retreat.

'I won't let you ... trample your feet ... on the Soviet government !' Makar roared through his clenched teeth, making for the crowd at a run.

'Smash him !'

'If only we had just one weapon !' Yakov Lukich wrung his hands and groaned in the back rows, cursing Polovtsiev's untimely departure.

'Cossacks ! Seize the brave man in your hands !' Marina Poyarkova's indignant, passionate voice rang out. She pushed the cossacks forward to meet the running Makar, and, seizing Diemid the Silent by the arm, hatefully demanded :

'Call yourself a cossack? Afraid, are you?'

Suddenly the crowd scattered in confusion, then started to run towards Makar. 'The militia !' Nastia Donietskova shrieked in a wild terror. Some thirty horsemen were streaming down from the hill slopes into the village. Clumps of spring dust spurted in light, translucent clouds from under their horses.

Within five minutes only Davidov and Makar were left on the open space before the granaries. The thunder of horse-hoofs came nearer and nearer. The riders were now to be seen on the pasturage. In front rode Pavel Liubishkin on Lapshinov's trotting-horse, at his right hand, armed with an oak cudgel, terrible in his resolution, was pockmarked Agafon Dubtsiev, while behind them in irregular order, on vari-coloured horses, were the collective farm workers of the second and third brigades.

In the evening a militia-man summoned by Davidov arrived from the district town. Out in the steppe he arrested Ivan Batalshchikov, Appollon Pieskovatskov, Yefim Trubachov and several other 'active' instigators of the trouble. Old Ignationok he arrested in her home. They were all sent, together with witnesses, to the District. 'Smoky' went voluntarily to give himself up at the village Soviet.

'So you've flown home, little pigeon?' Razmiotnov asked exultantly.

Staring at him, and sarcastically smiling, 'Smoky' replied :

'Yes, I have. There's no point in playing hide-and-seek, once I've lost the throw.'

'What throw?' Razmiotnov frowned.

'The throw when you play for points. Where am I going to now?'

'You'll be going to the District town.'

'But where is the militia?'

'He'll be coming in a minute, you needn't worry! The people's court will teach you how to beat up a Soviet chairman. The people's court will settle your arrears...'

'Yes, of course,' 'Smoky' reluctantly agreed, and asked with a yawn:

'I'd like to get some sleep, Razmiotnov. Take me to the shed and lock me up until the militia arrives, or I'll fall asleep. Lock me up, or I'll be running off in my sleep.'

The next day steps were taken to recover the stolen grain. Makar Nagulnov went from yard to yard visiting those who had taken grain, and without any preliminary greeting, averting his eyes, he asked in a restrained tone:

'Did you take any grain?'

'I did.'

'Will you bring it back?'

'I suppose I must.'

'Bring it back then.' And he left the hut without a word of farewell.

Many of those who had resigned from the collective farm had taken more grain than they had previously contributed. The distribution had been made on the basis of questions. 'How much wheat did you give up?' Batalshchikov had impatiently asked. 'Twenty-one' or 'Twenty-eight poods' might be the answer. 'Bring your sacks to the scales,' he would order. But in reality, when the seed grain fund was being collected the man had given up seven to fourteen poods less. Besides this, about a hundred poods had been carried off by the women in their aprons and sacks, without its being weighed.

By the evening the wheat was entirely recovered, except for a few poods. Some twenty poods of barley and several sacks of maize were still missing. The same evening the seed grain belonging to the individual peasants was distributed to them in full.

After nightfall a village meeting was held. Davidov spoke to an unprecedented gathering of people in the school:

'Citizens, what does yesterday's conduct on the part of recent collective farmers and some of the individual peasants mean?' he asked. 'It means that they have wavered in the direction of the kulak element! That is a fact, a shameful fact for you, citizens, who yesterday stole grain from the granaries, trod precious seed into the ground, and carried it off in aprons. You, citizens, shouted to the women to beat me up, and they did beat me up with anything that came to their hands. One citizeness even wept because I would not show any sign of weakness. I'm speaking of you, citizeness!' Davidov pointed to Nastia Donietskova, who was standing by the wall. As soon as Davidov began to speak of her she hurriedly wrapped her face in her kerchief. 'It was you who drummed on my back with your fists, and wept with annoyance because, as you said: "I beat and beat him, but the idol's like stone!"'

Nastia's hidden face burned with the fire of a great shame. All the meeting turned to stare at her, as, her eyes cast down with embarrassment and awkwardness, she only wriggled her shoulders, rubbing the whitewash from the wall with her back.

'You're squirming like an adder on a pitchfork, you reptile!' Diemka Ushakov could not control himself.

'She's wiped all the whitewash off the wall!' Agafon Dubtsiev supported him.

'Don't turn away, goggle-eyes! You knew how to use your fists, now know how to look the meeting in the face!' roared Liubishkin.

Davidov went on relentlessly, but a smile slipped across his broken lips as he said:

'She wanted me to go down on my knees, to ask for mercy, to give her the keys of the granaries. But, citizens, we Bolsheviks aren't made of dough, for anybody to knead into what shape they like. The Junkers beat me up during the civil war, but they couldn't beat anything out of me! The Bolsheviks never went down on their knees to anybody, and never will! Fact!'

'That's true!' Makar Nagulnov's quivering, agitated voice sounded stifled and hoarse.

'We, citizens, are ourselves used to making the enemies of the proletariat go down on their knees. And we shall make them!'

'And we shall make them on a world scale!' Nagulnov again intervened.

'And we'll do it on a world scale. But yesterday you wavered to the side of those enemies and gave them your support. How are we to regard conduct which broke the padlocks off the granary doors, beat me up, first tied up Razmiotnov, then shut him in a cellar, then dragged him into the village Soviet and tried to make him put on a cross as he went? That's out and out counter-revolutionary conduct! As they were dragging Razmiotnov the arrested mother of our collective farmer Mikhail Ignationok shouted: "They're dragging anti-Christ, a hellish Satan!" And with the help of other women she wanted to put a cross on a string around his neck, but, as a communist should, our comrade Razmiotnov could not allow himself to be made ridiculous. He told the dangerous old women who have been drugged by the priests: "Citizenesses! I'm not a believer, I'm a communist! Take your cross away!" But they went on insisting, and only left him in peace when he bit through the string with his teeth and began to resist actively with his feet and head. But what sort of conduct d'you call that, citizens? It's out and out counter-revolution! And the people's court will ruthlessly punish such scoffers as the mother of Mikhail Ignationok.'

'I'm not answerable for my mother! Let such a mother go to the devil! She has her own right to speak as a citizen, let her answer for it!' Mikhail Ignationok shouted from the front rows.

'And I'm not speaking about you, I'm speaking of the types who raised a howl about the closing of the churches. They didn't like it when the churches were closed, but when they try to force a cross on to a communist's neck, that's nothing! Well, they've shown up their own hypocrisy splendidly! Those who were the insti-gators of these disorders and took active part in them have been arrested. But the others, who have been caught on the kulaks' hook, must come to their senses and realize that they've gone wrong. That I tell you as a fact. An unsigned note has been handed up to the table, and it asks: "Is it true that all who have taken grain will be arrested and exiled, and their property taken away from them?" No, that is not true, citizens! The Bolsheviks are not vengeful, they mercilessly punish only their enemies. But we do not regard you as enemies, although you have left the collective farm, yielding to the kulaks' arguments, and although you have stolen grain and beaten us up. You are wavering middling peasants who've temporarily gone wrong. And we shall not apply any administrative measures to you, but shall open your eyes.'

A subdued hum of voices passed through the schoolroom. Davidov continued:

'And you, citizeness, don't be afraid! Uncover your face, nobody will touch you, although you did give me a healthy whacking yesterday. But if we go out tomorrow to sow and you work badly, then I'll give you a few whacks to go on with, remember that! Only I shan't hit you on your head, but lower down, so that you won't be able either to sit or lie down, damn you!'

The diffident laughter increased, and by the time it reached the back rows it had become a relieved, thunderous roar.

'You've had your little game, citizens, and enough of that! The fallow land is lying, time's passing, we must get down to work, and not play the fool. Fact! When we've finished sowing, then we shall have time to fight and struggle! I raise the question sharply: those who are for the Soviet government will go out to the fields tomorrow; those who're against, they can chew sunflower seeds! But those who don't go out to the fields tomorrow – we, the collective farm, will take their land from them and sow it ourselves.'

Davidov stepped back from the edge of the platform and sat down at the table. As he reached for the carafe, from the back rows, from the twilight dimly lit by the orange flame of the lamp, someone's warm, cheery bass voice movingly said:

'Davidov, you're a great lad! Dear old Davidov! Because you don't bear malice in your heart, and don't remember the evil ... The people here are touched ... we don't know where to look, we feel so ashamed. And the women are all upset. But we've got to live together ... Let it be like this, Davidov: those who recall the past can clear out! Ah?'

Next morning, fifty-seven of the former collective farmers

handed in requests to be taken back again. The individual peasants and all three collective farm brigades went out to the steppe at dawn.

Liubishkin proposed that a guard should be placed over the granaries, but Davidov laughed and said:

'I don't think it is necessary now.'

Within four days the collective farm sowed almost half its fallow land. On 2 April the third brigade transferred its activities to spring ploughing. During all this period Davidov was only once in the office. He sent out to the fields all who were capable of work, and temporarily released old Shchukar from his duties as coachman, assigning him to the second brigade. He himself spent all day from early dawn riding out to the various brigades, returning to the village after midnight, when the rousing crows of the cocks were already sounding in the yards.

Chapter 36

Giving a Lead

In the grass-grown yard of the collective farm office it was as quiet as on the pasturage outside the village. The rusty tiles of the granary roof gleamed warmly and dully under the noonday sun, but in the shade of the sheds, heavy molten grains of smokily lilac dew still hung on the trampled grass.

Hideous in its scragginess, a mangy sheep stood in the middle of the yard, its soiled legs straddled wide, while on its knees at her side, a lamb, white-woolled like its mother, eagerly struggled for her teats.

Liubishkin rode into the yard on a little mare. As he passed the shed, he angrily lashed at a kid which was staring at him from the roof with green, devilish eyes, and barked: 'You're always wanting to climb up on top, you unclean spirit! Get down from there!' After his bay mare ran a thin-legged foal with swollen pasterns, its fluffy tail flying out behind it. The bell tied to its neck tinkled

326

hollowly. The mare was so small for Liubishkin that the dangling stirrups swung about almost below her knees. It looked as though the bowed horseman were carrying his feeble little mare between his heroic legs, as happened in the fairy-tale. As he stood on the porch watching Liubishkin, Diemka Ushakov waxed merry.

'You look like Jesus Christ riding into Jerusalem on an ass!' he remarked. 'Terribly like!'

'You're an ass yourself!' Liubishkin snarled, riding up to the porch.

'Lift your feet up or you'll plough the earth with them!'

Not deigning to answer, Liubishkin dismounted, tied the rein around the balustrade, and harshly asked:

'Is Davidov here?'

'Yes. He's sitting and longing, but not daring to hope to see you. He hasn't eaten or drunk for three days, and all he says is: "Where's my unforgettable Pavel Liubishkin! My life is empty without him, and I find no joy in living."'

'Say another word about me! Go on! I'll tread on your tongue!'

Diemka took a sidelong glance at Liubishkin's whip and said no more, while Liubishkin strode into the hut.

Davidov, Razmiotnov and representatives of a women's meeting had just finished discussing the question of organizing a crèche. Liubishkin waited until the women had gone, then stepped up to the table. His calico shirt, unbelted, and dusty across the shoulders, smelt of sweat, sun and dust.

'I've come from the brigade . . .' he began.

'What for?' Davidov raised his brows.

'There's nothing coming of it! I've got twenty-eight men capable of work, but they don't want to, they're loafing about . . . I can't find any way of handling them. Only twelve ploughs are at work at the moment. I've had to force the ploughmen to work. Kondrat Maidannikov is sweating like an ox, but Akim Beskhlebnov, Samkha Kuzhenkov, that throaty splinter Atamanchukov and the others are only bitter tears, and not ploughmen! You'd think they'd never held the plough handles before in all their lives. They plough like the devil knows what. They do one furrow, and then they sit down to smoke and there's no moving them.'

'How much are you ploughing up in one day?'

'Maidannikov and I are turning over three-quarters of a hectare, but the others average half a hectare. If we go on like that we won't be able to sow the maize until the Feast of the Intercession.'

Without saying a word Davidov knocked the end of his pencil on the table. Then he asked in a wheedling tone:

'But what have you come in for? For us to wipe away your tears?' His eyes gleamed angrily.

Liubishkin bridled up.

'I haven't come with tears,' he replied. 'Give me more men and ploughs. I know how to joke without your showing me!'

'You know how to joke, that's a fact; but how to get work going, that you're weak at! And you're a brigade leader, too! You can't manage loafers! It's a fact you won't, when you've let discipline slide and you allow them to do what they like!'

'You find the right discipline then!' Sweating with his agitation, Liubishkin raised his voice. 'Atamanchukov's the man at the bottom of it all. He's setting the others against me, inciting them to leave the collective farm. But if you kick him out he'll take others out with him. And what are you laughing at me for, Siemion Davidov? You've given me a lot of cripples and weaklings, and then you dare to ask about work? What am I to do with old Shchukar? The talkative old devil ought to be stood up in the melon plot to frighten the birds instead of a scarecrow. But you've shoved him into my brigade, fastened him on to me like a gipsy mother to her son. What's he good for? He can't manage a plough, and he's no good as a driver. His voice is like a sparrow's. The bullocks don't regard him as a man, they've got no fear of him at all. He hangs on to the rein, the devil, and falls down a dozen times while he's doing one furrow. First he stops to tie up his boots, then he lies down and sticks his legs above his head and sees to his rupture. The women all leave their bullocks, braying and bawling: "Shchukar's rupture's dropped!" And they run headlong out of curiosity to see how he shoves it back in its place. It's a show, and not work! Yesterday we made him cook because of his rupture, but he's no good at that either, and he's even dangerous. We gave him some fat to put into the meal, but he gobbled it all up himself, then he oversalted the meal and cooked

it with some kind of scum on top of it. What am I to do with him?'
Liubishkin's lips quivered furiously beneath his black whiskers.
He raised his whip, revealing a circle of dirty shirt, faded and
rotting with sweat, under his armpit. 'Take the brigade leadership
away from me! I haven't got the patience to hang around with
such a lot as they are; they've hobbled me in my own work.'

'Don't come here playing the armyless leader! Fact! We know
when to take you off your job! But now get out into the fields,
and see that twelve hectares are ploughed by this evening. But
if you don't get it done, don't get upset! I'll be along in a couple
of hours to see how you're getting on. Off with you!'

Liubishkin slammed the door behind him and ran off the porch.
The mare tied to the balustrade stood gloomily. In her eyes, violet
with golden speckles, the sun was reflected. Adjusting the saddle-
cloth stretched from the bare, hot saddle-bow, Liubishkin slowly
mounted the horse. Screwing up his eyes, Diemka Ushakov venomously asked:

'Has your brigade got much ploughing done, comrade Liubishkin?'

'That's nothing to do with you.'

'Perhaps it isn't ... Look here, I'll take you in tow, and then it
will be!'

Turning round in the saddle, Liubishkin clenched his sinewy
brown fist until the fingers swelled, and promised:

'You only turn up! I'll put your eyes straight for you, you
squinting devil! I'll send them to the back of your head and teach
you to walk arse forward!'

Diemka spat contemptuously.

'I've found a doctor!' he said. 'You cure your own ploughmen
first, so that they plough more quickly.'

Liubishkin galloped out of the gate and dashed off into the
steppe as though riding into an attack. The sobbing tinkle of the
bell tossing on the foal's neck had hardly died away when Davidov
came on to the porch and hurriedly told Diemka:

'I'm going out to the second brigade for a few days. I leave
you in charge. Watch over the construction of the crèche, and
give them a hand. Don't give out any oats to the third brigade,
d'you hear? If there's any trouble come out to me. Understand?

Harness a horse, and tell Razmiotnov to drive round for me. I shall be in my quarters.'

'Perhaps it would be best for me and my group to transfer to the virgin soil to help Liubishkin,' Diemka suggested. But Davidov furiously cursed, and shouted :

'A fine idea ! They ought to be able to manage by themselves ! I'll go and twist their tails for them, if any of them only plough half a hectare when I'm around. Fact ! Harness up !'

Driving one of the management stallions harnessed into a drozhki, Razmiotnov went to pick up Davidov. He found him already waiting, standing by the gate with a small bundle under his arm.

'In you get. What are you taking with you, food?' Razmiotnov smiled.

'It's underclothes.'

'What underclothes? What for?'

'Why, a change of underclothes.'

'What are they for?'

'Come on, whip them up ! What are you standing for? I'm taking underclothes in order not to breed lice, understand? I'm going out to the brigade, and I've decided to stay there until the ploughing's finished. Close your mouth and get a move on.'

'You haven't gone out of your mind, have you? What will you do there till the end of the ploughing?'

'Plough !'

'You're leaving the office and going out to plough? That's a fine idea !'

'Drive on, drive on !' Davidov frowned.

'Don't be in such a hurry !' Evidently Razmiotnov was beginning to get annoyed. 'Explain what you're up to ! Can't they get on out there without you, or what? Your job is to direct, and not walk behind a plough ! You're the chairman of the collective farm ...'

Davidov's eyes glittered with fury.

'Well, go on !' he said sarcastically. 'You're teaching me ! First and foremost I'm a communist, and only afterwards chairman of the collective farm ! Fact ! Here's the ploughing going all wrong, and have I got to stay here ...? Get on, get on I tell you !'

'Well it's nothing to do with me! Here, are you asleep, you devil?' Razmiotnov galvanized the stallion with the knout. The unexpected jolt as the animal started threw Davidov backward, and he struck his elbow painfully against the drozhki as the wheels gently began to rattle over the summer track into the steppe.

When they had left the village Razmiotnov slowed the stallion down to a walking pace, and wiped his scarred forehead with his sleeve.

'You're being stupid, Davidov!' he began again. 'See them get the work on to its feet, and then come back. It's no miracle to be able to plough, brother! A good commander oughtn't to be in the line, but ought to command intelligently; that's what I tell you!'

'Drop your examples, please! I've got to teach them how to work, and I will teach them! Fact! That's directing properly! The first and third brigades have finished their corn land, and here we've got this breakdown. It's clear Liubishkin won't manage it. And you prate about "a good commander" and all that sort of thing. What are you throwing dust in my eyes for? Do you think I've never seen any good commanders? The good commander is the one who leads by his example when there's a failure anywhere. And that's the way I've got to lead.'

'You'd do better to send them two ploughs from the first brigade.'

'And men? Where are the men coming from? Get a move on, do!'

As far as the range of hills they drove in silence. Piled by the wind, a dense mass of cloud stood in the zenith over the steppe, obscuring the sun. Its white curling edges glistened snowily, but its sombre depths were menacing in their heavy immobility. From a rift in the cloud, and from the orange, sun-lined fringe the sunlight fell obliquely in a broad fan of rays. Slender and lanceolate in the expanse of heaven, they spread in streams as they approached the earth, and, lying on the distant barrier of brown steppe extended along the horizon, they decked it in beauty, wildly and joyously rejuvenated it.

Smokily darkened by the shadow of the cloud, the steppe silently and humbly awaited the rain. Already breathing out a scented, rainy humidity, the wind sent a grey column of dust whirling on the road. And a minute or so later a rare, fine rain began to fall. The hard, cold drops pierced into the road dust and were transformed into tiny crumbs of mud. The marmots whistled warningly, the drumming of the quails sounded more distinctly, the tensely passionate, challenging cry of the bustard died away. A low wind whipped across the millet stubble, and it bristled and rustled. The steppe was filled with the dry murmuring of last year's undergrowth. A raven floated eastward under the very foot of the cloud, heeling and catching an aerial current with its outspread wings. There was a white flash of lightning, and, uttering a throaty, baritone cry, the raven suddenly dropped precipitously downward. Caught by the sunlight, for a second it flashed like a tarry torch set aflame; the air could be heard rushing with a whistle and a stormy roar through the feathering of its wings. But, some hundred yards before it reached the earth, the raven sharply righted itself and flapped its wings, while at the same moment the thunder broke with a dry, deafening crash.

The camp of the second brigade had come into sight on the ridge of the hills when Razmiotnov noticed a man hurrying towards them under the slope. He was walking along off the road, jumping the ditches, occasionally breaking into an aged, broken trot. Andrei turned the horse in his direction, and when still some distance away he recognized Shchukar. The old man came towards the drozhki. From all the signs it was obvious that something unpleasant had happened to him. The hair on his head was flattened down with the rain, and his eyebrows and little wet beard were thickly covered with boiled millet. He was almost blue with pallor, and looked terrified, so that Davidov was troubled by the surmise that something had gone wrong in the brigade.

'What's the matter?' he demanded.

'I've had to run for my life!' Shchukar panted. 'They wanted to kill me...'

'Who did?'

'Liubishkin and the others.'

'What for?'

'They just felt like it! There was a row about the porridge. I'm a rash man in my speech, and I couldn't stand it ... Liubishkin seized a knife and came after me ... If I hadn't been nimble I'd have been spitted on a knife and baking now.'

'Go on to the village. We'll get to the bottom of your story afterwards,' Davidov ordered, sighing with relief.

But what had really happened in the camp half an hour before was this. The previous evening old Shchukar had oversalted the porridge, and had resolved to get himself back into the brigade's good books. In the evening he had gone off to the village and had spent the night there. Next morning he had taken a sack from his home, and on his way to the brigade had slipped into Krasnokutov's threshing floor, stealthily hiding himself behind a heap of chaff. His plan had the simplicity of genius: he intended to lie in wait for a hen, cautiously catch it, and decapitate it in order to cook it with the porridge, so winning the brigade's honour and respect. He lay there, holding his breath, for a good half-hour; but, as though of set purpose, the chickens rummaged around by the fence, showing no intention of coming near the chaff heap. Then old Shchukar quietly began to call them. 'Tweet, tweet, tweet!' he whispered, as he hid like an animal behind the chaff. Old Krasnokutov happened to be in the neighbourhood of the threshing floor, and, hearing someone's wheedling voice calling the chickens, he slipped behind the fence. The hens trustfully approached the pile of chaff, and at that moment Krasnokutov saw a hand come round the chaff and seize a speckled hen by the leg. With the speed of a polecat Shchukar strangled the chicken, and was just thrusting it into his sack when he heard the quiet question: 'Feeling the chicken?' Then he saw Krasnokutov appear above the fence. Shchukar was so confused that he dropped the sack out of his hand, removed his cap, and very unseasonably greeted Krasnokutov with: 'Your good health, Afanasii Pietrovich!' 'Thanks be!' the other replied. 'Interested in the chickens?' 'That's just it!' Shchukar assured him. 'I happened to be passing and I noticed that speckled hen. And she's got such an unusual variety of feathering that I couldn't go by without looking at her closer. "I'll catch her," I thought, "and see what strange sort of bird she is." In all my years I've never seen such a curious bird.'

Shchukar's cleverness was completely lost on Krasnokutov, and he put an end to it with: 'Don't lie, you old gelding! You don't put chickens in sacks to look at them! Tell me what you were stealing it for!' So Shchukar confessed and explained that he wanted to treat the ploughmen of his brigade to porridge with chicken. To his astonishment Krasnokutov said not a word against his plan, but only remarked: 'The ploughmen can have it, there's no sin in that. Now you've done in that one put it in the sack, and knock another down with your stick and drop it in, too. But not this one; take that one with the comb, she isn't laying. You won't get enough for the brigade out of one chicken. Catch another quickly and clear off sharp, or – by God, if my old woman starts brawling at us she'll make us both feel sick!'

Satisfied beyond words with the turn events had taken, Shchukar caught another hen and made off across the fence. Within two hours he arrived at the camp, and by the time Liubishkin had returned from the village the water was already boiling in the great cauldron, the cooked millet was bubbling merrily, and the lumps of chicken were oozing fat. The porridge was a glorious success. All old Shchukar was afraid of was that it would smell of the stagnant water which he had taken from a nearby shallow pond, where the standing water was already covered with hardly perceptible green. But his fears were groundless. Everybody ate and praised the porridge fervently, and even brigade leader Liubishkin said: 'I've never eaten such tasty stuff in all my life. I thank you on behalf of the whole brigade.'

The cauldron was swiftly emptied. The most dexterous began to fish lumps of meat and the thicker soup from the bottom. Then something occurred which for ever ruined Shchukar's career as a cook. Liubishkin fished out a lump of meat, and was about to carry it to his mouth. But he suddenly stepped back and turned pale.

'Here! What's this?' he menacingly asked Shchukar, holding a piece of white, well-stewed meat by the tips of his fingers.

'It must be a wing,' Shchukar calmly answered.

Liubishkin's face slowly flooded with a purple flush of terrible anger.

'A wing!' he roared. 'Well, look here, you porridge boiler!'

'Oh, my dears!' groaned one of the women. 'It's got claws on it.'

'You're too fast with your tongue, curse you!' Shchukar turned on the woman. 'Where do you find claws on a wing? You look for them under your own skirt!' He threw his spoon down and stared: in Liubishkin's trembling hand was dangling a brittle little bone adorned at one end with membranes and tiny claws.

'Brothers!' exclaimed the startled Akim Beskhlebnov. 'It's frog we've been eating.'

Everyone reacted to the announcement in a different way. One of the squeamish women jumped up with a groan, and, pressing her palms against her mouth, disappeared behind the field hut. Kondrat Maidannikov glanced at Shchukar's eyes, which were almost falling out of his head with astonishment, and fell on his back. Rolling with laughter, at last he shouted: 'Oh, women! You've broken the Lenten fast!' The less fastidious of the cossacks took up his jest. 'You won't be able to take the sacrament now!' Kuzhenkov roared with simulated horror. But, annoyed by the laughter, Akim Beskhlebnov furiously began to bawl: 'What are you laughing at? Shchukar ought to have a good hiding!'

'How could a frog have got into the cauldron?' Liubishkin wondered.

'He got the water from the pond, and didn't look to see what he was doing.'

'You son of a bitch! You grey-headed eunuch! What have you given us to eat?' Aniska, daughter-in-law of the Donietskovs, squealed. Then she howled at the top of her voice: 'And I'm carrying! If I have a miscarriage through you, you scoundrel ...!' And at that she threw the remains of the porridge on her plate at Shchukar.

A tremendous hubbub arose. The women rushed to seize Shchukar's beard, although the bewildered and terrified old man stubbornly shouted:

'Cool down a little! It's not a frog! True Christ, it isn't a frog!'

'Then what is it?' Aniska demanded.

'You only think you see it! It's your imagination!' Shchukar tried to be clever. But he flatly refused to swallow the 'imaginary' bone which Liubishkin offered him. Perhaps the matter would have ended there, if, infuriated by the women, Shchukar had not shouted:

'You piddle-tails! Satans in petticoats! You're after my snout, but you don't realize that it isn't an ordinary frog, but an oyster.'

'A what?' the women asked in amazement.

'An oyster. I'm talking good Russian to you! A frog's unclean, but the oyster's got blue blood. A relation of mine, who was orderly to general Filimonov himself under the old regime, told me that the general used to swallow hundreds of them even on an empty stomach. And he ate them alive! The oyster would still be in its shell, and he would fetch it out with a fork. He'd jab the fork into it and it would be "good-bye" to that one. It would squeal miserably, but he would shove it down his throat. And how do you know that this isn't one of the oyster family, too? The generals liked them, and maybe I cooked it on purpose for you fools, put it in for flavouring...'

At that Liubishkin could stand no more. Grabbing the copper ladle, he rose to his feet and roared at the top of his voice:

'Generals? For flavouring? I'm a Red Partisan, and you feed me on frogs as though I was some bloody general!'

Shchukar thought Liubishkin had a knife in his hand, so he turned and fled as fast as his legs would carry him, without one look back.

Davidov heard all the story when he reached the camp, but meantime, dismissing Shchukar, he asked Razmiotnov to whip up the horses, and arrived at the camp soon afterward. The rain was still pattering down over the steppe. From Gremyachy Log to the distant pond a bowed, colourful rainbow stretched across the sky. There was not a soul in the camp. Davidov took leave of Razmiotnov, and walked to the nearest stretch of ploughed land. Unharnessed oxen were grazing close by it, and, too lazy to go back to the camp, the ploughman, Akim Beskhlebnov, was lying in a furrow, his head covered with his coat, dozing beneath the lisping patter of the rain. Davidov awoke him and asked:

'Why aren't you ploughing?'

Akim reluctantly rose, yawned and smiled:

'You can't plough when it's raining, comrade Davidov,' he explained. 'Don't you know that? A bullock's not a tractor, and

336

as soon as his hair gets a little wet the yoke rubs his neck until the blood comes. And then you're finished work with him! It's true, quite true!' he ended, as he noticed Davidov's distrustful look. Then he advised: 'You'd better go and separate the two warriors over there. Kondrat Maidannikov has been shouting at Atamanchukov ever since first thing this morning. And there they are fighting now on that section. Kondrat orders the bullocks to be unharnessed, and Atamanchukov answers: "Don't you touch my harness, or I'll break your head!" They're all but at each other's throats even now.'

Davidov looked across to the far end of the second strip of ploughed land, and saw that something very much like a fight was certainly going on. Maidannikov was handling an iron bar as though it were a sword, while the tall Atamanchukov was thrusting him away from the yoke with one hand, and holding his other fist clenched behind his back. Their voices could not be heard from where Davidov was standing. Hurriedly making towards them, he shouted long before he reached them:

'Hi, what's all this?'

'Why, this is what it is, Davidov!' Maidannikov shouted. 'It's raining, and he's ploughing. That way he'll rub the bullocks' necks into sores. I tell him to unharness them until the rain stops, and he curses at me and tells me it's nothing to do with me. Then who is it to do with, you son of a bitch? Whose business it is, you hoarse devil?' he turned to Atamanchukov and swung the bar at him.

Evidently they had already managed to come to blows, for Maidannikov had a bluish black bruise like a plum above one eye, while Atamanchukov's shirt collar had a slanting rent, and the blood was running down over his swollen, shaven lip.

'I won't let you do harm to the collective farm,' Maidannikov shouted, emboldened by Davidov's arrival. 'He says they're not his bullocks, but the collective farm's. But even if they are the farm's, does it mean you've got to flay them alive? Stand back from the bullocks, you enemy!'

'Don't you order me about! And you've got no right to fight. I'll pull out the scraper and I'll alter your mug for you! I've got to plough my allotted amount, and you're standing in my way!'

the pallid Atamanchukov hoarsely cried, fumbling with his left hand at his shirt collar in the attempt to fasten it.

'Can you plough when it's raining?' Davidov asked him, taking Kondrat's iron bar away and flinging it down.

Atamanchukov's eyes glittered. Twisting his thin neck, he angrily hissed:

'You can't plough when it's for yourself, but you've got to when it's for the collective farm!'

'Why have you got to?'

'In order to carry out the plan. Rain or no rain, plough! And if you don't plough Liubishkin will be biting at you all day like rust into iron!'

'You're full of talk! Did you plough your share yesterday, when it was fine?'

'I did as much as I could.'

'He turned over a quarter of a hectare,' Maidannikov snorted. 'Look at the bullocks he's got! You can't reach to their horns. But what sort of ploughing has he done? Come and look, comrade Davidov.' He seized Davidov by the wet sleeve of his coat, and led him along the furrow. Leaving his sentence unfinished in his excitement, he muttered:

'We decided to plough not less than seven inches deep, and how much is this? Measure it for yourself.'

Davidov bent down and thrust his fingers into the soft, sticky furrow. From its bottom to its soddy top it measured not more than three or four inches.

'Is that ploughing? That's scratching the earth, and not ploughing! I wanted to give him something this morning for such work. Go over all his furrows and you'll find they're the same depth all the way.'

'Hi, come over here! You, I mean! Fact!' Davidov shouted to Atamanchukov, who was reluctantly unharnessing the bullocks. He lazily, unhurriedly came across.

'What d'you call this, ploughing?' Davidov quietly asked, baring his teeth.

'Well, what more do you want? A furrow sixteen inches deep?' Atamanchukov angrily screwed up his eyes, and, removing his cap from his shaven head, he bowed. 'Thank you! You try ploughing deeper yourself! We can all talk big, but we're missing when the work's to be done!'

'I'd like to kick you out of the collective farm, you scoundrel!' Davidov cried, turning scarlet. 'And we shall turn you out!'

'By all means! And I'll leave of my own will! I'm not condemned to work myself to death here! Wearing myself out and for the Lord knows what!' Whistling, he walked off to the camp.

As soon as all the brigade was gathered in the camp that evening, Davidov said:

'I ask the brigade this question: what ought we to do with that false collective farm member who cheats the farm and the Soviet government, who, instead of ploughing seven inches deep, spoils the earth by ploughing only three inches? What shall we do to the man who deliberately wants to ruin the bullocks by working them when it's raining, but only does half his task when it's fine?'

'Kick him out!' said Liubishkin. His proposal found especially zealous support among the women.

'You've got such a collective farmer, such a wrecker among you here. There he is!' Davidov pointed to Atamanchukov, who had seated himself on a cart shaft. 'All the brigade is here. I put the question to the vote: Who is in favour of kicking out the wrecker and loafer Atamanchukov?'

Out of twenty-seven present, twenty-three voted in favour of the proposal. Davidov counted the votes twice, then drily told Atamanchukov:

'Get out! You're no longer a collective farmer. Fact! We'll consider the matter again after a year. If you've changed we'll take you back. And now, comrades, listen to the few but serious words I've got to say to you. Almost all of you are working badly. Very badly! With the exception of Maidannikov, nobody's doing his task. That's a shameful fact, comrades of the second brigade! At that rate we shall be dirty with smuts! With such work we may find ourselves on the black list, and there we shall stop. A collective farm named after Stalin, and we've got a monstrous state of affairs like that! We must radically alter the position!'

'The task is too big and beyond our strength. And the bullocks can't manage it,' Akim Beskhlebnov declared.

'Beyond your strength? Too much for the bullocks? Nonsense! Why isn't it too much for Maidannikov's bullocks? I shall remain in your brigade, take Atamanchukov's bullocks, and show you by a living example that in one day you can plough one and even one and a quarter hectares.'

'Ah, Davidov, you're smart! You know what you're talking about!' Kuzhenkov laughed and squeezed his short grey beard in his hand. 'With Atamanchukov's bullocks you could plough out the devil's horn! I could plough a hectare with them...'

'But you won't do it with your own?'

'Never in my life!'

'Well, let's change over. You take Atamanchukov's, and I'll have yours. Agreed?'

'We can try,' Kuzhenkov replied seriously and cautiously, after thinking it over.

Davidov spent a restless night. He slept in the field hut, and was awakened again and again by the thundering of the sheet iron roof under the wind, the midnight cold which crept in beneath his wet raincoat, and the fleas which densely populated the sheepskin spread under him.

Kondrat Maidannikov aroused him at dawn. He had already called up the rest of the brigade. Davidov sprang out of the shed. In the western sky the stars were dimly shining, the young moon, curved like a bow, adorned the steely grey mail of heaven with a golden score. Davidov washed in water from the pond, while Kondrat stood close by, and, biting the end of his whiskers, told him:

'To plough more than a hectare is a day's good going. You overdid it a bit yesterday, comrade Davidov. So long as you don't make a fool of yourself...'

'Everything's in our hands, everything's ours! What are you afraid of?' Davidov encouraged him. But he was thinking: 'I'll die at the plough, but I'll do it! I'll plough at night by the light of a lantern, but I'll plough a hectare and a quarter. I mustn't do less! It would be a disgrace to the whole working class.'

While Davidov was rubbing his face dry with the edge of his hempen blouse-shirt, Kondrat harnessed his own and Davidov's bullocks. To the squeak of the plough wheels he explained to

Davidov the simple principles of bullock ploughing as they had been worked out over generations. Then he added:

'We've decided to plough like this: we allotted each his section, and let him get on with it! At first Beskhlebnov, Atamanchukov, Kuzhenkov and Liubishkin began to plough one behind another. "Now we're in a collective farm," they said, "and that means we must plough one behind another." And they did. Only I saw that that wasn't the way to work. If the first plough stops they've all got to stop. If the first plough takes its time over it, the others have got to, willy nilly. And so I revolted. "Either let me go in front," I said, "or allot every ploughman his section." Then Liubishkin realized that the other way wouldn't work. You couldn't see how much each had done. So we split the land up into sections, but I left them behind, and I gave them a ten-point start, the devils! Every section is one hectare, 370 yards long and thirty-five across.'

'But why don't you plough cross-ways as well?' Davidov asked, glancing at a ploughed section.

'I'll tell you why. You finish the long-ways furrow and turn your bullocks on the headland, don't you? If you turn them sharply you rub their necks with the yoke, and then they'll soon be no use for ploughing! So you plough long-ways, then you raise the ploughshare and go thirty-five yards without ploughing. The tractor can turn sharply, with the front wheels at right angles under the engine, and then go back on its tracks. But you won't turn three or four yoke of oxen like that. You've got to handle them like soldiers in line turning on the left leg, so that they can plough back without fault. And that's why you can't plough big sections of land with bullocks. The longer the furrow the better with a tractor, but with bullocks I plough 370 yards long-ways, then the plough has to go unused across the section. Here, I'll draw it for you,' and, coming to a standstill, Kondrat drew a long section on the ground with the sharp end of the scraper.

'Say this is a piece of land four hectares – 370 yards long and 140 yards wide. I plough my first furrow long-ways, look! If I plough one hectare at a time, I've got to go thirty-five yards across on the headland without ploughing. But if I plough the four hectares at once I've got to go 140 yards across. And that isn't practical. D'you see? It's a waste of time ...'

'I see. You've shown me very practically.'

'Have you ever done any ploughing?'

'No brother, I've never had to. I know the plough more or less, but I don't know how to use it. You show me; I'm quick at picking things up.'

'I'll set your plough for you, do a couple of furrows with you, and then you can try your hand at it yourself.'

Kondrat adjusted Davidov's plough, reset the draught-chain on the hake, fixing the depth of the furrow at seven inches, and, imperceptibly adopting a more familiar tone, explained as he worked:

'We'll start ploughing, and then you'll see. If it's too heavy for the bullocks, you raise this a couple of notches. We call it a hake. You shift the hake like this and the share swings over a little, goes slantwise, and cuts a layer of earth not with all its width, but only with part, and that makes it easier for the bullocks. Well, we'll start. Gee up, baldhead! Don't spare your belly, comrade Davidov!'

Davidov's driver, a young lad, cracked his stockwhip, and the bullocks suddenly took the strain. With some trepidation Davidov set his hands on the plough handles and followed the plough, watching as, cut by the coulter, the rich black layer of earth slipped from under the share over the polished mouldboard, turning over on to its side like a sleepy fish.

At the end of the furrow, on the headland, Kondrat ran across to Davidov and told him:

'Lean the plough over to the left so that it slides along; and so as you don't have to stop to clean the mouldboard you do this. Watch!' Kondrat bore heavily on the right handle, swinging the plough, and a layer of earth rode heavily and obliquely over the mouldboard, wiping off the mud sticking to it. 'That's the way to do it!' Kondrat let go of the plough handles and smiled. 'There's a technique in this, too, you see. If you didn't do that you'd have to clean the mud off the mouldboard with the scraper while the bullocks were going along the headland. Now your plough's as clean as if it had been washed, and you can make yourself a cigarette for the satisfaction of your soul. Here you are !'

He stretched out his rolled pouch, then made a cigarette for himself, and nodded his head towards his own bullocks. 'Look how my wife's handling that plough ! The plough's set well, it only bumps up now and then, she could plough by herself.'

'So your wife's your driver?' Davidov asked.

'Yes. It's easier working with her. If I let fly a curse at her she doesn't get upset, or if she does, it's only till night comes on. Then we make it up; after all we are each other's.' Maidannikov smiled and went off with long, uneven strides across the furrows.

In the first shift before breakfast Davidov ploughed about a quarter of a hectare. He half-heartedly sipped at his porridge, waiting for the bullocks to finish feeding, and winked at Kondrat with :

'Shall we begin?'

'I'm ready. Aniutka, drive up the bullocks !'

And again, furrow after furrow, the crumbling soil, untouched for centuries, turned over, cut by coulter and share. The upturned, mortally twisted roots of the grass stretched skywards, the broken, turfy top was hidden in the black depths of the furrows. At the side of the mouldboard the earth rocked and heaved as though fluid. The mouldering smell of the black soil was invigorating and sweet. The sun was still low, but the fading hair of the side bullock was already darkening with sweat . . .

By the evening Davidov's feet, chafed in his boots, were smarting painfully, and his back ached at the belt. Stumbling, he measured out the section he had ploughed, and smiled with his baked, dust-blackened lips. In the one day he had ploughed a hectare.

'Well, how much have you turned over?' Kuzhenkov asked with a sneer and a hardly perceptible smile, when, dragging his feet, Davidov came into the camp.

'And how much do you think?'

'Did you manage half a hectare?'

'No, damn you; a hectare and a furrow.'

After rubbing marmot grease on his leg where the teeth of a harrow had torn the flesh, Kuzhenkov went off to Davidov's section to measure it. He returned half an hour later, when dusk had settled in heavy shadows, and seated himself some way off from the fire.

'What are you silent for, Kuzhenkov?' Davidov asked.

'My leg's hurting me ... And there's nothing to say. You've done the hectare ... well, then you've done it! Not bad!' he reluctantly replied, and lay down by the fire, drawing his coat over his head.

'That's shut your mouth up, hasn't it? You won't open it so much now, will you?' Kondrat laughed. But Kuzhenkov was silent, as though he had not heard.

Davidov lay down by the hut and closed his eyes. The smell of wood ash came from the camp fire. Worn out with walking, the soles of his feet burned fierily, there was a nagging weight at his knees, and, no matter how he arranged his legs, he was uncomfortable and continually wanting to change his position. He had hardly been lying a moment when the black soil was again disturbingly flowing before his eyes, the white blade of the share was noiselessly sliding along, and at its side, the earth, changing its configuration, was boiling and seething like tar. Feeling rather dizzy and sick, he opened his eyes and called to Kondrat.

'Can't you sleep?' Kondrat asked.

'No. My head's swimming, and I can see the earth under the plough all the time ...'

'It's always like that,' a sympathetic smile sounded in Kondrat's voice. 'You're staring down at your feet all day, and that makes your head swim. And then the smell of the earth is devilish; it's clean, and it makes you drunk. Don't stare so much down at your feet tomorrow, Davidov, but take more interest in things around you.'

That night Davidov knew nothing of the biting of the fleas, or the snorting of the horses, or the noise of a belated flock of wild geese spending the night on the ridge of the hills. He slept as though dead. Just before dawn he happened to wake up, and saw Kondrat, wrapped in his coat, coming towards the hut.

344

'Where have you been?' half-asleep, Davidov raised his head and asked.

'I've been to have a look at your oxen and mine. They've been feeding well. I drove them into a valley where there's some fine grass.'

Kondrat's hoarse voice began to pass into the distance, and faded. Davidov did not hear the end of the phrase; sleep threw his head back on to his dew-drenched sheepskin, and he was lost in oblivion.

By the evening of that day he had ploughed a hectare and two furrows. Liubishkin ploughed exactly a hectare, Kuzhenkov a little less, and, to everybody's amazement Antip Grach, who hitherto had been among the group of backward workers whom Davidov had derisively called the 'weakling command', came out on top. He had Titok's lean oxen to work with, and at the noonday break he did not say how much he had done. After dinner his wife, who was acting as his driver, fed the oxen from her apron, putting in the six pounds of concentrated fodder allotted to the animals. But Grach even swept up the crumbs of bread left on the homespun cloth, and put them into his wife's apron to feed the oxen. Liubishkin noticed his action and laughed:

'You're tightening things up very fine, Antip!'

'And I'm going to! Our family isn't the last when it comes to work,' the swarthy Antip, still blacker with the spring sunburn, challengingly answered. And he did! In the evening it transpired that he had ploughed a hectare and a quarter.

But Kondrat Maidannikov did not drive his oxen into the camp until dusk had fallen. To Davidov's question: 'How much?' he hoarsely replied: 'One and half except for one furrow. Give us some tobacco for a cigarette . . . I haven't had a smoke since noonday.' And he looked at Davidov with weary, but triumphant eyes.

After the evening meal Davidov summed up the results.

'Comrades of the second brigade, socialistic competition has developed among us to further orders! The rates of work are highly satisfactory. Bolshevik thanks from the collective farm management to the brigade for its ploughing. We shall get out of our hole, comrades. Fact! And why shouldn't we, when the possibility of carrying out the allotted task has been proved in practice? Now we must fling ourselves into the task of harrowing. And we simply must harrow in teams of three. Especial thanks to Maidannikov, our finest shock worker.'

The women washed up the utensils, the ploughmen lay down to sleep, the bullocks were driven off to graze. Kondrat was already dozing off when his wife crawled under his coat, jostled him, and asked:

'Kondrat, Davidov called you ... it sounded as though it was praising you ... But what is a shock worker?'

Kondrat had heard the term many a time, but he could not explain it. 'I ought to have got Davidov to make it clear,' he thought, a little chagrined. But to leave his wife without an explanation, to lower his dignity in her eyes, was impossible, so he explained as best he could :

'A shock worker? Ah, you're a fool of a woman! A shock worker? Hm! Well, how can I make it clear to you? The shock worker is the most important figure in the collective farm, don't you see that? And now go and sleep and don't come crawling in with me !'

Chapter 37

A Fortnight of Changes

BY 15 May the sowing of corn was finished in the main throughout all the district. By that date the Gremyachy 'Stalin' collective farm had completely fulfilled its sowing plan. By noon of the tenth the third brigade finished sowing the remaining eight hectares with maize and sunflowers, and Davidov at once sent a horse courier urgently to District headquarters with a report to the District Committee on the completion of the sowing.

The shoots of the early wheat were very satisfactory, but in the second brigade section were about a hundred hectares of Kuban wheat which had been sown during the first few days of May. Davidov was afraid that this belated sowing would give poor results, and Liubishkin shared his fears, while Yakov Lukich declared with the utmost confidence:

'It won't come up! It won't come up for anything! Do you want to go on sowing all the year round and expect it to grow? It's written in books that they sow twice a year in Egypt and get a harvest each time. But Gremyachy Log isn't Egypt, comrade Davidov, we have to keep strictly to the sowing periods here.'

'What are you preaching such opportunism for?' Davidov grew angry. 'It's got to come up for us! And if we find it necessary we'll get two harvests a year. It's our earth, it belongs to us, and we'll squeeze out of it just what we want to. Fact!'

'You're talking like a child!'

'Well, we'll see. Your speech shows a rightward deviation, citizen Ostrovnov, and that is an undesirable and harmful deviation for the party. That deviation has been thoroughly branded, don't forget that!'

'I'm not talking about deviations, but about the earth. I don't know anything about your deviations.'

But while Davidov hoped that the Kuban wheat would come up, he could not dispel his own doubts. Every day he saddled the management committee stallion and rode out to look at the well worked, but alarmingly lifeless black stretch of land lying parched under the sun.

The earth had dried out quickly. Such seed as germinated was poorly nourished, and not strong enough to throw its shoots upward. Tender and weak, the sharp blades of the shoots lay feebly beneath the crumbling clumps of warm, sun-drenched earth, struggling towards the light, but unable to pierce the caked, dry earthy crust. Davidov dismounted and, going down on his knees, tore up the earth with his hand. As he stared at the tiny grain of wheat with the fine shoot emerging from its kernel, he felt a bitter feeling of pity for the millions of seeds buried in the earth, so tormentedly struggling towards the sun, and all but condemned to death. He was frenzied by the consciousness of his own impotence. Rain was wanted, and then the wheat would spread a green plush over the land. But rain did not come, and the soil was thickly overgrown with strong, vital, and unfastidious weeds.

One evening a delegation from the old men came to see Davidov in his room.

'We've come with a humble little request,' old Akim the 'hen-feeler' said, after greeting Davidov and vainly looking for an ikon before which he could cross himself.

'What sort of request? You won't find an ikon, daddy, so don't look for one.'

'Shan't I? Well, I'll manage ... But our request from the old men is ...'

'Well, what is it?'

'The wheat in the second brigade's section isn't going to come up, that's clear ...'

'So far, nothing is clear, daddy.'

'Well, it isn't clear, but it looks very much like it.'

'Well?'

'We need rain.'

'You're right there!'

'Allow us to send for the priest to hold a service.'

'What's that for?' Davidov's face turned a rosy hue.

'You know what for – so that the Lord should send the rain.'

'Well, that's a bit too ... clear out, daddy, and not another word about that to me!'

'Why not? The wheat's ours, isn't it?'

'It's the collective farm's.'

'Well, and who are we? We're collective farmers.'

'And I'm the chairman of the collective farm.'

'We understand that, comrade. You don't recognize God, and we don't ask you to go with the sacred banners, but to allow us believers to.'

'I won't allow you. Has a collective farm meeting sent you?'

'No. We old men decided on our own.'

'Well, now you see. There are only a few of you, and the meeting wouldn't allow it in any case. We've got to do our farming with the aid of science, daddy, and not with the aid of the priests.'

Davidov spent a long time talking circumspectly to the old men, trying not to offend their religious feelings. They were silent. Towards the end of their visit Makar Nagulnov came in. He had heard that a delegation of believers from the old men had gone to ask Davidov's permission to hold a service, and hurried to see what was happening.

'So we can't?' Akim sighed and stood up.

'You can't, and there's no reason why you should. There'll be rain without that.'

The old men went out, and Nagulnov followed them into the porch. He tightly shut the door to Davidov's room, and whispered to them:

'You hoary old sinners! I know all about you: you're always trying to live your own way, you're the stubbornest of devils! You'd like to celebrate all the saints' holidays, and drag out into the steppe with the ikons, and tread down the grain. If you bring the priest here and go out into the fields off your own bat I'll ride after you with the fire brigade, and we'll play the hoses on you until you're wetter than water. Understand? And it would be better for the priest if he didn't turn up! I'll shear him with fleecing shears in front of all the people, the hairy stallion. I'll shear him to shame and then let him go. Understand?'

Then he went back to Davidov, and sat down on the chest, morose and discontented.

'What were you whispering to the old men about?' Davidov suspiciously inquired.

'We were talking about the weather,' Makar answered without winking an eyelid.

'Well?'

'And they've decided not to hold a service.'

'What did they say then?' Davidov turned away to hide a smile.

'They said they realized that religion is opium . . . But what are you sticking to me like this for, Siemion? You're as bad as the ringworm: you hang on and there's no getting away from you! What did I talk about and what did I say? . . . I talked, and that's sufficient. With your arguments and entreaties you're encouraging them to be too democratic. And that's not at all the way to talk to such old men. They're all infected with a dangerous spirit, all soaked in dope. So it's no use wasting words on them, but just order them to quick march and put the lid on them!'

With a laugh Davidov waved his hand in despair. Makar was simply incorrigible!

He had been expelled from the Party for two weeks, but during that period there had been a change in the District Party leadership. Korchinsky the secretary and Homutov the head of the Organization Department had been removed from their positions.

On receiving Nagulnov's appeal, which was sent to him from the Regional Control Commission, the new District Party secretary sent a member of the Bureau to Gremyachy Log to make a further investigation, and afterwards the Bureau decided to rescind its decision to expel Nagulnov from the Party. The decision was rescinded on the ground that the severity of the sentence was not justified by Nagulnov's conduct, and moreover because a number of the charges against him (the 'moral disintegration' and 'sexual licentiousness') had to be withdrawn after the second investigation. Makar was reprimanded, and there the matter ended.

When Davidov, who had temporarily taken over the duties of nucleus secretary, handed the position back to Makar, he asked:

'Learnt your lesson? Going to deviate any more?'

'Learnt it only too well! Only, who deviated, I or the District Committee?'

'Both you and the committee. You both went wrong a little.'

'But I consider that the Regional Committee is also deviating.'

'How, for instance?'

'Like this! Why didn't they issue orders that the collective farm members who resigned were to be handed back their cattle? Isn't that compulsory collectivization? Of course it is! Here you've got people leaving the collective farm, and they're to have neither cattle nor implements. It's clear that they've got nothing to get a living with, nowhere to go to; and they'll be crawling back to the collective farm. They'll squeal, but they'll crawl back.'

'But the cattle and the implements have gone into the farm's indivisible fund.'

'What the devil do we need such a fund for, if they're going to be forced into the collective farm again? Why not tell them: "Here you are, guzzle and choke yourselves with your implements!" I wouldn't let them come anywhere near the collective farm. But you've let in such turncoats by the hundred, and I suppose you think they'll become intelligent collective farmers! Not on your life! They'll live inside the collective farm, the enemies, but until their dying day they'll have their eyes fixed on the life of the individual peasant. I know them! And your not giving them back their cattle and implements is a leftward deviation, and your taking them back into the collective farm is a rightward deviation. I've become politically developed, too, brother, and you won't be able to chew me up now!'

'How can you call yourself politically developed, when you don't even understand that we can't settle our accounts with the former members at once, but have got to wait until the end of the agricultural year?'

'Yes, I do understand that.'

'Ah, Makar, Makar! You can't live without taking leaps. Your piss gets too much to your head, that's a fact!'

They argued for a long time, finished up by swearing at each other, and Davidov went off.

During those two weeks there had been many changes in Gremyachy Log. To the great surprise of the whole village, Marina Poyarkova took her brother-in-law, Diemid the Silent, for husband. He moved into her hut, harnessing himself to a cart one night and shifting all his few belongings, and closely boarded up the door and windows of his own hut.

'Marina's found a good mate! The two of them will get more work done than a tractor!' Gremyachy said of them.

Dumbfounded by the marriage of his sweetheart of many years' standing, Andrei at first concealed his feelings. But after a time he could stand it no longer, and, keeping out of Davidov's way, began to drink. One day Davidov noticed it, and warned him:

'Drop that business, Andrei! It's not the thing for a Party member.'

'I'll drop it! Only I feel insulted beyond words, Siemion. Who has she changed me for, the bitch? Who has she changed me for?'

'That's her personal affair.'

'But it's insulting to me!'

351

'Be insulted then, but don't drink. This isn't the time for it. It'll be weeding time soon.'

But, as though intentionally, Marina more and more frequently happened across Razmiotnov's path, and always seemed to be satisfied and happy.

Diemid set to work like a prize ox on her small farm. In a few days he put all the yard buildings in order, dug a cellar ten feet deep in twenty-four hours, carried ten-pood beams and the plough on his back. Marina washed, sewed, and mended his clothes, and when talking to her neighbours could not sufficiently praise Diemid's working powers.

'He's the man to have about the house, women!' she declared. 'He's got the strength of a bear, and whatever he picks up boils in his hands. And even if he doesn't say much, what does that matter? We shan't quarrel so much...'

When the rumours of Marina's contentment with her new husband reached Andrei's ears, he mournfully whispered to himself:

'Ah, Marina! Couldn't I have mended your shed, or dug a cellar for you? You've ruined my young life!'

The former kulak Gayev returned to Gremyachy from exile. The Electoral Rights Commission restored his rights of citizenship, and as soon as he, accompanied by his numerous children, arrived in the village, Davidov summoned him to the collective farm office.

'What do you think of doing to get a living, citizen Gayev?' he asked. 'Will you be an individual peasant, or will you join the collective farm?'

'However I can!' replied Gayev, who had not got over his resentment at his illegal treatment as a kulak.

'But what do you think?'

'It's clear I can't avoid the collective farm.'

'Then hand in a letter of application.'

'But how about my property?'

'Your cattle are in the collective farm, and your agricultural implements, too. But we distributed your lumber. It will be more difficult to get that back. We can give some back, and you will receive payment for the rest.'

'You've milled my grain.'

'Well, that's easily put right. Go to the manager; he'll tell the warehouseman to let you have ten poods of flour to carry on with.'

'He's collecting everybody from the highways and by-ways into the collective farm,' Makar indignantly exclaimed, when he heard that Davidov intended to accept Gayev's application. 'He may as well put a notice in the paper that he'll take all exiles into the collective farm as soon as they've served their sentence,' he said to Andrei Razmiotnov.

After the sowing period the Gremyachy Party nucleus doubled its membership. Pavel Liubishkin, who had worked three years for Titok, Nestor Loshchilin, a member of the third brigade, and Diemka Ushakov were all accepted as candidates. The day the nucleus meeting accepted Liubishkin and the others, Nagulnov proposed to Kondrat Maidannikov:

'Join the Party, Kondrat. I'll gladly support your application. You served under me in the squadron, and just as you were a heroic cavalryman then, so you're a first-rate collective farmer now. I can't help wondering why you remain outside the Party. It's reaching the point where the world revolution is likely to come at any moment, and you're still a non-Party man after all this time. It isn't good enough. Apply to join.'

Kondrat sighed, and spoke in his innermost mind:

'No, comrade Nagulnov, my conscience won't let me join the Party just now. I'll fight again for the Soviet government, and I'll work in the collective farm with all my might, but I can't put my name down for the Party . . .'

'But why not?' Nagulnov's face clouded.

'I can't, because even now I'm in the collective farm I'm sick with longing for my property.' Kondrat's lips quivered, and he added in a swift whisper: 'I'm sick at heart for my bullocks, and I'm sorry for them . . . They don't get the care they ought to get. And Akim Beskhlebnov chafed my horse's neck with the collar during the harrowing. When I noticed it I couldn't eat all day because of it. Is it right to put a big collar on a small horse? And that's why I can't join. If I still haven't got rid of my desire for my property, it means my conscience won't allow me to be in the Party. That's how I see it.'

Makar thought a moment, then said:

'Yes, you're right there. Wait a little then, don't join yet. We'll fight relentlessly against all shortcomings in the collective farm; all the collars will be fitted to the right horses. But if you see your old bullocks in your sleep, then you can't be in the Party. You must come into the Party without any suffering over property. You have to come into the Party when you're clean all through, and are driven by the one thought of achieving the world revolution. My father was comfortably off, and he got me used to the farm from my childhood. But I wasn't in the least attached to it, the farm meant nothing to me whatever. I gave up a well-fed life and four yoke of oxen to be a poor labourer. So don't you join until you've got clean rid of that scab of property.'

The rumour that Liubishkin, Ushakov and Loshchilin were joining the Party quickly spread through Gremyachy Log. One of the cossacks jokingly remarked to Shchukar:

'And why don't you apply to join the Party? You're one of the active workers, you put your name forward. They'll give you an official job and you'll buy a leather document case, put it under your arm and go riding about.'

Shchukar thought it over. And as soon as it was dark that evening he went to Nagulnov's room.

'How are you, Makar?' he opened the conversation.

'And how are you? What do you want?'

'There are people joining the Party ...'

'Well, what then?'

'And then, perhaps I want to join. I don't want to spend all my life looking after stallions, brother. I'm not married to them!'

'So what do you want?'

'In good Russian, I want to join the Party. I came to see what job I'd get, and so on ... You tell me what to write and how to write it.'

'So you ... you think people join the Party in order to get jobs?'

'All our Party members have got jobs.'

Makar controlled his feelings, and changed the conversation.

'Did the priest visit you at Easter?' he asked.

'Of course.'

'Did you give him anything?'

'Why, of course! I gave him a couple of eggs, and a lump of fat pork, about half a pound.'

'So you still believe in God even now?'

'Yes, of course, not very strongly. But if I fall ill, or something goes wrong, or if the thunder sounds too loud, for instance, then I pray, naturally I turn to God.'

Makar wanted to deal politely with Shchukar, to explain in detail why he could not be accepted by the Party. But he failed to provide himself with a sufficient stock of patience when he launched Shchukar into the conversation, and so he suddenly burst out:

'Go to the devil, you old cesspool! You give the priests eggs, you dream of jobs, but in fact you don't know how to make up a mash for the horses properly. D'you think the Party needs any old rubbish? What d'you think you're doing, playing a joke? Your job is only to wag your tongue, and tell lies. Clear out and don't get me worked up, for I suffer with my nerves. My health won't let me talk to you quietly. Clear out, I say! Well, are you going?'

'I didn't get him at the right moment. I should have seen him after dinner,' Shchukar disconsolately thought, as he hurriedly slammed the wicket gate behind him.

The last news to agitate Gremyachy Log, and especially the girls, during those two weeks, was the death of 'Smoky'.

Yefim Trubachov and Batalshchikov, whom the People's Court sentenced to terms of forced labour, wrote that on the way to the station 'Smoky' yearned for freedom and Gremyachy Log, and tried to escape. Three times the militia-man escorting the prisoners shouted, 'Stop!' but he bent double and ran across ploughed land towards the forest. Only some forty yards separated him from the first bushes when the militia-man went down on one knee, threw his rifle to his shoulder, and at the third shot brought 'Smoky' down dead.

Except for his aunt, there was nobody to grieve over the orphan lad, or if the girls he had taught the simple arts of love grieved for him, it was not for long. 'The affair grows old, and the body cold.' And maidens' tears are like the dew at sunrise.

Chapter 38

An Energetic Manager

THE 'dead season' in agriculture, the period between the spring sowing and the haymaking, was first abolished in 1930. In former years, when the peasants lived in the traditional way, those two months were not called the 'dead season' for nothing. When they had finished their sowing the farmers leisurely made ready for haymaking; the oxen and horses grazed over the pastures, gathering strength, while the cossacks planed rakes, or repaired carts and reapers. Rarely did anyone drive out to plough up the virgin soil in the heat of May-time. The villages reposed in an oppressive silence. Not a soul was to be met in the lifeless street at noonday. The cossacks were either out on journeys, or resting in their huts or their cool cellars, or idly wielding axes. And the sleepy women were comfortably settled in a cool spot, catching their fleas. An emptiness and drowsy peace reigned in the villages.

But the very first year the collective farm existed the 'dead season' was violated in Gremyachy Log. Hardly had the grain begun to shoot when weeding began.

'We shall weed three times, so that not one weed will be left in the collective farm fields,' Davidov announced at the meeting.

Yakov Lukich rejoiced. Energetic himself, and never sitting still, he was highly delighted by this demonstration of good management, which would put the entire village in movement, in activities and bustling occupation. 'The Soviet government's flying high; we'll see how it settles! The grain to be weeded, and the fallow to be turned over, the cattle to feed and the implements to mend! But will the people work? Will they force the women

356

to weed? That's unheard of. In all the Don area the grain was never weeded in the old days. But they were fools to leave it unweeded. The harvest would have been richer. And I should have weeded my fields, old fool that I am! My devils of women hung about doing nothing all the summer,' so he thought; and grieved to think that he had not weeded his grain in the days when he was working his own farm. As he was talking to Davidov about it, he told him:

'We shall be loaded down with grain now, comrade Davidov! But in the old days we'd throw the seed out and wait for it to come up! It would come up together with rye grass, and quitch, and thistles, and wild oats, and spurge, and heaven knows what other filthy stuff. When you threshed it the grain seemed good enough, but when you weighed up the amount you'd got from a hectare there'd be only forty poods or even less.'

After the incident of the unauthorized distribution of the seed grain Davidov had intended to dismiss Ostrovnov from his position as manager. He had been troubled by a deep suspicion of him, as he remembered that he had seen him among the crowd around the granaries, and that the old man's face had worn an expression not only of distraction but of malicious, smiling expectation. So at least it had seemed to Davidov. Next day he had summoned Yakov Lukich to his room and sent out everybody else. The two men had talked in undertones.

'What were you doing around the granaries yesterday?' Davidov had demanded.

'I was trying to argue with the people, comrade Davidov! I was trying to persuade the enemies to come to their senses, and not take the collective farm grain arbitrarily,' Yakov Lukich had replied without a moment's hesitation.

'But the women...? Why did you tell the women that I must have the keys to the granaries?'

'Why, what are you saying? Good God! Who did I say that to? I never said such a thing to anyone!'

'The women told me you did as they were taking me...'

'It's lies! I'm ready to swear it! It's slanders! They've got their knife into me!'

Davidov had been shaken in his resolution. And shortly

afterward Yakov Lukich began to display such fervent activity in the preparations for weeding and for collecting the means for communal feeding, and he showered so many soundly economic plans on the management, that Davidov was once more vanquished by his energetic manager.

Yakov Lukich proposed that several new ponds should be made in the brigade field areas. He even indicated spots in the ravines where it would be easiest to dam the spring water. In his view the new ponds needed to be constructed in order to ensure that the brigade animals would not have to go more than half a kilometre for water. Davidov, and for that matter all the other members of the management committee, had to admit the value of the project, for the old ponds had been made by no means with an eye to future collective farm activities. They were scattered haphazardly over the steppe, and during the spring it had been necessary to drive the animals two to three kilometres from the brigade camps for water. The loss of time had been enormous. Almost two hours had been spent each time the tired oxen had been driven to the water and back, and in that time it would have been possible to plough or harrow more than one hectare. The management committee agreed to the construction of new ponds, and, taking advantage of the break in field labour, Yakov Lukich began to get timber ready for the dam.

Nor was that all. He proposed that a small brick works should be started, and had no difficulty in convincing the doubters of the profitable nature of such an undertaking, for to have their own bricks for building a large stable and cattle-sheds was incomparably better than carrying them the twenty-eight kilometres from the District town, and paying 4½ roubles per hundred in addition. Yakov Lukich also persuaded the members of the third brigade to fill in a ravine, from which year after year flood water washed away the rich lands on which millet and marvellously sweet and juicy water-melons grew splendidly. Under his direction the ravine was enclosed with piles, filled in with brushwood and dung, and rubbled with stones, while young poplars and willows were planted along the channel, in order that their roots should interlace and strengthen the crumbling soil. In this way no small area of land was saved from being washed away.

All these circumstances together stabilized Ostrovnov's shaken position in the collective farm. Davidov firmly resolved that on no account would he be deprived of his manager, and that on all hands he would support his truly inexhaustible initiative. Even Nagulnov adopted a more friendly attitude to Yakov Lukich. 'He's alien to us in his spirit, but he makes a fine manager,' he said one day at a nucleus meeting. 'Until we have developed one of our own men to know as much, we shall support Ostrovnov as the manager. Our Party is unlimited in its wisdom. There are millions of brains in it, and that's why it is so keen-witted. An engineer may be a reptile and a secret counter-revolutionary. He ought to have been set against a wall long ago for his spirit, but they don't do it. Instead, they give him work and tell him: "You're an educated man! Here's money for you. Eat enough for three, buy your wife silk stockings for her pleasure, but get your brain-box working, and do your engineering for the good of the world revolution!" And he does. He may set his eyes longingly on his old life, but he does his job. Shoot him, and what do you get from him? Worn trousers, and perhaps he may leave a watch with a pendant. But now he works and brings benefit to many thousands. So with our Ostrovnov. Let him dam up the ravine, let him dig ponds. It will all be for the benefit of the Soviet regime and bring nearer the world revolution.'

Ostrovnov's life once more acquired a certain equilibrium. He realized that all the forces which had stood behind Polovtsiev and directed the preparations for the rising had lost for the time being. He was firmly convinced that now there would not be a rising, for the moment had passed, and there had been a change in the attitude even of the cossacks most hostile to the Soviet government. 'Evidently Polovtsiev and Lyatievsky have fled across the frontier,' he thought. And his keen regret that there had been no opportunity to shake off the Soviet regime was tempered by a tranquillizing joy and satisfaction: henceforth there was no one to threaten the well-being of his existence. He no longer experienced a sickening fear when he saw the militia-man arriving at Gremyachy Log, whereas formerly the very sight of a black militia uniform had caused him inexpressible alarm and made him tremble.

'Well, will this heathen government be done for soon? Will

ours be arriving soon now?' his old mother once asked Yakov Lukich point-blank.

Agitated beyond all bounds by the untimely question, he answered bitterly and irritatedly:

'What does it matter to you, mother?'

'That's just it, that it does matter. They've closed down the churches, and treated the priests as kulaks, and is that right?'

'You're getting on in years, you pray to God ... But don't meddle in worldly affairs. You're very scrupulous, mother!'

'But where have the officers vanished to? Where has that good-for-nothing, one-eyed, smoking chimney flown off to? And you asked for my blessing, and now you're again serving this government!' Quite unable to understand why her son had not done anything to 'change the government', the old woman would not be appeased.

'Oh, mother, you make my blood freeze! Drop your silly talk! What are you raking all that up for? You'll blurt it out in front of other people. You'll be the cause of my losing my head, mother! You've said yourself that "whatever God does is good". And now live and be quiet. You've got two nostrils to your nose, snort down them and shut up! You're not being robbed of your piece of bread. And what else do you need, God be thanked?'

After one such conversation Yakov Lukich dashed out of the room as though he had been splashed with boiling water, and would not calm down for a long time. Then he gave a strict order to his son Siemion and the women.

'Watch grandmother with all your eyes!' he said. 'She'll be the death of me! If any stranger comes to the door lock her up in her room at once.'

They began to keep the old woman locked up day and night. But she was let out unhindered on Sundays, and then she would go along to her friends, decrepit old women of her own age, and weep as she complained to them:

'Oh, my dears, my good friends! My son and his wife, they lock me in now. And they feed me on dry crusts, and I eat the crusts and drink my own tears. But when the officers, Yakov's commander and his friend, were living with us in Lent, I was given cabbage soup and sometimes even stewed fruit. But now they've got so angry with me ... so angry ... my son and my daughter-in-law. Oh-o-o-ooh ! The things I've come down to, my dears ! My own son so furious with me, and what about I haven't the least idea. He came and asked my blessing on his work to destroy this heathen government, but now if I say a word against it he swears and curses away at me ...'

Chapter 39

Off with the Old Love ...

DURING the sowing period the gay and wanton woman Lukeria, Nagulnov's former wife, began to work in the fields. She was assigned to the third brigade, and she willingly took up her quarters in the brigade field hut. During the day she worked as driver to Afanasi Krasnokutov, but at night, outside the red field hut in which she lived, the balalaika was strumming until dawn, the basses and the upper register of the two-rowed accordion groaned and whined, the young men and women danced and sang. And all this merry revelry was directed by Lukeria.

For her the world was always sunny and simple. Not a single frown of care or anxiety ever showed on her thoughtless face. Raising her gracious brows, she walked through life easily, confidently, expectantly, as though every minute hoping to meet with some new pleasure. She ceased to think about Makar the very day after their separation. And Timofei was somewhere a long way off, and was it for Lukeria to grieve over her lost lovers? 'There are enough hounds in the world to last me my lifetime !' she said contemptuously to the girls and women who pointed to her grass-widowed state.

Certainly there were enough and to spare ! The lads and the younger married men of the third brigade vied with one another in soliciting her love. Under the blue and hazy light of the moon, in the camp outside the hut the mud and dung flew from the cossacks' boots as they danced the 'Krakoviak' and other dances.

But frequently the ploughmen, sowers and harrowers dancing and seeking to be in Lukeria's immediate presence would break into a volley of curses and start a bitter fight. And all because of her. Apparently she was only too accessible, the more so as all the village knew of her shameful relations with Timofei, and each man was flattered by the prospect of occupying the place Timofei involuntarily and Nagulnov voluntarily had vacated.

Agafon Dubtsiev attempted to reason with Lukeria, but it was a pitiable failure.

'I'm all right at my work, but nobody's going to forbid me to dance and make love. Don't get angry, daddy Agafon, pull your coat over your head and sleep. Or if you get jealous and want to share in the fun, come along. We accept even the pockmarked. They say pockmarked men make very hot lovers!' Lukeria laughingly jeered.

The very next time Agafon was in Gremyachy he appealed to Davidov for assistance.

'It's strange arrangements you're making, comrade Davidov,' he indignantly began. 'You've put old Shchukar into Liubishkin's brigade, and shoved Lukeria Nagulnova into mine. Have you put them in to act as wreckers, or what? Come out one night and see what's going on in the camp. Lukeria's turned all my lads' heads. She smiles at them all and makes promises, and they fight over her like young cocks. And they dance at night until the earth groans, until you're sorry for their heels, they kick them so mercilessly against the ground. Close to the hut they've beaten out a bare spot – you wouldn't believe it was possible. There's still a noise like a market going on in our camp even when the Great Bear's fading in the morning. During the German war I lay wounded in a Kharkov hospital, and when I was well enough the nurses took me to listen to the opera. It was a terrible mix-up: someone was howling away in a silly voice, someone else was dancing, and a third was sawing away on a violin. You couldn't understand anything of what was going on! It was such awful music that it made you clutch your throat. And that's how it is in the camp: they sing, and they bang their instruments, and they dance ... It's a dog's wedding! They go mad until the dawn's coming, and then what sort of work can you expect to get out of them all day? They fall asleep as they're walking, and lie down under the oxen. Either remove this infection Lukeria from the camp, or tell her to behave herself like a married woman.'

'What do you think I am?' Davidov stormed. 'What am I? Am I your teacher? Clear out and go to the devil! Coming here with such filthy ... What am I to do? Teach the woman modesty? If she works badly, turn her out of the brigade. Fact! What is this habit of running to the management as soon as the least thing happens? It's nothing but "Comrade Davidov, a plough's broken," or, "Comrade Davidov, a mare's fallen ill." Or like in this case: a woman flings up her tail, and according to you I've got to teach her better! Damn you! If a plough wants mending, go to the smith. And there's a veterinary surgeon for the horses. When will you learn to develop some initiative of your own? How long am I to go on helping you? Clear out!'

Agafon went off strongly dissatisfied with Davidov, who, after the brigade leader's departure, smoked two cigarettes in succession, slammed the door with a bang, and fastened it.

Dubtsiev's story disturbed Davidov. But he had not shouted and fumed at him because the brigade leaders had not shouldered their responsibilities, and had overwhelmed him with requests for decisions on all sorts of trifling administrative issues. He had flown into a temper because Lukeria, in Dubtsiev's words, 'smiled at everybody and made promises'.

From the day when he had met her outside the office, and she, concealing a smile beneath the lashes of her drooping eyelids, had first asked him to find her some 'cast-off' husband, and then offered herself to him as his wife, Davidov had changed his attitude towards her. More and more frequently he caught himself thinking of this essentially captious and unusually empty-headed woman. Previously he had had a faint feeling of negligent pity and indifference for her, but now he had altered considerably. And Dubtsiev's stupid complaint about her served as only a purely superficial pretext for his curses.

He was attracted by Lukeria, and that at a most untimely moment, during the most intense period of the sowing campaign. Undoubtedly the fact that all the winter he had lived in a 'state of monasticism', as Andrei Razmiotnov jestingly called it, conduced to the development of this feeling. And maybe the

363

spring had a strong effect on the mortal flesh of the irreproachable chairman of the Gremyachy collective farm, who had successfully handled all the farm's administrative and political campaigns.

More and more at night he awoke without cause, smoked, painfully frowned, listened to the singing and gurgling twitters of the nightingales, wrapped his head in his baize blanket, and lay until dawn, not shutting his eyes, pressing his broad, tattooed chest against the pillow.

But in the passionate and quickly maturing spring of 1930 so many nightingales settled in the orchards and groves of the riverside, that they not only filled the mute emptiness of the night with their music, but were not to be stilled even during the day. The brief spring nights were not long enough for the nightingales' love delights. 'They're singing in two shifts, the blighters!' Davidov whispered one early morning, as, in the grip of tedious exhaustion, he valiantly struggled with his sleeplessness.

Lukeria remained with the brigade until the sowing was finished. But the day the brigade returned to the village she went to see Davidov in the evening.

He was lying in his little room after supper, reading the newspaper *Pravda*. There was a quiet scraping, almost like a mouse, at the door, then a woman's soft voice asked:

'May I come in?'

'Yes.' Davidov jumped off his bed, and threw on his jacket.

Lukeria entered, and quietly shut the door behind her. A black shawl aged her weathered, swarthy face. Burnt deeper by the sun, the fine, numerous freckles showed more distinctly on her cheeks. But under the dark curtain of the shawl drawn over her forehead her eyes laughed and glittered even more clearly.

'I've come to see you . . .' she began.

'Come in and sit down.' Astonished and delighted by her arrival, Davidov pushed forward a stool, buttoned up his jacket, and sat down on his bed. He was expectantly silent, and felt awkward and uneasy. But she walked at her ease across to the table, with a graceful, unostentatious movement tucked her skirt under her to avoid creasing it, and sat down.

'Well, how are you getting on, collective farm chairman?'

'All right; I'm managing.'

'Not longing for anyone, are you?'

'No time to long for anything, and nothing to long for.'

'Not even for me?'

The usually self-possessed Davidov went a vivid scarlet, and frowned. With exaggerated modesty she lowered her eyelids, but a smile flickered in the corners of her lips.

'You've imagined a fine thing!' he answered a little uncertainly.

'So you haven't been longing for me?'

'Of course not. Fact! Have you something you want to see me about?'

'I have ... What news is there in the papers? What news of the world revolution?' Lukeria leaned on her elbows, and her face adopted a serious expression appropriate to the conversation, as though her lips had not worn a devilish smile only a moment before.

'All sorts of things ... What is the business you've come to see me about?' Davidov plucked up courage. He sat as though on hot coal. His situation was quite impossible, absolutely intolerable. Undoubtedly the mistress of the hut was listening at the door. And tomorrow she would tell all Gremyachy Log that Makar's former wife visited her lodger at night, and ... Good-bye to his spotless reputation! The slander-loving women would begin to gossip everlastingly at the corners and around the wells, the collective farmers would laugh knowingly when he met them. Razmiotnov would begin to sneer at his comrade who had been caught by Lukeria, then it would be carried to the District, and, worst of all, in the Agricultural Department they would link up one thing with another, and say: 'So that's why he didn't get the sowing finished until the tenth, because women were visiting him! Evidently he was more occupied with his petty love affairs than with the sowing.' And the Regional Committee secretary had well said when seeing the mobilized workers off to the districts: 'The authority of the working class – the advance guard of the world revolution – must be maintained at the highest level in the villages. You must behave with twice as much caution, comrades. I'm not speaking of the bigger things, but even in matters of detail you must have foresight. Have only a kopek's worth of drink in the villages, and there will be talk about it to the value of a hundred political roubles.'

Davidov began to sweat as he swiftly realized all the possible consequences of Lukeria's visit, and of this free-speaking conversation. He was faced with the open menace of being compromised! But Lukeria sat completely unaware of his tormented sensations. A little hoarse with his agitation, he harshly asked her:

'What is it you've come to see me about? Tell me and go, I haven't got any time to spend on trifles with you. That's a fact!'

'But d'you remember what you told me when I asked you? I didn't ask Makar at the time, but I know what he thinks all the same. He's against . . .'

Davidov jumped to his feet and waved his arms:

'I haven't got the time! Afterwards! Later!' At that moment he was ready to press his palm over her laughing mouth in order to keep her quiet.

She understood, and contemptuously raised her eyebrows as she said:

'Oh, you . . . ! Well, all right. Give me a paper, one that's interesting. I haven't got any other business with you except that. Excuse me for troubling you . . .'

She went out, and Davidov sighed with relief. But the next moment he was sitting down at the table, ruthlessly clutching his hair, and thinking: 'What am I such a fool for? I've got no strength. It's of great importance what anybody says about it! Can't women come and see me, then? Am I a monk, or what? And whose business is it? I like her, and I can spend time in her company if I want to! So long as the work doesn't suffer I can spit on the rest! But now she won't come again. Fact! I was very rough with her, and besides, she noticed that I was a little frightened . . . Oh, damn you, what mess have you got into now?'

But his fears were unfounded: Lukeria by no means belonged to the class of people who are easily turned from the plans they have made. And her plans included the conquest of Davidov. After all, why should she link her life up with some Gremyachy lad, she thought. What for? In order to grow withered by the stove in her old age, and forgotten on the steppe with the bullocks and ploughing? Davidov was a simple, broad-shouldered and good-natured chap, not at all like Makar, who was worm-eaten with affairs and expectation of the world revolution. Nor was he like Timofei. He had one small defect: the gap in his teeth. And it was right in front, in the most prominent spot. But Lukeria reconciled herself to this shortcoming in her favourite. In her brief, but richly experienced life she had learned that his teeth were not the most important thing to be considered in a man.

The next day at dusk she turned up again, this time dressed in her finery, and still more provoking. She made the newspapers the pretext for her visit.

'I've brought your paper back. Can I have another? And you haven't got any books, have you? I'd like to read something interesting ... about love.'

'Take a newspaper. I haven't got any books; this isn't a library,' he replied.

Without waiting for the invitation, she sat down and began a serious conversation about the sowing carried out by the third brigade, and the irregularities she had noticed in the recently-organized dairy. With a naive absence of cunning she adapted herself to Davidov, and to the sphere of interests in which, as it seemed to her, he must live.

At first he listened to her distrustfully. But then he began to find the conversation interesting, and talked of his plans for the dairy, informing her among other things of the latest foreign technical achievements in working up milk production. Not without a note of bitterness he ended:

'It's a peck of money we want. We ought to buy several calves born of mothers with a high milk yield, we ought to get a pedigree bull ... And we've got to do it as soon as possible. You see, a well-organized dairy farm will provide an enormous income. It's a fact that along those lines the collective farm can balance its budget. But what have we got in the dairy at the moment? An ancient separator which isn't worth a brass farthing, which simply can't deal with the spring milk yield, and nothing else. Not a single churn, and the milk is poured out into pots just as it used to be. Is that efficient? You were just saying the milk turns sour. But why does it turn sour? Probably they pour it into dirty utensils.'

'The pots are not properly baked to clean them, and that's why it turns,' she remarked.

'Well, that's just what I was saying: they don't look after the utensils properly. You take the business in hand, and put things in order. Do whatever needs to be done, and the management will always help you. As things are at present the milk will always be spoilt, if there isn't proper inspection of the utensils, and if the milkers milk as I saw one doing recently. She sat under the cow, and didn't wash the udder; all the teats were covered with mud and dung. And she hadn't washed her hands, either. The devil knows what she might have been up to beforehand, and she gets under the cow with her dirty hands. I haven't had time to take the matter up myself. But I shall now! And instead of you powdering and beautifying yourself, you might take over the management of the dairy, will you? We'll make you the manager, you'll go and take a course and learn how to run the dairy, and you'll be a qualified woman.'

'No, let them manage without me,' Lukeria sighed, 'they've got people there to put things in order without my help. I don't want to be a manager. And I don't want to go and take a course. It means too much trouble. I like to do light work, so as to have more time to live, and work is fond of the fools.'

'Now you're talking nonsense again,' Davidov angrily said. But he did not try to argue with her.

Shortly afterwards she got up to go. He went to see her home. For a long time they strode side by side along the street without speaking, then Lukeria, who had been unusually quick to learn all Davidov's cares, asked him:

'Have you been out to see the Kuban wheat today?'

'Yes.'

'Well, what's it like?'

'Bad! If there isn't rain this week I'm afraid it won't come up. And d'you see how all this will fit together? The old men who came to get my permission to hold a service will be delighted. Fact! "Aha!" they'll say, "he wouldn't let us hold the service and God wouldn't give the rain." And God has got nothing to do with it once the barometer gets stuck at "fine"! But they'll be strengthened in their stupid beliefs. It's a downright pity! Fact!

Partly we're to blame ourselves. We ought to have let the melons and part of the fallow land wait, and got the wheat sown quicker. That's where we went wrong.' Davidov spoke with more animation and, again riding his hobby-horse, would have gone on enthusiastically for a long time. But Lukeria interrupted with obvious impatience.

'Oh, stop talking about the grain,' she said. 'Let's sit down and rest a little ...' She pointed to the ridge of a ditch showing blue in the moonlight.

They went across to the ditch. Lukeria tucked up her skirt, and thoughtfully proposed:

'You might spread your jacket on the ground; I'm afraid of getting my skirt dirty. It's my holiday skirt ...'

When they were sitting side by side on the jacket, her face, suddenly severe and strangely beautiful, drew close to his smiling face, and she said:

'Enough of the grain and the collective farm! This isn't the time to talk about them. Can you smell the scent of the young leaves on the poplars?'

There Davidov's vacillation ended. Though attracted to Lukeria, he had feared that his association with her would undermine his authority ...

Afterwards, when he rose, and a dry crumble of clay trickled with a rustle into the ditch, Lukeria continued to lie on her back, her arms thrown out, her eyes closed wearily. For a moment they were silent. Then she sat up with unexpected vitality, clutched her bent knees with her arms, and shook with a paroxysm of silent laughter. She laughed as though someone were tickling her.

'What's that for?' Davidov, a little umbraged, asked in astonishment.

She as unexpectedly stopped laughing, stretched out her legs, and, stroking her thighs with her palms, meditatively said in a voice that was happy and a little hoarse:

'I feel so light now ...'

'Stick a feather in you and you'll fly away,' Davidov grew angry.

'No, you needn't ... you needn't get wild. My belly suddenly feels as though it's lost all its weight; it's gone all pleasant and light. And that's why I laughed. Had I got to cry then, or what, you strange man? Sit down. What have you jumped up for?'

Davidov reluctantly obeyed. 'What am I to do with her now? I shall have to formalize it, somehow, or it'll be awkward in front of Makar and generally ... I was without worries, so the devil supplied me with a few!' he thought, glancing sidelong at Lukeria's face, which was tinged a greenish hue by the moonlight.

Without putting her hands to the ground she agilely rose, and asked, screwing up her eyes:

'I am nice-looking, aren't I?'

'What d'you expect me to say?' Davidov answered indefinitely, embracing her slender shoulders.

Chapter 40

An Exile Returns

NEXT day, after a heavy downpour during the night, Yakov Lukich rode to the Red Grove. He had to go to the grove to mark the oaks to be cut down, for the following day almost the whole of the third brigade was to begin preparing timber suitable for the dam.

Yakov Lukich set out in the early morning. Swinging its sensibly-plaited tail, the horse took its own pace. Its unshod forefeet slipped on the greasy mud, but Yakov Lukich did not once raise the whip: there was no need for him to hurry. He dropped the reins over the saddle-bow and smoked, gazing at the steppe stretching around Gremyachy, where he had known and been fond of every little hollow, every valley and marmot hole ever since his childhood. His eyes rested with pleasure on the crumbling fallows swollen with moisture, on the grain washed and bowed down by the rain, and with intense bitterness and annoyance he thought: 'That gap-toothed devil said there'd be rain. Now the Kuban wheat will come up. You'd say God himself

370

was on the side of this accursed government. In the old days it was nothing but harvest failures and crop failures, but since 1921 the grain's been marvellous! All nature is on the side of the Soviet government, and at that rate when shall we see it worn out? No, if the allies don't help us to push the communists out, we'll never be able to do anything of ourselves. All the Polovtsievs in the world won't be able to resist them, no matter how clever they are. Force smashes force, and what can you do against it? And then the damned people are dangerous these days. One tells on another, all sorts of denunciations get made. So long as he can live, the son of a bitch, he doesn't care what happens to anybody else. These are miserable days to live in, and the devil knows where we shall be in a year or two. But it's clear I was born under a lucky star, otherwise my business with Polovtsiev wouldn't have ended so fortunately. The old ox would have been due for the poleaxe! Well, glory be that everything was settled so smoothly and cleanly. We'll wait and see what's going to happen further. This time we weren't destined to say good-bye to the Soviet government, but maybe we'll have better luck next time.'

On the blades of the grass spread beneath the sun, on the shoots of the virile grain the dew trembled like threaded glass beads. The westerly wind shook it off, and the drops broke away, glittering with rainbow hues, and fell to the rain-scented, desired and gracious earth. Still unabsorbed by the soil, a rainy moisture lay in the ruts of the roads, but above Gremyachy Log the rosy morning mists had already risen higher than the tops of the poplars, while in the dull azure of the sky, washed clean by the downpour, the young silver moon was fading, overtaken by the dawn. The moon was clearly outlined, and canted on to its back, which promised an abundance of rain. And as Yakov Lukich glanced at it he finally decided that the harvest would be good.

He arrived at the grove about noonday. He hobbled the horse and left it to graze, drew the small carpenter's axe from his belt, and went to notch the oaks of the section the forester had allotted to the Gremyachy collective farm.

At the edge of an out-running spur of the grove he marked six oaks, and moved on to the next. A lofty, spreading oak, as tall as a mast and unusually upright of line, stretched its branches over the low-growing immemorial, dwarf and flowering elms. In its very crown, amid the dark glossy green of the leaves, a rook's nest showed as a dark, gloomy patch. Judging by the girth of the trunk, the oak was almost the same age as Yakov Lukich, and, spitting on his hands, he regarded the condemned tree with a feeling of sadness and regret.

He made a notch in the trunk, wrote G.C.F. with a copying pencil on a spot stripped of bark, and, kicking away the damp, sappy chips, sat down to have a smoke. 'How many years you've lived, brother!' he thought as he stared up at the canopied crown of the oak. 'And nobody ruled over you. But now it's time for you to die. They'll fell you, dismember you, hew off your beauty, your branches and twigs, with axes, and carry you to the pond, to use you for piles where the dam is to be. And you'll rot in the collective farm pond until you moulder away. Then in the spring the flood water will drag you down to the mouth of the valley, and that'll be the end of you.'

At the thought Yakov Lukich had a painful feeling of incomprehensible anxiety and alarm. He was far from his normal self that day. 'Shall I have pity on you, and not let them cut you down? Surely something must be saved from the maw of the collective farm!' With a sense of joyous relief he decided: 'Live and grow on! Show off your beauty! There are things life doesn't mean to you. No taxes for you, no self-taxation, no need to join collective farms! Live as the Lord ordained you!'

He hurriedly jumped to his feet, gathered a handful of sticky mud, and carefully rubbed it over his notch. He walked away from the spur of trees feeling satisfied and reassured.

Sixty-seven oaks in all were marked by the hyper-sensitive Yakov Lukich, then he mounted his horse and rode along the outskirts of the grove.

'Yakov Lukich, wait a moment!' someone called as he was riding out of the trees. Then a man in a black lambswool cap and an open jacket of military cloth appeared from behind a hawthorn bush. His face was black and weather-beaten, the skin over the cheekbones was tightly drawn with emaciation, and the eyes deeply sunken, while the black, fluffy whiskers looked as though etched with charcoal above the white, parched lips.

'Don't you know me?' The man took off his cap, and, cautiously looking around him, emerged into the open. Only then did Yakov Lukich recognize the stranger as Timofei, son of Frol.

'Where've you come from?' he asked, taken aback by this meeting and by the entire appearance of the terribly emaciated, unrecognizably altered Timofei.

'From where there's no returning ... From exile ... from Kotlas.'

'Surely you haven't escaped?'

'Yes, I have. Have you got anything with you, daddy Yakov? Any bread?'

'Yes.'

'Give it me for the love of Christ. For four days ... I've eaten only rotten wood-sorrel.' He made a convulsive gulping movement. His lips trembled and his eyes glittered wolfishly as he watched Yakov's hand draw a crust of bread out of his breast.

He attacked the bread with such ravenous fury that Yakov Lukich caught his breath. He tore at the dry, burnt crust with his teeth, rent apart the crumb with crooked fingers, and swallowed it greedily, almost without chewing it, his Adam's apple working painfully. He raised his drunken eyes, from which their previous feverish glitter had gone, to Yakov Lukich only when he had chokingly swallowed the last piece.

'You've been starving, my lad!' Yakov said commiseratingly.

'I tell you this is my fifth day without anything to eat. I'm eating rotten wood-sorrel, or last year's dry thorn when I can find any. I've got a bit thin!'

'But how did you get here?'

'On foot from the station. I came by night,' Timofei wearily replied. He had paled perceptibly, as though he had spent his last strength in the effort of eating. An uncontrollable hiccuping shook his body, and made him frown painfully.

'And is your father still alive? How is your family, all well?' Yakov Lukich continued his questioning. But he did not dismount from his horse, and from time to time he glanced anxiously around.

'My father died of inflammation of the inside, my mother and sister are still there. But how are things going in the village? How is Lukeria Nagulnova?'

'She's separated from her husband, my lad . . .'

'And where is she now?' Timofei suddenly showed signs of animation.

'She's living with her aunt, board free . . .'

'Look, daddy Yakov! When you get back, tell her to bring me food here this very day without fail. I've gone so thin I couldn't get to the village. I must lie down and pass the day here, I've overdone it. A hundred and seventy viorsts, and at night, through an unknown district – do you know how you go? You grope along blindly . . . Let her bring me some food, and as soon as I'm a little better I'll come into the village myself. I've mortally hankered after the old spots.' He smiled sheepishly.

'How do you think you'll manage to live now?' Yakov Lukich continued his pumping. He was unpleasantly disturbed by the meeting.

With a harsh expression on his face, Timofei replied:

'Don't you know how? I'm like a wolf now. I'll get a little rest, then I'll come to the village at night, and dig up a rifle . . . I've got one buried in the threshing floor. And I'll begin to earn my living! One road is cleary marked out for me. Once they've punished me, I'm going to do some punishing, too! I'll blow somebody's brains out, somebody will hear of me! Then I'll spend the summer in this grove, and with the first frosts I'll make my way to the Kuban, or somewhere else. The world is wide, and if you look you'll find more than one troop of men like me.'

'Lukeria Nagulnova's begun to make up to the chairman of the collective farm, it seems,' Yakov Lukich, who had more than once noticed Lukeria going to Davidov's room, irresolutely informed Timofei.

Thrown down by an unbearable pain in the stomach, Timofei stretched himself under a bush. But he declared, although in a broken voice:

'Davidov shall be the first . . . You can say prayers for him . . . And Lukeria's true to me . . . The old love is never forgotten, it's not just hospitality. I'll always find a way to her heart, the road isn't overgrown, I don't suppose ... You've given me a bad time with your bread, uncle ... my stomach's turning over and over ... You tell Lukeria ... Let her bring bread and dripping ... Plenty of bread!'

Yakov Lukich warned Timofei that felling was to begin in the grove the next day, then rode out of the wood and turned towards the fields of the second brigade, in order to look at the Kuban wheat. All the area of the recently coal-black ploughed land was gleaming with a tender green embroidery. The shoots were breaking through at last.

Lukich did not return to the village till nightfall. After returning the horse to the collective farm stables he made his way home, still oppressed with the impression left upon him by the meeting with Timofei. But at home a new and incommensurably more bitter unpleasantness was awaiting him. As he was standing in the porch, his daughter-in-law ran out of the kitchen and warned him in a whisper:

'Father, we've got guests ...'

'Who are they?'

'Polovtsiev and that other, the slant-eyed. They arrived as soon as it was getting dark. Mother and I were milking the cows ... They're in the best room. Polovtsiev's very drunk, and the other you can't understand at all. They're both in terribly ragged clothes. And the lice are boiling on them, even walking on their outside clothing!'

From the best room came the sound of conversation: coughing, Lyatievsky mockingly and caustically remarked:

'... well, of course! Who are you, your honour? I ask you, worthy Mr Polovtsiev! And I'll tell you who you are. All right? If you please! You're a patriot without a fatherland, a general without an army, and, if you find these comparisons too high-falutin' and abstract – a gambler without a single sou in your pocket.'

As he heard Polovtsiev's gruff bass voice replying, Yakov Lukich impotently leaned his back against the wall, and clutched his head.

The old was beginning anew.

PICADOR *Classics*

Louis Aragon
Paris Peasant £3.50

Outwardly a guided tour of the byways of 1920s Paris, *Le Paysan de Paris* is probably the most important prose fiction to emerge from surrealism. At its core lies the surrealist credo – that the world of the tangible conceals a quality of the marvellous awaiting revelation. Flights of lyrical beauty and passages of aggressive sarcasm, humorous anecdotes and delirious dream patterns, mock philosophical disquisitions and minute descriptions of places and things are all to be found in the pages of this surrealist masterpiece that transcends the movement that inspired it.

Translated by Simon Watson Taylor

'Aragon had, among the surrealists, an unmatched responsiveness to all that is quirky and uncanny in people and things, to all that betrays a hidden wealth of poetic resource beneath the hard, functional surfaces of the city' CAMBRIDGE REVIEW

Charles Baudelaire
Les Fleurs du Mal £5.95

These 'flowers of evil' are Baudelaire's supreme creation. Their recurring images of sea-voyage and the Orient stem from the poet's own journey to the East in 1841 Their inspiration was in no small part provided by his mulatto mistress, the coarse and rapacious Jeanne Duval Their decadent vision and distinctive voice inspired the work of Mallarmé, Rimbaud and Verlaine, lighting the touch-paper for the whole Symbolist movement. This bi-lingual edition contains the first-ever English translation of the complete text of a work that has changed the course of European literature.

Translated from the French by Richard Howard

'Will bring Baudelaire vigorously alive for English readers, and in the full range of his extraordinary gifts' THE GUARDIAN

Hermann Hesse
The Glass Bead Game £3.95

Eleven years in the writing and published three years before his Nobel prize award, this is Hesse's great novel, the epitome of his creative credo. Taking the form of a biography of Josef Knecht, it is set centuries into the future in the province of Castilia, a disintegrating society where an intellectual elite play out the game of the title – a quest for perfection that synthesises the *I Ching* and the astrologer's art. When Knecht rejects the esoteric in an attempt to resuscitate his dying homeland, his final suicide is at once a symbol of despair and an exemplary supreme sacrifice.

Translated by Richard and Clara Winston

'A new English version of *Das Glasperlenspiel* which lifts the whole novel onto a higher plane' THE TIMES

Jules Laforgue
Moral Tales £3.50

First published just a few months after their author's untimely death at the age of only twenty-seven, Laforgue's *Moralités légendaires* were acclaimed as a masterpiece and are still today his most celebrated work. The six poetic prose parodies of classic legends – *Hamlet, The Miracle of the Roses, Lohengrin, Son of Parsifal, Salome, Perseus and Andromeda,* and *Pan and the Syrinx,* – have been enormously influential, most prominently on French poets from Apollinaire to Prévert, but also on such major figures in modern literature as James Joyce and T. S. Eliot.

Translated by William Jay Smith

Henry de Montherlant
The Girls £4.95

Widely condemned as misogynist, this tetralogy remains as Montherlant's
masterpiece. Through four interrelated novels, Pierre Costals, writer and
rake, explores his relationships with four women – Andrée the virgin
intellectual, Thérèse the peasant girl possessed by religious mania, Solange
the ravishing bourgeoise beauty, and Rhadidja the teenage Arab mistress
who satisfies his ideal of simple sensuality. It is at once a savage attack on
the manners and mores of its time and a ferocious literary fusillade in the
battle of the sexes.

Translated by Terence Kilmartin

Robert Musil
Young Törless £3.95

Written while Musil was still a student, *The Confusions of Young Törless*
survives as the only completed novel by the author of *The Man Without
Qualities*. In a military academy on the eastern borders of the Austro-
Hungarian Empire, Törless is drawn into the vicious brutalities of his fellow
cadets in the secret attic that provides a torture chamber for sadistic
homosexual ritual. Musil's parable of power corrupted chillingly evokes the
tides of thought and action that were to plunge Europe into disastrous
conflict twice in less than half a century.

Translated by Eithne Wilkins and Ernst Kaiser

John Steinbeck
The Grapes of Wrath £3.95

The novel that won Steinbeck the Pulitzer Prize in 1940 endures as his masterpiece. His torrential narrative follows the destiny of the family Joad, loading their home into a beat-up truck and heading west out of Oklahoma towards the golden dream of California. It is the story of all those disinherited who came out of the dustbowl to find themselves in labour camps filled with hungry men and broken dreams, drawn into the black and bloody conflict of migrant worker against company thug. No novelist has so vividly evoked the America of Woody Guthrie and Joe Hill.

'This is a terrible and indignant book; yet it is not without passages of lyrical beauty, and the ultimate impression is that of the dignity of the human spirit under the stress of the most desperate conditions'
THE GUARDIAN

All Pan books are available at your local bookshop or newsagent, or can be ordered direct from the publisher. Indicate the number of copies required and fill in the form below.

Send to: **CS Department, Pan Books Ltd., P.O. Box 40, Basingstoke, Hants.   RG21 2YT.**

or phone: 0256 469551 (Ansaphone), quoting title, author and Credit Card number.

Please enclose a remittance* to the value of the cover price plus: 60p for the first book plus 30p per copy for each additional book ordered to a maximum charge of £2.40 to cover postage and packing.

*Payment may be made in sterling by UK personal cheque, postal order, sterling draft or international money order, made payable to Pan Books Ltd.

Alternatively by Barclaycard/Access:

Card No. ☐☐☐☐☐☐☐☐☐☐☐☐☐☐☐☐☐☐☐

Signature:

Applicable only in the UK and Republic of Ireland.

While every effort is made to keep prices low, it is sometimes necessary to increase prices at short notice. Pan Books reserve the right to show on covers and charge new retail prices which may differ from those advertised in the text or elsewhere.

NAME AND ADDRESS IN BLOCK LETTERS PLEASE:

....

Name————————————————————————————

Address————————————————————————————

————————————————————————————

————————————————————————————

————————————————————————————

3/87